"Maggie Ritchie has written an intense and satisfying story – an insight into the constraints on passionate and talented women in the Parisian art world at the turn of the century. It will haunt you." SARA SHERIDAN

"Jessie's adventures as a woman artist in 1880s Paris completely captivated me. A wonderful story." CARMEN REID

"*Paris Kiss* is a beautifully written evocation of the Parisian art scene of the late 1800s. It is a mesmerising canvas of love, friendship and betrayal." LAURA MARNEY

"One of the most thoughtful and intriguing books I have read for a long time. It evokes all the seduction and decadence of the Paris art world of the end of the nineteenth century... Beautifully and convincingly told [with] a great sense of place and time. This is an exceptional book which leads you gently into and through a more exotic world, which a 'respectable' woman enters at her peril." JANE MACKENZIE

PARIS
KISS

Maggie Ritchie

Published by Saraband,
Suite 202, 98 Woodlands Road
Glasgow, G3 6HB
Scotland
www.saraband.net

ISBN: 9781908643780
ebook: 9781908643797

Publication of this book has been supported by Creative Scotland.

ALBA | CHRUTHACHAIL

Printed in the EU on sustainably sourced paper.

2   4   6   8   10   9   7   5   3   1

FOR

MICHAEL

AND

ADAM

CHAPTER 1

SOUTH OF FRANCE

September 1929

I had searched for Camille for forty years. Now I was scared of what I would find. I had always believed we would meet again, but not like this.

As the train carried me through France towards my old friend, my thoughts were full of the past we had shared.

We were going to be great artists and live only for art and love. I smiled at my reflection in the carriage window as late summer wheat fields streaked past. We had been so young then, with no idea of what lay before us. My dreams had long ago been pushed aside by motherhood, and love had become as worn and comfortable as the sheets on my marriage bed. I looked across at my husband. He smiled at me and returned to his paper, and I went back to looking out the window, and remembering.

Camille. It had taken years to track her down, and then, a few months ago, a letter written in her hand arrived. She had not been ill, as I had been told, but locked away in a lunatic asylum. I squeezed my eyes shut so I could no longer see my reflection. Oh, Camille! Never, even in your darkest nightmares, could you have imagined this horrible fate.

The train slowed and the sign for Montfavet moved into the window. I twisted my gloves in my hands and watched the guard lift down our cases. I would see her again, in a matter of hours. Suddenly, I didn't want to get off the train. My husband put out his hand and I took it, grateful now that he had insisted on coming with me.

We stopped at our hotel to wash and eat, but the coffee was sour on my stomach and I couldn't force down the omelette they brought to our room. My husband spoke to the concierge about a car and a driver and within what seemed like minutes, we had arrived at the Asyl de Montdevergues, an austere building on a windswept hill above the village of Montfavet.

I stood in front of the asylum gates and tried not to look at the towering walls. A gusting wind tugged at my hat as if it wanted to rip it off and fling it into the valley below. In the gunmetal sky, a hawk rode the currents close enough for me to see its wing tips ruffling. I felt in my pocket for the letter that had brought me to this desolate place. It was dog-eared now and Camille's scrawl was blurred in places from my tears. I leaned my clammy forehead against the gate and wondered what awaited me. Camille had spent fifteen years locked up behind these walls. Fifteen years! Afraid I would be sick, I grasped an iron bar.

My husband called from the car: 'Jessie, are you all right?'

I turned and waved at him to stay where he was but he was already opening the door and getting out. He put his arm around me and I buried my face in the familiar warmth.

'You can't go in there alone, I'll come with you,' he said, but I shook my head.

'No, we parted so bitterly, I need to see her on my own.'

His arm tightened around my shoulders. 'But you don't know what you'll find – I've told you, these places can be upsetting.'

The nausea that had swept over me earlier had gone. I turned to face him in the buffeting wind and spoke calmly. 'Camille has endured this horror for years, I only have to bear it for a few hours.' I patted his lapels, a wifely gesture. I had known him most of my life. I felt a rush of tenderness towards him and kissed him on the mouth. 'Thank you for coming with me so far, but I'll be all right on my own now. I'm her friend and I have to help her. Camille doesn't belong here. You read her letter, I have to help her.'

He moved towards the car. 'Well, if you're sure, Jess.' He paused before getting in. 'But be careful. You know how volatile she always was. She'll be worse now she's ill. And I wouldn't be too ready to believe she doesn't belong here.' A wave of fury surged through me, staining my neck crimson. He knew how much Camille meant to me. I took measured breaths and fought to control my temper.

The wind whipped a strand of hair over my face and I had to raise my voice to be heard. 'You never liked her.'

'No, I can't say I did.' He studied me for a moment. 'And you know why. Camille Claudel didn't deserve your friendship. None of them did.' He closed the door.

I walked towards the car and he wound down the window. I relented. He was only trying to protect me, like always. I touched his dear face. 'Darling, can't you forgive her, after all these years? I have.'

'No, I'm afraid I can't. I can't forgive what she did to you. What they did to you. And I don't like all this raking over the past. No good will come of it.'

He spoke to the driver and the car moved off with a crunch of wheels and a cloud of dust. When it had disappeared around a bend, I pulled my coat tight around my neck and rang the bell. It was time to see Camille.

I was shown into a small, stuffy waiting room crammed with mismatched furniture. I sat down on a sagging armchair and waited. In the silence, my head filled with sounds from the past: the clatter and hum of a café, the haunting song of a *chanteuse*, Camille laughing softly in my ear while a man's hand kept mine captive under the table. A shaft of sunlight broke through the tall windows and fell across my lap and for a moment I was back in a Paris studio where dust motes swirled lazily in a sunbeam and two young women bent over their work, their hands covered in wet clay. I took off my gloves and looked at my hands. They were crosshatched with age now, the knuckles bony lumps that ached in the chilly room.

Someone coughed and I looked up, startled to see a figure standing in the doorway. The light was streaming in from behind and I couldn't make out more than the hunched silhouette of an old woman. She stepped forward and I made out her features. Hollowed eyes and a mouth scored into a downturn of despair. Her hair was sparse and white under a hat that was so misshapen that it would have been comical in another setting, and she wore an over-coat that swamped her over a long, stained skirt in the pre-War style. I smiled with relief: they had obviously brought the wrong patient to see me. Camille was a little younger than me and this woman was clearly in her eighties. I was about to say so to the orderly who stood behind her when the woman shuffled towards me and lifted her chin to stare into my eyes. She was so changed, so horribly, desperately, sadly changed, I wouldn't have recognised her if it hadn't been for her eyes, dark blue like the night sky over Paris.

Camille opened her ruined mouth and out of it came a mumble I struggled to understand. My French, once the language of my dreams, had become rusty over the years.

'I'm sorry, what did you say?'

She clicked her tongue in irritation and moved closer. I'm ashamed to say I took a step back.

'Who are you? What do you want?' she rasped. Her eyes, her once beautiful eyes, narrowed and she spat at my feet. '*He* sent you, isn't it so? That son of a whore! I know who you are – you're one of Rodin's spies. You can't fool me, *moi que je suis* Camille Claudel.' She banged her chest with her fist and planted it on her hip in a gesture so familiar it made me want to weep.

I reached out to her as if to implore her to come back to me. 'Camille, it's me, Jessie. Don't you remember me? The studio in Paris?'

She scowled and once again I caught a glimpse of the Camille I had known more than forty years ago.

'You can't be Jessie; she is pretty with skin like a peach and hair like bronze with the fire from the forge reflected in it. You, you are not my Jessie…' Camille was pointing at me when she caught sight of her hand, as I had earlier. She studied the fingers for a moment, as if this old woman's claw did not belong to her. When she lifted her eyes to me, they were clouded with tears. 'Excuse me, *Madame*, I am confused sometimes.' She folded her hands in front of her. 'What did you say your name was?'

My throat was heavy and I had to cough before I could speak. 'Jessie, you knew me as Jessie Lipscomb. I wrote to you and told you I was coming. Don't you remember?'

She frowned. 'I knew a Jessie once, an English girl, a good friend, my best friend. But I lost her. We fought and I lost her. I wonder what became of her. If only she were here now. I am so alone, I have been alone for so long.' She hid her face in her hands and began to cry.

I crossed the room in two paces and took her hands. They had always been calloused and scarred, strong sculptor's hands, but now they were soft, the bones as fragile as those of a bird. I put my arms around her and felt how thin she had become; it was like holding a ghost.

'Hush now, hush my darling, don't take on so,' I murmured. I'd comforted her like this once before, a lifetime ago, and it must have been this that jolted her memory at last. Like a blind man, she touched my face, tracing the contours as Rodin had taught us.

'Jessie Lipscomb from Peterborough – it is you! *Ma petite anglaise.*' She stroked my cheek with papery fingers and the hole in my heart that had pained me for all these years finally closed over.

She put her fingers to her mouth and her eyes widened. 'But Jessie, what has happened? You look absolutely terrible!'

I laughed with relief to hear her sounding more like the Camille I remembered. 'Forty-five years has happened to me, that's what!'

She laid her head on my shoulder and sighed. 'I can't believe it is really you.'

'Nor I you.' I tightened my arms around her and we stood like that together, bathed in sunlight.

When she spoke, her voice was dreamy, like a child getting ready for sleep. 'So many years I've been here! I can escape this nightmare only by going into the past. When I can't bear it here, I close my eyes and I am in Paris again.' She lifted her head and looked at me. 'Jessie, do you remember the first time we met?'

'I do, my darling, as if it were yesterday.'

But it was the day I met Rodin that came back to me – a memory I'd kept alive over the years, revisiting it during stolen moments alone like a miser crowing over a prized nugget of gold.

CHAPTER 2

Paris

June 1884

It was my first summer in Paris. Camille and I were in our studio and I remember the model kept fidgeting.

Camille waved her sculpting tool at her. 'Marie-Thérèse! *Tu m'embêtes!* What is wrong with you? Do you need to take a piss?'

The model pouted but resumed her pose and Camille bent her head once more to the clay. She could always become absorbed in her work in an instant, while it took me a while to get going. I started sorting through my materials and changed the position of the rotating table.

Camille sighed loudly. 'Jessie! You're like a dog circling its basket.'

I tied my hair back with a strip of cloth and unwrapped the batch of clay. My hands rested on the cool, wet mass and I looked at Camille. I'd known her for only a few weeks but already we were firm friends. I'd never met anyone like her before. I studied the shape of her head, how she scowled as her fingers dabbed and smudged the clay and, ignoring the model, began to work until I had the outline of her head. I grew excited as the sculpture came to life between my hands and Camille's features emerged from the rough clay. It was the best work I had ever done – the likeness was good, the proportions exact. Hours passed as we became absorbed in our work, the only sounds the ticking of a clock and the rustling of our skirts as we moved around the tables.

I needed a finer sculpting tool and moved to the corner of the room to find one. I heard the curtain that kept the dust from the marble cutting room out of the clay studio being pulled back. I turned round and saw a man about my father's age. He was short but had a powerful barrel chest and a commanding air. His hair was cut brutally short, *en brosse*, in the military style, but he wore his beard wild and long. His suit was dusty and his waistcoat was daubed with clay. He carried an ebony walking stick topped with silver, which he planted in front of his feet like a theatre impresario. I was standing in the shadows and he seemed unaware of my presence. He was staring at Camille and held out hands in grey kid gloves, like a supplicant, towards her.

'Camille, *ma chère ...*'

Camille started, as if woken from a dream. She nodded a warning towards me – so slightly I would have missed it if I hadn't been watching her carefully – and he dropped his hands as I stepped out of the shadows.

'Monsieur Rodin,' Camille said loudly. 'Allow me to present your new pupil, Jessie Lipscomb.'

So this was the great Rodin, the reason I had come to Paris. I had almost given up hope of meeting him as the days wore on and no tutor appeared. I studied him closely. Few of the general public had heard of Rodin in those days, but his name was touted in art circles as a powerful sculptor who broke all the rules. Alphonse Legros, my tutor in London, had impressed on me that Rodin, his former pupil, was an extraordinary genius.

'Auguste will free you from the English *politesse* that binds your work like a corset,' Legros had told me.

He had a direct way of speaking but fortunately was more restrained when I took my father to meet him so he could persuade him to let me go to Paris on my own to study with Rodin. Papa had been against the scheme at first; he'd heard the usual stories of women ruined by disreputable artists and, like everyone, he'd read *Trilby* and seen *La Bohème*. But Legros assured him I would be well looked after at the home of one of Rodin's most promising pupils, Camille Claudel, and that her family was respectable, from the *haute bourgeoisie*. When my father looked sceptical, Legros appealed to his parental pride.

'She has outgrown the women's classes here at South Kensington with their ridiculous restrictions on modelling from life. Your daughter is suffocating here, Monsieur Lipscomb,' Legros said. 'She is an artist; she needs to breathe, to be taught by the best of the best. She needs to go to Paris or she will be desperately unhappy.'

That clinched it: Papa could never bear to see me, his cherished only child, sad.

'If you really want to go, Jessie, you may,' Papa had said, laughing as I flung myself into his arms. 'Your mother will be furious with me, but she'll come round. We both know you're a sensible girl.'

A few months later I was stepping off a train at Gare du Nord and into my new life in Paris.

Legros had called Rodin a man of passion and I could see at once that he was one of those men who draw women like moths to a lamp: the air in the studio crackled with the energy that radiated from him. On the other side of the room, like a cat craving attention, the model tossed her hair and arched her back so that her nipples, now hard as pebbles, pointed at the ceiling. I noticed Rodin's eyes slide towards them.

Camille snapped her head round and barked at the pouting Marie-Thérèse. 'Time's up! Go on, get your clothes on and get out. Do you think I'm made of money?'

The model smiled lazily and strolled past Rodin, not bothering to cover up her buttocks, which rolled luxuriously as she walked. She trailed a dirty peignoir behind her, and cast him a last smouldering look before slipping behind the screen. Camille muttered what sounded like *Salope!* and turned back to Rodin and me.

'*Maître*,' I said. And oh, the thrill of using that word! 'I'm so pleased you could take me on as your pupil.'

Rodin inclined his head over my hand and dropped it in the French manner I still find slightly disconcerting – at once intimate and dismissive. He smoothed his beard and studied me. His eyes were the startling blue of glaciated ice but when he took off his thick glasses to clean them, he blinked like a mole coming out of the ground.

'Mademoiselle Lipscomb, it will be my pleasure to teach you. Alphonse wrote to me and had nothing but the highest praise for your talents.' He smiled and I basked in the sunlit warmth of his attention. Rodin rubbed his hands together – oddly, he had not taken off his gloves – and walked over to my table. 'Let me have a look at your work. This head is yours?'

I was filled with alarm. 'I have only just started it, *Maître.*'

'Good. I like to catch a piece early, before it takes the wrong direction.' He circled the table, examining the figure from all angles. He stopped and closed his eyes. Like a blind man, he placed his hands gently on the clay face and felt its contours, as if he were caressing a lover. I felt like a houseguest who has stepped into the wrong bedroom. I glanced at Camille and saw she was transfixed, her mouth parted and a flush on her cheek. Rodin dropped his hands and stepped back, breaking the spell. He leaned on his stick for a moment as if considering his response, and I held my breath while I waited.

Rodin banged his stick on the wooden floor and I jumped as the crack sounded around the room.

'While the piece is technically proficient ...'

I steeled myself for the codicil.

'... it is dead.'

I gasped as if winded and thought for a moment I was going to be sick.

Rodin circled the bust, which I had been so proud of only a few moments earlier and could now see was the work of a fraud, and pointed at it with his stick. 'I may as well be looking at a photograph of Mademoiselle Claudel.'

He said *photograph* as if it were an insult. The technology was in its infancy then and many artists feared it would make our profession redundant. I decided not to tell my tutor that my young man William had been showing me how to use his camera and how I'd started experimenting with reflections and lighting.

Rodin was in full swing now. 'You have, it is true, caught Camille's likeness, but in doing so you have killed her, just as if you had stuck a pin through her heart. She is like a butterfly in a glass case – beautiful but dead.'

He pounded the floor again with his stick and I flinched at every ricochet.

9

'Where is her energy?' *Bang!*

'Where is her spirit?' *Bang!*

'An artist stands naked before the world. What do you feel when you look at your friend? Admiration? Jealousy? Desire? Hatred? I see nothing in this piece – only technique, which I do not decry, but it does not make you stand out. Mademoiselle Lipscomb, you must sculpt from your gut as well as your head. Then, and only then, will you become a true artist.'

Rodin was right, of course, I know that now, but his comments rained down on me like burning embers from Mount Vesuvius. I wasn't used to being eviscerated in this way. My tutors at South Kensington had always been effusive about my work, said it was like that of a man – the highest praise a woman artist could hope for in those days. Now my shame burned all the brighter in front of Camille, who stood silently at my side. I glanced at her. Was that a shadow of a smirk? I clenched my fists so my nails dug into my palms and told myself this was why I was here – to learn. My dismay must have shown in my face and Rodin softened his tone. He laid his hand lightly on my shoulder and, to my horror, tears pricked my eyes; I tried desperately to blink them back.

Rodin ran his hand down my arm and squeezed it. 'I would not say this if I did not think you had real talent – why would I waste my breath? You are one of the few who has the potential to make it in this cruel game. Legros was right!'

The clouds parted. I smiled through my tears. '*Merci, mon maître.*'

He smiled and patted my shoulder. 'Now, watch carefully and I will show you how to improve this mannequin and turn it into a real, living, breathing person with fire in her belly.'

He whipped off his gloves to reveal calloused labourer's hands scored with burns and I wondered if that was why he kept them covered, through shame. Most sculptors I knew were proud of their marked hands, but then few had clawed their way up from the back streets, as Rodin had. Soon I was too busy watching the great Rodin at work to care whether he wore gloves or fur mittens. In a few deft moves he smudged my careful refinements, pinching the cheeks to make them fuller and more childlike, smearing the lips so they seemed about to talk, always, always keeping the surface rough so you were never in any doubt that although this was a creature of clay, as he said, it was a living, breathing creature.

Camille came to life before our eyes and the real Camille gasped beside me and reached for my hand as we watched our *maître* create a masterpiece in a matter of minutes. It was true what they said: Rodin was a genius, the greatest sculptor since Michelangelo.

He wiped his hands down the front of his waistcoat, careless of the grey smears he left behind. 'Now, Mademoiselle Claudel, it's your turn.'

I remember thinking fleetingly that he had called her Camille when he had come into the studio, but now he was using her title and the formal 'vous'. The thought slipped away as I waited to see what he would say about Camille's work. In the weeks I had been sharing a studio with her it was already clear she was a far more talented artist than I could ever hope to be. Rodin, I was certain, would have nothing but praise for her tender sculpture of a young girl in her first flush of innocence – a quality she had spotted in Marie-Thérèse despite the model's brash ways. I waited glumly for Rodin's praise; it would make my humiliation all the keener.

Camille, her hands clasped behind her back and her features set in concentration, stepped aside to allow Rodin a better view. He peered through his spectacles at the figure from all angles, running his hands over the young girl's flanks like a farmer at a horse market. He stepped back and I heard Camille's breathing quicken. Rodin shook his head and raised his stick and brought it down with a sickening squelch through the soft clay. I heard myself cry out as he lashed out again and again with the stick and turned the delicate sculpture into pulp. The violence of his action stunned me into silence and I waited, my mouth still covered and my eyes wide, for Camille to explode. I was already familiar with her temper and sure she would not stand for this. But she appeared unmoved.

'You are right, *Maître*, the leg was awkward, the pose stiff and contrived.' I was amazed by her even tone. 'Thank you.' Camille began to salvage what was left with movements as quick and confident as Rodin's, smoothing away the savage rips in the clay. Rodin watched, his eyes never leaving her hands. I watched too as the sculpture took on the shape of a young girl awakening to desire, pulsating with longing, her back arched like a cat, an eagerness in outstretched arms that made you want to turn away to spare her shame. None of us turned round when the model called out that she was leaving.

'And don't think I'll come back to work in this madhouse in a hurry,' she said. 'Destroying a perfectly good sculpture! I sat for hours getting cramp in my arse – and for what? Nothing! You're all lunatics!' The door slammed behind her.

The windows were a blaze of copper from the setting sun when Rodin put his hand over Camille's. 'Stop! She is perfect now. Never overwork your piece, always leave some life in the clay.'

And he tipped his hat and left.

Camille and I stood looking at each other in the silence he left behind. Then we both grinned and I grasped her hands and swung her round.

'Rodin says I have talent!'

Camille laughed and pushed a strand of hair out of my eyes. 'Of course you have talent, Jessie Lipscomb from Peterborough. Do you think I would let any old riff-raff share my studio? Come on, let's celebrate.'

She sat down with an '*ouf!*' on one of the rickety chairs we'd grouped around an old tea chest we'd covered with a silk shawl. I fetched the coffee pot from the stove and a bottle of brandy Camille had stolen from her mother's kitchen. Once we were sipping our laced coffee, Camille pulled a silver case from her pocket and lit Turkish cigarettes for both of us. It had taken me a while, but I'd soon got the hang of smoking by copying Camille.

She squinted at me through a cloud of aromatic smoke. 'Oh, that's good,' she sighed.

Hooking her heels over the packing case, she stretched her arms above her head. I heard her back crack and felt in my own bones the familiar weariness of the sculptor. We often spent twelve hours at a stretch in the studio, hefting clay, mixing plaster and working from the top of a ladder – all in a corset and bustle, our long skirts dragging behind us under cumbersome dustcoats. I looked down at my sage-green dress that I had picked out so carefully in London and twitched its skirts out of the dust in irritation; it was ruined.

Camille, who in her workman-like navy blue dress with white collars and cuffs always made me feel overdressed, pointed at my filthy hem. 'Your fine skirt is dirty.'

All at once I was fed up being trussed up like a butcher's goose. Nobody knew me here and I could do exactly as I pleased without fear of scandal or upsetting my parents. I could sit in a café without a chaperone and work when I liked in my own studio with undraped models, and learn from the most revolutionary sculptor of my time. Legros was right: in Paris, I could be free. I stood up and ripped off my dustcoat and started to unfasten my high-necked jacket. Camille helped me, laughing as we struggled with the tiny row of buttons. She peeled it away from my arms, her breath warm on my neck. I unhooked my skirt and it fell to the floor. I stood facing her, my arms folded, waiting. Camille shrugged and in a few minutes we were both in our bloomers. We stood at the studio window and watched a flock of starlings swoop and turn in the violet sky.

When it was time to go home, we locked up and went downstairs. Outside, in the rue Notre-Dame-des-Champs, most of the *atelier* windows were open to let in the last of the light, and the warm air was full of the sound of hammering. Camille walked with a slight limp and she stumbled on the uneven cobbles. I slipped my arm through hers without comment and she pressed her weight against me.

'You know, Jessie, finding a new friend, it's like falling in love.'

'Yes. Just like falling in love.'

CHAPTER 3

ASYLUM OF MONTDEVERGUES

September 1929

In the milky light that spilled into the waiting room, Camille looked for a moment like her young self. She held on to my hands as if reluctant to let me go.

'How could I not have recognised my own Jessie?'

'Well, it's been a long time.'

'A lifetime ago, another world,' she said with such sadness that my heart contracted. 'The first time I saw you I knew we would be friends. How beautiful and proud you were, when you walked into the studio in all your finery. You were all dressed up like a fashion plate; do you remember that ridiculous hat with the stuffed bird?'

'You mean my *merle bronzé*, if you don't mind!' How I had loved that hat. It was the fashion then for hats to be decorated with whole birds and this one had a blackbird with iridescent amber and blue feathers. The cloches now are elegant and give a neat silhouette, but I still sometimes hanker after the extravagances of the Eighties. I tried not to look at the battered black hat crammed on Camille's head. She had been so beautiful with her tight black curls tucked under a simple boater. But her dark eyes gleamed with some of her old spirit and it was good to hear that guttural laugh again. The longer we were together, the more she seemed to become her old self, as if our friendship and the memories of our youth in Paris gave her strength. I wanted to prolong this moment and I laughed with her.

'I soon learned to dress like a true bohemian – I blame you for that,' I said.

'And I like an English lady. Do you remember the stripes you persuaded me to buy, and the hat with its ostrich feather?'

'What about the Japanese embroidered silk jackets we bought together in that funny little shop?' I said. 'We must have looked a sight.'

Camille touched my face again, as if to smooth away the marks of time. 'My Jessie, you were always so strong and straight and true. You haven't changed at all.'

I smiled. 'If only that were true.'

'*Ah, bouf!* Me, I know I have changed. Remember the pretty bust you made of me? The one Rodin was so cruel about?' I flinched and she laughed again. 'Still hurts, *hein*? Always so competitive, Jessie!' She sighed and looked at her worn hands. 'We were so young, we never imagined one day we would be old like this.' Her voice trembled and I covered her hands with my own. She looked up at me with her navy blue eyes. 'I have lost everything. But you, Jessie, you are the same.'

She was wrong; I wasn't the same woman who had walked into Camille's *atelier* all those years ago. How could I be? I was sixty-eight on my last birthday and nobody gets to that age without being dealt a few blows by life. At twenty-two, when I arrived in Paris, I was going to be a great artist. Nothing else mattered. But that ambition was ripped away from me, and it was Camille who had been to blame. The old bitterness rose up again, rushing through me like lava in a volcano. I still had a temper, but over the years I had learned to keep the old rage deep down inside me. I mustn't give into it now, not with Camille standing before me so frail and diminished. No, it was best not to think about the rift that had split apart our world, the golden world of our Paris youth. The muffled tick of the wall clock reminded me that I didn't have much time with Camille. There was so much I wanted to ask her, but I would have to be careful not to tip her into the mania I'd caught a terrifying glimpse of earlier. I looked around the dingy room, at the walls streaked with damp, the shabby furniture. In the corner there was a glass door leading to a garden with a stone bench.

I nodded towards the French window. 'Shall we step outside? It's a bit stuffy in here.'

As we walked towards the bench, Camille leaned on me but there was no weight to her. The wind had risen and she shivered despite her shapeless coat. Her limp was worse than ever and I tightened my arm around her.

'Are you cold? Do you want to go back in?' I said.

'No, no, I like the wind.' She closed her eyes and put her face up to the sun. 'Let's sit and talk a while.'

We sat on the bench and watched a hawk, perhaps the one I had seen earlier, high above the asylum walls. Wings outstretched, it rode the updraft looking for prey. It plummeted out of sight only to reappear, a small bird fluttering in its claws. The wind moaned as it hurtled around the desolate garden and I crossed my arms to fend off its cold embrace. Beyond the forbidding walls, I knew the deep valley fell away in a murderous drop. It was as if Camille and I were the only people left alive, perched at the edge of the world.

Camille rested her boots one on top of the other. She turned her face up to the grey vault of a sky and closed her eyes, as if relishing the watery sun.

'I wonder what happened to Georges?' she said.

I nearly cried out. She had caught me unawares; I was dismayed that his name still had an effect on me even after all these years. Damn him. Rosa had told me it would get better: one day I would think of him and not be able to recall his name. But I had never forgotten Georges. At first I thought that Camille meant to hurt me, but she had spoken so casually. I remembered then that I had never had the chance to tell her what happened between Georges and me. Our friendship had broken in two by then.

I brought my breath under control and kept my voice light. 'Georges? I have no idea. He's happily married, no doubt, with a troop of grandchildren.'

Camille shook her head and laughed. 'A grandfather! Not our Georges! Perhaps, if you'd stayed…' She turned to me, her eyes sharp in her ruined face. 'He never got over you, you know. Pestered me for months after you left Paris, mooning about the studio and interrupting my work with questions about you, wanting to know if he should follow you and bring you back.'

I was furious that he still had the power to hurt me after all these years. This time I didn't try to hide my anger.

'But he didn't follow me, did he? Typical of him to talk big and do nothing.'

Camille shrugged. 'I don't know why you're so angry. You were lucky, you were able to run away, please yourself as you always did and abandon your friends without so much as a goodbye.'

I bit my lip. Camille must know that this wasn't true, that it was she who had abandoned me. But she didn't give me a chance to speak and carried on in a rush.

'I, on the other hand, was trapped. Rodin would not let me go – he hounded me until the day he died.' She wrenched her eyes from the hawk and glared at me, as if I were to blame for her sorrows. 'It was his gang of murderous thieves who put me in this living grave.'

Without warning, Camille howled and leaped to her feet. Her hands clutched the air, pulling and pinching at it as if she were sculpting an unseen face from invisible clay. I jumped up and tried to calm her but she pushed me away with a surprising strength so I nearly lost my footing. Her eyes were wild and she spat on the ground.

'*La bande de Rodin!* I knew it! They sent you here to get my secrets! You don't think I know their game? They try to poison me still, even though he's dead and buried, God rot his soul. It's why I won't take the meals they try to feed me in this prison. I know their game, every plate poisoned. It's why I eat only boiled potatoes and eggs that I cook myself in my room.'

Camille was starving herself to punish Rodin. It explained why she was as frail as a bird, her hair thin, and her eyes sunken, and the stale smell that came off her. She was muttering now and pacing back and forth in a tight circuit. She pulled at her clothes and slapped her face. I was worried she would hurt herself and tried to lead her back to the bench, but she shrugged me off.

'But Camille,' I said. 'Nobody is trying to poison you here. The nurse who showed me in here, she seemed kind.'

'Don't be fooled, Jessie, they are all in Rodin's pay.' She grabbed my arm and pulled me towards her. Her breath was sour and I could see her lips, like dry leaves rubbing together.

Her voice took on the metallic quality I'd noticed earlier when she was raving. 'The doctor, Charpenel, he pretends to be a doctor, but he's really one of Rodin's lackeys. He can't fool me, I know what he's up to, giving me art materials, saying he wants me to sculpt, to sketch, that it'll be good for me. Good for me! Good for Rodin more like, that bastard.' With astonishing agility she jumped onto the bench and shook her fist at the asylum walls. I clutched at her coat, hanging onto her so she would not fall, and begged her to come down.

Camille ignored me and stretched her arms wide. She shouted into the wind: 'I will never work again, do you hear me, Rodin? I know you have told this so-called doctor to steal my ideas. You have always stolen my ideas, always, right from the start, when you pretended to love me.'

I felt her sag and caught her and helped her down so she sat on the bench, slumped against me. She looked up at me with eyes that were almost black, as if she were not seeing me but looking far back, into our past.

'Rodin,' she whispered. 'The great man. But he stole his greatness from me.' She clutched at me and I held her more tightly. 'He never had an idea in his life that didn't come from me.' She began to sob. 'Now I am forgotten, hidden away in this place full of lunatics, just like he always wanted.'

I wanted to remind her Rodin was long dead, that he couldn't hurt her now, and that he had no part in putting her away. But it was no use: her mind had drifted free of its mooring and it would only upset her if I tried to use reason. And, in truth, there was a kind of logic in her ravings. Rodin had taken what he wanted from her. I knew only too well the power Rodin had over her – over both of us. After all, we were only young women, his pupils, and he was the Great Artist. And a man. Camille was not the only one who had been betrayed by Rodin. He had promised me so much, but like Camille, my talent had not been allowed to blossom.

No, I would not defend Rodin to poor, broken Camille. Instead I began to talk quietly to her of our early days in Paris, when we were giddy with our own power and believed we could do anything.

CHAPTER 4

Paris

June 1884

That evening, after I had met Rodin for the first time, Camille and I walked through the streets of Paris as the sky deepened from purple to black and the lamps were being lit. As she slipped her key into the front door of her family's top-floor apartment, I was telling her about life class at South Ken.

'The poor girl had been educated in a convent school and there she was, faced with her first nude model. As soon as he unwrapped the draperies she turned white as a sheet and rushed to the lavatory. You should have heard *Maître* Legros curse her as she crept back to her easel. It was fortunate that the nuns hadn't taught her much French beyond *la plume de ma tante*.'

Camille laughed, loud and unabashed, showing her teeth and the redness of her wide mouth, as a man would. I was learning that she was a woman of big emotions; she cared nothing for modesty and I loved her candour. I had never met anyone like Camille before. But I found out how ruthless she could be when the maid, Eugénie, appeared looking thunderous. She snatched our coats, glared at Camille and turned on her heel. I was taken aback: my mother would never have tolerated such behaviour from one of our maids, but Camille seemed unfazed.

'The little bitch still hasn't forgiven me for stealing her room for my studio,' she said. 'What a fuss! I'm sure the bed in the corner of the kitchen is just as comfortable and far warmer.' Camille called after her. 'Don't pout, you little idiot, it'll only give you wrinkles.'

The maid disappeared down the corridor and Camille flicked her wrist. '*N'importe quoi*, she'll get over it. Let's eat, I'm starving. It's a shame Papa is away working in the countryside, but you'll meet him soon. I think you'll like him, he's a terrible tease.'

We went into the dining room where the maid was stalking around the empty chairs, ladling out fragrant portions of some kind of stew. Camille sat down and tucked a napkin into her collar. 'Eugénie, even when you're sulking, you cook like a goddess.' The maid's lips twitched as if she were suppressing a smile and Camille winked at me, her mouth already full.

'Camille! Where are your manners? How many times do I have to ask you to behave like a lady and not a street urchin?' Camille's mother was standing in the doorway, dressed in joyless black, her hair scraped back in a severe low bun.

'*Mais maman, j'ai un faim de loup!*' Camille said. 'You know I'm always famished after a day at the studio. Don't be cross.' Camille went to her mother and put her arm around the stiff back and kissed her cheek but, unlike my own darling Ma, she did not return the embrace and shrugged her off. Camille stepped away from her and sat down with a thump. I could see she was upset by the rebuff. Her mother seemed to be the only person who could hurt Camille with her coldness. I squeezed Camille's hand under the table and smiled brightly at the old ogre.

'Madame Claudel,' I said. 'I'm sorry. It was my fault. I couldn't help myself. I was so desperate to taste this dish. Camille was only keeping me company, as her guest. Dinner here is always so mouth-watering. I wonder if I might have the receipt for my mother?'

She flushed and I could see the Ice Queen had begun to thaw. Madame C was a consummate housewife – what the French call *une bonne femme* – and praising her household was a sure way to please her. I clasped my hands together and gushed shamelessly, eager to deflect her spite away from Camille.

'I'm so grateful for your hospitality, you've treated me with such kindness since I came to Paris.'

'My dear child, you are most welcome.' She spoke sharply to Camille again. 'You should be more like your friend, Jessie. She at least remembers her manners.' But she patted her daughter's hand and sat down, with a creaking of stays and a great deal of sighing, as if the weight of the world were on her shoulders. She was a martyr as a well as a tyrant, always complaining of her lot, looking after her three children alone while her husband lived it up in the countryside. Living under her roof made me appreciate my own gentle and loving mother. Her persecution of Camille was fierce, and it made me all the more determined to be a loyal friend.

Camille's brother Paul wandered into the dining room with his nose in a book, as always. He was a tall, thin boy, and as shy and awkward as Camille was bold and friendly. But in his own earnest way, he was as passionate as his big sister.

'Good evening, Paul,' I said, to which he reddened and dropped his book.

'Ah, um, g-g-g...'

Camille laughed. 'You should be flattered, Jessie, my little Paul stammers like that only when he talks to a pretty girl.'

Paul's blush spread to the roots of his hair and I kicked Camille under the table. To distract him, I picked up the book he had dropped and looked at its cover before handing it back to him.

'You are reading Verlaine? I'm afraid I find him rather difficult.'

Paul's expression grew eager, his earlier embarrassment forgotten. 'Oh, but you must persevere! The meaning is not important but the sound, the music of the words. And you must try Mallarmé and Rimbaud, too.'

'Les poètes maudits,' I said. I loved Verlaine's name for the scandalous young bloods: the cursed poets.

He looked surprised. 'You have read them, then?'

Camille snatched the book from Paul's hands and began leafing through it. 'Don't underestimate Jessie, little brother. She has fire in her blood, like you and me.' She slid the book across the table at him and whispered: 'You'd better not let Maman catch you with this.'

They both darted a look at their mother, but she was busy with the maid.

Paul shrugged and resumed reading. 'Maman never reads my books.'

I don't know if it was his bookishness or his shy good manners, but I warmed to Paul straight away. I'd always wanted a younger brother to mother and fuss over, and he was so sweet natured and shy. I soon discovered that he was intensely religious, which struck the only note of discord between him and the scornfully atheistic Camille. He took me to Mass and lent me copies of Christian writings and during our walks to church, I discovered he was as passionate about Cardinal Newman as he was about the scandalous Rimbaud.

Louise, on the other hand, I found harder to like. She came in late to dinner, but where Camille would have been reprimanded, her mother fussed over her and helped her to a big ladleful of food. The baby of the family, Louise was a petulant, spoiled creature who looked remarkably like a prissy doll I'd detested as a child and had dropped on her annoying little porcelain face. Louise Claudel was a prettier but more insipid version of her older sister. She had the same dark curls, but they were carefully arranged in glossy ringlets and decked in ribbons, and her dress was a froth of lace and more ribbons. She was seventeen, only two years younger than Camille, but already she had acquired the feminine wiles of a much older woman. Louise dimpled at her mother but rudely ignored me. I was her elder at twenty-two, but she treated me like an insignificant paying guest. I had taken an instant dislike to her.

Camille narrowed her eyes at her sister. 'What have you been doing today, Louise? Let me guess, you have been grappling with important affairs, such as whether to line your new dress with silk or *broderie anglaise.*'

Louise stuck out her tongue. '*Tais-toi*, Camille. You always think you're so clever.'

'Cleverer than you, but then that wouldn't be hard.' Camille turned to speak to me and I saw Louise shoot her sister a venomous look. There was a murderous rivalry between them that shattered my illusions about sisterly love. Perhaps there were some advantages to being an only child, after all.

Camille placed her palms on the table. 'Maman, please can we eat now?'

The long day in the studio had left me ravenous too – we often forgot to stop to eat – and I was grateful when everyone took up their spoons. By the end of the meal, the earthenware dish lay empty and my corset dug into my waist. Madame Claudel tried to interest us in a game of cards but Camille noticed my drooping eyelids and we made our excuses.

I loved the little bedroom I had been given. Compared to my huge bedroom at home, it was cramped, with barely enough space for the cast-iron bed and the armoire. But when I opened the full-length windows, the lights of Paris spread out before me like a jewelled skirt.

Camille came to stand beside me at the iron balcony. 'I love it here,' she said. 'I couldn't live anywhere else now.'

She helped me unpin my hair and with the cumbersome task of taking off my corset. When I was in my chemise and bloomers, she laughed.

'I think today you started a new trend in studio costume for young lady artists, *petite anglaise*.' Camille put her arms around me and I leaned into her embrace. Her cheek was soft against mine and I closed my eyes and smelled the clay in her hair. I knew in that moment that I had found the perfect friend, one I would love all my life.

CHAPTER 5

That first summer in Paris! Every day was an adventure shared with Camille. We were each other's constant companions. There were two other English women who also shared the *atelier*, Amy Singer and Emily Fawcett, and they were pleasant enough, but Camille and I preferred to be alone. We went to the studio when we knew Amy and Emily would be out. Camille and I worked furiously, encouraging each other to get through difficulties and breaking off for coffee and cigarettes around our rickety tea chest. I still miss those conversations, as intimate and absorbing as a dance. I've never since been able to talk so freely and deeply to anyone. I took it all for granted then, the ease between Camille and me, and assumed we would be friends for life. I can still see the careful way she listened to me, her intelligent eyes fixed on mine as I talked, the way she would pause with that slight frown while she considered her response.

When we weren't working in the studio, we explored Paris, copying the Masters in the Louvre and the Luxembourg Palace, visiting the prison where the inmates would sit for us for a few *sous*, or sketching the cadavers at the anatomy school in a fug of chemical fumes.

That long, happy summer took on a dangerous, but more exciting, edge when we met Rosa. Camille and I were in the Bois de Boulogne sketching in the suffocating heat of a closed cab. If you were a woman artist, it was hopeless to try and work *en plein air* and capture the street scenes. Within minutes, men would gather round like a cloud of gnats, asking idiotic questions and making lewd remarks. I had tried it once and given up in disgust when some oaf tried to put his hands on me. The only way to work in peace was in a cab, but the day was hot and we were sweating in our corsets and heavy skirts. It was torture to be in the *fiacre*, which smelled of stale cigars and perfume, instead of under the cool green canopy of a chestnut tree. The sun climbed higher into the whitening sky making it impossible to concentrate. When a charming family – the women in white muslin dresses, the men in linen suits and boaters, and their children pushing hoops – stopped at the riverbank in front of us and laid out a white cloth for a picnic, Camille nudged me.

The heat had made me irritable. 'Watch out, you nearly knocked the charcoal out of my hand.'

'Never mind that. Do you see that person? There, under the willow tree, sketching the family? It's Rosa. The fiend! I've a good mind to report that *salope* to the police.'

I poked my head through the window but could make out only a slight man in plus-fours holding a sketchbook. 'What am I supposed to be looking at?'

Camille pushed her head out of the window too, so we were crammed together, shoulder-to-shoulder. 'Look more closely, the artist. Do you see now? *C'est une artiste, pas artist … tu comprends?*'

'Oh, I see now. Are you sure it's a woman? I suppose he is rather small.'

'It's Rosa Bonheur all right. It's not fair. I don't know how she gets away with it.'

I sat back in the stifling cab and pulled at the high collar chafing my throat. The buttons were too small to undo without a hook. 'Good for her! What harm is she doing? Better than being cooped up in this sardine tin.'

She narrowed her eyes at me. I regarded her coolly; I loved her passionately but Camille didn't intimidate me. I think it's why she loved me back.

She flopped back in the seat and fanned herself with her notebook. 'Rosa may be a pain in the neck, but I admit, *elle a du coeur au ventre.*'

'I'm not sure your mother would approve of your choice of words, but you're right, your friend does have guts.'

Camille opened the cab door and called out: '*Hein! Monsieur l'artist!* I want you to meet a friend of mine.'

As the figure drew closer, I craned my neck for a closer look at Rosa Bonheur, who at that time was all the rage in England, with Queen Victoria a great admirer of her animal paintings. Hands in her pockets, Rosa strode over. She made a remarkably convincing *flâneur*. Up close, her face was lined and she appeared older than my own parents, perhaps in her sixties, but her eyes were bright, giving her the air of a much younger woman – or man.

'*Eh bien, mes petites,*' she said, her voice a husky contralto. 'What are two such lovely ladies doing out without a chaperone? Shall I protect you from the wolves of Paris?'

Camille opened the door. 'But Rosa, how are you dressed? You look completely absurd, even for a man.'

Rosa rolled her eyes at me. 'Camille has no taste. *Ma chère* Camille, if you had the least idea about fashion you would know this is *le Style Anglais*. Why, everyone, but everyone, is wearing it in London.'

'Jessie is from London, let's ask her.'

They both looked at me. I hesitated.

Rosa took my hand and made a great show of kissing it. 'Well, Jessie, I can tell that you, unlike this little country mouse, are a woman of the world, *au courant* with Savile Row and Jermyn Street, where I buy all my clothes, naturally. So tell me, do you not find me *tellement chic*? I'm sure you can see me strolling along the Strand in this elegant ensemble, which is, by the way, what I wore to play golf with the Queen's charming but incomprehensible man, John Brown. Later I took tea with Her Majesty and I could tell she had eyes only for me. And can you blame her?' Rosa spread her arms and struck a manly pose.

I laughed. 'Well,' I said. 'It's not exactly what you see on the streets of Mayfair, but perhaps on a shoot at a country house.'

Rosa grinned in triumph. 'You see, Camille, I am the fine English gentleman killing the little birds.' She bowed to me. 'Thank you, my dear Jessie. I like this costume even more now. I will wear it when I'm next at a *chasse* to paint the horses and hounds.'

A gendarme walked past in his *kepi* and short cloak. Camille ducked down and tried to pull Rosa inside the cab.

'Get in, you fool, before you're arrested for dressing like a man,' she said.

But Rosa shook her off and called out: '*Monsieur l'officier! Ça va?*'

The policeman doffed his cap. '*Ça va bien, Mademoiselle Bonheur.* Allow me to congratulate you on your costume. You are quite the most alluring artist in Paris, even in trousers.'

Rosa, it turned out, was within the law. She had acquired a permit from the police to dress as a man so she could paint at horse fairs and cattle marts.

After she had waved him off, she insisted we get down from the cab. 'I have finished my work for today and I starve like the poor little bohemians in their attics. Let's eat.' Rosa took us to a little kiosk, tipping her hat to women as they walked past and calling out flowery compliments so archaic they provoked giggles rather than outrage. 'Mademoiselle, you are slim as a palm tree. I beg you to throw me one of your coconuts.' In between her sallies, she gave us a running commentary of salacious asides. 'This one is a little peach, how I'd like to squeeze her.'

Camille batted Rosa on the arm. 'Enough! Your compliments are nearly as ridiculous as that suit. You sound like my *grandpère*. Don't you have any modern compliments?'

'You want modern? Try this. Eh, Mademoiselle!' she called out to a startled woman on a bicycle. 'Those legs would be better wrapped around *my* saddle.' She turned to us, satisfied. 'You can't get more modern than a bicycle, now, can you?'

At the café she ordered iced lemonade for us and I gulped mine down gratefully, not caring how unladylike I looked. People were already staring at us thanks to Rosa's outrageous appearance, but they soon turned their attention to a raucous group who arrived and sat a few tables away from us. The women were attractive in a dishevelled way that wasn't quite respectable, and one, her hair tumbling free over her low bodice, sat in an older man's lap, who had his back to us.

Rosa caught me watching them. '*Grisettes* – artists' tarts who like to call themselves seamstresses.' She pointed with her chin at the girl with the loose hair. 'That one's a sight to gladden the eyes of any red-blooded male. Auguste is a lucky dog.'

The older man turned his head and I recognised Rodin, who was laughing as the model ran her fingers through his beard and kissed his upturned face. Camille turned to see what we were talking about.

She let out a small cry and stood up. 'Let's go. Now.'

Rosa shrugged and put some coins on the table. But instead of leaving with us, Camille turned on her heel and marched over to the other table. Rodin rose, tipping the woman off his lap, and tried to say something. When he put his hand on Camille's arm, she pulled away from him and stormed out. Rodin stared after her.

'What's going on?' I said to Rosa as we watched Camille climb into the cab and slam the door.

Rosa gave a low whistle. 'Can't you guess? The little cat! Rodin has his work cut out for him there.'

I looked at Rosa's knowing face and it dawned on me what I had just seen. It was the first I knew of the love affair between Camille and Rodin.

CHAPTER 6

ASYLUM OF MONTDEVERGUES

September 1929

'Who could forget Rosa! That scoundrel!' Camille was laughing softly, her distress forgotten as we reminisced about our old friend. Then I ruined it all with an ill-judged remark.

'Only Rosa could get away with behaving like that.' I meant her eccentric dress sense, but Camille's face darkened and the frightening metallic voice was back.

'Of course, it was all right for Rosa to walk about in trousers, smoking on the streets and living openly with her woman lover,' she said. 'Unnatural as she was, Rosa was welcome in all the smartest Paris salons. But me, what was my crime? I fell in love with Rodin and lived my own life apart from my family. And then when I dared to break free from him and make it on my own as an artist, they dragged me away by force from my studio and locked me up with the lunatics.'

I was alarmed when she began to pace up and down, muttering to herself: '*Toute seule! Toute seule! Abandonée!*' When I tried to bring her back to the bench, she shook me off and screamed at the banked grey clouds, cursing Rodin.

'Camille, please.' I pulled her into my arms and stroked her poor thin hair, murmuring to her as I used to when she couldn't sleep. She clung to me and began to cry again.

'What is wrong with me? Why am I here? Oh, Jessie, help me, please help me.'

I began to cry too. 'I will, I promise.'

Dr Charpenel shook his head and for a moment forgot to address me in his impeccable English. '*Je suis desolé, Madame.* What you ask, it's impossible without the family's permission.'

I leaned my hands on his desk. 'But, what good is it doing keeping her here? She should be with people who love her. I would take care of her, Camille could live in my home, she would want for nothing.' She would sculpt again; we would work together as we once had. I would make her whole and bring her back. Camille, my Camille.

'Madame Elbourne, please understand that your visit has already upset the patient. Her only other visitor over the past fifteen years has been her brother.'

I closed my eyes. When Paul finally replied to all the letters I'd written him during my search for Camille, he did not tell me she had been abandoned here alone all that time, cut off from everything and everyone she loved. It was monstrous; unforgivable.

'While it is admirable that you care about your friend,' Charpenel said. 'I must insist that you do not raise her hopes of being released. That is simply out of the question – the Claudel family has always been adamant that she remain in our care.' He closed her file as if the matter were settled.

I would not give up. 'You yourself said that she would get better if she were cared for by people who loved her. I love her. Let me try at least. I can talk to her family, convince them that Camille is not mad.'

'My predecessor made a clear clinical diagnosis. Mademoiselle Claudel is in the grip of delusions that she is being persecuted, based on mostly false interpretations,' he said.

I seized on his choice of word. '*Mostly* false? It sounds as if you believe there might be some truth to her so-called delusions. I would also feel persecuted if I'd been taken against my will and locked up in an asylum.'

He refused to meet my eye. 'All I can say, Madame Elbourne, is that, historically, the asylum system has sometimes been abused by families who want to get rid of troublesome women.'

I waited.

Charpenel sighed and stared down at this desk with its neat piles of buff-coloured files. 'When she was first admitted, she wrote letters every day complaining of her wrongful incarceration, to the newspapers, to influential friends, until her mother gave strict orders she could not send or receive correspondence from anyone outside the family. Madame Claudel died earlier this year, and the ban is no longer in force – it is why you were able to write to her.'

I thought of the letters I had written over the years to Camille at her family's address; they had all gone unanswered. Now I knew why. All those years I had thought she was ignoring me, too busy with her own life to bother with me, and all the time she was here, shut up alone. No wonder she was so broken.

I put my hands on Charpenel's desk so he was forced to look up at me. 'Doctor, I implore you as a man of compassion, let me try to help Camille.'

'Even if you were to obtain permission, the outside world would be an enormous shock to Mademoiselle Claudel. Everything has changed so dramatically since she came here in 1914 from the psychiatric hospital of Ville-Évrard. She was transferred with the rest of the patients when the Germans began advancing on France.'

The mention of that year made me flinch. My sons were among the first to join up. They were different when they came back, but at least they came back. Camille would know nothing about the Great War, other than whispers from beyond the asylum walls.

Charpenel rubbed his chin. 'It would be too dangerous for her to travel to England, and I cannot in all conscience recommend this course of action.'

I began to protest but he held up his hand and continued. 'However, I do believe she would be happier and calmer under supervised freedom and the right medication in her family home.' He began to scribble on a pad. 'What I will do is recommend in the strongest possible terms that Mademoiselle Claudel be released into the care of her sister, Madame de Massary, who lives in the patient's childhood home in the country. Perhaps now that the mother is dead, the family will reconsider their position.' He put on his glasses and picked up one of the files.

'Thank you, Doctor.'

Charpenel stood up and led me to the door. 'Please do not expect miracles. Families in such cases are often reluctant to take on the responsibility of caring for an elderly relative.' He paused at the door and shook my hand. 'I will also forward your offer to care for the patient, but I can do no more. After that, it is up to the family.'

I held onto his hand. It seemed so unfair that Camille's fate should be decided by the same people who'd condemned her to this living hell in the first place. But there was no point railing at this reasonable man.

'Thank you,' I said. 'If you don't mind, I'll wait while you write the letter and take it to Louise myself.'

Camille and I waited outside in the dying afternoon sunshine for my husband to pick me up. If he was as appalled as me when he saw Camille, he hid it well. He talked of the weather and his cheerful good manners seemed to have a calming effect on her. When he suggested a photograph, she sat meekly next to me while he fussed over the camera. I reached for Camille's hands, which she kept folded in her lap, like an obedient schoolgirl. She was quiet, defeated, and she seemed somehow absent, as if her soul were elsewhere. It upset me more than anything to see the awful emptiness in her eyes.

I kissed her three times, the Parisian way she'd once taught me. 'I'll come back, Camille.'

She smiled blankly at me. 'That would be nice. Thank you for coming such a long way, Madame.' Her pupils were huge. They must have given her something while I was with Charpenel. A nurse led her away, and Camille was once again just a small bent old woman. I wanted to run after her, bundle her into the car and take her far away from this place.

When the gates clanged behind us, I turned to my husband. 'I have to go to Paris.'

He sighed and rubbed his temples. 'I knew this was a bad idea. What about our trip to Italy?'

'You go. I can't leave her here.'

'Very well, Jessie, do what you have to do. You've always done exactly as you wish.'

Had I? I had always been so sure of the path my life would take, but that all changed when I became entangled in the affair between Camille and Rodin.

CHAPTER 7

Camille brushed off my attempts to talk about what had happened in the Bois de Boulogne and the next time I saw Rodin was in our studio. He talked pleasantly enough to me about my work, but I could tell his attention was on Camille, who was ignoring him.

Rodin waited for her to look up but she dug into a lump of clay as if she wanted to destroy it. After a few minutes of uncomfortable silence he rapped his stick on the floor.

'Come now and rest, *Mesdemoiselles*. We shall have some coffee with a little something for inspiration.' Rodin took a silver flask from his coat pocket and sat at our tea chest.

'You know how to boil water, I expect,' Camille said, sitting opposite him.

Rodin eyed her with amusement and she stared back, coolly.

I was uncomfortable, but when I started to leave Camille cut her eyes towards me, and I knew I had to stay and witness the silent drama between them.

'I'll make the coffee,' I moved to the stove and measured the grounds into a ceramic percolator. I set the mismatched cups on the table and Rodin tipped viscous green fluid from the hipflask into them.

He smacked his lips. 'This absinthe has killed the last of the little worms wriggling about in my head from the terrible wine they serve in the Bois de Boulogne.'

'From what I could see, you found other consolations in the Bois,' Camille bit back.

Rodin laughed uncomfortably and glanced at me. I dipped my eyes and took a gulp of the absinthe and nearly choked. It was vile.

Rodin pressed his hands together and looked at us in turn. 'I have a proposition for you both. I've lost two assistants recently and a big commission has just come in. So, I'd like you to work in my main *atelier* at the *Dépôt des Marbres*. What do you say?' He sat back and waited.

I put down my cup with a clatter and realised my hands were shaking. It was unprecedented for women to work in a male sculptor's studio, let alone one of Rodin's standing. I looked at Camille, but she was staring at Rodin.

'The new commission,' Rodin continued calmly, as if he'd merely invited us for a promenade. 'Is from the *mairie* of Calais. It will be a lot of work, but it's prestigious and will be displayed in the town centre. Mademoiselle Claudel, you will work on the hands and feet, and Mademoiselle Lipscomb, Legros tells me you are one of the few young sculptors to have really mastered draperies, so that will be your job.' He spread out his hands. 'Well, will you come and work for me?'

I wanted to shout: 'Yes! Yes!' It was the chance of a lifetime and more than I could ever have hoped. Working in Rodin's studio would open doors and be the making of my career. I glanced at Camille, expecting to see her fizzing with excitement, but she was studying her cup, as if considering her options. Only the flush creeping up her neck betrayed her emotion.

Finally, she looked up. 'I want to accept, but there are difficulties. Everything depends on Jessie.'

I frowned at her. 'Why on me?'

Camille put her hand in mine. 'I can't attend Rodin's *atelier* on my own – my parents would not allow it. But, together it would be possible for two unmarried women to work in a man's studio – unorthodox but possible if my father gives his permission. And he will be more likely to do that if we chaperone each other. So, everything depends on your agreement, Jessie, and whether you can help me persuade my parents to give us permission.' She waited, as still as a cat.

Rodin poured some more absinthe into my cup. I took another drink, feeling his and Camille's eyes upon me. My limbs felt loose and there was a giddy fluttering in my stomach. I held out my cup and Rodin filled it again.

'Of course we must do it,' I said.

I caught the look between them and wondered for a moment if they had planned this. It would explain why Camille was so unfazed by the offer. But the thought left my fuzzy head and I smiled and raised my cup.

'To us!'

They laughed with relief and patted me on the back. We were like conspirators. I could hardly believe we would soon be working in Rodin's studio.

Rodin put his hands on his thighs and stood up. 'I will leave you now. It's getting late and as my new employees I order you to get some rest.' He bowed to us in mock formality while we clapped and called out *au 'voir, au 'voir*.

When we were alone, Camille clutched my hands and beamed at me, her eyes shining.

'Can you imagine? Rodin's studio! Oh, Jessie, I bless the day you came to me.'

CHAPTER 8

Camille's father was expected home the following Sunday and she planned to ask his permission then. That week we worked on in a fever of excitement. When Sunday morning finally arrived, I woke early to the clamour of church bells. The Claudels' apartment was quiet and at first I thought the dining room was empty when I went in. I was startled when Paul stood up.

'G-g-good morning, Jessie. M-m-may I say how charming you look?' He had a slight stutter that made his shyness even more endearing.

I smiled to put him at his ease. 'I'm glad to see you; Camille is still asleep and I thought I would have to break my fast alone.'

'My sister has never been an early riser.'

We ate in companionable silence for a while, but there was something about the way the sun came in the windows and pooled over our breakfast that reminded me of Sunday mornings at home, and, for the first time since I had arrived in Paris, I was struck by a wave of homesickness. It caught me by surprise and I couldn't stop the tears filling my eyes. At home, the bells from St Botolph's would be calling my parents to worship in the simple little thirteenth-century church with its carved wooden pews and cross-stitched hassocks. They would be at breakfast now, spreading Cooper's Oxford on their toast, Papa grumbling over the newspaper while Ma scolded him for scattering crumbs.

Paul noticed my distress and passed me a napkin to wipe my eyes. 'You miss your family.'

'I do, very much. Paris is wonderful but ...' I couldn't go on.

Paul waited until I had composed myself. 'I'm glad you are here, Jessie, you are good for Camille.'

I looked up, surprised. 'It is she who is good for me – she has such talent.'

'It is true, she has an immense talent, but she benefits from your steadiness and from your gentleness. She is a lot less bullet-headed since you came to live with us. Camille has always known exactly what she wants – and how to get it. She is an irresistible force of nature.' His laughter held a note of resentment.

I buttered my bread and waited for him to go on. This was my chance to find out more about Camille.

Paul shrugged, his face sweet and open once more. 'But, I'm being unfair to my sister. Life in our family is not easy for her. Maman likes to blame Camille for our move to a cramped apartment in an unfashionable part of Paris.'

'Why would it be Camille's fault?'

He explained that she had outgrown her tutors in the village where she had grown up and one had recommended a move to Paris so she could attend art college, and Paul one of the city's finest *lycées*.

'So, you see, the move was for me too. But Maman chose to blame Camille – her story is that she bullied the family into moving to Paris. Unfortunately, Father cannot leave his business in the country, so Maman is unhappy. It's easier for her to blame Camille than to go against her husband. My poor sister, she would never admit it, but she suffers most from our mother's coldness. Maman does not easily give those little gestures of affection that seem to come so naturally to other women.'

I thought of my own mother, who had always stroked my hair and put out her arms to me as a child, covering my face in kisses, who hugged me still. There was a world of difference between Madame Claudel and her martyred air and Ma, who had a tough life working as a barmaid in a railway hotel before Papa met her but was always cheerful. She would have had little patience for Camille's mother, who was always complaining about living in Montparnasse.

'And do you like it here?' I said. 'Or do you miss your childhood home?'

'The countryside near our village, Villeneuve, is beautiful, but it is a backwater. There is nowhere quite like Paris.'

I smiled. 'You're right – as much as I miss my home in England, there isn't anywhere I'd rather be now than Paris.'

We heard the front door open and a man's voice speaking to the maid in the hall.

Paul turned his head towards the noise, his face apprehensive. 'Papa is home,' he said. 'He'll want to put us all through our paces. He's ambitious for all of us, you see, even for Louise. He wishes her to play the piano to concert level. Can you imagine?'

We shared a smile.

'I got the impression she prefers visiting the milliner to practising her scales,' I said.

'You have the measure of her, I see.'

We heard more voices coming from the salon, and after a while the dining room door flew open. It was Camille.

She spoke quickly. 'Jessie, there you are! Papa is here. I told him about Rodin's proposal. He is not against it, but Maman is being impossible.' She spotted her brother and pulled him to his feet. 'You must help me persuade her, Paul, you are the favourite and she will listen to you.'

In the salon, a sharp-featured man with mutton-chop whiskers wearing a fez stood near the window. He regarded our entrance with amusement.

'Ah, here come the revolutionaries, the rebellious artists ready to scandalise the good ladies of Paris. And here is their knight errant, *le petit* Paul. What do you have to say about this latest scheme of Camille's?' He held out his arms to his son, who embraced him stiffly.

'Oh, Papa,' Camille said, dancing around her father. 'You must let Jessie and I do this. Just think how much we will learn in Rodin's studio! He has promised me the hands and the feet. *The hands and the feet!*'

Madame Claudel observed her daughter coolly from where she sat next to the window, a hoop of embroidery on her lap. 'It's out of the question.'

Camille grasped Paul's elbow and looked at him beseechingly to intercede, but he only blushed and turned away.

Her husband said, 'Now, my dear. Let us consider this proposal rationally. I presume, Camille, that this is your new friend, Mademoiselle Lipscomb?'

Monsieur Claudel came towards me and shook my hand. He looked me up and down with a wry smile. 'The English are such a practical race, I'm sure we can trust your judgement in this matter, Mademoiselle. What do you have to say about Monsieur Rodin's extraordinary proposal? I know my wife trusts your steadying influence on our wayward girl.' With his back to Madame Claudel, he winked at me and I understood my role at once: to persuade Madame Claudel our virtue would not be sullied.

I cleared my throat. 'It is an unorthodox proposal, yes, but it is also a great honour. Monsieur Rodin has assured us that all due proprieties will be followed.' I took a letter from my pocket. 'I have written to my own parents, who give their permission.'

I handed the letter to Monsieur Claudel, who read it and gave it to his wife. We waited while Madame Claudel finished reading.

She folded it carefully, her lips a thin line. 'Jessie's parents obviously trust her, and I suppose we must show the same tolerance. You may go, Camille, but I expect you to behave correctly.' She picked up her embroidery. Monsieur Claudel grinned and motioned that we should leave the room.

In the hall, Camille grasped my hands. 'Oh, Jessie, you were wonderful! You have opened the door for us, a door that is locked to other women.'

We swung each other round. We would no longer just be Rodin's pupils, but professional artists, his colleagues!

The rest of that memorable Sunday was taken up with a noisy family lunch that lasted four or five hours. *Père* Claudel took centre stage. I watched quietly as his children sought his approval, like flowers turning their faces to catch the sun's warmth. Despite what she'd said earlier, Camille was clearly his favourite and he beamed with pride while she told him about her latest sculpture. With Paul he discussed poetry and urged him to read us one of his own. Even Madame Claudel thawed a little, batting away her husband's hands when he squeezed her waist. For Louise he had a gentle, bullying tone, forcing her to sit at the piano where she played some of Mozart's and Brahms's more popular pieces, running her languorous white hands up and down the keys.

'Very pretty, my dear. Now, tell me, have you mastered the Debussy I gave you on my last visit home? He is one of France's most exciting new composers. I'm interested to see how you interpret his *L'Enfant Prodigue*.' He settled himself into a chair and steepled his hands expectantly.

Louise pouted and stood up from the piano. 'Oh, Papa, that tiresome modern music is too difficult for me. The key changes all the time.'

Monsieur Claudel's face hardened and his mocking affability disappeared. 'You must stretch yourself if you want to become a real musician. There are to be no amateurs in this family, only real artists. Look at your sister, and your brother, how hard they work at improving on their creative gifts.'

Louise looked mutinous. As she scowled I could see her resemblance to her older sister. Her father turned his back on her abruptly and began to talk to Camille about the forthcoming Salon exhibition. Louise bit her lip and went to sit beside Madame Claudel, from where she glared murderously at Camille.

That night, Camille and I sat on her bed talking. Through the open window we could hear distant music, a woman singing a love song. Camille rested her head on my shoulder and we listened for a while.

'Jessie, are you in love?'

Her curls tickled my nose. I smoothed them down, and wondered what to say. I suppose I was: I had known William since I was a child and couldn't imagine my life without him. But I had never experienced the heady emotions I'd read about in novels.

Camille prodded me. 'It's not a hard question. Do you have a young man?'

'Yes, I do, William Elbourne. Our families expect us to marry.'

She sighed and sounded wistful. 'You're so lucky not to have any impediments to your love, to know what lies ahead.'

I didn't say anything for a while. William was as familiar to me as the air I breathed, but sometimes I wished for more: a grand passion that would knock the breath out of me.

'And you, Camille, do you have someone?'

She hesitated and I thought she was about to tell me something about her obvious crush on Rodin – I did not suspect the seriousness of their affair then – but instead she stood up and walked over to the window. I went to join her and we leaned our elbows on the balcony railing and looked out over Paris, twinkling with lights. It was a clear night and the stars hung in the velvet sky like jewels in a cape. A cool breeze came off the Seine and I shivered; Camille put her arm around my waist.

'When shall we tell Rodin that we can work with him?' I said.

'Tomorrow we'll go to my old college, the Colarossi. One of the sculptors from Rodin's *atelier* attends the morning class. We can give him a message for Rodin.'

Camille pulled me towards the bed. 'Why don't you stay here tonight? I'm too excited to fall asleep just yet.'

I climbed under the sheets with her. We lay there without speaking for a while, listening to the *chanteuse*.

'I wonder what the men in Rodin's studio will make of us,' I said.

She shrugged. 'They'll just have to put up with it. What can they do? Rodin himself has appointed us.'

I wasn't so sure. At South Ken, the studio where the male sculptors worked sounded like a construction site, the men shouting above the racket, cursing like East End stevedores. They were notorious brutes to women. I didn't imagine the ones at Rodin's studio would be any different.

'We're in for a fight,' I said.

Camille took my hand and squeezed it. 'Are you frightened?'

I grinned at her. 'What, of a bunch of muscle-bound fatheads? Not a bit of it!'

Camille laughed and she grabbed my hand. We lay, our fingers intertwined, our faces close together on the pillow; in the moonlight her eyes were a fathomless black.

'*Ma petite anglaise*,' she said. 'Together we can do anything.'

CHAPTER 9

VILLENEUVE

September 1929

Louise had aged well. Her hair, an improbable blonde, was shingled in the latest style, her lips carefully painted crimson, and her skin powder-pale with rouged cheeks. She perched on a chaise longue, slim in a chic black jersey dress.

'Chanel,' she said when I complimented her, touching the silk scarf at her throat. Hermès, no doubt. 'Jessie! After all these years, it's incredible.' Her polite smile died when I told her why I was there. 'You want Camille to come and live with you in England?' I gave her Charpenel's letter. She took it in manicured hands, nails as red as her mouth.

'As you can see,' I said. 'The doctor says she's well enough to leave the asylum, with the right care.'

Louise shook her lacquered head. 'This is preposterous, out of the question.'

I had been expecting this. 'If you won't let me take her home with me, she could come and live here. It's so peaceful.' Birdsong filtered through the open windows. I leaned towards her. 'Please, Louise, you can't leave her in that place. Show some mercy. She's your sister.'

Louise screwed up the letter and dropped it on the rug. Her voice was hard. 'Who are you to lecture me? What do you know about Camille?'

'I know Camille like I know myself.'

'Oh really? Where were you when she started to behave like

a raving lunatic? And now you come marching in, telling me my duty. You have no idea what our family has had to put up with from Camille over the years, no idea. It's too much.'

She stood up and went to the bureau, returning with a bundle of letters. 'Don't you think we've been through all this before? It's not the first time the doctors at Montdevergues have tried to go against my family's wishes. These are from 1920, from a Dr Brunet. He wanted Camille to be let out on a trial basis, said she was calmer.'

She read from the letter. '*Her thoughts of persecution, though not completely gone, are much less pronounced. She would very much like to be with her family and to live in the country. I believe that, in these conditions, we could try to let her out.*'

She put them back in the drawer and slammed it shut. 'Maman saw right through that ruse, knew she'd been playacting for the gullible doctor. Camille is a sly one, they all are, it's part of their sickness.'

Louise had always been selfish and spoiled, but I thought she might have grown up. She clearly hadn't: she was as brittle and self-obsessed as ever. It was hard to listen to her, the way she spoke about Camille, her flesh and blood. I forced back my anger and tried again.

'Louise, if you could only see Camille, you would be able tell straight away that she is harmless. Won't you go and visit her at Montdevergues?' She turned her hard little face to the window. I had tried to rouse her compassion with a gentle appeal to her good nature, but she obviously didn't have one. I spoke more sharply. 'Dr Charpenel said Paul has been her only visitor in all these years.'

Louise flinched then composed her features into an icy mask once more. 'I can't possibly leave my family. It's such a long way, and I am not strong.' She pressed a lace handkerchief to her temples, as if to show me what a terrible strain she was under. It made me furious and I lost my patience.

'I've never heard anything so ridiculous. I made the journey from England to the South of France and back up to Paris, and you see I am still in one piece, even though I'm older than you. You're just making excuses.' I stood up, my fists clenched by my side, and Louise shrank back in alarm. 'And if you won't let Camille come with me, why don't you have her live here? There's nothing to stop you, there's plenty of room, and it is her family home too, after all.'

Louise looked horrified. 'Are you mad, also, Jessie? Camille cannot come here; she's not fit to live with decent people. I have children, and they can't be exposed to Camille's vices.' She returned to the bureau and found another document. 'We've had regular reports over the years. In this one it states that Camille had a period of calm, and then a relapse. The latest one says she's no better than she was when she was admitted.' She held out the piece of paper to me. 'You can read it for yourself if you don't believe me.'

I ignored the documents. 'Obviously she had a relapse, anyone would. Camille thought she was going to get out but when your mother refused to let her out then and made it clear she never wanted her back, all hope was taken from her. And now she's been abandoned in asylums for years, with no prospect of freedom. Can't you see it's a living hell for her?'

Louise threw the documents on the floor and screeched at me like a child who has run out of arguments and finds refuge in a temper tantrum. 'And what about me?' She stamped her foot and somehow managed still to look elegant in her black and white Chanel courts. 'It's all poor Camille this, poor Camille that. You have no idea what she was like, the things she did. What do you think my life would be like if she was free to roam around the village? How long before she ran back to Paris, to her foul drunken ways, sending obscene letters to the newspapers, accusing us of God knows what?'

I began to understand why Louise didn't want Camille back. Locked up, voiceless, her correspondence censored, the world would never know about the injustice she had suffered at the hands of her family. Released, there would be nothing to stop her stirring up a scandal. Dr Charpenel had also told me that when she'd first been put away, the papers had been full of furious letters from her support-ers. The furore had died down, but it would be reignited if Camille were given her freedom. They had too much to lose. Paul was a prom-inent diplomat, a poet and playwright, Louise, a respectable married woman, comfortably installed in the Claudel family home.

Louise marched across the room and opened the sitting room door to indicate our meeting was at an end. I took my time gathering my things. When I stood before her she'd brought her emotions under check again and her painted lips stretched into a sympathetic smile. She didn't fool me.

'I'm sorry if I spoke harshly, Jessie,' she said sweetly, placing a hand on my arm. 'But this is a painful subject for me. My poor sister! Fortunately, Camille is not alone, not at all, you are mistaken in this. Paul visits her when he's home from America and one of his daughters goes to see her *Tante* Camille from time to time. I believe they have grown quite fond of each other.'

I shook her hand off. 'Camille has been abandoned, and well you know it. She is desperately lonely and in despair. If you don't believe me, look at this.' I showed her the photograph my husband had taken of Camille in the asylum. I had asked him to develop it in Montfavet for just this purpose.

Louise stared at it for a long moment. At last, I saw tears in her eyes. 'Poor Camille.' But the moment was over and her voice was hard again. 'There is nothing to be done for her. I can't bring her here. I simply don't have the time to look after her. And even if I could, why would I? When she lived close to me in Paris, she never wanted anything to do with me. I didn't see her, not even once, while she was being hailed as a great artist, this "woman of genius".' She seemed to collect herself. 'Besides, Camille was always jealous of me when we were younger. She hated how close I was to Maman. All those old feelings of hers would return if she lived here, and it would be worse if she saw me again. Who knows what she would do?' She shuddered. 'I wouldn't be safe in my bed at night.'

I resisted the temptation to slap her and forced myself to speak pleasantly; it would do Camille no good if I were to antagonise her family. 'Please Louise, won't you visit her, just once? It would mean so much to her.'

She looked at the photograph again before handing it back to me. 'Yes, I promise, next summer, I'll take my two children to see their aunt. Poor Camille.' She shut the door behind me so quickly it nearly caught my back.

A car was waiting for me. The driver sprang out and opened the door.

'Take me to Paris,' I said.

I would find out what had happened to Camille. If I could prove that she had not been mad, that a terrible injustice had been committed, her family would be forced to take her out of that place. I would piece together the rest of her story. So far, I knew only part of it. I would find Georges; he would help me now, as he had done the first time we met.

CHAPTER 10

Paris

July 1884

Camille and I went early the next morning to the Colarossi Academy to get a message to Rodin and to hire a new model to replace Marie-Thérèse, who had inconveniently fallen in love with an artist and was refusing to sit for anyone else. The art college was the site of one of two model fairs, and if you got there early enough you could have your pick of the Italian and Jewish professional models who flocked to the city at that time.

A group of odd characters had gathered at the gates. An elderly man with an Old Testament beard, dressed in a robe and sandals, sat on his bundle paring an apple for a small boy with the rounded cheeks of a *putto*. His mother, a ripe peaches and cream blonde, reached out to slap the urchin's hand away from his nose. The lace trim on her eighteenth-century costume was grubby and the feathers on her large hat drooped. Nearby, two young women in peasant dress, one dark and one fair, both strikingly beautiful, stood chatting in Italian to a tall man, his shirt open to reveal a powerful chest. He had a handsome Slavic face with deep-set eyes and high cheekbones. Only his mane of dark curls betrayed his Italian origins.

Camille spoke to the old man. 'I suppose there's no need to ask what kind of work you do – I recognise you from half a dozen Bible scenes.'

'Mademoiselle, in my time I have been all twelve of the apostles, and I make a fine St Augustine. "Make me chaste but not yet", eh?' He leered at Camille.

Her tone was cool. 'This is your family?'

'My little grandson, Emile, and my daughter, Ruth. Abraham and his son is one of our specialities, while Ruth can be Delilah or the Madonna. She's versatile. And I've sat for all the most prominent artists and have many tales with which to enliven your *atelier* and amuse your guests.'

I took Camille by the elbow and spoke to her quietly. 'This is the last thing we need – a time waster who distracts us from our work. No doubt he has any number of tricks to cut down on his posing time.' I nodded at the athletic man with the peasant girls. 'What about him?'

'Undraped?' Camille asked.

'Undraped. I'm sure we'd cope.'

We grinned at each other.

'Why not?' Camille said. 'We'll be working in Rodin's studio and surrounded by men soon enough.'

'We should get to know the enemy, up close.' I said. 'How often have you had the chance to work on a male nude?'

She frowned.

'Exactly,' I said. 'A gap in our education – it's high time we filled it.'

Camille turned back to the man. 'Today, I'm looking for more of a David. Or a Goliath.' She nodded at the athletic man with the peasant girls.

Abraham stroked his beard. 'Ah, Mademoiselle, you have an eye for a good physique. That's Giganti. All the sculptors love him. You should see him with his clothes off, muscles that Michelangelo would have killed for. I hear Rodin wants to sign him up.'

Camille moved towards the young Italian. 'You are Giganti?'

The giant straightened up from where he'd been lounging against the wall. He towered over us, but his face was gentle when he smiled. '*Si, signorina.*'

Camille reached up and squeezed his bicep. 'We pay five *sous* a day. Can you come tomorrow morning?'

While I waited for Camille to hire Giganti, I listened idly to the conversation between the fair and dark women. When I heard

Rodin's name, I edged closer. I'd picked up enough Italian on trips to Florence to make out what they were saying.

'He's an old goat,' the blonde said. 'Do you know how he made me pose last time? Legs so wide I nearly got a chill in my…' She clutched at the skirt between her legs.

The brunette's laugh was throaty. 'Do you know what he said to me? "Next time, bring your sister, *la blonde*, and we can all have some fun." Dirty pig. He said he'd pay double to sculpt us both, you know, together.' She shrugged. 'I don't mind. Rodin always pays well. It's just a pity about that scratchy beard.'

So our *maître* was one of those artists who took advantage of his models. He wasn't alone – I'd heard stories, but it still wasn't right. Women like these depended on artists for their livelihood and were too poor to say no. It was little better than prostitution. Can you imagine the outrage if I or Camille took liberties with Giganti? I couldn't help smiling – it wasn't an unpleasant thought.

The life class was in a studio with a glass ceiling that made the most of the weak morning light. We hauled a couple of easels from where they lay stacked in the corner and dragged them to the front. Taking precious sheets of paper from our leather portfolios, we pinned them to the boards. I smoothed my hand over the coarse grain and took out my charcoal sticks. Camille stood at her easel, one hand on her hip, looking towards the door. She craned to see over the heads of the students coming in until she spotted someone and waved.

'*Eh, bien*, here is my friend, Georges,' she said.

He wore the uniform of the Latin Quarter art student: dark blonde hair swept back and worn long over his collar, tweed jacket over a loose shirt open at the neck. But there was a sleek elegance about him that belied his labourer's clothes and there was an aristocratic languor to his gait. He was the most exquisitely handsome man I'd ever seen. I couldn't take my eyes from him.

Georges sauntered over, his hands in his pockets. '*Salut*, Camille. What brings you here? I thought you'd outgrown us at the Colarossi now that you've got your own *atelier* with Rodin as your mentor.' He nodded at me. 'Who's your friend?'

Camille introduced us. Georges kept his hands in his pockets but he looked at me intently, as if I were the only person in the room. I was transfixed. If someone had shouted *Fire!* at that moment I would have stayed rooted to the spot.

'English?' he said.

'Yes.' I was furious to find myself blushing. His lips twitched into a smile and I dug my nails into my palm. Idiot!

He moved closer. 'Interesting.'

Camille looked amused. 'Yes, she is interesting. Jessie is a rising star, a protégée of Legros, and now, like me, of Rodin. You'd better look to your laurels, Georges.'

Georges leaned his hand on my easel. 'I work with Rodin, you know.' He addressed Camille but hadn't taken his eyes off me.

'That's exactly what we want to talk to you about,' Camille said. She wasn't used to being ignored and sounded cross. 'Rodin has invited me, I mean both of us, to work at his studio. We came here to ask if you would take a message to Rodin, that we accept his offer.' Camille poked Georges' hand with her charcoal. 'So, there's no need to make such a close study of Jessie – you'll be seeing a lot more of her when we become your workmates.'

Startled, Georges broke eye contact with me and concentrated on Camille. 'Rodin's studio, you say? Women working in the studio of the great man, now that is a new one.' He rubbed his face and grinned. 'I don't know if the lads are quite ready to embrace the fairer sex, well not in that way, at least. I, on the other hand, am more than ready to give it a go.' Camille punched him on the arm and Georges laughed. 'Don't worry, I'm only joking. Your virtue is safe with me, Camille. Your friend's on the other hand…' He looked at me and my stomach contracted. I was determined not to blush again and met his eyes.

'I'm not worried about my virtue,' I said with all the coolness I could muster.

Georges raised his eyebrows. 'Perhaps you should be. Be warned, I love a challenge.' The room had begun to fill up and he moved away to set up his easel at the other side of the model's dais. 'I'll come and find you after class,' he called over his shoulder.

I frowned and pretended to attend to my easel, but as soon as his back was turned I peeked around the side of it. He had stopped to talk to an aristocratic woman in sables, a wealthy Russian by the looks of her jewellery and the retinue that fussed around her, laying out materials. Georges whispered in her ear, and she laughed and laid a heavily ringed hand on his shoulder. No! The stab of jealousy was so strong it made me grip the sides of my easel. Georges glanced back and I ducked my head, hoping he hadn't caught me. I was acting like a fool; he was obviously a flirt and I had fallen for his charms like a silly servant girl. I began to fix paper to my board, determined to put him from my thoughts.

Just then, a timid model came in accompanied by another woman. She licked her lips and darted looks from under her hat around the crowded room.

Camille leaned towards me. 'Une ingénue. Prepare for some sport.'

The new girl stopped at the dais and looked desperately at her friend, who gave her a little shove and said: 'Go on, what are you waiting for? It's not so bad after the first time.'

A man called out: 'Take off your clothes. Let's see what you're made of.'

'She doesn't dare – her chemise is torn.' This time the taunting was from a woman. I was surprised and looked questioningly at Camille, but she seemed to be enjoying the show.

The students started chanting: 'Off, off, off!'

The girl looked as if she was about to cry. She stood uncertainly and all at once began tearing off her clothes. A raucous cheer rose around her. She stood naked before us, using one arm to cover her small breasts and the other she put between her legs.

'Look at her feet! The soles are as black as my husband's heart,' called another woman.

'Have you been walking far this morning, sweetheart? Your feet are so veined and red.' A man, this time, with a thick German accent.

'At least her breasts are firm. Give her a few years and she'll have a clutch of brats hanging off them. They'll look like empty slippers.' Another woman.

It was barbaric. Nobody deserved to be treated that way. 'We must help her,' I said to Camille.

'*Ah bouf*, Jessie. Stop being so soft-hearted. She needs toughening up otherwise she'll be no good as a model. She'll survive. You'll see, it'll be over soon.'

Camille was wrong: the poor girl's torment had just begun.

A man walked towards her, his hat pushed to the back of his head. He grinned at his friends, who called out their encouragement. 'Mademoiselle,' he said. 'We would like you to take up the pose of the Wounded Swan.'

'I'm sorry, Monsieur, I don't know this pose. But I have learned others.' She lay down on the chaise longue, her ankles crossed and her hands doing their best to cover her shame.

The man tutted like a disappointed schoolteacher. 'No, that won't do at all. Here, stand up. That's right. Now bend your arm, no this way. Stand on one leg. Turn it out, like so.'

'Twist your neck towards the window,' one of his friends called.

'Stick out your bony little bottom.'

'Lower your knee. Not that one, you fool, the right knee.'

The commands came fsaster and faster and soon she looked like a contortionist.

'She'll never sustain that pose, it's ridiculous,' I said.

'That's the point.' Camille's charcoal flew across the paper.

After a few minutes, the girl's limbs started trembling and she stumbled. She rubbed her calf muscles and began to wail.

I could bear it no longer and walked over to the girl's chief tormentor, prepared to tell him what I thought of his behaviour. Before I could say anything, Georges pushed in front of me. As he passed me he laid his hand on mine and shook his head slightly. He jumped up onto the dais, took off his jacket and put it around the girl's shoulders.

'Dry your eyes, Mademoiselle,' he said, giving her his handkerchief. 'They are only having some fun. Come, stop crying. Didn't your friend tell you that all the new girls get the same treatment on their first day? Well done, you have passed the test, you're a fully fledged professional model. Now, isn't that something to tell your mother about tonight?'

His actions seemed to calm the students, who began to cheer the little model, crying: 'Bravo! Bravo!' She smiled broadly and took a bow, her shame forgotten.

Georges said something to her and she arranged herself into a pose that was both challenging for us to draw and easy for her to hold. He stepped off the dais, carrying his jacket over his shoulder, and tipped his hat at me with a grin.

Camille spoke softly in my ear. 'Duchamp is a handsome devil. You could do worse.'

'I barely know him and, besides, I'm promised to William.'

She smiled. 'Ah yes, William, your childhood friend. If you say so, Jessie, but I think our gallant D'Artagnan,' she nodded towards Georges, 'is smitten with you. That's good – we'll need an ally in Rodin's studio.'

I picked up a piece of charcoal and began to sketch in the outlines of the figure, but couldn't stop thinking about Georges and how he had helped that downtrodden creature. It takes a lot to go against the crowd – I should know. He obviously didn't give a ha'penny about what other people thought of him. I'd been too hasty to dismiss him as a shallow flirt; there was more to Georges Duchamp than those casually rumpled – devastating – good looks.

At the end of class I was picking up some dropped charcoals when I felt rather than saw Georges crouch down beside me. His hand brushed against mine.

'I'm on my way to Rodin's studio. You can deliver your message in person. I'll take you there, if you want,' he said, using the familiar '*tu*'.

I met his eyes and the look in them stopped my breath. Georges held out his hand and, like a sleepwalker, I slipped my hand into his warm palm and followed him.

CHAPTER 11

Georges strode through the Latin Quarter and Camille and I had
to rush to keep up with him. We were out of breath, hairlines damp
and corsets digging into our ribs by the time we got to 182 rue de
l'Université. Rodin's *atelier* was in the *Dépôt des Marbres* where the
Government stored the marble for State commissions. Georges led
us into an open-air courtyard filled with dust and noise. I had been
in stone-cutting yards before but never one so large and busy; it was
like a small factory. Georges had to shout above the din of chisels
being hammered into marble and the rumble of wheelbarrows as
workmen moved blocks of stone around the yard.

'Eh, Jules,' he called to a wiry man up a ladder. 'Come down
from there and meet Rodin's latest slaves.'

The man slid down the outside of the ladder. He removed the
cotton kerchief he'd wrapped around his face, which was dusted
white and marked with two rivulets of sweat, like a weeping statue.
Jules Desbois, the senior *practicien* or stone sculptor, wiped a filthy
hand on his shirt and shook our hands.

'Women in the studio, I've seen everything now. But,' a shrug of
the shoulders, 'if Rodin thinks you're up to the job, who am I to go
against the *maître*?' He began to pace to and fro, his hands behind
his back as he delivered an evidently well-rehearsed lecture. 'I warn
you now, there won't be any allowances made for you. We work
twelve hours a day, sometimes sixteen. Rodin makes the *maquettes*
and we turn them into stone or bronze statues weighing a ton. We
work as a team here, there's no glory for anyone other than Rodin.
The pay is poor and Rodin can be difficult, but,' another shrug, 'he is
a genius.' He stopped pacing and put his hands on his hips. 'I'll treat
you like the men – no better, but no worse. You'll get a fair crack of

the whip. If you can take the pace, I'll have your backs. If not, you should leave now.'

Camille was the first to speak. 'We are not afraid of hard work, or of Monsieur Rodin. We expect him to be as exacting with us as with any of the men working here. You will find us their equal in stamina, if not strength. And as for talent, he has chosen Jessie and me out of his many students.'

'You think you're up to it?' Desbois rubbed his chin. 'One other thing – this is the coldest place on God's earth in winter. Enough to freeze your balls off, eh Georges?' He waited for our reaction. He wanted to shock us and it made me angry. If he imagined he could intimidate us with some coarse language, he was about to be proved wrong.

'I suppose that's where we have the advantage, Monsieur as, for-tunately, we have no balls,' I said with a sweet smile, spreading my skirts. Desbois looked stunned for a moment, and then he guffawed and slapped Georges on the back.

'A pair of cool customers. Where did Rodin find them? The lads better watch out, they've met their match with these two. I tell you what, come back next week and we'll see what you're made of.' He turned his back on us, whistling as he returned to his work.

Georges lit a cigarette. 'Well done. Desbois is not usually so easy to get round.' He looked at me through the smoke. 'You make quite an impression, Jessie.'

Camille scowled and pulled at his arm. 'Come on, we're wasting time. I thought you were going to show us around.'

Studio M, Rodin's main Paris *atelier*, was cavernous, with bare white walls and a flagstone floor. Light flooded in through arched windows onto plaster models of all sizes and in different stages of completion. On one table, the figure of a man was crouched over two small, lifeless bodies. It was Dante's Ugolino, an Italian noble-man who was imprisoned for treason and forced to eat his children's corpses before he too starved to death. I wrenched my eyes away from the gruesome tableau and looked around the room. It was almost too much to take in: every surface was crowded with plaster arms, legs and heads. At the back of the room, vast portals towered nearly to the ceiling. Figures sprang out of them and seemed to writhe in ecstasy. I walked towards the massive structure, as if in a trance, until I was close enough to study the yearning, tormented creatures. Each tiny face was contorted by a different expression of agony, lust or despair. I had never seen anything quite like it.

'The Gates of Hell,' Georges stood behind me, so close I could smell his lemon cologne and feel the warmth from his body. When he pointed at the giant doors, it was as if he embraced me. I tried to concentrate on what he was saying about the figure that topped the doors, a seated nude, his chin on his fist, as if deep in thought. I could not know then that *The Thinker* would become the world's most iconic sculpture.

'It is Dante, looking out over the circles of hell,' Georges said.

'No, it is Rodin.' My senses overwhelmed first by Rodin's masterpiece and then by Georges' physical closeness, I hadn't noticed Camille. Her words broke the spell and Georges took a step away from me.

His tone was irritable. 'You always sound so sure of yourself, Camille.' He shaded his eyes to peer at the statue where the ceiling cast a shadow. 'But the figure looks nothing like the *maître* – too young, for a start.'

'Don't be so damned literal, Georges. It's Rodin, I tell you,' she said, beginning to throw her arms about in an effort to explain. 'Can't you see? He's the archetype of all artists: he's Dante, Baudelaire, Balzac, Hugo and Rodin, above all, Rodin, dreaming into being his creations. But it is not an easy dream – look how every muscle in his body tenses with the effort of imagining, even his toes are gripping. It is Rodin as Creator.'

'Very perceptive, Mademoiselle Claudel.' We turned to see Rodin. He stood easily, hands in his trouser pockets, the master of his studio. 'Do you like my door to Hell? I hope you can both help me complete the infernal thing.' He smiled, pleased with his joke.

I was about to launch into an embarrassing gush of praise when Camille broke in, all business. 'It's all settled, we can join your studio.'

Rodin clapped his hands. 'Excellent, I knew you would find a way. And you have conscripted Georges to your camp, I see. Very wise! Now, allow me to give you a guided tour, with commentary by the artist.' He smiled affably and stretched out his hand to Camille; she ignored it and took my arm.

As he walked around the studio and talked about his work, Rodin worked away at a small piece of clay. He stopped at a pair of seated lovers locked in an embrace. Once again, I found myself looking at a masterpiece, one that would become famous as a symbol of romantic love. It is an extraordinary privilege to have been one of the first people in the world to have seen *The Kiss*, and one I still cherish.

We stood in awed silence in front of the sculpture. The couple were consumed with desire, lost in each other, the woman as hungry as the man. Tantalisingly, their lips did not meet. To look at them was to experience the thrill of the voyeur. Camille broke away from me and stepped closer to stroke the woman's haunch. Georges took her place next to me and placed a hand on my back.

'What do you call it?' Camille asked Rodin.

'The critics call it *The Kiss*, but the original title is *Francesca da Rimini*.'

'The adulterous lovers, Paolo and Francesca, from Dante's second circle of Hell,' I said. 'She fell in love with her husband's brother while they were reading the tale of Lancelot and Guinevere.'

'You know your Dante,' Rodin said, taking a well-thumbed book from his pocket and showing me the cover: *La Divina Commedia*. 'I take it with me everywhere.'

Camille was also transfixed by the sculpture. 'The woman is desperate for him, she is the man's equal in passion, pulling him close while he holds himself back. It is the moment before.'

Rodin and Camille shared a long look and once again I was the voyeur.

He opened his palm to show her a small, clay hand, its fingers curled in supplication. 'For you, because you know that the hands and the feet are the most expressive parts of the body.' Camille took the hand from him and studied it. Rodin turned to us. 'The models are about to return from lunch and I must get back to work. But please stay if you wish. Georges will look after you.'

Rodin went over to a noisy trio, who had come into the studio. It was the two Italian women we had seen at the Colarossi and Giganti.

Georges gave a low whistle. 'Two sisters – one fair as day the other dark as night. Rodin has a good eye, eh Camille?' He nudged her but she ignored him.

The sisters didn't bother with a changing screen and pulled off their cotton blouses and stepped out of their gathered skirts where they stood. Naked, they began to parade around the studio, as comfortable as if they were strolling fully clothed through a street market. Giganti kicked off his clogs and was soon as naked as the other two. His physique was breathtaking: an anatomist's dream of muscles and sinews. Rodin gestured to Giganti and he began tumbling like a circus acrobat. The blonde sister danced with abandon to music only she could hear, arms weaving. Meanwhile, the dark one squatted on a dais, careless of her modesty.

Rodin followed the models, walking round them to catch every perspective, drawing lightly, quickly, furiously. I had never seen anything like it and began to realise why Rodin's sculptures were so alive. It was a technique I adopted as my own and followed throughout my life, always placing models on a rotating plinth so they could be seen from all angles. As Rodin finished each sketch he let it drop in his wake. Georges began to gather up the papers and Camille and I went to help. We laid them out on a large table.

'He'll colour them later with ink washes,' Georges said.

I studied the drawings. The squatting model, whose pose could have been crude in a lesser hand, was transformed by Rodin's delicate pencil marks into one of nature's innocent creatures.

Camille traced the lines with her finger. 'She is like a wild animal, caught unawares.'

We were well matched, Camille and I; we saw with the same eyes. I knew at that moment that I had come to the right place and was with the right people. Paris was my home now.

As we left the studio, I paused for one last look and saw Rodin standing in the middle of the room. He was staring after Camille like of one of the tormented souls from *The Gates of Hell*.

CHAPTER 12

As Camille predicted, Georges became our ally, and, with Rosa Bonheur, the four of us were a gang. It was Georges who proposed the boating trip. The oars dipped in and out of the green waters of the Seine. I leaned back on cushions in the stern, my hand trailing in the water. I watched Georges through the veil of my hat as he rowed in his shirtsleeves. He had contrived for us to be alone together in the boat and I had let him do so. The attraction between us had been growing all summer and although I knew it was wrong of me, it was exciting and I didn't want to give it up. Not yet, anyway.

Georges stopped rowing and leaned on the oars. We watched a kingfisher dive under the water in a flash of blue and green.

'You and I are the same,' he said.

'How so?'

He pushed back his hat. 'It's obvious, surely. We are both artists and we neither of us give a damn for convention. I like how you stood up to Jules at the studio. You don't compromise, and you don't apologise for being what you are. I've never met a woman like you.'

I was of course thrilled by the compliment but tried to laugh it off. 'I'm hardly unique. What about Camille? She's not one for apologising or compromising either.'

'Ah, Camille, but she is completely mad.' He smiled. His teeth were white against his tanned face. He grew serious and laid aside the oars to be nearer to me. Our knees touched and he took my hands in his. 'You and I, we would make a perfect –'

We were jolted by a collision. I clutched the side of the boat to avoid being tipped into the water. I looked behind me to see Rosa shaking her fist at us from the prow of the other boat as Camille hooted with laughter behind her. A spray of water soaked Georges' shirt. Camille, wielding the oars, was laughing so much I was sure she'd fall in.

'*Hein*, look out, you maniacs!' Rosa called. She looked quite convincing in her white flannels and a Panama hat.

Georges reached out and pulled their boat alongside ours. 'The only maniac around here is you, Rosa,' he said when we were level.

'This boating is easy,' Camille said. 'I have mastered it already, although the fool Rosa is holding me back, she knows nothing about rowing.'

Rosa stood up and the little craft pitched dangerously. 'It is you who is the amateur. Give me one of those sticks and I will show you the expert's way.' She managed to wrest an oar from Camille and began rowing in one direction while Camille went in the other.

Georges took his hat off and ran a hand through his hair. 'It would help if you were sitting the same way instead of pulling against each other.'

'*Ah bouf!*' Rosa said. 'What do you know, you whippersnapper? An admiral had me out on the Seine before you were out of shorts.'

'Pity he didn't teach you to row as well,' Georges said.

'Impudent boy!' Rosa had stopped rowing while she talked, but Camille had not and the boat spun in a circle. 'Camille, *arrête-toi!* Before you drown us both.' Rosa put down her oar and blew out her cheeks. 'All right,' she called to Georges. 'You win. I admit I haven't the first idea about boating. Get us out of this thing, won't you? I'm hungry.'

I held the boats together while Georges rowed us to a small beach overhung by willows. He tied up the boats, working with quick, easy movements. He handed us out, except for Rosa, who glowered at him and jumped clear of the water and landed in the sand with a crunch of her brogues.

'*Ouf*, it's hot,' Camille said, taking off her hat and throwing herself down. I spread out a travel rug and joined her.

'I have the perfect antidote for this heat,' Georges said, pulling up two ropes dangling off the side of our boat. At the end of each was a bottle of champagne, cooled by the river.

'How clever you are, Georges,' Camille said. 'I don't suppose you have any glasses?'

He lifted a wicker basket stowed under the seat and started unpacking it. 'Glasses, baguettes, foie gras and,' he pulled out a tin with a flourish, 'caviar.'

'Bravo! Not just a pretty face, *mon vieux*,' Rosa said. She popped the champagne and poured it into the flutes.

Georges prised open the lid of the biggest tin of caviar I'd ever seen. 'I share an *atelier* with a Russian. His mother sends him a tin from St Petersburg every month in case he starves. He never has any money, but we always have caviar.'

Georges dug a long silver spoon into the glistening black roe and held it out to me. I went to take the spoon from him but he stopped my hand. His touch felt warm and dry. 'Close your eyes and open your mouth,' he said softly.

Camille nudged me. 'Go on, we'll make sure he doesn't make any sudden moves, eh Rosa?'

I did as he said and leaned towards him. He put a spoonful of caviar in my mouth; I could taste the sea as the tiny spheres burst on my tongue. 'Delicious,' I said with a sigh, my eyes still closed.

'Yes, you are, Jessie,' he said. His lips brushed my neck. I started away from him as they all laughed.

'Do you want me to hit him with an oar?' Rosa spoke through a mouthful of caviar and bread. 'That I can do.'

'No, I can take care of myself,' I said, pushing Georges away and settling my back against a tree. 'Let's eat, I'm starving.' I tore a chunk of baguette with my teeth and Camille grinned at me.

'What's so funny?' I said.

'You're supposed to make sure I behave. What would Maman say?'

I stretched and settled back against the tree trunk. 'We're grown women, not little girls.'

'Try telling that to Maman.'

We drowsed under the willows, the wind soft on our faces, the sounds of the river in the distance. From under my hat I saw a dog and some children splashing in the shallows. A little along the grassy bank, a young man in a striped costume sat with his legs dangling over the water. Couples strolled arm in arm along the riverside, and here and there artists sat at their easels under white umbrellas. My eyes grew heavy and I dozed while the sun sank lower into the sky. When I awoke, Georges was sitting next to me, smoking.

I sat up. 'Were you watching me?' I smoothed my hair and wondered if I'd been sleeping with my mouth open.

He smiled. 'Don't worry; you look like an angel when you sleep.' Strains of accordion music wafted through the trees. He pulled me to my feet. 'Can you hear that? Let's go dancing.'

Camille and Rosa had gone ahead of us down a towpath. The music grew louder until we came to a jetty where people were eating and drinking around a small dance floor. Couples danced to an accordionist and a woman who sang huskily about her broken heart. Georges held out his hand to me and we waltzed among men in open shirts and women in cotton print dresses. Georges held me tightly in the crowd so our bodies were pressed together and I wanted the waltz to go on forever. When the music changed all too soon to a spirited polka, Georges spun me around and we charged about in a breathless carousel. He led me in a gallop off the dance floor and into a small clearing behind the café. I hung onto him, laughing and trying to get my breath back.

'You dance well,' I said.

His hair was in his eyes and he pushed it back. 'All those wretched afternoons I suffered as a child at Monsieur Julliard's dance classes have finally paid off.'

'They certainly have.'

'Remind me to send him a case of wine,' Georges said. He stepped closer and his fingers found the nape of my neck. 'Here, let me help you, your hair is coming down.' Deftly he removed some pins and it fell in around my shoulders. With a sudden movement that made me gasp, he wound the heft of my hair in one hand and moved his mouth close to mine. '*Jessie, je meurs pour toi.*'

I knew I should stop him, that I should tell him I was not free, but it was the last thing I wanted to do. This was Paris, I was far from home and nobody need ever know. Instead, I drew Georges closer and we kissed. The warmth of his mouth! If I close my eyes, I can still feel it. He put his arms around me and I arched my back to fit into the curve of his body. He began to undo the buttons at my throat, his fingers fumbling with the tiny hooks. We heard voices and I put my hand on his. Someone was coming.

'They must be somewhere. Did they go back to the boats? I'll look behind here.' It was Rosa. Just as I was tucking my hair into a chignon, she came into the clearing.

'Here you are,' she said. 'We thought you'd got lost.' Rosa eyed me. 'You look a bit dishevelled. That's the polka for you. It's undone many a girl.' She winked and held out her arm. 'Come on, Jessie, my turn for a dance. Georges, look and learn – I'll show you some real dancing, *mon vieux*.' She waltzed me back into the throng and I watched Georges longingly over her shoulder, like a child being dragged from a sweetshop. I was gratified to see that his face was thunderous.

Rosa laughed and pointed at Georges with her chin. 'He looks like my cat when I've taken away a bird from its claws. Was he annoying you?'

'Oh no, not at all.'

She cocked her head. 'So it's like that, is it?'

I stiffened in her arms. I wasn't ready to tell anyone about what had just happened – I didn't know what to make of it myself. All I knew was it was wrong, and all the sweeter for that.

My voice was sharp. 'I don't know what you mean. It isn't *like* anything. Besides, I'm more or less engaged to someone back home.'

'More or less, *hein*? And no matter how more or less you are engaged, that won't deter our Georges. Quite the opposite, I'd say. If you were promised to the Prince of Wales and locked into a chastity belt, Georges would still come after you, having sweet-talked his way into getting a spare key. A man like that never gives up. The chase is on and when he finds out you're out of bounds, well, that will only make the game more interesting.'

'You're talking nonsense. Anyway, I can look after myself.'

'So you keep saying.' We had reached the edge of the dance floor and she stopped and looked at me seriously. 'You must listen to me, Jessie, before you get hurt. We are not in the tearooms of London now, but the jungle of Paris, where the wild beasts prowl. They may be exotic and beguiling, but the only rules they obey are their instincts and desires. Be careful they do not eat you up.' Rosa nodded towards Camille, who was sitting at a table, sketching the dancers. 'She is even more dangerous than Georges. She has no scruples at all, only an animal's instinct for survival.'

I dropped my arms and stepped away from her. 'That's ridiculous; Camille is my friend, she'd never hurt me.'

Rosa shook her head, exasperated. 'Your loyalty is admirable, Jessie, but you must be careful or you will be hurt.' She smiled and tucked an escaping strand of hair behind my ear.

We sat down and I tried to dismiss Rosa's warning, but I would have cause to remember it. Perhaps I should have listened to her, but would I have done anything different? I don't regret my time in Paris – how could I? Those days were in many ways the most vivid in my life, and now, after all these years, I am reliving those events as if they had only just happened.

Georges strolled over, his hands in his pocket. He started telling us an anecdote about a former art teacher and soon we were all capping each other's stories about eccentric tutors and the strange antics of models.

'Georges, do you remember old Pierre, the model who fancied himself a critic?' Camille said. 'He'd posed for all the great artists and would go around during his break giving us advice on technique.'

'Pierre was priceless,' Georges said. He adopted an old man's falsetto. 'See here, the anterior deltoids need a tad more definition.'

Camille frowned and wagged her finger. 'That's not the way Pissarro would do it. The maximal tibia is all wrong. And Renoir would use more Cadmium Red for the skin tones.' She laughed. 'That was Pierre – model, anatomist and tutor. A bargain, really, for five *sous* a day.'

Georges poured me a glass of wine and I smiled at him, grateful for his easy manner. 'You lot don't know how lucky you are,' I said. 'At South Ken, we "lady artists" were fobbed off with tramps dressed in dusty old costumes – drunken matadors, tipsy shepherdesses and toothless Pierrots. It was considered dangerous to expose us to the undraped form too often.'

Camille smiled at me. 'But you are here with us now.' She put her arm around my shoulder. George put his arm around the other.

'Yes, Jessie, you belong here,' he said, his eyes catching mine.

Rosa bit off the end of her cigar and spat it out. 'Models with their pretensions and whines – who needs them? That's why I stick to racehorses and cattle. They don't complain about the cold and they don't go to the *pissoir* all the time. And, best of all, you don't have to listen to them banging their gums about some artist cheating on them. Give me a horse market over a studio any day.' She looked at the end of her cigar and watched it glow red in the violet evening light. 'That's how I first met Rodin, drawing animals, when we were both starting out.'

The rest of us clamoured to know more.

'You never told me you knew Rodin then,' Camille said at the same time as I said, 'Tell us what he was like as a young artist. It's so hard to imagine him at our age.'

Rosa puffed at the cigar. 'Let me see, he was shy, I'd say, introspective, intense. More like a woman than a man, really.'

Georges grunted. 'That's hard to believe.'

Rosa shrugged. 'He's nearly fifty now – in his prime. What you see is the respected artist with a growing reputation. But in those days he was as hungry as you all are. And he was just as unsure of himself.' We made loud protests but she waved them away. 'You're all still wet behind the ears, mere babies to an old hand like me.' She resumed her story. 'Rodin had a hard time of it in the early days. He was rejected three times by *L'École des Beaux-Arts*. They failed him on his sculpture submission, can you believe it?'

She told us about the young Rodin, who had been sent as a child to *Le Petit École* to learn a useful trade in the decorative arts. His family had little money and he was expected to earn a living as a craftsman working on the ornamentation of the city's churches and public buildings. At sixteen he tried to get into the Beaux-Arts, but his sculpture was considered grotesque because he preferred to depict the beggars and cripples of the back streets of Gobelins where he'd grown up. When he couldn't get in to the Beaux-Arts, he went to work as an apprentice in the Sèvres porcelain factory.

'When I met him,' Rosa said, 'he hadn't given up his dream of becoming the world's most famous sculptor – that's how he put it, without a trace of humour. He would find ways to learn what he needed by himself, so he took anatomy classes at *L'École des Médecins*, hanging around with his drawing pad while the young doctors carved up cadavers.'

Camille and I exchanged a glance. I knew we were thinking the same thing: Rodin had had to educate himself, just like we did. If he could make it, against the odds, through hard work and determination, then so could we.

'For his work at the porcelain factory he needed to know how to render animal forms,' Rosa said. 'So he took lessons with Barye, the best animal sculptor of modern times – other than me, of course. By the time I met Auguste, he'd graduated from sketching animal skeletons in the basement of the Natural History Museum and had a permit to draw the carnivores in the *Jardin des Plantes*. I saw at once he was gifted.'

I imagined the young Rodin and his frustrations as he tried to gain a foothold in the art world.

'He had to struggle so hard,' Camille said. 'It's why he helps us, Jessie and me. Rodin knows what it's like to have talent, but have the doors slam shut in your face.'

I nodded. 'Camille is right – it's why he gave us a chance in his *atelier*.'

Georges smirked. 'Nothing to do with your pretty faces and pretty figures, I suppose?'

Camille and I turned on Georges, ready to tear a strip off him. He could always rile us, going from ally to cynical enemy in a capricious turn, as if to amuse himself with our furious reaction. But Rosa shushed us.

'No squabbling, *mes enfants*,' she said. 'Although, you must admit, girls, Georges does have a point – Rodin loves to be around attractive young women.' She raised her palms as we started to protest again. 'However,' and here she looked at me, 'I'm sure you can take care of yourself. After all, you have Georges to protect you – although that's a bit like putting a fox in charge of guarding the hens, eh *Monsieur Reynard*?' Georges looked so innocently pained we couldn't help laughing and our quarrel was forgotten before it began.

It grew dark and the café owner lit the lanterns hanging from wires above us. We did not notice how late it was until a sleepy busboy started sweeping around us and piling chairs onto tabletops.

Rosa stood up. '*Alors*, it's time these young women were safely in their beds and out of the clutches of rogues like us. What do you say, Georges? We don't want their reputations ruined – not yet anyway.' She winked at him and ground out her cigar on the sole of her shoe.

Georges slapped her leg down. 'Rosa, if you are going to dress like a gentleman, you should at least behave like one.'

'Oh ho! Am I to take lessons in *galanterie* from you, my pretty boy? Come, Jessie. As punishment I will deprive this pup of his little playmate on the way home. She stuck out her tongue at Georges and dragged me laughing out of my seat.

'You'll have to make do with me, *mon ami*,' Camille said to Georges. 'Shall I be English to pique your interest? Frightful weather we're having, old chap. Would you like a little *rosbif* and marmalade with your tea? How is Queen Victoria?'

'I had tea and crumpets with Her Majesty only last week,' Georges said in a ridiculous accent. 'She sends her regards and asks that you return her galoshes.'

'You are both preposterous,' I said. 'Not everyone in England is on speaking terms with the Queen, although Rosa is by her own account. You know, Rosa, I think I will walk with you after all.'

But on the way back to the river, Rosa stopped to tease Georges some more and Camille fell into step beside me. She stumbled a little and laughed when I caught her. I realised she was a little drunk.

'Jessie, do you want to have children?'

I laughed, but she pulled at my arm. 'I'm serious. Have you thought about it?'

'No, but then who thinks about it? Of course I want children.'

She shook her head. 'I don't know if I will ever be a mother.'

She sounded so sad that I squeezed her arm as we walked. 'Surely every woman wants to be a mother?'

'To have a child with the man I love – it's what I want, of course, but also what I most fear.' In the darkness I couldn't see her face, but her voice was thick with tears. 'It would mean the end of everything for me. You can't be an artist and have children. At least, that's what Rodin says.'

I bridled. It was the usual argument I'd heard a hundred times from male artists and critics, that women would never be great musicians or artists because of their need to have children. 'Stuff and nonsense,' I said. 'That may have been true for the last generation but these are different times. Think of how hard we've worked to get this far, why should we have to throw it all away as soon as we become mothers?'

Of course, I was young then, and childless, and knew nothing.

'Perhaps you are right, Jessie,' Camille said. But she still sounded so sad.

At the riverbank, Georges insisted we return to Paris in the same boat. 'Rosa, after your performance on the river I forbid you to touch the oars. I don't want Jessie at the bottom of the river.'

Rosa and Camille sat together with the travel rug over their knees, weighing down the stern, while I sat next to Georges and took an oar. He protested but I soon showed him I knew what I was doing.

'I've been on boats since I was a child. My father taught me,' I said.

'Don't tell me – you can shoot too,' Georges said.

'And ride – a horse and a bicycle.'

Rosa stood up again, making the boat sway. 'Behold the New Woman, Jessie Lipscomb,' she called to a pleasure boat as it washed past us. Some of the passengers cheered and waved.

Georges and I settled into a rhythm. Occasionally our arms brushed against each other as we turned the oars and we glanced at each other and looked away. Desire sat between us like another passenger as we rowed silently, the oars dipping in and out of the inky water trembling with reflected stars. Too soon we drew alongside streets with gas lamps that threw broken shards of light onto the river. By the time a cab deposited us at 135 bis boulevard Montparnasse it was well past midnight.

While the others were distracted, Georges caught my hand and pressed it to his lips. '*À la prochaine.*'

So he would try again. 'Yes, until next time,' I whispered.

Camille and I crept upstairs, holding our shoes in our hands. Madame Claudel opened the door to the apartment. She stood there, glowering at us, her arms crossed over her white cotton nightgown, a plait of grey hair over one shoulder.

'What time is this for two respectable girls to come in? I've been worried sick.'

'Maman, I'm sorry, but we had a boating accident,' Camille said. 'Our boat nearly sank and we had to wait for ages to get help.'

Madame Claudel looked at me. 'Is this true, Jessie?'

'Yes it is. Camille was extremely brave. I fell over the side but she pulled me to safety. You could say she saved my life.'

She narrowed her eyes. 'But your clothes are dry.'

I thought quickly. 'Fortunately, we were able to dry off in the sun.'

Madame Claudel looked sceptical but was obviously too tired to question us any further.

'I suggest you drink some warm milk before bed. I don't want you getting a chill. Now, I must go to bed, I can feel one of my migraines starting.' She turned to leave us, but stopped at the hall table. 'Jessie, I nearly forgot, an English gentleman called for you today. He left his card.'

I took it over to the gas lamp and went cold. The day before I would have been overjoyed to receive this, but now, after what had happened with Georges, a wave of guilt washed over me. The calling card was William's. And on the back, written in a familiar hand:

My dearest Jessie,

I wanted to surprise you but this will have to serve. I will call on you tomorrow morning.

> *Fondly,*
> *Your affectionate William*

CHAPTER 13

The next morning I waited in the drawing room for William to arrive. I was trying to read *Le Figaro*, but Louise was playing a Chopin étude over and over again and I couldn't concentrate. I kept jumping up to look out of the window.

Camille put down her anatomy book. 'What's got into you, Jessie? You're as nervous as a cat. I know he's your beau, but you've known William since you were a child.' She narrowed her eyes. 'Or is there something else bothering you?'

I wanted to tell her everything, how I had let Georges kiss me, how I had encouraged him instead of putting a stop to it. Now I'd betrayed William and misled Georges. I'd spent the night unable to sleep, thinking about what Georges had said: *you and I are the same... neither of us give a damn for convention... I've never met a woman like you before...* William too was unconventional, passionate about his calling, but when it came down to it, he was, well, William. I'd known him all my life and I couldn't imagine him not being there, but I didn't feel the same frisson of excitement with him that I did with Georges. I wondered if it were possible to love two men, at once. But everyone said – all the love songs, the novels and poems – there could only be one true love, the grand passion that was supposed to sweep all before it. I threw down the newspaper in disgust and buried my face in a cushion. Camille threw another at me and we both laughed. The doorbell rang and we froze.

Louise looked puzzled. 'That must be your William. It's Eugénie's day off. Aren't you going to let him in?' When I didn't move she crossed the room. 'I'll go, since you both seem to be stuck to your seats like one of those dreary statues you're always droning on about.'

I could hear the front door being unlocked, Louise prattling in the hall, the low murmur of William's voice. I pressed my hands together to stop them trembling and tried to compose my expression, but as soon as I saw his dear face peeking around the door I forgot all about Georges and rushed forward and threw my arms around his neck.

'Oof, Jess! What a welcome!' he said, staggering back like a music hall comic. He smiled and held me at arms' length. 'Let me look at you. Paris certainly agrees with you. You seem different, but I can't say in what way.'

'I've changed my hair.'

'No, it's not that.'

He searched my face and I cursed the heat I could feel blooming in my cheeks. I hoped he couldn't read the guilt in my expression and forced myself to meet his eyes. I would have to brazen it out. 'I'm probably as fat as a pig,' I said. 'The food is heavenly here.'

'You're as perfect as ever,' he took my hands and kissed them.

I turned to Camille. She was standing at the window, watching us.

'William, I want you to meet my friend, Camille Claudel.'

He strode towards Camille and pumped her hand. 'Mademoiselle Claudel! A pleasure, an absolute pleasure.'

She removed her hand and made a show of flexing the fingers. Her expression was unfriendly, her tone more so. 'Please, call me Camille. I hate these ridiculous bourgeois formalities, so like a straitjacket.'

'You're quite right, manners can be tiresome. Camille, then, and you must call me Monsieur Elbourne.' She scowled and William grinned. 'Just my little joke, please call me William.' He put an arm around my waist and Camille frowned. For a moment, I could have sworn she was jealous but William didn't seem to notice her coldness. He babbled on happily, pulling me closer all the while until I gasped and pushed him away with a laugh.

'My darling Jess writes so warmly about you,' he said to Camille, 'I feel as though we are already acquainted.'

Camille put her hands on her hips. '*Ah oui?* In that case, why don't we get to know each other better? Come with us now to the *atelier* and you can see where Jessie and I work.'

Camille was being imperious, trying to intimidate him. I had so hoped they would be friends, but my William had never been one to be overawed. I held my breath while he looked at her for a while. Then he bowed. William never bowed. He was teasing her again. I breathed out. William was too good-humoured and intelligent to be drawn into one of Camille's dramas.

'I should be deeply honoured,' he said with an affable smile. 'But, your studio will have to wait until later. First, I need to stretch my legs after spending yesterday on trains and boats and more trains.' He held out his arm to me. 'Jess, will you take a stroll with me? I haven't been to Paris for years. On the way, you can tell me all about what you've been up to.'

Before Camille could object, he gave the Claudel sisters a cheerful wave and pulled me out of the room. I could hear Louise laughing softly and Camille barking at her.

Once we were outside I said, 'William, you were teasing Camille.' 'Me? Never!'

'William Elbourne, don't you think I know when you're teasing?'

'Oh, well, she deserved it. She's quite a handful, and I pity any chap who takes her on, if there's one brave enough. Luckily, I've had plenty of practice dealing with bossy women.'

I pinched his arm, hard.

'Ouch! I didn't mean you of course, dearest heart. I have three formidable sisters and an even more formidable Mama. You, on the other hand, have a sweet and easy nature, except when you're doing your impression of an exploding volcano.' He batted his eyelids at me and I pushed him off the pavement. He skipped over a pile of horse dung. 'That's no way to treat your betrothed.'

'May I remind you that we are not engaged, not officially anyway?'

He waved his hand in the air. 'A technicality. Now, stop being so stuffy and give us a kiss.'

He pulled me into his arms. It was comforting, like going home. I was enveloped in his familiar smell of sandalwood soap. I kissed him back and a messenger boy on a bicycle whistled as he rode past.

'Eh, Monsieur, can I have a go next?'

William grinned. 'Cheeky beggar.' He didn't let me go. 'I've missed you, Jess.'

'I've missed you too.' But I wondered if that was quite true. I'd been too busy, too entranced with my new life, to give him more than a fleeting thought. I changed tack. 'I hope you can be friends with Camille. She is rather forthright, I admit, but she's been a good friend to me since I arrived in Paris, like a sister really. Besides, she's spirited and pretty – I thought you liked those qualities in a woman?'

William swung my hand as we walked. 'She's quite attractive, I suppose, if you like those dark, continental looks. I find them a little overstated. Give me a fine English girl any day.' He raised my hand to his lips. 'Jess, you haven't forgotten me, have you?'

'Of course not, how can you ask such a question? I love you as much as ever.' There was that wriggle of doubt again as I found myself comparing him to Georges. They were so different: William, clever, a crackling whirlwind of energy, who teased me like a brother and didn't always take me seriously; William who I had known since childhood. But Georges, Georges with his languid charm, who spoke to me as an equal and trained his attention on me like a lighthouse on a vessel out at sea, or, as Rosa would have it, a wild animal on its prey. He was dangerous, unknown, intriguing and left me breathless, excited, disturbed. William, on the other hand, I knew like I knew myself and he kept me safe, loved, untroubled. William would never hurt me.

I shook my head impatiently; the sun was shining and we were in Paris. I took William's arm. 'Where do you want to go?'

'I do of course want to see your work, so I'll obey Miss Claudel's imperial command, but first will you come with me to the *Jardin des Plantes*? I've been told there are some fascinating exhibits in the mineralogy museum.'

My heart sank: a dusty collection of rocks was a less than thrilling prospect. I was used to being free in Paris with no man my master. But I swallowed my resentment – after all, this was William's day and he should spend it as he wished. I would have plenty more days ahead of me to do as I wished I consoled myself with the thought that I would see where Rodin had spent his days as a young artist, drawing with Rosa. As we strolled through the Luxembourg gardens, the sun streamed through the leaves in a haze of green and gold and my mood lifted.

'Let's find a bench.' I said, leaning into William. 'It's so lovely to see you.'

We sat down and watched some children in starched white dresses and sailor suits chase a kite while their uniformed nannies chatted in the shade of a tree. Old men played boules in a sandy enclosure and the click of the balls mingled with birdsong and the children's cries. William fished inside his coat and handed me a bundle of letters.

'I nearly forgot,' he said. 'Letters from home.'

My mother had sent news of small hiccups in the rhythms of domestic life at Wootton House, while Papa asked about my work and suggested Paris exhibitions he had read about in *The Times*. William's sisters' cheerful letters were dotted with exclamation marks and heavily underlined in places. I laughed and dried my eyes as I read out snippets. Suddenly home seemed so far away.

William put his arm around me. 'You're a gentle girl, darling Jess. We all miss you. When are you coming home?'

'I'll be back in Peterborough next summer for a few months. Be patient, we both have our work – and the rest of our lives together.'

William heaved a dramatic sigh. 'You're right, duty calls. You must swan about in Paris with that she-devil to make Great Art, while I toil in my laboratory for the Advancement of Science. Give me strength for the battle ahead.' He leaned in for a kiss, pouting and closing his eyes.

I pushed him away with a laugh. 'Don't tease. You love your smelly laboratory as much as I love my dusty studio. Come on, let's go and see your minerals.'

As we left the park, an older couple passed us, their faces turned upwards to catch the sun bathing the gardens, and the man said, '*Régarde les jeunes amoureux.*' He raised his hat and William smiled at him and held my arm tighter. I remembered Georges' arms around me, the warmth of his throat as I kissed him there. I was such a fraud. I looked around the park, which was one of Georges' favourite haunts and dipped my parasol to hide my face; it would be awful if we met Georges. We'd be less likely to bump into him in the museum than out in the open. I quickened my pace and William hurried to keep up.

'Steady on, Jess, I had no idea you were so interested in mineralogy.'

'There's a lot you don't know about me,' I said.

CHAPTER 14

It was gloomy in the museum after the brightness outside. I stopped a sigh and tried not to think about an afternoon cooped up with bones and stones. But when we stopped at a glass case full of rocks, I was surprised to see how beautiful they were, split open like pomegranates to reveal whorls of astonishing purples, pinks and blues.

William leaned in for a closer look at an agate. 'Look, Jess, crystals, forged by unthinkable heat in the very belly of the earth. The Greeks weren't so far off the mark when they imagined Hephaestus hammering away underground – no man-made forge could create these gemstones.' He was filled with awe in the same way I was when looking at one of the Masters. William was passionate about unravelling the mysteries of the physical world and like many men of science in those days, he wrote poetry, exploring the wonders of the universe in verse as well as with beakers and experiments. Much as I admired his fervour, after the fourth case of agates – none much different from the other as far as I could tell – I stifled a yawn. When William fell into conversation with another chemist, I realised that a long scientific debate was about to ensue. I'd heard too many of those and I wasn't about to endure another. Not in Paris.

I started to move away. 'If you'll excuse me, I want to sketch some of the animals in the menagerie.'

'I'll find you there,' said William, turning back to his discussion about the saponification of fats.

There were already some artists at work at the *Fauverie*, the cages where the big cats – their pelts bedraggled and eyes dulled

– paced back and forwards in the tight enclosures. A lion lay panting in the heat, one giant paw protruding between the bars. Its spine was arched and quite different from Landseer's lions in Trafalgar Square, which have dipped backs like crouching greyhounds. At such close quarters, the wild civet smell from the wet straw was overpowering. A chimpanzee from the monkey house began to shriek dementedly and throw itself against the bars. Menageries are invaluable for teaching us about animals we would not otherwise see, but I've never liked the thought of a wild creature trapped in a cage, aand the screeching monkey and the frenzied pacing of the big cats were too much for me. I tore off my gloves and felt my brow. It was clammy.

I began to faint but felt an arm go round my waist as someone caught me. 'Jessie, Jessie, *qu'est-ce-que tu as*? You are so pale. Are you unwell?'

A tang of lemon verbena cologne sharpened the air. A face came into focus, brow furrowed and lips so close I could feel their breath on my cheek.

'Georges, what are you doing here?' I said.

'Rosa – who else? – dragged me to this appalling place. I find this obsession of hers with the animals tiresome.' Georges placed a cool brown hand on my forehead. 'You look a little better now. It must have been the heat in here.' He still had his arm about my waist and I leaned into him gratefully.

'What little butterfly have you trapped now, *mon vieux*? Jessie, is that you?' Once more, Rosa broke the spell of our embrace. She waved away the small knot of curious artists. '*Allons-y*, move aside you lot. Give the girl room to breathe.'

I had recovered enough to be amused by today's outfit on Rosa: jodhpurs, a tweed hacking jacket, riding boots and whip, her short hair tucked under a flat cap. She looked as if she'd left her horse tied up outside.

When Rosa dispersed the crowd, I could see William hurrying towards us and stepped away from Georges.

'Jessie,' William said. 'One of the attendants who spotted us together earlier told me you had fainted in the menagerie. Are you all right? What happened?'

'Don't fuss, I felt a little queasy, that's all. Silly of me, I'm not given to fainting in coils like Alice's Mock Turtle. Dearest, these are two of my new friends.'

When he heard the endearment, Georges shoved his hands in his pockets and grimaced.

Rosa stepped forward and put out her hand. 'Rosa Bonheur.'

William looked confused.

Rosa laughed. 'Don't know whether to kiss it or shake it, eh? With our friend Georges, however, there can be no room for doubt.' She slapped Georges on the back and he coughed and looked annoyed.

Georges took his hands out of his pockets. With a bow that was barely perceptible, he clicked his heels.

William looked amused. 'Ah, you're a military man, I see. My uncle is in the Diehards. He's never taken to the new name – The Middlessex – insists on calling it the 57th. But I don't suppose that'll mean much to you chaps over here?'

I elbowed him, more sharply than necessary. 'William, Monsieur Duchamp is an artist, not a soldier.'

Georges brushed a piece of invisible lint from his sleeve. 'Jessie is right. No regiment in its right mind would have me. I've picked up some rather irritating affectations from a Cossack with whom I share an *atelier*. But the Russians aren't all bad. Where we would be without their exquisite caviar, after all?'

Not only had Georges used my first name, casually, but, to my horror, he also winked at me when he mentioned the caviar. Thankfully, William didn't seem to pick up on Georges' outrageous behaviour, because he smiled pleasantly and shook his hand.

'William Elbourne. You're clearly a friend of, er, Jessie.'

Georges took out his cigarette case and offered it to William, who shook his head. He took his time fiddling with matches and exhaling. 'This place is getting on my nerves,' Georges said. He waved his hand wearily and I wondered what William would make of him. He hated affectations of any kind and I could see a frown appear between his eyes. 'I can't believe I let Rosa talk me into coming here. May I suggest a little champagne to revive the ladies? There is a delightful little bistro on the quai Saint-Bernard.'

William put his arm around me with such a proprietary air that I had to resist the urge to shake him off. An odd thing was happening: the more insouciant and French an air Georges affected, the more uptight and English William became. They were both being impossible.

'I'm afraid we don't have time,' William said in a clipped voice I didn't recognise. 'We're expected shortly at Jessie and Camille's *atelier*.'

But Georges was not to be deterred. Rosa was right about his love of the chase – William's presence on the field only seemed to sharpen his appetite for me.

'We'll come with you, won't we Rosa?' he said. 'I'm absolutely consumed with desire to see Jessie's work.'

Rosa tapped her boot with her whip. 'I too must admit to a certain curiosity. Jessie has hidden depths we'd both to like to explore, eh Georges?' She winked at me and I shook my head at her, furious at her indiscretion. 'In a strictly professional sense, of course,' she said with an innocent smile at William. 'Besides, Auguste is always talking about the genius of Camille, his little pot of gold he discovered. *Alors*, no more chit-chat! To the *atelier*, my dear Monsieur Elbourne, *tout de suite!*' She grabbed William's arm and marched him away. William looked over his shoulder at me with a helpless look.

I laughed and called after him, 'There's no use fighting, William – Rosa has a will of iron. You go with her; I'm feeling much better now anyway.'

Georges smirked and took my arm. 'Don't worry, Elbourne, I'll look after Jessie.' I pulled away and glowered at him. I was not a toy to be snatched from another child.

We walked through the reptile house where coiled and looped snakes flicked their tongues and crested lizards lay fatly on rocks. A turtle poked its nostrils at us from a foul-smelling terrarium and a black and yellow spotted snake spiralled slowly beside it in the cloudy water. The stench was appalling and I was glad to come out the other side. The Seine ran swiftly past and a cool breeze carried its river smell to us. We stopped at a small enclosure where moth-eaten yaks and bison mournfully chewed the cud, gazing at us with big, stupid eyes.

'It's like being watched by gaping onlookers while you paint,' Georges said with a shudder.

Rosa climbed up and leaned her elbows on the railing and made a kissing sound. One of the beasts ambled over and she scratched its mighty head. 'We ate some of these during the Paris Siege,' she said. 'The mob broke in here and carted off anything that looked remotely like a cow or a horse. Zebra *en daube* became quite a feature in Parisian households for a while.' Some people walking past turned their heads and frowned at her flippant remarks.

'Lower your voice, Rosa, no one talks about those times,' Georges said. 'Do you want to get us lynched?'

'Georges, don't be a bore. I lived through it so I've earned the right to joke. What are you getting your pantaloons in a knot about? You weren't even born then, pretty boy.' She gave the bison a final pat and jumped down. 'Let's find a cab. Jessie still looks a little pale, and she's so quiet, she can't have recovered fully.'

William hailed a cab with one arm and reclaimed me from Georges with the other. They were as bad as each other. I shook him off and climbed up myself. When the cab arrived at the studio an argument began between William and Georges, as they vied to pay the fare. I left them to it and ran up the stairs to the studio. The door was locked so I had to use my key to enter. When I pulled back the curtain that separated the marble studio from the clay studio, I froze.

CHAPTER 15

Camille was pinned to a wall by a man, her bare legs wrapped around his back, her ankles crossed where her high, buttoned boots began. He groaned and called her name. I recognised the voice at once. How dare he touch my beautiful Camille? I was filled with a molten jealousy that rose up from my core and erupted as I shouted his name: 'Rodin!'

They stopped and looked at me. I clapped my hand over my mouth and stared back at them. There were voices in the stairwell; I knew Rosa wouldn't turn a hair, but the men would be shocked, or worse. Camille would be ruined. I had to act quickly.

I called down: 'Could you go back and catch the cabby? I think I've left my favourite gloves on the seat.' Footsteps clattered down the stone steps and I heard Rosa whistling and shouting in the street. I pulled back the curtains again.

Camille was calmly working on a sculpture. Rodin stood in the shadows, both hands on his cane, watching her.

I pulled off my gloves and tucked them into my sleeves. 'I'm sorry we're early.'

Camille did not look up from her work. 'Did the others see?'

'No.'

She came over to me and put her arms around my waist. '*Merci*, Jessie, *merci*.' Her curls had come undone from the knot on top of her head. I smoothed them from her eyes and shook her skirts free of dust, like a maid of honour attending to a bride. The curtain moved and we turned to face it, side by side. William stepped into the room. He must have sensed the tension in the air and he looked at us for a long moment.

'No sign of your gloves, Jessie, I'm afraid. Camille, lovely to see you again.'

'Hello, William,' she said with a warm smile. 'There is someone I want you to meet.'

Rodin emerged from the shadows.

CHAPTER 16

I still have the photographs William took that day in the *atelier*, pre-served under tissue paper in an album alongside postcards of Paris, with passes to the Louvre and the Luxembourg Museum and a lock of Camille's hair tied with a faded navy ribbon. William had brought his pride and joy – one of the new portable Kodaks – and took pictures of Camille and me working and later on a break with our chipped cups of tea and cigarettes. He had shown me how to work the camera and I took a picture of Rodin's reflection in a mirror that hung in our studio. I wish I'd kept that photograph, but I sent it to Rodin years later.

The noisy arrival of Rosa and Georges and their idiotic banter had eased the tension. Rodin and William hit it off immediately and were soon laughing and slapping each other on the back and calling each other 'my dear fellow'. I was gratified at first, but the heartier and louder they grew, the more I began to resent William's intrusion. Rodin was my tutor and this was my time, my place. This was my and Camille's studio but they were treating it more like a man's club. Georges had passed around cigars and they were all puffing away, Rosa included. Any minute now I expected a steward to come out with a tray of brandies and ask Camille and me to step into the ladies' sitting room.

'A scientist?' Rodin was saying to William with his arm around him. 'I find this extremely interesting. We are both fascinated, you see, by the physical world, how the body works, how light plays on a surface, by density and perspective – it's all there in the nat-ural world. I adore scientists – science is at the core of everything we do, don't you find?' William nodded eagerly and I resisted the temptation to roll my eyes. Camille didn't seem to mind this show of male camaraderie and was listening to them intently as she perched on a stool and worked on a piece of clay. Rodin was in full flow and talking about Darwin now. 'I believe that Monsieur Darwin is right – we are animals with animal instincts and we must procreate or die; it is the urge that drives us. After all, what is sculpture but the art of the hole and the lump?'

Georges coughed on his cigar smoke and looked at me, his eyebrows raised. I shook my head slightly at him. I wasn't shocked but, perversely, I liked him being worried about me. William, on the other hand, was so entranced by his new friend that he merely gazed at Rodin in wonder, nodding enthusiastically in that irritating way young men suck up to older men.

'It's always a pleasure to meet a fellow Darwinian, sir,' he said, and this time I rolled my eyes.

Rodin planted a loud kiss on the side of William's face and beamed at me. 'I like this man, Jessie. Once again you have demonstrated you have excellent judgement. Monsieur Elbourne, I'd like to hear your opinion on the work here.' William looked bashful for a moment and I ground my teeth.

'I'm no judge, of course, but I would like to see Jessie's work.' He looked at me steadily. 'I'm keen to find out what you've been up to in Paris.'

I returned his look, keeping my expression neutral. 'You must look at Camille's work first,' I said. 'You're familiar with mine already.'

Georges had been listening. '*Hein*, Elbourne, why don't you try to guess which work is by Jessie and which is Camille's?'

William loved a challenge. He nodded at Georges. 'You're on.'

'Let's see you try. I'll bet you ten francs I can tell which is which better than you,' Georges said.

'Let's make it twenty. I know my Jess.'

Camille came to stand beside me. 'This is ridiculous,' she whispered to me.

'Absurd, isn't it? Let them have their childish game. I wonder if they'll be able to pick out our styles,' I said.

She shrugged. 'That should be easy.'

Rodin laughed. 'A bet, excellent!' He gestured with his stick at my mother and child group. 'What is your verdict?'

William didn't hesitate. 'This is yours, Jessie.'

He walked around my mother and child group. 'This is definitely Jessie's. The woman's expression is tender and the infant trusting, most affecting. The detail is so exact you would think they were about to move. Am I right?'

I nodded and Georges scowled.

William moved to the two busts of Giganti shrouded in damp cloths. I unwound them and he looked from one to the other.

'I'm sorry, Jess,' he said, shaking his head. 'For the life of me, I can't say which one is yours.'

'They are pretty rough,' I said. 'It's impossible to tell them apart at this stage.'

Georges stepped forward. 'Impossible? Not for a fellow artist who knows Jessie's work so intimately. This one is by the hand of Mademoiselle Lipscomb. It's obvious,' Georges said.

I was astonished. How did Georges know? Perhaps he was right and we did share a special bond.

Rodin whistled. 'Well, well, young Duchamp, I'm impressed. Even I could not tell one from the other.' He turned to William. 'This is why I took him on at my studio in rue de l'Université – he has the keenest eye in Paris.'

Georges smiled and it was William's turn to frown. Rodin led William away to another part of the studio where Rosa was peering at one of Camille's nudes. 'I take it you've already met the formidable Madame Bonheur,' he said.

Left alone with Georges, I kept my eyes on Giganti's feline smile. 'How did you know it was mine?'

'It was the way you were standing next to it, as if to protect it from the viewers. It's a dead giveaway for a card player like me.' Georges winked at me and I punched his arm. He caught my fingers and whispered my name. 'Jessie, my love, this is agony for me, to see you with another man.'

I pulled free but he looked so pained I touched the back of his hand lightly before moving over to the group gathered around Camille's piece.

Rosa was saying, 'Exquisite. It would be even more so in marble.'

'I've picked out a piece from the depot already,' Camille said. 'A piece of snowy Cararra, only lightly veined.'

'Mademoiselle Claudel is the most instinctive stone carver I have come across,' Rodin said. 'She's far more skilled with marble than I, making the first cut without hesitation. Rosa is right – marble will transform this peasant girl into a nymph.' His hand swept down the curve of the clay figure's back and came to rest on her waist. He smiled at William. 'My eyesight is poor but to appreciate a woman, the hands are better, don't you agree, Monsieur Elbourne?'

'Why don't you ask Rosa?' he said with a laddish grin; I wanted to throttle him.

'Mademoiselle Lipscomb, where did you find this man?' Rodin said. 'You must let me borrow him. I have some business that takes me to Montmartre. And every red-blooded man who comes to Paris must go to Montmartre. What do you say – are you game?'

'Well, Jess, am I to be let off the leash?'

William had hardly set foot in Paris and he was heading off to the notorious fleshpots of Montmartre. He was no better than all the other Englishmen who flocked to the cabarets to gawk at cancan girls flashing their bloomers. It was typical of William to be swept up by the prospect of an adventure. And the worst of it was that I'd kill to get the chance to go to Montmartre, to see the bohemian quarter where all the latest, most daring artists and writers met. All this was going on in Paris, right under my nose, but because I was a respectable woman, I wasn't allowed near it. I was furious with William for having that chance instead of me, and going off with Georges, Rodin and Rosa, leaving Camille and I behind like children in the nursery while the grown-ups went out to play. But I was damned if I was going to show him he'd hurt me. Besides, I was also itching to be left alone with Camille to confront her about what I'd seen. I passed my hand over my eyes – I couldn't get the image of them together out of my mind. William was still waiting to hear my response and I tried to remember why I was angry with him.

Montmartre, that was right. I shrugged the way Camille did when she was being cuttingly dismissive.

'You go, I have work to do here,' I said.

Rodin took Georges and William by the arm. 'It's settled then. We'll throw a bachelor party for our new English friend, eh Duchamp? You're coming too, of course. But Rosa – don't even think about it.'

Rosa was already pulling on her gloves. 'If you think you can get rid of me that easily, Auguste, think again. I've drunk you under the table many a time in our youth, and I'll do it again tonight.'

'I suppose there are stranger sights in Montmartre than La Bonheur,' Rodin said.

'But if the *gendarmes* catch her with her hands up a *cocotte's* skirts,' Georges said, 'she's on her own.'

The three men and Rosa laughed and moved to the door.

William grabbed his hat and blew me a kiss. 'See you at the Gare du Nord tomorrow, before my train goes.'

'Don't forget your camera,' I said, holding it out to him. 'You'll want a record of your adventure.'

He missed the sarcasm in my voice.

'Thanks, Jess, you're a good sport.'

He ran out of the studio with the others and I turned to face Camille. It was time she told me the truth about Rodin.

CHAPTER 17

Camille and I waited until we could hear the others spill out onto the street below. Now we were alone, I didn't know what to say to her. The image of her and Rodin returned and I couldn't get it out of my head. A crush on our tutor was one thing, but a full-blown and sordid affair was quite another. It made me sick to think of them together. But at least it all made sense now: her fury when she saw Rodin in the Bois, her sadness when she talked about being able to be with the one you loved. I couldn't understand why, how, she could allow Rodin to make love to her. I'd heard all the stories, of course, about women throwing themselves at him, his affairs with models and society women who posed for him, but I couldn't see the attraction. I was only in my early twenties then and he seemed so old to me, with his long grey beard and stained suits.

I couldn't look at Camille, so I moved towards the little stove. 'Tea?'

She nodded and pulled the silver case from her skirt pocket. 'Cigarette?'

Once we were settled around the table, our cigarette smoke blueing the air, Camille began to talk.

'I suppose you're shocked. I would be if I were you. *Enfin*, he is our *maître*.'

'What age is he – fifty?'

She picked a strand of tobacco from the tip of her tongue. 'Forty-nine. As if that matters – he is a genius. It is the artist I love, the man, his passion, age means nothing to me.'

I wondered if that ever worked the other way round, if Rodin would make love to a woman more than twenty years older than him; somehow I doubted it. That's what my worldly-wise mother would say, anyway. I shook my head – that kind of comment would only enrage Camille. But I had to make her realise she was playing with fire.

I took her hands in mine. 'Camille, think about the risks you are taking. If it got out, your family would disown you and you'd be ruined.'

'Jessie, please, I need you to understand, I need your help and I need you not to judge me, judge us. I can't lose you now I've found you. I couldn't bear it if we quarrelled. You mean everything to me.'

She kissed my hands; there were tears on her cheeks. I knelt beside her and wiped her face with my thumbs.

'Will you help me, Jessie, will you help us, Rodin and me?'

'You know I would do anything for you, but what can I do?'

'You could make it possible for us to meet somewhere safe. Not like this. You could take letters between us, arrange meetings, and keep guard so we are not discovered. With you as chaperone no one would suspect, and we would be safe – I would be safe.'

There was a piece of dried clay in her hair. I crumbled it between my fingers. 'Are you in love with him?'

I came to sit beside her and waited while she stubbed out her cigarette and struck a match to light another. She leaned her head on my shoulder and I held her while she told me about her affair with Rodin.

'It began last year. Rodin says he fell in love with me the first time he saw me. *C'était un coup de foudre.* It's a good expression and for me it was exactly like being struck by a bolt of lightning.'

So it was for me, the day I met Camille.

She told me Rodin had arrived at the *atelier* one day to replace her previous *maître*, Bouchon. Camille was eighteen and newly arrived in Paris.

'I was working on a bust of our old servant, Hélène. He stood in the shadow of the doorway over there for a while before I noticed him. Short, square, powerful as the Minotaur. *Je suis Rodin.* It's all he said. He walked up to the sculpture I was working on, the clay was still wet and it smeared his hands. Rodin looked at me with such intensity, as if I were one of his own works, and put his hands on my face, like this.' She reached up and touched my face, tracing the contours, and I wanted to catch her fingers and kiss them, one by one.

Camille sighed and resumed her story. 'Later, another day, he did the same, but this time he traced my neck, my breasts, stroked my arms and ran his hands over my hips. It didn't occur to me to move. He unbuttoned my bodice. I knew his intention but I didn't care. I felt the power in his touch – he moulded me like a piece of clay. He did such things to me that afternoon, I was enslaved. But so was he. It's perfect, we have a perfect love.' She looked at me again, as if waking from a dream. 'Don't you see, Jessie, it's what I've always wanted. Rodin is my lover. The great Rodin! Can you imagine?'

I saw limbs entwined: two nudes. But the lovers I conjured were not Rodin and Camille, but Camille and I.

She lit another cigarette and a spiral of smoke wound its way from her lips and hung in the still air between us. 'Afterwards I lay on a dustsheet spread on the floor, as unabashed by my nakedness as a child. He sculpted me then, and it seemed more intimate than what we had just done. Does that make sense?'

Camille's dark curls fell into her navy blue eyes as she looked up at me.

'Perfect sense,' I said. Camille had found her grand passion, and love trumped everything. What a bore I must seem, droning on about her reputation, when all that mattered was Love, the kind of love I'd never had. Of course, I loved William, and I was excited by Georges, but this was different, and I envied her.

'Will you help me?' Camille said. 'Help us, *ma petite anglaise?*'

I took her hands in mine and kissed the tips of each finger. 'Camille, you know I would do anything for you.'

I was rewarded with a fierce embrace. She unstopped the brandy bottle, tipped the liquor into our cups and raised hers. 'To Art and Love.'

'Love and Art.'

Camille drank until the cup was empty; she traced the familiar Willow pattern of lovers fleeing across the bridge, two doves flying above them.

'I'm meeting Rodin at the Louvre tomorrow morning, early, before it opens,' she said. 'Will you come with me? He wants to speak with you.'

I stiffened. 'So you were planning to ask me anyway, if I hadn't caught you here?'

'Yes. Are you angry?'

'No, it makes me feel better,' I said with a sigh. 'Now I know your hand hasn't been forced.'

She smiled. 'I'm glad there are no secrets between us any more.'

'No secrets.' I drank the rest of my brandy and wondered why I had agreed to help them. At least this way I would be close to Camille and I would be part of one of the world's greatest love stories; I would not be left out.

CHAPTER 18

We made our way through the eerily empty halls of the Louvre, our footsteps echoing on the stone floors. In the sculpture room the morning sun pooled around Michelangelo's *Dying Slave* and *Rebellious Slave*. We took out our notebooks.

'Look how he has exaggerated the size of the hands and feet – it breaks all the rules I was taught,' I said.

'And he's left the torso of the rebellious slave rough,' Camille said, 'while the skin of the dying slave is highly polished. Do you suppose it means he has reached some kind of divine state as he nears death?'

'More likely the money for the commission ran out before he got around to a final polish.' Rodin's voice gave me a start. He came to stand in front of me and planted the walking stick in front of him. He cocked his head to one side and smiled. 'Well, Mademoiselle Lipscomb, are you with us?'

'*Oui, mon maître.*'

Rodin held out his arms and I stepped into them. He pressed me against his chest. His coat smelled of clay and the cigars he smoked.

'I knew we could rely on you, *ma chère élève.*' He released me and became business-like. 'We must make practical arrangements.' He beckoned Camille over so we stood together like a trio of conspirators. 'There is a room at the studio that locks from the inside where we can meet in private. Jessie can stand guard and if someone comes, you can warn us, *d'accord?*'

He spoke to me as if he were giving orders to the men at his *atelier*. It rankled that he assumed I would do his bidding unquestioningly, like a good little woman.

'Not so fast,' I said. 'You must allow me to speak.' Rodin looked surprised, but he nodded. I gripped my sketchpad against my chest and took a breath. 'Have you thought about the consequences? What will happen to Camille if your affair is discovered? You're a man, your reputation will recover but Camille would be ruined.' It took a lot for me to stand up to Rodin, and he was not used to being challenged. He glared at me but I refused to drop my eyes. Camille was too important to me. She may not be able to think clearly, but my mind was not clouded with passion.

Camille broke the tense silence with a laugh. 'Oh Jessie, you use such bourgeois words – ruined! You know Papa would forgive me anything. And as for my so-called reputation, I couldn't care that for it.' She snapped her fingers.

Rodin chewed his lip, as if considering the situation, then smiled at me. 'Camille, this is important, and Jessie is right to be worried about you. My personal affairs are complicated at present but you, both of you, must trust me when I say they will be resolved. I would never abandon Camille.'

I dropped my shoulders. It was clear they were set on a path and nothing I could say would change it. I had no choice but to fold up my reservations and tuck them away. Camille needed me, and if, God forbid, it all did go wrong, she would need me even more.

I nodded and lowered my eyes. Rodin put his arms around both our shoulders. '*Très bien.* You will not regret your decision, you have my word. *Alors*, let us see what Michelangelo can teach us about breaking the rules of proportion.'

I moved away from his embrace and put my notebook in my satchel. 'Excuse me, *Maître*, but I have to meet William. Perhaps we may come here another day to resume the class.'

'Certainly we shall – for my two favourite and most gifted pupils there will be many opportunities to look at Michelangelo together. The doors of the Parisian art world have just opened wide for you, Jessie. But I must not keep you from your young man. Be gentle with him – his head may be a little sore after last night.' Rodin's laughter was good-natured.

Camille put her arm through mine. 'I'll come with you, Jessie. I'll wait in the cab while you say goodbye.'

The platform was crowded and it took me a while to find William. When he turned to greet me, his face was tinged with green.

'William, your eyes look as if they've been poached.'

'No need to shout, Jess. Feeling a bit delicate, that's all, must have eaten a bad oyster.'

'Oyster, my foot. Do you think I don't know what a hangover looks like?' I was still furious with him for rushing off to Montmartre at the first sniff of adventure; too annoyed to admit I would have done exactly the same in his place. 'What on earth were you drinking, anyway? I've never seen you look so ill.'

He put his hand over his eyes. 'Um, this green stuff, like perfumed syrup, bloody awful. What did Georges call it? A green pixy, I think.'

I rolled my eyes. '*La Fée Verte*? Don't tell me you've been drinking absinthe. It's supposed to send people mad.' I suppressed a smile. William looked about the same colour as the Green Fairy, a rather winsome name for this most evil of drinks.

'Absinthe, that's the chap.' He clutched his forehead, turning even greener. He groaned. 'I think that damned pixy is doing the cancan inside my head.' He brightened for a second. 'I say, those French dancing girls can kick their own height; you should take it up, Jess, better than calisthenics any day.'

'Shut up, you idiot.' But he was making me laugh, teasing me out of my bad mood, the way he used to when we were little and he left a spider under my water glass at dinner, a trick he was still fond of playing.

He took me in his arms. 'That's better, Jess. I love to hear you laugh.' He tried to kiss me and I pushed him away.

'Urgh, you smell like rubbing alcohol. Are you still drunk?'

'As a lord,' he sighed. 'But, I do have perfect recall, and I can report that I behaved like a perfect gentleman, despite the many and varied temptations on offer. Do you know, there was one girl who could put her leg behind her...'

I put my hand over his lips and he tried to bite my fingers. 'Please remember, I'm not one of your chaps. Keep your saucy tales for the men at your club.' I said.

'And tales are all they are.' He grew serious. 'You do know that you have nothing to worry about on that count, Jess? Nothing could tempt me away from you, my darling.' He moved his face close to mine and I let him kiss me a little before pushing him away again.

The whistle went and we began to walk towards the train.

'I wonder how Georges is feeling this morning,' William said. 'Now, there's one with an eye for the ladies.'

I gripped his arm tighter. I wasn't really worried about William: he was too decent to give into the temptations Montmartre offered. But Georges was different. I'd seen the way the models nudged each other and made excuses to get undressed in front of him, and the way he joked with a couple of them in a manner that made it clear they had been together. I wanted to ask William what he meant, what Georges had done, but he had moved onto Rosa.

'What a seducer! She was bowling them over with these elaborate compliments, treating the dancers like duchesses. One of them was quite smitten with her and they headed off together into the night. Bet the poor thing got a fright when Rosa's jodhpurs came off.'

I tried to smile but I was too distracted by the thought of Georges, and what he had been doing. William didn't seem to notice and he was still laughing when we stopped at the First Class carriage door. He clapped his hand to his head. 'I nearly forgot to give you this.' He fished in his pocket and pulled out a scrap of paper. 'We met this funny little chap, Henri I think his name was, an artist. He gave me one of his sketches and I kept it for you.' He handed me a crumpled piece of paper.

The signature *Toulouse-Lautrec* was scrawled under a few pen lines. I'd never heard of him before but the drawing was powerful: a dancer, so alive she seemed to move across the page. I folded it carefully and put it in my purse. A guard blew the whistle again and the train doors began to slam shut. William put his arms around me. Suddenly, I desperately didn't want him to leave.

'Can't you stay a little longer?' I said. 'I've hardly seen you.'

'I know Jess, I'm sorry. I shouldn't have dashed off to Montmartre like that, but you do see how one couldn't resist? You know that I do love you, don't you? Enjoy Paris, but remember always come back to me, because no one could love you more than I.' He stroked my face. 'We may be two different metals, but together we make a perfect compound.'

The guard blew the final whistle. William kissed me hard on the mouth and jumped onto the train just as it started to move off.

I wiped my eyes and walked to the cab, my heavy heart lifting with every step that took me nearer to Camille.

CHAPTER 19

PARIS

1929

After I left Louise in Villeneuve, it didn't take me long to track down Georges. In Paris, I asked around a few of the galleries and one of the owners recognised his name.

'You show his work here?' I said.

'No, Madame, but he is one of our best customers. Monsieur Duchamp has an excellent eye. He comes to all the openings with his wife.'

His wife. Of course he had a wife. I spent a long time wondering what to wear. In the end I went to Chanel and bought one of the new jersey dresses that had been so elegant on Louise. It was flattering but as I fixed my stockings, I realised Georges had never seen me in a short skirt. The last time he'd seen me I'd been in my twenties. I turned from the mirror in disgust: I was an old fool.

Georges sent a car for me. The uniformed chauffeur drove me to a wide boulevard in the Embassy district and a starched maid showed me into a smart apartment. I couldn't move for chairs encrusted with ormolu and porcelain figurines of shepherd-esses. The air was sweet with the scent of roses – vase after vase of flowers too perfect to have grown in any garden. My reflection looked back at me over and over from mirrors lining the walls: a faded tabby cat, out of place in all this opulence. It was so vulgar; I couldn't understand why he lived here, how he could bear it. The answer walked into the room. She was breathtaking, and around forty years younger than me.

'Charlotte Duchamp, but you can call me Lotta, everyone does.' She had dimples. The clear forehead and look of a stunned hare pointed to a brain untroubled by deep thought. Georges had snared himself a fat little rabbit: diamonds dripped from her ears and encircled her unlined neck, and there were diamond clips in her glossy black hair. It was sickening – not even the hint of grey. But there were creases at the corners of her eyes. She must be about twenty-nine or thirty: jumped off the shelf just in time. This one must have been embroiled in a scandal for her parents to have married her off to an older man. I looked at the ostentatious wall hangings and gilded furniture, so obviously not Georges' taste, and realised it was she who had brought the wealth into the marriage. Georges had been bought off, unable to resist a much younger woman with a fat dowry.

'I'm afraid Georges is, um, getting dressed.' She tittered and coyly glanced at a hideous onyx and gilt clock disgracing the mantelpiece. It was four o'clock, the time Parisians reserve for making love.

Charlotte – I couldn't bring myself to call her Lotta – made unending small talk while I smiled and thought desperately: 'How could he? How could he?' By the time Georges walked in, cheeks still pink from his bath and smelling of lemon verbena, I had decided to leave. He was a little heavier in the jowl and his waist was thicker, but Georges was still a handsome man with a head of thick silver hair, and the same way of pushing his hand through it and letting it drop into his eyes. I didn't care about the lines in his face; he was still my Georges.

'Jessie! It's wonderful to see you.' He kissed me three times, and whispered: 'Please don't go. I haven't had a decent conversation in a year.'

I wanted to hold onto him, for him to lead me away into a bedroom and make love to me again and again. I closed my eyes and brushed my lips against his earlobe, remembered the first time we'd danced together, a clearing in the woods, his hands in my hair. We must have embraced too long because there was a small cough. I stepped out of his arms and turned back to the rabbit. She looked put out. I sat down on a hard chaise longue and she made sure she sat next to me so Georges had to sit across from us. I didn't listen to a word as she twittered away about people I didn't know; all I wanted to do was be alone with Georges and talk about the past, our past. We looked at each other in agony, murmuring politely as the rabbit nibbled away at one of those dainty biscuits so beloved of the French, a *langue du chat*, and sipped her coffee. Finally, after what seemed like an age, she excused herself and reappeared in a blonde mink coat and a cloche hat. A Pekingese peered out glumly from her arms.

'*Je m'excuse*, Madame, I have so much to do today, you have no idea! A fitting, then the hairdresser's and a manicure, all before cocktails at six. Now Georges, remember you have to take our little baby for walkies.' She kissed the Pekingese and it licked her mouth. I suppressed a shudder. 'Now, don't keep your old friend too long, she looks tired.'

Cheeky little bitch.

She was still talking while she fiddled with her hat and pouted at her reflection in one of the ridiculous mirrors. 'Now don't forget Plon-Plon, will you?' She made kissing noises in the air at Georges and disappeared in a cloud of *Je Reviens*.

I stood up from the chaise longue and fought my way through the forest of occasional tables to stand over Georges. 'Plon-Plon? Is that you or the dog?' I said. Poor Georges – how could I stay angry at him?

'You kick me when I'm down – how cruel you are, and how I've missed you.' He pulled me onto the overstuffed sofa and I disappeared into a mass of feather cushions. 'It's not funny!'

'But it is!' I said, hitting him back. 'This place, and the young, wealthy wife, it's like a Feydeau farce. Should I jump into a wardrobe when she comes back?'

He groaned. 'Don't, Jessie.'

Georges looked so miserable I stopped teasing him and told him why I'd come.

'You found Camille? But this is impossible! Last I heard she was ill, had had some kind of nervous breakdown and been hospitalised.

It was before the War, and then, you know, that terrible time, it damaged us all.' He held up his right hand. 'I can't move the fingers. The nerves were severed.'

I hadn't noticed. I took his paralysed hand in mine and stroked it. I had laughed at him only a few moments before and now I wanted to cry for him.

He took back his hand and put it in his jacket pocket. 'I can't sculpt, or paint, or draw, but what the hell – I have all this, don't I?' He gestured with the other hand. I looked at him and we both started to laugh again, leaning against each other, tears rolling down our cheeks in a crazed outpouring of all our emotions: the sadness of what we had lost and the barbarous cruelty of this brave new era that had been scarred by a war terrible beyond our worst nightmares. It wasn't our century; we belonged in the last one.

When we were calm once more, Georges poured us brandy and sodas. 'Tell me more about Camille. How is she?'

I hesitated. I didn't want him to imagine her the way I'd seen her. 'She hasn't been well, but the doctors say she'll be better soon once she's had a rest. The thing is, Georges, I want to find out about her, about her work. There's so much I don't know about her life. We lost touch when I went back to England.'

He looked into his glass. 'I remember when you left.'

'Yes.' I moved away from him slightly so we were no longer touching.

'I'm sorry,' he said.

'Never mind all that now. Tell me about Camille's work after I left; did she have the success she so deserved?'

'Oh yes, for a while, before she fell out with everyone. You know what she was like, so hot-headed. After Rodin, she broke off her friendships one by one. There was always some reason – we were all in cahoots with Rodin, trying to steal her ideas, some nonsense or other. Rosa stuck it out the longest, but even she gave up eventually. It's a shame; she could have been one of the greats.' Georges went to the mantelpiece and took down a small bronze piece hidden among all the shepherdesses. He put it into my hands. '*La Valse*, she called it.'

A man and a woman, naked, clutched each other in ecstasy as they danced, intoxicated with passion, swooning against each other to a silent waltz. I traced the lines and imagined the imprint of the artist's hand in mine.

'Camille's?'

Georges nodded. 'It's quite rare, one of the originals. The Government refused her a marble commission unless she dressed the figures. She did it, reluctantly, and then they refused the commission anyway.' He sighed. 'Camille never did understand the rules of the game. She should have known those stuffed shirts would never commission such a piece by a woman. She showed me the letter, which complained about the "closeness of the sexual organs", its "surprising sensuality". Camille was furious, but Rodin talked her down, persuaded her to dress the woman, and he made sure it was shown. Even so, the critics sneered, said the couple looked as if they were about to jump into bed together. Poor Camille, she couldn't win. I knew she'd never make it. She had some spirit, though. So do you, Jessie.'

He put his good hand on mine and our fingers intertwined, as if they had a will of their own.

'Do you remember your first day at Rodin's studio? How you and Camille stood your ground against all those men?'

I smiled. 'How could I forget?' I squeezed his hand. 'You were a good friend, Georges.'

'Don't say that; it only makes me feel worse.'

CHAPTER 20

RODIN'S STUDIO, PARIS

July 1884

Camille and I hovered at the door until I spotted Georges standing over a table of sketches with his sleeves rolled up. When he looked up, I waved, but he only frowned and bent his head again.

'Don't worry,' Camille said to me. 'His pride has been hurt after seeing you with William, that's all. Watch this.' She called across the room to him: '*Salut*, Georges!'

He put his hands in his pockets and came over. '*Bonjour, ma belle* Camille.' He gave me the briefest nod. 'Mademoiselle Lipscomb.'

Georges was being absurd. He had no right to be sulky with me. After all, it wasn't as if I had promised him anything. I made to walk away, but Camille caught at my arm and smiled at him. When she wanted to, she could always turn on the charm and now she looked up at Georges through her fringe.

'Won't you help us, dear friend? We need you to show us around on our first day of school. Please?'

He rolled his eyes but his expression softened. 'Camille, you are irresistible. Only, I thought Jessie already had a champion – why don't you get William to show you around the studio?' He looked so like a truculent schoolboy that I wanted to laugh. Besides, I was secretly flattered by his jealousy.

'Don't let's quarrel,' I said, touching him lightly on the arm, 'it's a bore to fall out when we have such fun together.' He took my hand, turned it over and traced a finger down my lifeline. I closed my hand and trapped his finger. Georges grinned.

'Well, all right, since you'll both be eaten alive otherwise. It would be an act of cruelty to throw two dumb animals to the wolves.'

I pinched his finger and Camille rounded on him, fists on her hips. 'Who are you calling dumb animals?' she cried and I added: 'The only dumb animal around here is…' He put up his arms as if fending off a couple of street thugs and begged for mercy. Suddenly he was the Georges we knew again, our ally and friend.

'A truce, I beg of you vixens! Come on, I'll show you where to leave your hats and coats. It's not much, I'm afraid, but it's relatively private, it's where the models change.' He led us to a dressing screen in a corner of the vast room. Georges pulled the screen back to reveal a packing case and two enormous coats hanging from a couple of nails. 'The only dustcoats we have are for men,' he said. 'We're not used to women in this *atelier* – no Turkish rugs and cups of tea here. You'll have to rough it with the rest of us. This is where the real work begins.'

I didn't like the way he was talking down to us as if we were simpering debutantes and was about to tell him exactly what he could do with his dustcoats when Camille pressed my side in warning.

'Georges, we know you are the senior assistant here and we the lowly newcomers, but we also know you've never roughed it in your life. I'll bet you have a secret supply of luxuries stashed away somewhere. Confess!'

He pushed a hand through his hair. 'Am I being a pompous imbecile? Don't answer that – I can tell by Jessie's face.'

I made myself calm down. I would have to learn Camille's trick of charming a man into treating her as an equal; it seemed to work better than confronting them shrilly as I and other firebrands had done in England to such little effect.

Georges sat down on a crate and tapped its side. 'Camille, you know me too well. There's a bottle of cognac, English water biscuits and coffee in here, and, of course, a tin of caviar from my Cossack friend.' Georges winked at me and I widened my eyes in warning; he'd already nearly given the game away like that once before. He gave me a lazy smile. Now that he had stopped being so bombastic, I allowed myself to smile back at him. Like Camille, he wielded charm like a weapon.

'Georges, I'm disappointed in you,' I said. 'No champagne?'

'Ah, for that we have to go out. But don't worry, I know...'

'A charming little bistro around the corner,' we choroused.

'Am I so predictable?'

'Thankfully, yes,' I said. I sat next down next to him. He casually slipped his arm behind my back and I leaned surreptitiously into him. Georges groaned when Camille began to take off her hat.

'Camille! Not that awful straw boater again. If you want to learn how to wear a hat with style, only look at Jessie's, how it tips over one eye and there's the mink trim that frames her face.' He unpinned my hat and smoothed a strand of hair behind my ear. 'And it's perfect with the little cape she is wearing.' He ran his hand down the embroidered peacock feathers on the sleeve of my dolman and let his hand rest in the swansdown cuff. 'Exquisite,' he murmured.

Camille was watching us closely, a smile threatening. 'Jessie has a weakness for fine things.'

Georges lit a Turkish cigarette and eyed me through coils of aromatic tobacco. 'As do I,' he said.

This was getting out of hand. Georges was maddeningly used to seducing women, but I was not one of his easy conquests, an impressionable *grisette* who would give in to him after a clutch of compliments. I stood up and briskly pulled on a dustcoat, folding back the sleeves.

'Right,' I said. 'Let's get to work.'

I nearly laughed again when I glanced at Georges. He looked like a fox that has just seen a plump hen disappear into the safety of the chicken coop.

He sighed. 'I'll show you what Rodin wants you to do.'

We stood among *The Burghers of Calais*; the six larger-than-life figures loomed over us.

Georges was all business again. 'The hands and feet are unfinished – that's where you come in, Camille. Rodin believes the hands and feet are the most expressive parts of the body. There are some examples in here that will start you off.' He pulled open a drawer, compartmentalised like those used for storing butterfly collections. It held rows and rows of clay hands and feet, tiny and minutely detailed, modelled from men, women and infants. Camille picked up a baby's hand, chubby fingers outstretched as if reaching for its mother. She cradled it in her own palm, as if it were an injured bird, before carefully replacing it.

Georges glanced at me. 'Rodin says you have an eye for drapery, so you are our wardrobe mistress. The technique here is to sculpt the bodies naked and then dress them. Rodin believes it breathes life and movement into the sculptures. Here are the designs.' He handed me some papers and held onto them a fraction too long, so I had to pull them out of his hands. We looked at each for a long moment before he released the papers and walked away.

Camille laughed and started to climb the ladder to work on a burgher whose hands were meant to clutch at his head. 'Watch out, Jessie, I think Georges is getting to you.'

'Oh please, he's behaving like a child.'

She smirked and I flicked some clay at her.

I stood with my hands resting on a mound of cold clay, studying the Burghers. They stood in different attitudes: one stared resolutely outwards; another bowed his head, as if filled with dread. It felt wrong to cover up their bodies, their muscles tense with life, as if they were about to break into a walk. At first I worked tentatively, but my confidence grew as the sculpture began to take shape. I was working on a particularly tricky fold of cloth when I became aware of someone watching me. I turned around to see Rodin.

'Don't stop what you are doing, Mademoiselle, I like to observe my assistants as they work. But do not expect praise – I have no time for such niceties. If I say nothing, you are doing well.' He circled his stick in the air. 'Please, continue. While you work, I'll tell you the story behind the sculpture.'

Rodin leaned on his stick. 'It is 1347, the Hundred Years' War. The English have Calais under siege, its people are broken, starving. Mothers have no milk to feed their babies and children are dying, their bodies lying in the streets like so much rubbish. Fires rage outside the city walls and missiles rain down on the citizens. Finally, exhausted Calais surrenders to the English king.'

He laid a hand on one of the clay giants' backs. 'These men have come forward to hand over the keys of the city to Edward, willing to sacrifice themselves to spare the lives of their fellow citizens. They walk in a slow procession towards certain death, each man facing his fate in his own way.' I had grown still as I listened to Rodin, whose arms traced the events in the air. 'A year after Calais fell,' he went on, 'the Black Death swept into England, killing a third of the people. God must have been on our side.'

Rodin considered me. I could see why Camille had been drawn to him. He could train his entire attention on you as if you were the only person that mattered to him and the effect was mesmerising.

He looked up at Camille, whose dark eyes were watching us from the top of the ladder. 'You have both worked hard this morning and made a good start. Pack up your tools now and come to lunch.'

Camille came down and stood beside me, wiping her hands on a rag as we watched Rodin walk out of the studio into the courtyard. We held hands briefly.

'Are you ready?' Camille said to me. 'Let's go and meet our colleagues.'

In the courtyard, the hammering had stopped. The *practiciens*, their arms and backs strong from carving marble, were pushing trestle tables together to make one long banqueting table. They lifted oak benches into place while an army of assistants emerged, wiping the sweat from their necks, laughing and calling to each other. Barefoot boys ran in and out with baskets of bread and tureens of soup. The men sat down and began tearing off chunks of bread and dunking it into the thick soup. Camille and I stood together and some of the men nudged each other and pointed. Soon forty faces turned to stare at us.

'The little dark one would be pretty if she cracked a smile.'

A big man with a black beard and a red kerchief tied around his thick neck waved his hand. 'Are you blind, Henri? Can't you see the other one has a better body? Hey, gorgeous, show us your titties.'

At first I'd been paralysed, but now I was enraged. I marched to the table, my eyes on the steaming soup tureen, ready to throw it over Black Beard; he would regret he'd ever opened his mouth.

Camille caught up with me and whispered, 'Don't do it, Jessie. You'll play into their hands. It's what they want – if you do something foolish, it's you who Jules Desbois will fire.'

She was right. They were waiting for me to take the bait.

'Let me handle this,' Camille said.

One of the younger men giggled and Camille walked over to stand behind him. She put her hands on his shoulders and he looked uncertainly at the other men.

'This one is a handsome specimen,' she said. 'What do you think, Jessie? Shall we sit either side of him? That way we can both get a feel of these magnificent arms.' She pinched his biceps as if she was at an agricultural show viewing a prize bull.

The young boy, who looked about sixteen, blushed to the roots of his blond hair and muttered a response. The rest of the men roared with laughter and his companions slapped him on the back.

The *practicien* with the beard shuffled up the bench and patted the space next to him with a beefy arm. 'Sit next to me, *chérie*. I like a girl with a bit of spirit,' he leered at Camille. She hesitated and I could see her courage wavering. I didn't know if we were going to pull this off. Where was Georges? I could see now why Camille had been so eager to enlist him as our ally. With a surge of relief I saw him sauntering out of the studio.

Georges stood a moment, taking in our plight, and beckoned to us. 'There's plenty of room down here.' Black Beard stood up. He must have been about six foot three, nearly as tall as Giganti.

'Butt out Duchamp, they've already got seats, next to me.'

'Not a chance, Rodolphe. Camille and Jessie don't want to be bored to death by you droning on about chiselling techniques. Rodin will be along shortly to check on the progress of his new assistants and he won't want to find them asleep in their soup.' There was laughter and groans of recognition from the other men.

Rodolphe glared at them. 'What are you idiots laughing about?

Everyone knows I'm the finest *practicien* with the best technique in the whole of Paris.' A noisy argument erupted and we took the opportunity to slip onto the bench on either side of Georges.

'You took your time,' Camille said to him. 'I thought we were going to be eaten alive.'

'Nonsense, they're quite harmless,' he said, beginning to eat his soup. 'You're both quite capable of looking after yourselves. Look at you, Camille, a rough country girl, who grew up scrapping with the village boys. I don't believe you could be afraid of a mere *practicien*, a lumbering brute of a stone carver.' He turned to me. 'Then there's the formidable Jessie, a daughter of the British Empire. I can just see her cycling single-handedly across the Gobi desert or scaling the Himalayas with only an umbrella for protection. Ouch! No punching my arms, girls, or I shall put you next to the charming Rodolphe.'

As Georges talked on, giving us snippets of gossip about the *practiciens* – who were highly respected for their skills but also arrogant and fiercely competitive – his dark eyes sought mine and I nodded in gratitude. My heartbeat slowed and I grew calm enough to look around. That disgusting pig Rodolphe was watching us. He'd been put in his place and couldn't hurt us now, or so I thought. I shouldn't have underestimated him: he would take the first chance he could to pay us back for his public humiliation.

With Georges sitting between us, I began to enjoy the busy hum from the *atelier* workers. They talked with their mouths full, drawing on the table with nubs of pencils fished from their pockets. Sitting on my other side was a *metteur-au-point*, whose job it was to do the first rough cut of stone. He was shouting across the table at a *practicien* who was anxious to take over and complete the piece.

'I tell you, it's not ready. Another day, perhaps two, and she's all yours.'

'Two! What's taking you so long? I can't hang about with my thumb up my arse waiting for you. I've finished polishing *Ugolino*. Any more and his cock will be worn away.'

'Keep your hair on. The arms are a real bitch on this one – twined above the head. Tell you what, why don't you come and work on the bottom half? You can carve her a sweet little … oh, *je m'excuse*, Mademoiselle.' He held out a dusty hand to me. 'I'm Pierre.'

'Jessie Lipscomb,' I said, amused he was anxious not to offend me; he wasn't so brave now he wasn't part of the mob. 'What are your working on, Pierre?' I talked shop with him for a while before I asked why Rodin had not joined us at table.

'*Maître* never eats with us. He goes home and has lunch with his wife.'

I stopped eating. 'I didn't know he was married.' I looked at Camille to see if she had heard, but she was busy laughing at something Georges was saying.

Pierre nodded at the doorway where an older woman stood waiting with a basket over one arm. 'That's her over there. They say she was a stunner in her day.'

I studied Rodin's wife. Standing patiently, she looked like a servant in her wooden clogs and shawl. Her face was lined but her bone structure was fine, with the remnants of beauty. Her chestnut hair was streaked with silver and piled on top of her head, as if she were still proud of her crowning glory. At that moment, Rodin joined her and took the hat and coat she was holding for him. He kissed her as he did so and she brushed some dust from his shoulders. They shared the comfortable intimacy of a long-married couple. I glanced at Camille again: she had grown quite still and stared at the pair as they left arm in arm.

'Who is that with Rodin?' I said to Georges.

He looked up from his plate. 'Oh, that's Rose Beuret. The men call her Madame Rodin, and I suppose she is his wife in all but name. She was his young model when he was starting out. Now she keeps house for him.'

'They are not married?'

Georges laughed. 'No. Our *maître* doesn't believe an artist should marry, says it dissipates creativity. They have an eighteen-year-old son but Rodin hasn't given him his name. Shame really, she supported him as a seamstress when he didn't have a *sou*, but it doesn't stop him bedding every model he can, eh, Camille?'

He nudged her, but she ignored him and began talking about

work, as if the subject of Rodin and his family were of no interest to her. It was a convincing performance, but she was unusually sub-dued for the rest of the meal and kept glancing at the door.

After lunch we went back to the Burghers and worked in silence for a while, before Camille threw down her cloth and climbed down to sit on the bottom step of the ladder. She dug at the floor between her boots with her knife.

'Did you see the way she was pawing him? Fussing over him like a mother hen? He hates that. It must be torture for him to be tied to that old witch.'

I was taken aback. I'd been expecting tears of shock or indigna-tion, but she seemed to have convinced herself that this woman was unimportant. I couldn't bear to listen to her deluding herself.

I kept my voice gentle. 'Camille, they have a son together.'

She threw the knife down and the metal blade rang against the stone. 'What of it? She trapped him with a child. It's the oldest, dirt-iest trick in the world. I would never do that, never! Anyway, what is a son without his father's name? A bastard, that's what. If Rodin loved this woman they would be married, it's as simple as that. This Rose means nothing to him, I know it.' She picked up the knife, climbed back up the ladder and began hacking at the clay.

At the end of the day, Rodin came to inspect our work. Camille scowled at him and walked away, her limp more pronounced than usual. He followed her and I could see them talking and gesticu-lating. Rodin grabbed Camille by the arm and opened the door to a back room. She tried to shrug him off but he held on and pulled her inside.

I looked around the *atelier* to see if anyone had noticed, but it was empty. I tried to carry on working but couldn't concentrate and made a hash of a rope tied around the neck of one of the suppli-cants. I was still trying to fix it when there was a tap on my shoulder. I turned round. When I saw who it was, the carving tool fell from my hand with a clatter.

'I am Madame Rodin. Who the hell are you?'

CHAPTER 21

Rose Beuret folded her arms and waited for my answer. I tried not to look at the locked door behind her in case Rodin and Camille chose this moment to re-emerge.

'Well?' she said.

'I'm Jessie Lipscomb. I work here.'

'*Anglaise, hein*? You speak French like a *parisienne*.' My dustcoat was unbuttoned and she flicked it open to expose my raspberry and cream striped dress. 'What's a fancy lady like you doing in this bear pit? You'd better watch out, some of the boys can be bit rough. But perhaps you like that?' She pushed her face close to mine. Her bone structure was extraordinary; there was an almost masculine strength to it. She narrowed her eyes. 'Or maybe your tastes run to older men, like my Auguste.'

Dear God, she must think I was having an affair with Rodin. It had been a difficult day and I'd had enough of being attacked by strangers: first the *practiciens* and now this has-been model. I didn't care who she was married to, or not married to, I was going to let her have it. There was something delicious about letting my temper explode like a firework popping into a cloudburst of stars.

I drew my shoulders back and looked her in the eye. 'Madame, you insult me. I'm an artist, here for purely professional reasons. Monsieur Rodin is my tutor and employer, nothing more. If I were a man you would not dare speak to me like that. And if I were a man, I would teach you a lesson you would not forget.'

She pushed back her sleeves. 'Don't let that stop you, you little *salope*.' She was about to spring at me when Georges chose that moment to come looking for me. He broke into a run when he saw us circling each other.

'Madame Rodin, I see you have met our new recruit.' He stepped between us, lifted Rose Beuret's hand to his lips and offered her his most charming smile and put his arm around me, all in a neat series of moves. 'Jessie, surely you have heard of *la belle Rose* – the most intoxicating flower in all Paris.'

Rose Beuret patted a lock that had fallen out of her enormous pile of hair and smiled at Georges, 'It is true, Auguste used to call me his "wild flower".'

'And who could blame him? They were all mad for you: Courbet, Cézanne, Monet, Renoir. I wish you'd pose for me but I would not dare quarrel with the *maître*. We all know that Monsieur Rodin guards his treasure jealously.'

Rose giggled like a schoolgirl. 'Ridiculous boy! I'm old enough to be your mother.' She sighed. 'But you're right, in my day, none of the other models could hold a candle to me. Everyone wanted me to pose, but I belonged to Rodin. I was only eighteen when I met him. I had breasts like ripe peaches and hair so long I could sit on it.'

'You're still the most stunning woman in all of Paris.' He lowered his voice and glanced at me. 'But I confess, my heart has been captured by another.' I was about to protest when I realised he was playing a clever game to deflect Rose's anger from me.

Rose beamed at us both. 'Aha! So, it's like that, is it? I like a love story. Playing hard to get is she, Georges? The little English minx!' To my alarm, she pinched my cheek and shook my head from side to side. 'Well, let's see if your lady friend the *professional artist* is worthy of your attentions. Show me your work – what was your name again?'

I opened my mouth to give her a sharp reply but Georges gave me a warning look. I stepped reluctantly aside so she could see the half-draped figure I'd been working on all day.

Rose, who seemed to be enjoying her role as the boss's wife, frowned and tapped a finger over her mouth. 'Let's see if you're as good as you think you are, English girl.' She put her head to one side and considered my work like an art expert. I rolled my eyes at Georges who shook his head at me. 'This is good, very good,' Rose said. 'You have a feel for the clay, and for the hang of cloth. But be careful to allow the drapes some movement. Leave them a bit unfinished – that's what Rodin likes. I should know – I've been around his work for half my life.'

I was pleased, in spite of myself. It was ridiculous to care about her opinion, but any artist who says they don't lap up praise like a thirsty dog is lying.

Rose rearranged her shawl. '*Au revoir, mes enfants.*' She wagged her finger at us. 'Be good, you two, and if you can't be good, be careful.' Her laugh was guttural as she winked at me. '*Hein*, little fancy pants, stop playing so hard to get and take pity on this gorgeous man.' She grabbed his face in one hand and it was Georges' turn to suffer. Rose sighed again and smoothed the front of her bodice. 'It all goes, as you'll find out for yourself in good time, English Miss. You think you'll always be young, then one day you wake up and you don't look so peachy any more. Enjoy it while you can.'

She left and I became aware of Georges standing so close to me I could smell his citrus cologne. His forearms were brown like a labourer's, the fine hairs golden in the afternoon sun.

'So, are you going to take Rose's advice?'

I began packing up my carving tools. 'Thanks for coming to my rescue again, even if it meant she has the wrong idea about us.'

'Has she?' He bent down to help me put away my things. 'Rose Beuret's pretty astute. It's a mistake to underestimate her. You should warn Camille to be more careful.'

I froze. 'What do you mean?'

He gave me a slow smile and offered me his arm. 'Let me walk you to the door. You've worked quite hard enough for your first day.'

At the models' screen he helped me off with my dustcoat and took down my dolman from its peg and held it out for me. He wrapped it around me and held me for a moment.

'Jessie, I'm sorry if I was rude this morning, when you came in. I couldn't help it, seeing you with that fool, William.'

I turned to face him. 'William is not a fool.'

Georges held up his palms. 'I know he isn't. I don't know why I said that. Yes I do, and so do you.' He rubbed his forehead. 'The truth is, I didn't behave very well with him. When we were in Montmartre, I tried to distract him, you know, with some of the women. I'm sorry.'

Georges could make me warm to him one moment and make my blood boil the next. I remembered what William had told me about Georges' behaviour in Montmartre.

I stepped away from him. 'I'm surprised you had time to tempt William, I hear you made yourself more than agreeable with the dancers.' Georges' eyes gleamed and, too late, I realised my mistake.

'Are you jealous, Jessie,' he said. 'I do hope so.' He grinned. 'Why, I believe you're blushing.'

'Nonsense, it's just a little hot in here.' But when I put my hand to my cheeks, they were hot.

He laughed. 'Come on, wildcat, I'll walk you home.'

Camille caught up with us in the street, eyes bright and her hair coming loose. She looked ravishing. I tried not to think of Rodin's hands all over her, and hoped Georges wouldn't notice that her blouse was buttoned up wrong.

He offered Camille his arm. 'What a healthy glow you have. You must have been doing those calisthenics that are so fashionable with the young ladies of Paris.'

'It's so hot today,' I said, in a rush. 'No wonder Camille is warm. It's all right for you in your shirtsleeves, think of us in our bustles and layers of petticoats and bloomers.'

'I think of nothing else, I can assure you,' Georges said with a wicked smile.

Camille groaned. 'Listen to me, and stop being such an idiot for once. I've had the most brilliant idea. Why don't we all go to the Madwomen's Ball? Have you ever been, Georges?'

'Once or twice,' he said. 'But there's no need to make a special outing to see mad women now that I work alongside you, *ma petite folle*.'

Camille scowled at him. 'Shut up, Georges. Seriously, it would be good material. I'll bring my sketchbook. Will you take Jessie and me?'

'All right, as long as I get locked up in a cell with Jessie for at least an hour, no, make that two hours.' He put his arms around our waists and squeezed.

'We'd better ask Rosa, too,' Camille said, pushing him off. 'I'm not playing gooseberry while you run around after Jessie all evening with your tongue hanging out.'

Georges threw up his arms. 'But, of course we must have La Bonheur there. She'll make the poor demented crazies feel quite sane and sensible when she turns up in top hat and tails.'

'I would love to see Rosa in white tie,' I said. As we walked, they told me the ball was held in La Salpêtrière, the Paris insane asylum for women. I shuddered, imagining Rochester's wife and Miss Havisham in her rotting white gown. 'Won't it be dangerous?'

'Don't worry, they don't let the violent ones attend,' Georges said. 'Most of them aren't mad, at least not the way you'd imagine, with staring eyes and disordered hair. Now I think about it, a look not dissimilar to the *toilette* of our own dear Mademoiselle Claudel. Camille, will you stop hitting me? Save your strength for the nurses when they try to take you back to your cell after the ball with your lunatic *copines*.'

As we walked home, exultant after our first day in Rodin's studio and talking about the ball, the sun was low, bathing the green rooftops in gold, and the sky stretched above us a wash of purple ink.

CHAPTER 22

Paris

1884

I sprawled on the bed in my breeches, watching Camille get ready for the ball. Her mouth full of pins, she cursed as she struggled to put up her hair in an elaborate style. I went to help and tucked it into a loose knot.

'There,' I said. 'You should have dressed up as a boy, like me, much easier than squeezing into stays and fiddling about with hairpins.'

Camille was in dark blue silk, which shone like a blackbird's wing against her pale skin. She ran her hands down the bodice that pushed her breasts up into tight little domes, caught me looking and grinned. 'Not bad, eh?' I undid a button on my cambric shirt so it bared my shoulders. Camille pulled at it and gasped when she saw I was bare-breasted underneath it. She sighed. 'You're so lucky not having to wear a corset with your costume.'

'Caravaggio's *Boy with a Basket of Fruit* would have looked a little odd in one,' I said. We admired our disguises in the dressing table mirror: me, a young Italian boy, my hair tied back with a ribbon, and Camille, Artemisia Gentileschi, the seventeenth-century artist who had dared to paint herself as Judith beheading Holofernes. 'You look magnificent,' I said. 'Have you got the sword?' In answer she picked it up from the floor, pushed me onto the bed and pressed a wooden sword to my throat, its tip red with gore. We tussled until I gained the upper hand and threw her off. I took the sword and touched the bloody end. It was still tacky. 'Is that what happened to my Cadmium Red? The tube was completely empty.'

'And I used up the Venetian Red on the severed head.' Camille nodded at the dressing table. On it sat poor Holofernes' head, which she'd made with wire and papièr-maché.

'Pig.'

'*Salope*. Here, I'll make it up to you.'

Kneeling on the bed, Camille took out a small tin and rubbed her finger in it. She dabbed a slick of rouge on her lips and then on mine. I looked at my reflection and when I smiled my teeth were white against the red. Camille sat next to me, the little pot of rouge still in her hand, and looked at me in the mirror.

'You know,' she said, 'some of the models put rouge on their nipples.'

'No! Why do they do that?'

She shrugged and grinned at me. 'Do you want to try?' I hesitated then opened my shirt to reveal my breasts. She dipped her finger in the rouge and smeared it on my nipples. They tingled and the skin puckered under her touch. Camille held out the pot to me. 'Your turn.' She pulled down her corset and I rubbed on the make-up. I saw her nipples harden and had an urge to take them in my mouth. I screwed the lid back on the pot and avoided her eyes in the mirror.

'Let's have a cigarette before we go down,' I said.

Camille took two from the enamelled silver box on the dressing table and put one in my mouth. 'Want to keep Georges waiting, eh?'

Georges was waiting in the street below to take us to the Madwomen's Ball, but there was no rush this evening – we could stay out as long as we wanted. Camille's mother had gone to the Claudels' country house. She had left instructions with the maid to act as our chaperone, but Eugénie was only too happy to leave us to our own devices. Four glorious months of freedom stretched ahead of us.

I lit our cigarettes. 'It won't do Georges any harm to cool his heels for a bit.'

Camille laughed in her throat. 'That's right, you show him who's boss.' She blew out a stream of smoke and we sat for a while in silence. When she turned to face me, she looked troubled. 'I've been meaning to speak to you, about Rodin.'

I didn't want to speak about their affair, think about them together, but I said, 'Yes, go on.'

'I want you to know that he does love me, truly, and only me.'

I knew she was thinking about Rose Beuret. We hadn't talked about her since that day at the studio, but she had been troubling me. The situation was already fraught with danger, and now there was another woman involved, a woman who insisted on calling herself Madame Rodin.

Camille took a deep breath. 'The other day in the studio, when we saw that woman, Rodin's, you know, I was shocked. I didn't know about her either.'

I looked at her sharply. 'You must have known. Didn't he tell you he wasn't free?'

She shook her head but wouldn't look at me. 'Not until now. But he explained it all to me. You see, the problem is, that he can't leave her, this Rose, not until their son gets on his feet. They're having trouble with him, Rodin says. The boy had a fall when he was a child and has never been normal. Rodin won't say any more, says he can't just walk out on her, not yet anyway. But he says she means nothing to him.'

'Are you sure about that? I wouldn't underestimate her.'

Camille straightened up and looked at me. 'What do you mean?'

'She cornered me when you were … when you were with Rodin.'

'You never told me. Why didn't you tell me?'

My temper sparked. 'Well, I'm telling you now!'

'D'accord, calme-toi.' She squinted at me through the smoke. 'So, what's she like, this so-called Madame Rodin?'

'Formidable. She thought I had designs on Rodin and warned me off.' Camille sniggered. 'I'm serious,' I said. 'You should have seen her – I'm sure she would have struck me if Georges hadn't turned up and convinced her I didn't have my claws in her man.'

Camille put her arm around my shoulder. 'I can just imagine how he did that. Did he tell her you were his?' I nodded and she laughed. 'Any excuse! You really ought to put Georges out of his misery. He won't leave you alone until you do.'

I shook her off, irritated. I couldn't seem to make her understand the threat from Rose. It was like watching from a distance, powerless, as Camille walked too close to a cliff edge, oblivious of the rocks below. It would take only one false step and she would fall. I tried again. 'The problem here is not Georges. The problem is Rose Beuret. I don't think you know what you're up against. You should have seen the way she challenged me; she'd have been at my throat if Georges hadn't stepped in.'

Camille threw up her hands. 'You see what Rodin has to put up with? He says she's jealous of everyone, accuses him of sleeping with all the models – as if he would bother with those empty-heads when he has me!' I wasn't so sure Rodin had given up his taste for models. I'd seen the way he touched the two Italian sisters whenever he got the chance, the sly little strokes and pinches. Camille had grown more strident, as if to drown out any doubts she had about Rodin. She threw her cigarette butt on the floor and ground it beneath her heel. 'He's promised me he will leave Rose, and I believe him. It's just the time isn't right.' Camille glared at me, daring me to challenge her version. I stared back at her and she put her head in her hands. She groaned. 'Listen to me, I sound like an idiot. How often have you heard the *grisettes* bleat out the same excuses for their married lovers? The truth is I don't know whether to believe him. Jessie, I don't know what to do.' She began to cry and I gathered her in my arms.

'Hush now, hush.'

'I love him,' she said, her voice muffled.

'I know you do. It'll be all right, you'll see.'

I could feel her tears on my neck, and then her lips, soft and open. I shuddered and her mouth found mine. Perhaps it was being dressed as a boy, or the emotion of the last few days, but I didn't pull away and kissed her back. Our mouths opened, the tips of our tongues hot and soft; such warmth. We shifted closer, our hands exploring, when a pebble cracked against the window. We jumped apart and looked at each other, our breath coming in short gasps. Camille was the first to recover.

She laughed and pushed her hair out of her eyes. 'I don't know what came over me. You must not pay me any mind, Jessie, I'm not myself.'

I should have been relieved – after all this was the sort of thing curious schoolgirls did – but instead I was disappointed to hear her dismiss our embrace as an aberration. I shook myself. Camille was right: it meant nothing.

I stood up and buttoned my shirt. 'That'll be Georges.'

We went out onto the balcony and a figure stepped into the circle of light cast by a street lamp. Camille put her arm around my waist and we waved. From the street we must have been a strange sight, me in my breeches and Camille in her dress.

'Jessie!' Georges called. 'What's taking you so long? Come down!'

We touched up our rouge in the mirror. I met Camille's eyes and bit my lip. 'Let's go. Georges is waiting.'

CHAPTER 23

'Guess who I am? Let me give you a clue.' Georges held out his arms, showing off lace cuffs stained red. He wore a powdered wig under a tricorn hat, a tight black suit and white stockings.

'Are you a revolutionary?' Camille said.

'The most revolutionary of them all,' he said with a bow. 'Some called me *le dicatateur sanguinaire.*'

She clapped her hands. 'Robespierre!'

'Bravo! And tell me who you are supposed to be – someone biblical by the look of that sword and, ugh, is that a severed head? Delilah? No, don't tell me. Salomé!'

'Artemisia Gentileschi.'

Georges groaned. 'Of course, I might have known it – one of the first women artists. She has a lot to answer for, encouraging you harridans. And you, Jessie, let me see you.' He held out his hand and I stepped into the lamplight. Georges whistled softly between his teeth and made me turn around, I suspect so he could see the full effect of the breeches. After he'd had a good look, he said: 'The fruit basket gives it away – the Caravaggio that hangs in the Villa Borghese.' I was surprised he'd made the connection. In those days Caravaggio had fallen out of favour and few studied his work, but he was my favourite painter. George took a bunch of grapes from my basket and put one in his mouth. 'You make a handsome boy,' he said. 'Be careful, or you'll have Camille falling for you.' Camille and I laughed uneasily and Georges smiled. His instinct for people's tender places was uncanny. 'We all look crazy enough to fit right in with our hosts at the insane asylum,' he said. 'But just wait till you see La Bonheur's disguise.'

We walked to the cab, where standing in full military regalia, hand tucked into his waistcoat, stood Napoleon Bonaparte.

Rosa gave a suitably napoleonic scowl. 'Salute your emperor, my loyal subjects.' She touched her general's hat. 'I thought *les folles* would like this, since most of them think they are married to Napoleon anyway. Who knows? I might get lucky with a tasty little lunatic tonight.'

Georges pulled me forward. 'At least Jessie will be safe from your advances, Rosa, as she's dressed as one of Caravaggio's boys, and a pretty one at that.'

Rosa whistled. 'You make a delectable boy, Jessie. But as my tastes run to the fairer sex, I'll have to make do with Camille, who is looking just as edible, I must say, in that tight bodice. Don't tell me…Artemisia Gentileschi?'

La Salpêtrière was more like a city within a city than an asylum for women. On the way, Rosa explained that the ball was one of the curiosities of Parisian life, drawing fashionable people curious about the insane, but it was also supposed to help the patients by giving them something to look forward to. I didn't know what to expect, but I was not immune to the low thrill of voyeurism. We were all jittery and talking loudly, but as the cab passed through the forbidding, high walls, we fell silent.

Once we were inside, the ballroom was a surprise. It was brightly lit and cheerfully decorated with flowers and plants. An orchestra on a central podium was playing a waltz and there were women dancing together. Two benches along the walls held the more unfortunate inmates who wore their afflictions in their distorted expressions and deformed bodies. But even they sat quietly watching the spectacle. It was the guests – the sane – who appeared most excitable, shrieking and cackling over each other's costumes, as if the mad house had released them from their everyday social restraints. We huddled together uncertainly until Rosa broke free, swooping on a pair of dancers and claiming one as her partner. The woman left behind looked lost among the circling couples. She was dressed as a Pierrot, and looked sad despite her painted-on smile. I touched her on the shoulder and she jumped.

'May I have this dance?' I said.

She kept her head down while I led her around the dance floor, but by the third turn of the room she was studying me.

She cleared her throat, as if she was not used to speaking. 'You are a sculptor.' It was a statement, not a question.

'How can you tell?'

'Your hands, they're calloused and rough.'

'I could be a laundress or a housemaid,' I said.

Her laugh was a dry bark. 'And what would a laundress or a housemaid be doing at The Ball of the Incoherents?' She looked around her and whispered. 'That's what the doctors call it. I know because I listen at doors and at night I break into the office and read their notes.' She put her head to one side. 'What's your name?'

'Jessie.'

'I am Hersilie.'

We stopped at a buffet table covered in delicacies. In the glow from hundreds of candles, little cakes dusted with sugar sparkled and fish mousses quivered. I watched her pile her plate high.

Hersilie spoke with her mouth full, her eyes roving over the table. 'Me, I'm also an artist.'

'I see,' I said.

She could tell I didn't believe her. She stopped pushing food into her mouth and gripped my arm with greasy, bony fingers.

'I swear to you, I'm a painter. I ought to know, that's why they put me in here.'

I shook her off and rubbed the red marks she'd left on my skin. I tried to feel compassion for her, but there was something abrasive and unlikeable about her.

I took a breath and tried again. 'How long have you been here?'

'Let's see, I was twenty when my brother had me locked up.' She counted on her fingers. 'Fifteen years.' That made her only thir-ty-five but she looked much older. Her hair was grey and her skin heavily lined under the white powder. She brushed some crumbs from her mouth and grinned, showing rotten and missing teeth. 'Do you want to know why they put me in here? I bet you do, you all do.'

I shook my head unable to take my eyes from her.

'I'll tell you anyway. It was because I lived on my own, dared to earn my own living as an artist. Too ambitious, you see, for a mere woman, I must be mad, no other explanation.' She laughed softly. 'Want to stay single and paint for a living? You must be suffering from *acute monomania with hallucinations*. Added to that, the neighbours hated me and called me an unfriendly bitch, a witch, an oddball. When my half-brother put me away, those bastards couldn't wait to line up and testify against me to the quack paid to commit me.'

Her breath was rancid and I wanted to step back, but I was mesmerised. 'That's monstrous! Why would your brother do a thing like that?'

'Half-brother. When our father died, he wanted my share of the inheritance. He robbed me!' Hersilie shook her fist but tucked it behind her back when a nurse looked our way and jangled her keys in warning.

I told myself there must have been another reason. This woman was odd in her speech and manner, but put Rosa in here for fifteen years, or Camille, or I, and I doubted we would be any different. I thought of what Camille and I had done earlier this evening, of my feelings for her, and for Georges, and in the background, like a reproach, William. Their mouths had all been on mine and I had hungered for each of them. Perhaps there was something wrong with me. Perhaps other women didn't go through this, not if they were normal. If a doctor could read the thoughts that swirled inside of my head, he would condemn me as vicious, an overheated hysteric. And there was Rosa, swaggering about dressed as a man but with the sympathies and nature of a woman. Compared to us, Hersilie was quite sane.

She was talking again, as if once she'd begun to speak, she could not stop. The poor creature told me of her life in the asylum, stories that would come back to haunt me years later, about her first day when she was forced into a bath with an iron cover that left only her head free and doused with bucket after bucket of freezing water. The punishment continued every morning until she finally recanted and gave up her ambitions to live from her art.

'They call it hydrotherapy,' she said. 'More like drowning. Those infernal baths! If you struggle, the metal cuts your neck.' She leaned her head to one side and showed me her scars.

I gasped and went to touch them, stopped and put my hand to my own throat. 'That's torture. You must complain to one of the doctors.'

Another dry bark. 'Who do you think came up with the water treatment if not one of those demons who call themselves doctors? You are shocked, Mademoiselle, but then nobody knows what goes on here behind locked doors. You are an artist like me, a free spirit, so I shall tell you everything and you will tell everyone else – don't forget to inform the President and the Holy Father in Rome – and I shall be released.'

She gabbled at me in a low voice and the horror of her life crept into my ears. A bath could take between one hour and twelve hours, depending on a patient's level of madness and how long they took to recant. The doctor evidently thought Hersilie one of the saner ones, or she was quick to give up her ideas as the fantasies of a lunatic. But she still suffered, she told me, for crimes such as helping another inmate who had fainted, forgetting to return a pair of scissors to a nurse and writing a few words on the wall. In punishment, Hersilie had been chained by the neck and fifty buckets of water emptied over her head, and she was often forced into a straitjacket and tied to her bed. I could hardly bear to listen and wanted to get away from her, to leave this place with its smiling nurses in their white head-scarves pinned neatly behind their heads, the doctors in their suits, conferring in little groups, while the women patients twirled round and round the dance floor. But I could not tear myself away from Hersilie and instead moved closer to catch her muttered words.

'See that girl over there – the imbecile?' She nodded at a young woman with a wide smile that never wavered and vacant eyes. 'They tie her arms behind her back so tight the rope cuts her and push her head into a bucket of water. What good can that do? She's like an infant, thinks it's a game, laughs when she sees them coming and puts on the rope herself.

'The worst punishment – they call it a treatment of course – is to be isolated in a cell. You lose track of the days, of the months. They're not supposed to do it any more, but they do it in the extreme cases, to incurables like the *tribades*.' My French was by now faultless and I had often been told I spoke like a native, but this word was new to me. My forehead creased and she realised I had not understood her meaning. Hersilie spoke in a hoarse whisper. 'You know, women who make love with other women. Like your friend over there.' She was looking at Rosa, who had her arms draped around her dancing partner, a thin woman with hollow eyes. 'I see she's with Monique, one of the masturbators. Her hands are usually cuffed.'

I started back, embarrassed. 'What?'

'You know, to stop her touching herself.' Hersilie leered at me. 'You are shocked? *Excusez-moi, j'appelle toujours un chat un chat.*'

This Monique had not been caught doing anything out of the ordinary, according to Hersilie, but her doctor had picked up *classic signs of onanism*, which left women thin with a blue tinge to the eyelids.

'What nonsense!' I said. I was beginning to doubt this woman's account; such things were not talked about in those days. Her mouth twisted. 'It is nonsense, of course, you are right. These doctors have their heads stuffed with crazy ideas. The real reason Monique is so skinny is simple – she's sad and that's why she won't eat. Her husband abandoned her and had her committed when he took up with their housemaid. Poor Monique pretends it hasn't happened, of course, always talking about Charles this and Charles that, how good he is to her and how she must hurry and get the house clean and his dinner ready.'

Hersilie had learned to survive by pretending to the alienists – that's what they called themselves then, the doctors who treated sick minds – she'd given up her dangerous illusions. To them she was a success story, docile and hardworking. They were considering her release but meanwhile her days were filled with the backbreaking laundry and tedious needlework believed to be beneficial for women with damaged minds.

'When I get out, I'm going to tell the whole world about what goes on in here, but I don't know when that will be, so it's up to you,' she said.

'But, why don't you write to the authorities now and complain?' I said.

'They read all our letters and punish us if they don't like what we write. I learned that the hard way,' she said, rubbing her wrists. 'But I have my helpers who smuggle letters out for me. I keep one on me all the time. Will you take it and make sure it's posted? It's addressed to the only person who can help me.'

'Of course I shall.'

'Here, shake my hand.' Hersilie slipped me a piece of paper, which I shoved into my pocket. She raised her voice. '*Au revoir, Mademoiselle.*'

I nodded at her and she mouthed: 'Tell your friend to be careful.' She nodded towards Rosa, but the warning could as easily have been for Camille.

I pushed my way through the crowd of Parisians in their elaborate costumes. They guzzled champagne and screeched with laughter while the inmates looked on, their expressions glazed. Someone pulled at my arm and I turned. A young woman held out a bundle of rags to me, her hands scarred with burn marks.

'Do you see my baby? Isn't he beautiful? His name is Alphonse, *mon petit Alphonse.*'

I looked into the bundle and saw a piece of wood, crudely drawn features. I tried to smile at her, but found myself running across the room towards Camille and Georges.

Georges was leaning against a wall, looking bored, but straightened up when he saw me. 'Have you had enough? Do you want to go?'

I nodded, not trusting myself to speak. I would tell them about Hersilie later.

Camille put away her sketchpad. 'It's horrible here, isn't it? I've been in prisons and in orphanages, but there's something depressing about this place, I don't know what it is. I thought they would be strange, different somehow from normal people, but instead they just seem so hopeless, and so sad.'

Georges shrugged. 'Let's go, then. The morgue is more cheerful. I'll see if I can prise Rosa away from her latest conquest.'

In the cab I took out the letter Hersilie had given me, intending to show it to the others. It was folded and sealed with candle wax. I turned it over. Scrawled across it in a shaky hand were some words in rusty red ink. I sniffed and smelled the unmistakeable metallic tang of dried blood. It was addressed to Jeanne d'Arc. So, she was mad, after all. I crumpled up the letter and threw it out of the window. I watched the walls of La Salpêtrière recede behind us, vowing I would never set foot in a hellhole like that again.

CHAPTER 24

Paris

1929

I shifted slightly on Georges' ridiculous sofa, and managed only to sink further into the pile of cushions.

'Georges, do you think she was mad?'

'Who, that woman at the ball? *Fou à lier, je dirais.* Sane people don't have a correspondence with Joan of Arc.'

'No, I meant Camille.' He was silent for a while. I took one of his hands, the one that still worked. It was liver spotted, like mine, but his touch felt the same as it had more than thirty years before. 'You know what happened to her, don't you?' I said.

He nodded without looking at me. 'We all did. She wrote to me, to her agent, to all her friends in the art world. There was a brouhaha for a while, of course. I did what I could, wrote to her brother, to the newspapers. Then the letters stopped and after a while the articles dwindled. War broke out the following year and I, well, I forgot about her.'

I slipped my hand under his so we were palm to palm. 'You saw things no one should see. It's understandable.'

He closed his fingers over mine. 'I survived, others didn't. But when I came back, I couldn't sculpt.' He held up his useless hand. 'My inheritance lasted until a few years ago and then I met Lotta. She'd had an unfortunate affair with a married man and his wife was threatening to tell all of Paris. I was a friend of her father, and he made me a generous offer if I'd make an honest woman of her.' So, I'd been right. He hadn't changed a bit. Georges met my eyes and winced, as if he knew what I was thinking. I tried to take my hand away but he held on. 'Jessie, don't look at me like that. What else was I supposed to do? Can you see me working in a bank?' I shook my head. 'So, no,' he said. 'I didn't do anything about Camille. I forgot about her. We all did.'

I relented, and smiled at him. 'You did what you could, and Paul had the law on his side.'

'*Quel connard.*'

I squeezed his hand. 'Georges, I'm trying to help her now, to build a case to get her out. If I could only find out if he had any grounds to put her away…'

'Don't tell me she's still in an asylum?' I nodded and he closed his eyes. 'My God! All these years! Poor Camille. I thought I had suffered, but can you imagine?'

I shook my head. 'I can't. I try not to. Will you help me? I last saw her when we were all so young, and she was confined just before the war. Let me see…' I counted on my fingers. 'She would have been nearly fifty. Georges, I need you to tell me what she was like when you last saw her. Was she mad?'

Georges stood up and went to a table that held decanters and glasses. He poured brandy and splashed soda into our crystal tumblers. He stared into the middle distance, as if remembering. 'For a while, in the late '90s, Camille had a good run. She seemed to get out from under Rodin's shadow, forged her own way with smaller pieces, delicate little things with unusual subjects. There was one I particularly liked, an intimate group of women, and behind them a tidal wave threatens while they are oblivious to the danger. Extraordinary – such a small piece and this overwhelming sense of peril.'

He swirled his brandy and thought for a moment. 'I bumped into her one day, must have been '97, at the Salon. I remember the year because I had a piece in too. Camille told me she'd left Rodin and was working on her own in a studio. I almost didn't recognise her – she was plastered in make-up, like a terrible painted mask. Her voice was strange too, dull, and mechanical. She had put on a lot of weight. Remember how beautiful she was once, with that perfect '90s figure? I miss that shape – the young girls are so flat nowadays.'

I shot him a look and he cleared his throat. 'Sorry, yes, where was I?'

'Camille, you were talking about when you saw her last.'

'Ah yes.' He stared into his drink again and went on.

Sensing she was isolated, Georges had called on her at her studio at boulevard d'Italie. Camille had been friendly enough. She was looking out of the window and singing some street ditty when he arrived with a basket of peaches and a bottle of vintage champagne. Camille had laughed at his extravagance and let him in, teasing him like in the old days. She showed him what she was working on and they talked shop.

'She seemed out of touch with what was going on, wanted to hear the gossip from the Latin Quarter, who was showing where and, in particular, who was being commissioned. The studio was a hell of a mess – none of those feminine touches I remember from your *atelier* at rue Notre-Dame-des-Champs. But, then, Camille was never exactly *bonne femme* material.' Georges took a sip and wiped his moustache. 'When I left she promised to call on me, but I didn't hear from her for months. Finally, she sent me a note saying she'd been ill and she'd get in touch when she was better, but she never did. Soon after, the stories started about her odd behaviour.'

'Odd in what way?'

'Accusing her friends of plotting against her, wild irrational outbursts and raving letters. She couldn't keep a model, kept sacking them. She said they were stealing her ideas. You know what models are like – word went round and soon nobody wanted to work for her. And there was this terrible, public rift with Rodin over one of her pieces, an important commission. I heard he used all his powers to block it when he saw it in her studio. I spoke to him about it and he wouldn't discuss it other than saying the sculpture was a personal affront and an invasion into his private affairs. I must say, when I eventually saw it myself I wasn't surprised.'

I couldn't believe what I was hearing; Rodin had always been our supporter, and he'd adored Camille, hailing her in public correspondence as *une femme de génie*, and had always praised her courage in sculpting subjects that were not then considered suitable for a woman.

'Are you sure about that?' I said. 'The Rodin I knew would never object to a sculpture. I can't imagine him censoring Camille, when he was so revolutionary himself.'

'It's better if I show you.' Georges fetched a catalogue and opened it at a photograph. 'Here it is, see for yourself.'

In the picture, captioned *L'Age Mûr*, I saw a young woman, on her knees, begging a middle-aged man – obviously Rodin – not to leave her. He was being led away by a naked crone who looked cruelly like Rose Beuret, with sagging bosoms and a drooping stomach. There could be no doubt about it to anyone who knew about their story. It was there for anyone to see, their triangular dance of love, guilt and hatred exposed to the world.

I passed my hand over the picture of the young girl. 'It's powerful. But I can see how he might object.' Georges sat down next to me on the sofa and we looked at the picture together. I remembered all the times we had stood in front of sculptures and paintings like this.

'Camille managed to get it shown, eventually,' Georges said, interrupting my thoughts. 'She always insisted the piece wasn't autobiographical but an allegory about youth and age. Rodin didn't see it that way, said she was making a fool of him, washing their dirty linen in public. You know how he hated to have his affairs discussed, thought it diminished his standing to be gossiped about in the cafés and salons.' He sighed and closed the book. 'In a way I don't blame Camille for being so bitter – he never did leave Rose Beuret despite all his promises, and strung her along for years. The sculpture made it all public and Rodin never forgave her.'

Georges told me that when it was shown at the 1903 Salon, *L'Age Mûr* was poorly received and lambasted for being a shabby copy of Rodin's work. It seemed Camille was destined always to be compared to Rodin.

'The last time I saw her was in her new studio, on L'Île St Louis, in the early 1900s,' Georges said. 'It was peaceful out there on the banks of the Seine, surrounded by trees, the scent of apples coming off the barges as they floated down the river to market. She was even heavier by then, her face bloated and prematurely aged, her hair greasy and in disarray, but her eyes were bright and she seemed content. She was working on a new sculpture on the theme of Perseus and the Gorgon. From what I could see, Camille wasn't mad, no.'

Georges couldn't tell me any more. We talked a little longer about people who might be able to fill me in about Camille's last days in Paris.

'You know who is still around and remembers the old days?' he said. 'Remember Suzanne Valadon? She was a wild one! I'll give you her address – she still lives in Montmartre.' He walked me to the door.

I put my hand on his chest. 'I'm sorry, Georges, that you had to stop sculpting. It must have been hard.'

His smile was rueful. 'If I'm honest, I don't think I would have ever made it as an artist. Without money behind me, I wouldn't have stuck at it. Unlike Camille, I didn't have the stomach for it – the rejections and scrabbling about for commissions. But that's all in the past now. I do have one regret, though. Jessie, I've always wanted to tell you how sorry…'

'Please, Georges, don't. Let's just say goodbye. We didn't get a chance last time.'

I put out my hand to shake his, but he folded me in his arms and held me. And, for a moment, I was twenty-two again in a studio in Montmartre.

CHAPTER 25

September 1884

The first time I met Suzanne Valadon was at Henri's studio. Of course, everyone knows the name Toulouse-Lautrec now, but at that time he was young, only twenty and, like us, still making his way as an artist. Georges had taken Camille, Rosa and I to his new friend's studio in Montmartre.

'You'll like Henri,' he said as we waited in front of the door at the top of a grubby tenement stair. 'His *five o'clocks* are legendary for going on all night. And his work is interesting, *avant garde*. I think he'll go far.'

Rosa snorted. '*Un avant gardist?* Not one of those tedious pointillists, I hope. Paris is full of myopic painters messing about with dots. It hurts my eyes to look at them.'

'No, he's completely different.' Georges said. 'Wait and see.'

Camille frowned. 'Lautrec? How is it I've never heard of this oh-so-promising artist, if he is as good as you say he is?'

'It's Toulouse-Lautrec, Henri de Toulouse-Lautrec, from one of France's oldest families, a true aristocrat. He's quite a character.'

I was about to say William had met Toulouse-Lautrec and had given me one of his sketches, but held my tongue. I had been careful not to mention William in front of Georges since our quarrel, and I didn't want to spoil the party mood. Besides, England was a world away and I was in Montmartre, a wild neighbourhood, or so I'd heard, the haunt of criminals, prostitutes, artists and intellectuals, according to my Paris guide, which warned it was No Place for a Respectable Lady. I was thrilled.

Toulouse-Lautrec opened the door to his studio. Before us stood the most extraordinary man I'd ever seen. Georges had prepared us for his deformity and warned us not to stare. His torso was that of an adult's, but he had the legs of a child as a result of a hunting accident when he was twelve. What I had not expected to see was a small bearded man dressed as a Japanese geisha, in a kimono and a wig jiggling with hair ornaments. In his arms he cradled a yellow porcelain doll, swaddled in embroidered silk.

Catching me staring at him, he bowed. 'Henri de Toulouse-Lautrec, *à votre service.*'

I closed my mouth.

Georges clapped him around the shoulder. 'Henri, allow me to present Mesdemoiselles Jessie Lipscomb and Camille Claudel, two talented sculptors who work with me at Rodin's studio.'

Toulouse-Lautrec refastened his monocle and peered at Camille and me. '*L'atelier* Rodin, eh? You must be good. Women working with men, *quel scandale!* I met the great man in Montmartre not so long ago with Georges, do you remember, *mon vieux*? What a night! There was this absolutely charming Englishman with you – I am a shameless anglophile, you know, it's my chief weakness – who told me all about the science of stones. He talked with such *passion*; I'll never put on a pair of diamond studs again without thinking of him.'

'Ah, that would be the redoubtable William.' Georges' tone was dry.

'But he was fascinating, fascinating! And so lively and handsome, he made quite an impact on our crowd of dissolutes. All the little *demimondaines* couldn't get enough of him and his amusing accent.'

'Yes, he was the typical Englishman in Montmartre, goggling at everything and everyone,' Georges drawled.

I glared at him before turning back to Toulouse-Lautrec. 'William is a dear friend of mine, and he speaks well of you, Monsieur Toulouse-Lautrec. In fact, he gave me one your drawings and I have it still. I thought it was powerful – simple, yet so expressive.'

He gave a small bow. '*Merci bien.* Praise from a fellow artist is rare but all the more welcome when it comes.' He kissed my hand. 'I insist you call me Henri and I shall call you Jessie – such exotic names you English ladies have!'

In those days, before the drink had really taken hold of him, Henri was gregarious and warm, with the rare knack of instantly putting people at their ease. I was to discover that when he was among artist friends at his studio parties, rather than hiding his strange appearance, he would draw more attention to his oddity by dressing in outlandish costumes, a habit he'd learned from his eccentric father. It worked as a distraction and made it less awkward for everyone. I was charmed by him and he seemed to take to our little group immediately. And when Georges introduced Rosa, Henri's eyes lit up. That evening, she looked as if she'd stepped off a tennis court, in cream flannels and a panama hat. She was also smoking a clay pipe.

'You must be Madame Bonheur,' he said. 'I had heard about you and your unmistakable dress sense, but the reports don't do you justice. *Enchanté.*' He made a show of shaking her hand as if she were another man. 'You must allow me to give you the name of my tailor – he's a genius when it comes to dressing the, ah, more unorthodox figure.' He spread the sleeves of his kimono and smiled warmly. We laughed but Rosa was not to be won over so easily.

She took the pipe out of her mouth and pointed it at him. 'I keep hearing your name, Henri de Toulouse-Lautrec. Georges here raves about you, but what does he know? More significantly, my old friend Cormont tells me you have potential.'

'You know my former *maître*?' Henri said.

'Young man, I know everyone. Now, show me your pictures and I can decide for myself what all the fuss is about.'

'With pleasure.' He called across the attic room: '*La belle* Suzanne! These are my delightful new friends, Jessie and Camille, and of course you know the handsome Georges. Will you look after them while I show Madame Bonheur around?'

A beautiful woman lying on a chaise longue waved at us and returned to her conversation with two young men, who sat at her feet as if in adoration of The Sphinx.

'That's Suzanne Valadon,' Georges said in an undertone to Camille and me once we were alone. 'She's a model, but also an artist. She sat for all the great artists and they say she's been to bed with most of them. Renoir is completely smitten, apparently. He makes love to her and in return she insists on painting lessons.'

I looked more closely and with a jolt recognised the girl in the red bonnet from Renoir's *Dance at Bougival*.

'A model who paints?' Camille said with a sneer. 'She doesn't look as if she has a single intelligent thought in that pretty head.'

Georges and Camille sniggered and it made me furious. They were as bad as the *practiciens* with their outdated ideas. This was 1884, after all.

'Just because a woman is a model, it doesn't follow that she's a fool or a slut,' I said. 'Anyway, I'm sure most of the gossip about models comes from male artists bragging about imaginary conquests.'

Georges only laughed harder. 'Oh, Jessie, I don't know what's more charming, your naivety or your faith in the virtue of your fellow women, which is admirable, but sadly misplaced. You see, Suzanne Valadon may only be nineteen but she already has an illegitimate brat. Everyone in Paris knows the story.'

'Well we don't. Tell it to us at once!' Camille said.

I crossed my arms and glared at Georges, but I couldn't fool him; he knew I was intrigued.

He beckoned us closer and lowered his voice. 'Well, you must first know that little Maurice was born nine months after La Valadon had been sitting for Renoir. She goes to the great man with the baby in her arms and he takes one look at it and says: "He can't be mine, the colour is terrible." Next she goes to Degas, who says: "He can't be mine, the form is terrible." In despair, she tells the Spanish artist Miguel Utrillo about her troubles and he says the baby can have his name. "I would be glad to put my name to the work of either Renoir or Degas."'

Camille and Georges roared and clung onto each other. I tried not to smile but their laughter was infectious. I punched Camille on the shoulder.

'You're supposed to be on the side of women artists,' I said.

She wiped the tears from her eyes. 'I know, but it's so funny. Georges, you are a scandal and a terrible gossip, which is why we love you so.'

Georges put his arms around us. 'It's a good story, and I don't feel bad telling it to you because I heard it from Suzanne herself. Come on, I'll introduce you to her, she's great fun.'

Up close, Suzanne Valadon's skin was luminous, like porcelain held up to the light. Her eyes were sleepy, as if she had just made love, and her lashes looked as if they had been dusted in charcoal. With her strong jaw and dark eyebrows, she had the kind of almost masculine beauty that awes women as much as men. I couldn't take my eyes off her.

She shooed the young adorers away and beckoned us to sit down. 'They were trying to get me to pose for them, but I'm too busy with Henri. He's booked me up for weeks, and I'm learning so much from him.'

'You're an artist as well as a model?' I asked. I desperately wanted to be open-minded but I confess I was shocked that she posed naked. In those days it wasn't acceptable for a woman artist to take off her clothes and pose, not if she wanted to be taken seriously. But somehow, like Rosa, Suzanne got away with her eccentricities through the force of her personality. She was both bold and guileless, and had the devastating confidence of the truly beautiful. And she was always treated with respect, despite her reputation for sleeping around.

Henri came over with Rosa. 'I love making new friends and now we must celebrate,' he said, waving a bottle and a clutch of glasses at us. 'I've developed a taste for American cocktails and you must try my own invention, *le Tremblement de Terre*. And I promise you it will live up to its name, in your language, Jessie, the earthquake.' The English word rolled luxuriously from his mouth like a train from a tunnel. He began pouring from different bottles. 'Four parts absinthe, two parts red wine and the merest hint of cognac for flavour.' He stirred the murky liquid in our glasses and handed them out to us. He drank his down as if it were water. 'Simple but delicious!'

'Simple but lethal,' Georges said, tipping the contents of my glass into his own. 'I think Jessie and Camille will stick to wine.'

But Camille was too quick for him and took a gulp. She went pale and then green. I thought she was going to be sick, but she recovered.

She gritted her teeth and swallowed. 'You should sell this recipe to *L'École d'Anatomie*. It would be excellent for preserving the cadavers. Why don't you…'

Suzanne stretched languidly and placed a soft, white hand on my arm, like a cat putting out its paw for attention, and spoke across Camille as if she were not there. 'I believe Jessie was asking if I was an artist. Yes, I am, although one that is still learning. Luckily, I have the best tutors in the world: Renoir, Degas, Puvis de Chavannes and, of course, Henri, who is the rising star. I sit for them and pay close attention while they work, and so they teach me everything they know.'

Camille scowled at Suzanne who ignored her and gave Georges a slow smile, leaning forward so her breasts nearly spilled out of her low-cut bodice.

'I'm sure you have much to teach them too,' he said, practically salivating. If he were a dog he'd have rolled onto his back for his belly to be scratched. I wanted to kick him in the shins. Suzanne smiled at him like an indulgent mother and he gazed at her adoringly. It was my turn to scowl. Camille snorted; she had clearly taken against Suzanne and didn't bother to hide her contempt.

Suzanne turned her head slightly at the sound and looked coolly at Camille, as if weighing up an enemy. 'You're Camille Claudel, aren't you?'

'What of it?'

'I've heard about you. I understand you too are the pupil of a great artist.'

'Rodin is my tutor, yes.'

Suzanne winked at Camille. 'Then we are the same, you and I.'

Camille coloured and opened her mouth to speak, but Rosa got in first. She made a space for herself on the chaise longue next to Suzanne, who reluctantly moved over. 'Don't waste your time on

Duchamp, he's only a beginner,' Rosa said. 'When are you going to pose for me? Or am I to be the only artist in Paris not to paint La Valadon?'

Suzanne flicked her cool gaze back to Rosa. '*Ah, non, chèrie*, you paint animals – cows and horses and hunting dogs – not beautiful women. But I have an idea, why don't you paint my cats? They are adorable!'

Suzanne uncoiled herself from the chaise longue and tossed back one of Henri's lethal cocktails in one go. She became animated and began to regale us with preposterous tales about a goat she kept in her studio to eat up her bad drawings, and about her cats, which she fed caviar, but only on Fridays, because they were good Catholic cats. I wasn't sure if I believed her, but her stories made me laugh so much I forgave her outrageous flirting with Georges. We were all soon in fits except for Camille, who sulked while the rest of us egged on Suzanne. La Valadon turned out to be excellent company, witty and self-deprecating, but when we plied her with questions about Renoir and Degas, she batted them away.

'Boring! Who wants to talk about technique? Look at their paintings. All you need to know is there on the canvas. Now, have you ever met a rabbit with a taste for Chinese food and wine? No? Well, I have…'

Camille cut across her rudely. 'Henri, where did you get your costume?'

'Oh, do you like it? Isn't it just adorable – so original?' He stood up and did a little twirl. 'At one of those Japanese importers. They even had the proper wooden *zori* shoes and white silk *tabi* socks.'

'I'm interested in Japanese art,' Camille said. 'Do you know the Goupil print shop in rue Coulaicourt?'

Henri pressed his hands together under his chin and closed his eyes. 'Know it? I practically *live* there. I adore those Japanese block prints. I've been trying out some new techniques I've borrowed from them. Would you like to see?'

Paris in those days was full of shops that brought in ceramics, prints and curios from Japan, which had recently opened its doors to European traders. I found the Japanese design too pared down and clung to the ornamental, realistic style I'd been trained in, but Camille was intrigued by the block prints and had been talking about sculpting in jade or onyx.

Henri held out his hand to Camille. 'Come and see my pictures. You're not easily shocked, I hope?'

'Nothing shocks me, other than the banal,' she said.

But he was right to warn us. Henri's paintings, even then when he was first developing his unique style, were not for the faint-hearted. They were desperately sad, these frank scenes from cafés and brothels: the women's bodies were fleshy with drink, their faces haggard as they sprawled half-undressed on dirty beds, in poses at once enticing and repellent. I wanted to concentrate on Henri's work and walked on ahead of the others and stopped in front of one of the paintings. Two *filles de joie*, a redhead and a brunette with hard, knowing faces, were negotiating with a top-hatted gentleman. With growing horror, I realised that the man was William: my William. His ears were tinged red with excitement, his expression eager.

'Ah, your English friend. I told you he'd made an impact.' Henri had arrived quietly at my side. I wondered if he knew about William and me but his smile was open and trusting. 'He had such an expressive face, I couldn't resist sketching him.'

Rosa called over with a question, and Henri hurried away. I studied the painting more closely. There was no doubt in mind: it was William. I trembled with rage and wanted to tear it off the wall and grind his 'expressive' face beneath my heel. How could he? I knew only too well that Paris was full of temptations and heady liberties, but I had resisted tasting them, while William had succumbed on his first night. He had been whoremongering when he could have been with me. I looked around to see if any of my friends had noticed the painting and saw Georges watching. After a moment, he turned his attention back to Henri, who was explaining his technique.

'I thin the oil paint with turpentine to give flatness, and use bold outlines, like the Japanese woodblock prints.'

Camille was nodding but Rosa only sniffed. 'Yes, yes, I see all that, but why on God's good earth would you want to paint this seedy lot? I mean, I like a popsy in a petticoat as much as the next man, but these ones look as if they're already dying of the pox. I'd rather paint a prize bull or a horse any day.'

Georges sighed. 'This again? Rosa, please remember that not everyone shares your obsession with dumb animals. I'm still recovering from the day you dragged me along to a livestock auction. It took me weeks to get the stench out of my clothes.'

'Nonsense, you enjoyed it until you stepped in dung and the farmers laughed at you.'

Camille doubled over with laughter and Georges looked put out. 'I don't know why you're laughing – remember that time we went to the country with Rosa and she made you climb over a fence and hold a cow by its horns so she could sketch it?'

Camille wiped the tears from her eyes. 'I do indeed, Georges, and I remember your face when it lifted its tail.'

Suzanne smiled at Georges and put her arm through his, blocking off Camille. 'How brave to be in a field at all,' she cooed. 'I find the countryside absolutely terrifying.' She pointed at a line drawing. 'This one's of me. Henri sketched me after I'd been out on the tiles all night. Just imagine drawing me with a hangover, the little swine. But he's so amusing that I can't stay cross with him for long.' She laughed throatily and put a strand of hair the colour of cognac in her mouth and looked up at Georges.

Camille stomped over and handed me a glass of wine. 'I can't stand another minute of that simpering half-wit's conversation,' she whispered. 'Why don't we...' She stopped and stared at the painting of William. 'Is that...? No, it can't be! Oh, Jessie.' She put her arm around me. 'Is it really him?'

I nodded, too miserable to reply. I took a sip of wine; it tasted thin and sour. I turned my back on the painting, but I couldn't get the women's raddled faces out of my mind. I was gripped by nausea every time I thought of William's red ears and foolish grin.

Camille called to Georges. 'Jessie's not feeling well. Will you get us a cab?'

He broke away from Suzanne and came over. He put his palm on my temple; his touch was cool.

'You're burning up,' he said. I couldn't help looking at the painting one last time and he saw what I was looking at. He took a moment to study the picture, his face grim.

'I'm sorry, Jessie, that you had to find out like this about William,' he said. 'I didn't tell you because I didn't want to see you hurt.'

I thought I was going to be sick.

Georges put his arm firmly around my waist. 'I'll take you home. Rosa, are you coming?'

Henri said: 'You're leaving so soon? But you haven't seen my paintings of racehorses.'

Rosa beamed. 'Racehorses you say, now that I'd like to see.' She turned to Georges and shooed him away. 'You three go on without me. Don't you worry about me, I can look after myself.'

It was cold outside and the early-morning sky was as pink and gold as a Rubens nude. Georges took off his jacket and wrapped it around my shoulders. The tweed was rough against my cheek, but it still held the warmth from his body. In the cab, Camille fell asleep where she sat opposite me, next to Georges. As the cab bumped over the cobbles of Montmartre, I studied his face, as I had studied William's only a few moments earlier. He had taken off his hat and pushed his hand through his hair, which was the colour of dark honey. His eyes were cast in shadow and I couldn't tell if he knew I was staring at him; I didn't care if he knew. All this time, I had been holding back, William had been unfaithful at the first tawdry opportunity thrown his way. When Georges came to sit beside me I leaned into him.

He tilted my chin towards him and paused. 'Jessie,' he murmured. I wanted him to say my name again.

I put my arms around him and he bent his head and kissed me, long and deep; this time I didn't push him away.

CHAPTER 26

MONTMARTRE, PARIS

1929

Suzanne poured me some wine. All around us, on every wall of her studio, La Valadon's younger self was immortalised by some of the world's most famous artists. She was still handsome for a woman in her sixties, but her beauty had faded. It was disconcerting to see how the years had changed everyone. Meeting Georges in particular had taken it out of me and I'd rested up for a day before going to Montmartre to find Suzanne.

She pointed at two of the portraits. 'That one was painted by my son, Miguel Utrillo, and that by my husband, André Utter.' She smiled over the rim of her glass. 'He's my second husband. Unlike Camille, I never had any problem persuading men to marry me. You did come here to talk about Camille, didn't you?'

I put down my glass untouched; I was too old to drink cheap wine. 'Georges told you.'

She shrugged and smiled coyly. I wondered if they'd slept together, and supposed it was more likely than not. 'He wrote me a note to tell me you were coming, something about finding out more about Camille.' She made a face at the wine. 'This wine would thin paint, but if I buy the good stuff Miguel or André just polish it off.' She knocked it back anyway and wiped her mouth with the back of her hand. 'So, what do you want to know about that stuck-up bitch? I'm sorry, she was your friend. But I never had much time for Camille. She was a man's woman.' My eyebrows shot up and she had the grace to laugh. 'I know, I know, I'm one to talk. But I've always been loyal to my friends, and Camille, well, she was a cold one.'

I was surprised – I had never thought of Camille as cold. Passionate, yes, and hot tempered, but never cold.

Suzanne frowned. 'I know you always thought she was your friend, Jessie, but I never trusted her, and in the end, the two of you fell out, didn't you? What was it over, a man?' I made a noncommittal noise. I didn't want to talk about that now; it was buried in the past. Suzanne shook her head. 'Camille was ruthless when it came to getting her own way, and she couldn't stand not to be in the limelight.'

A skinny black cat jumped into her lap and butted her with its head. She stroked it and it settled into a purring cushion. 'I'll try to help you, for old times' sake,' she said, 'but I don't know how much I can tell you. We were never close, as you know, but we did run in the same circles, particularly when she became Rodin's official mistress.' She looked up at the portraits and sighed. 'It seems so long ago. It was a different world before the War.'

'Anything you can tell me about Camille and her life before she disappeared would be helpful,' I said.

Suzanne picked up her palette and began daubing green and violet onto the nude she was working on. 'You don't mind, do you?'

I shook my head. Her work was bold, colourful, coarse, even. She'd become a successful artist since I'd known her, the first woman painter admitted to the Société Nationale des Beaux Arts. Mind you, it couldn't have hurt that her former lover Puvis de Chavannes was president. I was being uncharitable – her work was undoubtedly powerful, better than some of the portraits by prominent artists that hung on her walls. Camille used to say Suzanne slept with artists to get what she wanted, but that was unfair. It was inevitable her lovers would be other artists when she mixed so freely with them. I'd often wondered if Camille's antipathy to Suzanne stemmed from the fear that she too would be known only as Rodin's lover, rather than the artist, Camille Claudel.

Another cat, a tabby, wound its way around my leg. I scratched it behind its ears and its chest began to rumble. 'How did you do it, Suzanne?'

'Hmm? What?'

'Become an artist and be a mother. Camille always said you couldn't do both. I didn't believe her, until I had my own children.'

Suzanne swivelled around from her easel and glared at me. 'You think I got by on my looks, is that it?'

'No, of course not. I didn't mean to offend you, I was curious, that's all.'

But Suzanne crashed on as if I hadn't spoken. 'I know that's what Camille used to say – that I was only a jumped-up model and the only reason I got anywhere was by opening my legs. What? You don't think I heard her vile slanders? *Quelle salope!* As if she was any better! You think my life has been easy?'

Suzanne didn't wait for me to answer. She picked up her glass and drained it before pouring another. Her speech was thickened but otherwise she didn't show the least sign of being drunk. 'I got here by my talent, through sacrifice and hard work, just like all the other artists who made it, and that's the simple truth. Camille, she could talk the talk but she wasn't tough enough. She wasn't brought up on the streets like me,' she thumped her chest. 'Me, the bastard daughter of a sewing maid, I was sent out to work in a milliner's workshop when I was eleven, a mere child. By the time I was sixteen, I was a model and the plaything of every artist who thought painting my body gave them the right to fuck me.'

I flinched, more at her bitterness than at her language. I realised the same well of bitterness lay inside me, the dark waters a deep and constant reminder of what I had not achieved because of my sex. A beam of sunlight came through the studio window and lit up Suzanne's face, showing her jowls and the red veins spidering across her cheeks, the grey roots showing underneath the brown dye. I pitied us both: two disappointed old women who had once dreamed of greatness. My sadness must have shown because Suzanne's mood changed abruptly. She laughed, that great shout of laughter I remembered so well, still as joyful as ever.

She patted me on the knee. 'Jessie, don't feel sorry for me. I've had a marvellous life, full of art and love and adventure. Did you know I used to be a circus acrobat, walking the tightrope? Can you imagine?' I shook my head and smiled. But I could just picture Suzanne balanced on a rope between two lampposts with the fire-eaters and jugglers who performed in the streets of L'Opera, posing on one leg above a gasping crowd. She guffawed. 'You should have seen me – Berthe Morisot herself painted me on the tight-rope when I was fifteen.' She waved her glass in the air and some of it spilled on the sleeping cat. 'Ah Berthe, she was something else. Those were the days – I knew all the greats, the artists, writers and musicians of our time. So what if my heart was broken a few times along the way?' She slapped her thigh and the little cat lifted its head and mewed. 'I broke a few myself, mind you. Erik Satie never got over me after one night together, the poor little thing.' She smiled at the memory, and grew serious again. She leaned towards me and the cat wriggled off her lap and landed lightly on the floor. 'What I'm trying to say to you, Jessie, about Camille, she thought she was better than me, but in the end, she was no different.'

The wine was taking hold, and I thought Suzanne was going to drift off into her reminiscences again. I prompted her. 'Camille was no different?'

'Yes, we were the same, you know, her affair with Rodin, and wasn't she with Debussy too?' She waved her hand and began to slur. 'The thing is, the thing is, Camille, she wasn't strong enough to do what I've done, live my own life, an outsider and the rest of them can go to hell. Respectable society? Pah! What did I ever care for those bastards? They couldn't touch me because I didn't care what they thought of me.' She burped gently and slopped some more wine into her glass. 'I did try it once, the respectable life, but it wasn't for La Valadon. My first husband – God rot him – was a stockbroker. I moved out of Paris and became the dutiful wife, but it nearly killed me. Then I met André and he saved my life.' Her eyes swam and I thought she was going to cry. She wiped her eyes and carried on. 'He brought me back to Montmartre, where I belong. But Camille, she was different. She came from the bourgeoisie, and that lot, they'd eat their own children before they'd let them taint the family name. She never stood a chance, the poor bitch.'

I thought of Camille in the asylum, her hands clasped in her lap, staring out over that desolate valley, shut up and abandoned. I wondered if Suzanne was right, if her family had shut her away because she was an embarrassment.

'But Camille had friends, powerful friends,' I said. 'Surely Rodin would have protected her.'

Suzanne shook her head. 'She played it all wrong. You could see how things changed between Camille and Rodin – at first she was the young beauty with all the power, he the desperate older man. Then she made the mistake of falling in love with him.

'By the time she realised she was his creature, his little ape, it was too late. No one would take her seriously, and then, once it was too late, she tried to strike out on her own, without a patron. She had no income of her own – her family gave her a pittance, hardly enough to pay for marble and forge fees. This life,' she gestured around the studio, 'it's a hard one, full of little failures and disappointments, a constant struggle to pay the bills. Camille wasn't strong enough. It's enough to drive anyone mad.'

Suzanne could be right – after all, there were artists who took their own lives because they couldn't face failure and the grim poverty that came with it. There was one who was found frozen to death in his studio, his jacket wrapped around his sculpture to save it from being damaged by the cold. But I knew that Camille, the Camille I knew, would not have cared about poverty or discomfort, or what the critics said; she would have carried on working in her studio as long as she could. She had been ripped away from everything she loved. I thought again of Camille in that place, living out her days locked up, far from Paris, when she should be in a studio like this, working.

'Camille, she should have what you have, Suzanne,' I said. 'And I, I'm jealous, too, of your life as an artist.'

She stared at me, her eyes hard. She was more sober than I'd realised. 'Are you really, Jessie? Think carefully before you wish to swap places with me. I have earned my name, but after all these years of hard work, I'm overshadowed by my son's fame, the son whom I taught to paint when he became a drunk, neglecting my own work to care for him. Now all I hear is: *There goes Utrillo's mother! Used to be a stunner in her day, slept with all of them, Renoir, Toulouse-Lautrec, de Chavannes.* And that's how I'm remembered, my work forgotten while people gossip about who I fucked.' She shrugged and went back to her canvas. 'I don't care what those *connards* say about me. I live by my art and that's enough for me. And unlike Camille Claudel, I survived.'

I stood up to go and asked the question I'd put to Georges. She took her time considering it.

'No, I don't think she was mad. Weak, yes, and angry, but not mad. Maybe you should talk to her brother. I hear he's in town.'

'I didn't know Paul was in Paris. Thank you, Suzanne.' I put out my hand.

When I was at the door, she looked up from her painting. '*Hein*, Jessie, we had some good times, didn't we? Remember that night at *Le Chat Noir*?'

I looked at a painting of Suzanne bathing, her famous bottom shaped like a cello. 'How could I forget – you and the banister?'

She laughed and slapped her solid haunch in its unflattering checked skirt. 'I think I still have the splinters in my magnificent arse.'

CHAPTER 27

The three of us – Camille, Georges and I – had just finished a long shift at Rodin's studio. The little café at the end of the street was already closing when we arrived looking for a meal, so Georges suggested we go to his studio instead.

'It's not far – across the road, the door by that street lamp. There's bread, cheese, wine and, of course, caviar.'

Camille yawned. 'Why not? No one will know, unless you tell on us, Georges.'

I hesitated. It was one thing to be alone with Georges in Rodin's studio, where we were colleagues, or out and about in public with Rosa keeping a sharp eye on him, but quite another to be alone with him in the privacy of his *atelier*. And since the night we'd kissed in the cab, Georges had been making it clear he wanted more with a little touch on the arm here, a lingering look there. And I'd been encouraging him, furious at William.

Camille tugged at my arm. 'Come on, Jessie, don't just stand there, I'm starving.' She crossed the street ahead of us, but still I didn't move. Snow began to fall and flakes came to rest in my eyelashes. I blinked them away, shivered and pulled my short cape more tightly around my shoulders. Georges unbuttoned his overcoat and wrapped it around me. It was lined with rust-coloured fur and I couldn't help stroking the collar.

'What is it?' I said.

'Russian wolf.' He pulled the deep collar around my neck. 'It suits you – it's the same colour as your hair.' He took off his gloves and held my face between his hands; they were warm. 'Jessie, *viens avec moi.*'

I thought back to William in the painting, of his betrayal of the friendship we had shared since childhood. He had no right to sully it, no right at all. Why was I holding back when he had not? I tilted my face up to Georges, and he kissed me lightly, so lightly, on the lips, and led me through the deepening snow.

Camille was waiting for us in the doorway. 'What took you so long? My feet are like ice.' She stamped her boots. There was snow in her dark hair and her skin shone pale as a moonstone.

Georges unlocked the door and went over to an iron bed. He put his hand on a lump under the sable counterpane and shook it. 'Sasha, wake up. We have company.'

A tousled head poked out of the fur and peered at us with cross little eyes, like a bear emerging from hibernation. 'What time is it?'

'Early. Just after midnight. We have guests.'

Georges' Russian studio partner threw off the cover and stood in his longjohns. He scratched his tow-coloured head and grinned, pulled on a jacket with military frogging over his bare chest, and padded over to us.

He bowed and tried to click his stockinged feet together. 'I am Aleksandr Cheburko Ivanovich. But you can call me Sasha.'

Camille laughed. 'Well, Sasha, I am Camille and this is Jessie, and we are hungry enough to eat your fur bedding.'

'No need! I have caviar and vodka.' Sasha swept a shaving kit and jars filled with paintbrushes off a tea chest onto the floor. He beamed at us again and fetched a bottle of clear liquid, a tin of caviar and a hunk of bread and laid them out on his makeshift table. He indicated the bed. 'Please.'

Camille and I sat down and Georges squeezed in between us, spreading the fur over our legs.

'You girls can keep me warm,' he said. 'What a feast, Sasha. But vodka is rather strong for Jessie and Camille. I have a couple of bottles from my father's vineyard, will you fetch them?'

The Russian brought the wine and a chair, which he sat astride. 'You should try vodka. In my country, women drink it too. Is good for keeping out cold.'

'I'd like to try it,' I said.

Camille seemed to catch my reckless mood. She grinned as Sasha handed us small glasses of clear liquid. I took a sip and made a face as it burned a path down my throat.

'No, no, like this.' Sasha threw back his head and emptied his glass.

Camille copied him and fell into a coughing fit.

Georges patted her back. 'I told you it was strong. Why must you always try to outdo the men? I swear, Camille, you'll come to a bad end. Why don't you just accept that women are the weaker sex?'

'Never!' Her defiance was spoiled by another bout of coughing.

Georges took the glass from my hand. 'You should be more like Jessie, she knows how to behave.'

Well, I was sick of being a good girl – it hadn't done me any favours so far. I took back my glass and swallowed the contents in one fiery gulp. The warmth spread through me and my courage returned: I was in Paris, alone. I could do anything I wanted. Anything. All those rules I'd been taught, the ones that applied to women but not men, could go to hell. William could go to hell.

'Another,' I gasped, holding out my glass to Sasha.

Georges shook his head. 'You are both to eat something, straight away.'

'Yes sir,' I said and giggled. Camille belched and we laughed.

Georges rolled his eyes and muttered something about women not being able to hold their drink, but when we'd both eaten some briny caviar on rye bread, he poured us more vodka.

'*Santé*,' Camille said.

'Bottoms up,' I said in English.

'Bottom? What is bottom?' said Sasha.

'*Ton cul*,' Camille said, and we snorted with laughter, silly now and careless.

'In Ukraine we say *Budmo*,' said Sasha. 'And we must shout, *Hey!* We do three time and everyone empty glasses each time.'

'Hey! Hey! Hey!' And down it went.

'Jessie, you are English, *da*?'

I nodded, unable to speak. My tongue seemed too big for my mouth and I couldn't feel my jaw. Sasha seemed unaffected and poured himself another drink.

'I read many fine English books, Mr Dickens, Mr Hardy. You like famous Ukrainian writer Gogol? Dostoyevsky said we are all coming out from beneath Gogol's overcoat.'

'No, no, no! No book talk. I forbid it,' Camille said. She wriggled off the bed and pulled Sasha to his feet. 'Show me your work, Sasha, I want to see your work.'

He held out his hands, palm upwards, in surrender. 'French women – so commanding, is irresistible.'

'Bossy, more like,' Georges said, leaning back on his elbows on the bed. 'Don't take any nonsense from her, Sasha. If Camille annoys you, put her over your knee. She likes that.'

Camille turned and stuck out her tongue at Georges. 'It is you who needs punished, *coquin*.' She squinted and shook her finger at me. 'See to it, Jessie.'

Sasha opened a curtain over a doorway into the next room, where I could see canvases stacked against the walls.

He shook the bottle he still held. 'First, I must buy more vodka, there is tavern near here.'

Camille noisily insisted on going with him and they both tumbled out into the cold. The door closed behind them.

Georges shifted on the bed to face me and pushed a strand of hair out of my eyes. 'Do you also think I need punished, Jessie?'

I pretended to consider the matter. 'Well, you don't always behave like a gentleman.'

'I don't care about any of that, all those rules for people of our class, about how we should behave.'

He sat up and took one of my hands in his. I thought he was going to take me in his arms and make love to me.

'You seem troubled, Jessie, ever since that night at Henri's studio. Has something happened?'

This was what made him so different from William. Georges paid attention to me, studying me like an artist studies a rival's painting, looking carefully at the brushwork, at the colours used, at the composition. William reserved that concentration for his work. He loved me in a distracted, amused way more suited to a sister than a lover. Georges made me feel like he was interested in me, and only me, above everything else. He took me seriously, sought my opinion and treated me as an equal despite his jokes about women artists. And he was handsome in a careless, ruffled way that made me catch my breath. It was a devastating combination.

He was still looking at me, patiently waiting for me to speak, and I found myself talking about the painting, about William *negotiating* with those women. At one point, I began to cry and tried to take my hands from his to dry my eyes but he held them firm and kissed the tears from my cheeks with his warm mouth.

'Jessie, if you were mine I would never look at another woman. With you it would be different. He must be mad to let you slip from his hands. Me, I would never let you go, never.'

He tightened his grip on my hands and I cried out. Then his mouth was on mine. I resisted at first but he put his hands in my hair and pulled me towards him. His shirt was open at the neck and his chest was smooth. I felt the muscles in his back flex and ran my fingers down the groove of his spine. The heat from the alcohol pulsed through me as Georges put his hand on my thigh and pushed it to one side. I knew it was wrong but I didn't care. It would be a relief to give in and take what I wanted, just as William had. I stopped thinking and lay back on the bed. Georges leaned over me, his eyes searching mine. He stroked my face.

'My God, you are beautiful, like a Bellini nymph, carved from the whitest marble.'

There were voices at the door. We looked at each other with a wolfish hunger before leaping apart. I rearranged my clothes, my fingers clumsy.

Camille and Sasha were still fumbling with the lock and laughing. Georges put his hand on mine and spoke quickly.

'Jessie, I know Rosa and Camille, they joke about me, and how I have an eye for the girls. It's true, or at least it was true, until now. I'd give up everything for you, I swear to it. *J'en mettrais ma main au feu.*'

Camille burst in with Sasha, laughing as they stumbled into each other in the doorway, but she stopped when she saw us.

'Jessie, your eyes are huge. And Georges, I don't know. You look like one of those tormented couples from Rodin's *Gates of Hell*. Have you quarrelled?'

'I think I've had too much to drink, that's all,' I said. 'Georges was telling me not to have any more.'

'Time for us to go.' Camille removed Sasha's arm from her shoulders. 'Georges is right, no more vodka for you,' she said, firmly.

I followed her as if in a dream.

We walked home in silence, but when we reached our street, Camille turned to me.

'What really happened in there?'

'Georges kissed me,' I looked down. 'And more. I don't know how far it would have gone if you hadn't come in.'

I heard her gasp.

'Did you want to?'

'Yes.' I groaned and put my face in my hands. 'Yes I did. I've never wanted anything so much.'

We stopped under a street lamp and faced each other. Camille's eyes were as dark and cold as the bottom of a lake. Rodin called her his dream in stone, after the Baudelaire poem, and now I knew why. She was angry, jealous even. It was the same for me when she told me about Rodin, when I pictured them together, naked, touching. I was seized by an urge to take Camille in my arms in the empty street and kiss her like we had before the ball. But my blood was up and this time I knew I wouldn't stop.

Camille laughed abruptly, the sound like the snap of a sail, and the moment was over. She quickened her pace and her limp became more pronounced. She could never disguise it when she was angry. I hurried to catch up with her.

Her voice was dangerously light. 'I'll bet Georges told you he'd mend his ways, settle down and be a good boy for you.' I didn't say anything but she looked at me sharply. 'Ha! Don't be a fool and fall for it, *ma petite anglaise*, he says that to all the girls, believe me, I know, I've had enough broken-hearted models wailing on my shoulder about him. A word of warning: Georges is amusing – and handsome of course – but you'd be a fool to fall for his fine words. You'd be better to stick with your William, much safer.'

'But what about love, Camille?' I said, hurrying to keep up. 'What about love?'

'Ah, love.' She stopped and looked at me sadly. 'Love always gets in the way.'

CHAPTER 28

MONTMARTRE, PARIS

December 1884

'*Bon anniversaire, nos vœux les plus sincères, Que ces quelques fleurs vous apportent le bonheur...* ' The song was drowned by cries of '*Santé!*' as we raised our glasses to Camille in *Le Chat Noir*, where we were celebrating her twentieth birthday. She threw her head back and drank deeply to raucous cheers from the other tables. I watched her white throat move and a trickle of red wine snake down her chin. The candlelight threw shadows on the faces around the table, like a scene from a Caravaggio. Rosa, in full tails, leaned back in her chair and applauded. Suzanne, now besotted with Henri, was pressing sticky red kisses onto his forehead. Henri was entertaining us with gossip about the Prince of Wales' adventures in the Paris brothels, where the whores had adopted Henri as a sort of mascot.

'The girls at *Le Chabanais* tell me that Bertie is delighted with his new chair, a most *unusual* chair. Madame Kelly sneaked me into his room to have a look at it. Shall I go on?'

Camille banged her empty glass on the table. 'It's my birthday! I demand to hear all the details.'

Henri looked at me and raised his eyebrows at Georges, as if asking his permission. No one had said anything yet, but that night Georges was making it clear we were a couple. He was bareheaded and his hair stuck up at an angle where he'd pushed his hands through it. I wanted more than anything to sit on his lap and kiss him, feel his mouth open under mine. Georges draped his arm over my shoulder and frowned at Henri.

Rosa called across the table. 'Jessie's her own woman. I'm sure she can cope with a few saucy tales.'

Georges looked at me. 'It's up to you, Jessie.'

I shifted in my chair so that I was a little closer to him. 'The papers at home are always full of tittle-tattle about the Prince of Wales. If Henri has inside information, who wouldn't want to hear it? Come on, tell all – spare us nothing!'

Henri grinned. 'Very well, but do not blame me, *Mesdemoiselles*, if you become faint when you hear the juicy details.'

Suzanne pinched his cheek. 'Get on with it, you devil!'

He kissed a strand of her hair. 'Well, first you must know that his Royal Highness' coat of arms always hangs above this massive bed at *Le Chabanais*, where he has his own room. And there's a copper bath of immense, whale-like proportions, in the shape of a woman, or a mermaid or something. The girls fill it with magnum after magnum of champagne before jumping in with him. Can you imagine? And, this is the best bit, because he's so fat, they've built a special chair for him, a *siege d'amour*, so it's more comfortable when one of them kneels down in front of him to pleasure him while the other straddles his enormous ...'

'All right, Henri, that's enough,' Georges said, to a chorus of protests from Camille, Suzanne and I.

'What a spoilsport you have become all of a sudden, Georges, I can't think what's got into you,' Suzanne said, winking at me. She began one of her silly anecdotes, I think it was about her pet goat, but I wasn't paying attention. I could feel Georges staring at me. I was afraid that if I met his eyes and he asked me now to go away with him, I should get up without a word and follow him. Everything had changed between us – and all because of that one night at Georges' studio.

'Jessie.' His lips brushed my cheek and his breath tickled my ear. 'We need to talk about this. I want to know how you ...'

We were distracted by a heated exchange that flared up between Henri and Camille, who were both drunk. Camille had been watching Rodin at the bar, where he was talking to a gallery owner, and Henri, spoiling for a fight, had taken offence.

'I fear I do not have your complete attention, Camille. But then, who can concentrate in the presence of the towering, the monumental, the unbearably *expressive* Rodin?'

Camille scowled at him. 'You have the gall to mock Rodin? You'll never be half the artist he is.'

'Sadly, this is true. If only my legs had continued to grow apace with the rest of my body... But let me tell you, there's nothing wrong with the most important part of me.'

Suzanne gave out a shout of laughter and Rosa nudged her in the ribs. 'Lucky bitch!'

Camille rolled her eyes. 'Are you still peddling that story, Henri? I don't believe a word of it.'

A woman called over from the next table. 'The little man speaks the truth – he's well endowed where it matters.' A cackle. 'We girls call him The Tripod.'

Another cackle, from her friend this time. '*Merde*, you made wine come out of my nose, you ginger bitch. Tripod. That's a good one.'

There was something familiar about the two women and I turned in my seat to study them. They were street girls, *femmes des boulevards* paid to lure men into cafés for a couple of overpriced drinks and maybe more. Either that or *filles de joie*, who let themselves be picked up by customers. Rosa had explained the difference to me, but I still didn't understand the nuances. In any case, they were clearly prostitutes – my father would have called them floozies – their hard faces powdered white, mouths scarlet, hats trimmed with grubby ostrich feathers, black velvet chokers around their necks and indecently low necklines. One was a redhead in a grubby sage dress and the other a brunette in stained grey. Where had I seen them before? With a lurch I recognised them: they were the two women from Henri's painting, the ones with William. I stood up, I couldn't help myself. I wanted to know what had happened that night; I wanted to hear the details, no matter how sordid.

'Georges,' I said. 'I'm going to talk to those women. I want to ask them if they'll pose for me.' I was too ashamed to tell him the real reason, but luckily he didn't seem to recognise them.

Georges shook his head. 'It's not a good idea, Jessie, they're rough street girls.'

'It's all right, I'll be fine.'

'At least let me come with you.'

I squeezed his shoulder. 'Thank you, but I'd rather go alone.' I walked over to their table and took a deep breath. They looked up at me.

'What do you want?' the hard-faced brunette said.

'May I sit down?'

She shrugged, but their hostility was palpable.

The other one, the redhead, sneered at me. 'Why would a fine lady want to drink with the likes of us? Aren't you afraid your precious virtue will be spoiled? Or perhaps you're one of those rich bitches who like slumming it, *hein?*'

I would have to appeal to them woman to woman and open my heart. I told them how I'd seen Henri's painting, about William and how we'd known each other since we were children; that we were expected to marry but now everything had changed. How I wanted to confront him, but I needed to know the truth. It was torture not to know for certain, would they help me? When I'd finished, I could see their shoulders drop.

The ginger topknot placed a grubby hand on my glove. 'Oh, *ma mie*, you're in love with him, aren't you?'

I didn't want her to touch me. I thought of her fingers burrowing in William's clothes. I took my hand away under the pretence of wiping my eyes. Up close, there was nothing attractive about these women, their skin was mottled under the heavy make-up and their hair greasy and thick with powder. I couldn't understand how men, well-bred and cultured men like William, could want these women, who were more to be pitied than desired.

The redhead patted my hand and told me her name was Claudine. 'Ah, there, there, don't cry now, *petite*. Yvette, do you know who she's talking about?'

When Yvette put her arm around me, the smell of stale sweat mixed with cheap perfume rose from her armpits. 'He is English, *ton petit ami?*'

I nodded and she screwed up her eyes as if trying to remember. She gave a cry and pointed at Rodin. 'Was he with that one, over there by the bar?' I nodded again and she prodded her friend. 'The artist, you know, the one who always pays us so well to watch us eat each other, the filthy beast.'

Claudine grimaced. 'How could I forget? It took me days to get the taste out of my mouth.'

'The dirty dog – no class, not like the Englishman. Now, he was a real toff,' her friend said.

So they had been with William. I stood up, sickened, but Claudine pulled me down by the skirts. Her laugh turned into a wet cough and she spat on the floor before she could speak again.

'Hear us out, Mademoiselle. By the way, you wouldn't have a few *sous* for a poor working girl? My glass is empty, and that's never a pretty sight.' I dug in my purse and handed her some coins and she pocketed the money. 'He was a handsome bastard, right enough, for a *rosbif*,' she said. 'I like 'em dark like that, broad with a big chest you can sit astride. He looked strong. I bet he has to take his weight on his elbows, eh?' She nudged me and I flinched. 'Otherwise he'd drive you into the mattress, that one.' She cackled again.

The brunette, Yvette, said: 'Get on with it, the show's about to start.'

Claudine wiped her nose on the back of her hand, taking her time. 'He was a right handsome bastard, and healthy looking too. I'd have given it to him free, eh Yvette, eh?' Another cackle and another glare from the brunette. 'All right, keep your wig on.' She yawned and hiked up her skirts to scratch her thigh. 'But he was a waste of time when we collared him together.' She laughed and imitated an English accent: 'He says, *desolé modomazelle* but he's got a girlfriend.'

'When did that ever stop any of them?' Yvette said. 'But you don't have anything to cry about, *chérie*, your English boyfriend stayed true to you, a proper gent, like I said. Not like some of the degenerates we get in here. Up against a wall in an alley one minute, the next they're knocking you about or mooching the price of a *vin blanc* off you.'

I rubbed my forehead, trying to block out the raucous sounds from the other tables. I had been wrong about William. How could I have doubted him? William, who as a boy had chased me through the orchard to torment me with a frog he'd found, and when I'd fallen and skinned my knee had comforted me and pressed dock leaves on the graze; William, who had listened to my dreams of becoming a sculptor and encouraged me to follow them; William, who was still the man I'd always known and loved. The pain that had been sitting in my chest lifted. I put more coins on the table and thanked the two women, but they had already turned their attention to the stage, where red velvet curtains twitched.

'Oooh, look, Yvette, the show's about to start. The Irish tart is on tonight, the one who sings dirty nursery rhymes, you know, with the little cat. She made me laugh so much last time, I pissed my knickers.'

I went back to our table and sat next to Camille, across the table from Georges. She looked at me questioningly and I mouthed *research* at her. She nodded, satisfied, and turned her attention back to the stage. I was glad when the lights dimmed and I could press my hands to my burning cheeks to cool them down. Alone, in the dark, I faced up to what I had done with Georges out of anger with William, but also because I had wanted to. I could see Georges' silhouette across the candlelit table, his head turned towards me. Had he deliberately misled me? No, he must have been mistaken. Confused, I looked away and tried to concentrate on the show.

The curtain went up and the proprietor, Salis, jumped onto the stage and called for hush. '*Mesdames et Messieurs, votre attention s'il vous plaît. Je vous présente le formidable, l'unique Aristide Bruant!*'

A cold horror crept over me as I remembered something else – the letter! I'd dashed off a furious letter to William, telling him I didn't want anything more to do with him, accusing him of horrible acts of depravity, and, worst of all, telling him I'd fallen in love with Georges, that things had gone too far to back off now, that I'd compromised myself, that he wasn't the only one who could give into his base desires. Oh God, had I given it to Eugènie to put in the post? In my turmoil, I couldn't remember. If William read it, he'd assume the worst. He was an enlightened man, but he would never forgive me if he thought I'd lost my honour. I screwed my eyes shut and tried desperately to remember what I'd done with the letter. With relief, I pictured it where I'd left it, on my dressing table.

I opened my eyes and realised the crowd were going wild. They clapped and stamped and there were cries of 'Bruant! Bruant!' A man in a black cloak lined with scarlet and a fedora swept into the spotlight and stood waiting for quiet, his hawkish features disdainful. In a harsh growl, he began to sing a *chanson réaliste*, one of the street ballads about the harsh lives of the poor. A hush fell on the café and I listened carefully to the story he was telling. Bruant sang about the *faubourgs*, about the prostitutes who loved their sadistic pimps and drank to forget their abandoned children, about an orphan wandering the streets, begging and performing circus tricks for a few *sous* before in turn selling his young body. By the time Bruant fell silent, I could see one of the women I'd talked to was sobbing, head buried in her thin arms while her friend looked stricken, her ghostly make-up streaked with tears. I rubbed my own eyes. The melancholic song had tapped into my own troubles and unleashed a torrent of sadness I had stopped up with anger. Soon I was crying as openly as the two prostitutes I'd so despised moments earlier. In the end, we weren't so different; I had been a snob to recoil from their touch. My life in England had been sheltered, but now I was experiencing real life, how we are all touched by pain and joy, no matter how lowly or highly born. This is what I needed to see, to feel, for my work to come alive, to breathe and move as Rodin's and Camille's did. When the lights came up, I clapped until my hands ached.

To lighten the mood, Salis brought on the dancers, who cartwheeled and kicked their way through a stirring *galop infernal*, the women flashing their frothy petticoats and bloomers, spinning their legs in the *ronde de jambe*, then performing backflips and jump splits. They were dancing *le chahut*, the original, wilder version of the cancan that has now become little more than a titillating show for tourists. One of the dancers jumped down off the small stage and pulled a man in evening dress into the troupe. She stood in front of him, her hands on her hips and suddenly kicked her leg high and knocked off his top hat. When the audience whooped their appreciation, she flashed a cheeky smile, turned round, bent over, and threw her skirts over her back to thunderous applause.

After the dancers had finished, a strange creature skipped onto the stage. The gas footlights distorted her white face and painted cheeks into a grotesque parody of an innocent child. She wore a mobcap and cotton nightdress and held a black kitten with a blue bow tied around its neck. She lisped her way through a nursery rhyme full of filthy double entendres that made people shriek with laughter.

Georges slipped into the chair next to me. 'That's May Belfort, the star turn. Henri has quite taken her under his wing. He's been asking his friends if any of them has a tomcat to mate with her *petite chatte*. Suzanne wants to send her one of her cats, says it will be a proper wedding ceremony and we are all invited. Can you imagine?' He laughed softly and kissed me in the dark. I desperately wanted to push him away, and at the same time for him never to stop, just like that night. Things had moved too quickly, and now I didn't know how to undo them. I shouldn't have gone to his *atelier*. He would never let me forget what had happened between us. I had been a fool, worse than a fool.

In *Le Chat Noir*, I studied Georges' profile as he laughed at the singer's saucy ditty about Mary and her not-so-little lamb. He smiled warmly at me and took my hand, as if everything were settled between us. Somehow I had to tell him everything had changed, and that I still loved William.

I pressed his hand. 'Georges, I need to speak to you.'

He looked at me curiously, just as the café doors burst open. A whistle rang out and voices shouted: '*Attention tout le monde! Police!*'

One of the floozies at the next table shrieked: '*Les flics!*' Tables and chairs were knocked over as people scrambled towards the door. There was a sound of breaking glass and women's screams. May Belfort, now down to a pair of bloomers, picked up her kitten and hugged it to her pink-tipped breasts before jumping off the stage into the panicked crowd. As she ran past me I heard her shout: 'Jesus, Mary and Joseph, it's the fecking peelers!'

Across the room I saw Suzanne sliding down the banisters egged on by Henri, who was wielding a riding crop and galloping down the stairs clinging to the back of a dancer, his face scarlet. Suzanne landed in a flurry of petticoats at the *gendarmes'* feet, her legs in the air. She wasn't wearing any underwear.

Georges pulled me to my feet. 'It's a raid.'

'Why?' I shouted over the uproar.

'There are laws about decency. The prostitution they don't care about, but the shows are too public.' He pulled Camille to her feet and called to Rosa. 'Get the girls out of here! Go over the stage, that way. There's a back door. I'll deal with the *gendarmes*. I know the chief of police. *Vite! Va t'en!'*

Rosa led us into a back alley and out into the thronged main street away from the café, where she whistled through her fingers for a cab. It was a crisp clear night and I shivered. We had left our capes in the rush to get out, but Camille didn't seem to feel the cold. She spread her arms wide and spun round in a circle, laughing up at the velvet-black sky embroidered with stars and a full moon.

'What a birthday! What a life, eh Jessie?'

CHAPTER 29

Christmas Eve, 1884

'Well, are you going to open it?' Camille picked up a brown parcel tied with string, from which dangled a white card. It said in Georges' writing: *I'll never forget that night with you in my studio. Tout mon amour du tout mon coeur. Mille bisous. Je t'aime.*

'All his love from all his heart, eh? And not one but a thousand kisses. And an *I love you*. Such ardour! Such persistence!' Camille said. 'You have to admire him for it.' She handed me the parcel. 'Quick, quick! Open it before I die from curiosity.'

We were dressing for dinner in Camille's bedroom at her family's country home in Champagne, in the little village of Villeneuve-sur-Fère. I put the parcel down and fiddled with the catch on my pearls to buy myself some time. I hadn't seen him since the night of the raid. I had been too cowardly to let him know that things had changed. When we'd got home from *Le Chat Noir*, I had rushed upstairs and been relieved to find the angry letter I'd written to William still on my dressing table where I'd left it. I tore it into pieces and dashed off another to him, full of declarations of love, saying I'd missed him and I was sorry for not writing to him for so long. *Sorry, sorry, sorry*, I'd written and covered the letter in kisses before sealing it and putting it in the hall to be posted.

But I had not put a stop to Georges' feelings for me; perhaps I didn't want to.

I was still fiddling with my pearls while I thought it all through, and finally Camille tutted with impatience and came over. She lifted my hair away from my neck. 'Here, let me do that for you. There you go, all done. Now, the parcel – no more excuses!'

I sat on the bed with the package in my lap, smoothing the brown paper, half afraid of what I would find inside.

Camille groaned. 'Jessie, *tu m'enmerdes!* If you don't open it, I shall.'

I unstuck the paper. Inside was a framed sketch in ochre chalk of a young woman. Her eyes were bold, her rosebud lips full of promise. I caught my breath. Georges must have drawn it from memory, but it was full of tender details, from the charcoal flick of mischief at the corners of the mouth and eyes to the contours of the face delicately smudged by his fingers.

Camille took the picture off me and studied it. 'He's not a bad draughtsman. He's caught your expression well.'

I tried to cover how thrilled I was by looking at it critically. 'It doesn't really look like me – my cheeks are not so full and he's flattered my nose somewhat.'

'Why always so exact, Jessie? It's a love poem from an artist, it's how he sees you – and what he wants from you.'

Camille handed it back to me. There was no signature, but I knew Georges' hand. It was such a simple gift, which cost nothing more than the artist's skill and thought, but I had never been given anything so romantic.

Camille leaned in for a closer look. 'Well, Georges has surprised me, I must admit. I've never seen him so serious about anyone before. Perhaps I was wrong to warn you off and he really is ready to change his ways.'

I closed my eyes and tried to think. It had been so clear-cut only days earlier: William had betrayed me and I had nearly given into Georges, but pulled back because he was a womaniser who could not be trusted. Now everything had changed again and I was more confused than ever.

There was a knock at the door and Louise's sharp little face appeared. 'Come on you two, what's keeping you? It's time to gather around the *sapin de noël* to open presents.' She made a face at her sister. 'Is that what you're wearing? Maman will have a fit.'

Camille stood up and looked down at her plain blue serge dress with its white cuffs and collar. 'What's wrong with it?'

'It's not even clean – there's a stain on the bodice and the cuffs are grubby.'

Camille shrugged, but dabbed at the mark with a linen towel she'd dipped into the washing jug.

Louise said: 'For goodness sake. You're making it worse. Come into my room and I'll lend you something to wear.' When Camille refused she began to whine. 'Don't ruin Christmas again. Just this once, can't you try to please Maman? And Papa likes it when you dress up.'

'*D'accord, calme-toi*,' Camille said. 'But only if I can borrow your grey dress with the mother-of-pearl buttons; everything else you have is too *froufrou* for me. Jessie, I'll see you downstairs. I'd better go with the little ninny before she starts crying.'

When the sisters had left and I could hear them squabbling in the corridor, I turned over the portrait, looking for a message. At the bottom were two words: *Choose me.* I pressed the words to my lips and put the sketch and Georges' card in my jewellery box, my feelings once more in turmoil. I hadn't had the chance – or the courage – to speak to Georges. I had told Camille about William, that he hadn't been with those girls in the café, but there was something else I hadn't told her about. There was another package, from England. Inside was a velvet box with an emerald pendant. The gem cast a green glow, like absinthe in candlelight. The note said: *Remember me.*

I took out the necklace and tried it on against my neck, noticing how the emerald made my hair blaze like copper. Then I thought of Georges leaning against the doorframe at Rodin's studio, his sleeves rolled up, laughing at something I'd said, and I put the emerald necklace back in its case and shut the lid of my jewellery box.

Downstairs, Louise was still whining. 'Oh Jessie, Camille is *affreuse*. She says I look fat in my new evening dress, what do you think?' She pouted and placed her hands around her tiny waist – the bodice was fashionably low, revealing all of her shoulders and a good deal of her breasts.

Camille snorted. 'She looks like a barmaid. Watch out, kitten, next time you see Monsieur Renoir he'll put you in one of his paintings for the whole of Paris to goggle at.'

Camille's snobbish barb rankled, but I bit my tongue. After all, I had not told her that my mother had once been a barmaid.

Louise stuck out her tongue and pinched Camille on the tender part of her arm.

'Ouch! You little…' Camille lunged at her sister, her hands like claws.

Louise screamed and ducked. 'Maman! Maman! Camille tried to scratch me.' Madame Claudel rushed into the room and Louise ran to her and showed her a faint red mark on her face.

Madame Claudel snapped at Camille: 'Apologise to your sister at once. Any more of this behaviour and you'll spend Christmas Eve in your room and miss *Le Réveillon.*'

Camille looked mutinous but muttered an apology; we had fasted all day and she didn't want to miss the feast after Midnight Mass. Earlier we had peeked into the kitchen to see Marie, the cook, preparing goose and *boudin blanc.* A large chocolate and chestnut Yule log lay enticingly on a marble pastry table and Marie had chased us when she caught Camille breaking off a piece.

On the way to the village church, the Claudels were on their usual form: noisy, argumentative, amusing, exasperating. The night was cold, and I was glad of my furs as I walked arm-in-arm with Camille. It was pitch black, the stars hidden by snow clouds, our path picked out by the swaying yellow beam from Paul's lantern.

The church was ablaze with candles and the air heavy with incense. A choir of small boys decked in white and red cotton sang like young angels while families crowded in a side nave to admire an elaborate nativity scene. The village of Villeneuve was laid out in miniature with replicas of the *boulangerie* and the *patisserie,* the tiny square bustling with housewives and stallholders hawking their wares. In the foreground, larger figures of shepherds and the Magi knelt in adoration before an empty manger. I sat through the Mass, soothed by the priest's chanting and the congregation's murmured responses. I prayed for guidance, and for the strength to resist temptation and do the right thing. After he carried out the final blessing, the priest brought out the Christ Child, crafted exactingly down to the creases in its plump wrists, and cradled the baby in his hands while the villagers lined up to kiss its feet. I stood next to Camille. When it was her turn, she pursed her lips together and whispered something to the little plaster baby.

CHAPTER 30

Christmas Day, 1884

I woke at first light with a sense of foreboding. I still had a headache from the night before. The Claudels had been in high spirits, chatting and teasing each other. By the time we'd eaten our way through the rich midnight feast, I'd had enough. It's easy to feel lonely with another family at Christmas. I found the Claudels' constant bickering enervating and missed the quiet affection of my own parents. I was relieved when Madame Claudel broke the party up at three and I could slip away to bed.

I stretched under the linen sheets; they were damp with cold. It was too early for the maid to have built a fire and the air was icy. I sat up in bed, the blanket still under my chin, and saw that Camille was standing at the window in her nightdress and bare feet.

'I love it here,' she said without turning round from the bleak landscape that stretched before her. 'When Paul and I were children we spent every day out there.' She came to sit on my bed. There were dark shadows under her eyes and she looked drawn in the grey light. 'I want to show you something, out on the moors. Will you come with me? I'm fed up being stuck here with my family. I can't breathe.'

I knew I wouldn't go back to sleep. Perhaps a walk would clear my head. I had spent a restless night and was tired of going round in circles about Georges and William. I threw back the covers and got dressed as quickly as possible.

The world was blurred by fog and I shivered despite wearing my warmest walking dress, a thick woollen coat and sturdy boots. Camille was wearing her stained blue dress again and a man's tweed overcoat.

'Papa's old gardening coat – as he never gardens he won't miss it,' she said. Dwarfed by the shabby coat, her small face upturned and vulnerable in the morning light, she looked like a child.

The ground was uneven and hard with frost and I noticed Camille was finding it difficult. She paused and winced, her hand on her hip.

I caught at her arm. 'Are you all right? We can go back, if you like.'

She shook her head. 'It's nothing. I only get pain sometimes, in my hip. I was born with one leg shorter than the other.'

It was the first time she'd talked about her limp and I'd been careful not to mention it. I knew Camille hated showing any weakness.

I nodded. 'Can you manage?' I put my hand under her arm, but she pulled away.

'Of course I can manage. Didn't I run wild here all my days as a child?' She walked on. 'Come on, it's not far now.'

After a while, we reached a bleak terrain scattered with massive boulders, which the elements had worn into strange shapes. The fog had grown thicker and wisps of it were gathered around the base of the rocks.

Camille stopped and caught her breath. '*La Hottée du Diable.*'

'Is this what you wanted to show me?'

She nodded, her mouth pinched white with fatigue.

I sat down on a smooth boulder and she joined me with a small sigh.

'Why is it called the Devil's Basket?' I said.

'There is a legend that the Devil promised to build a convent in one night in return for someone's soul – the builder's I think. But a rooster woke early and started crowing, so Satan ran off, dropping these stones from his basket.' She kicked at a small stone with the pointed toe of her thin Paris boots. She was vain about her small feet and hadn't changed into walking shoes.

I pulled my coat tighter around me. Camille's coat swung free, unbuttoned, but she didn't seem to notice the cold. She started climbing one of the rocks that was as big as an elephant. Halfway up, she beckoned to me. 'This one has a cave inside it. Paul and I used to climb into it when Maman was in one of her moods. Come and see.'

I felt my way up the rock after her, fumbling for foot and hand holds. Camille sat at the top, her legs dangling into a black hole. Suddenly, she disappeared from sight.

I scrabbled up to the top and called into the darkness: 'Camille! Are you hurt?'

She laughed. 'It's quite safe, Jessie. Just slip down. It's like being on a helter skelter.'

Her pale face glimmered in the darkness below and I could see her grinning. 'Are you frightened?' she called.

I could never resist a challenge; I hitched up my skirts and followed her through the rushing blackness. I landed on a springy bed of dried brush, my skirts tangled about my waist.

I pulled twigs from my hair and blew out my cheeks. 'Some helter skelter!' We laughed and my sombre mood lifted. It was cosy in the cave. We were sheltered from the wind that raced around outside, moaning as it passed over the cave entrance.

Camille pulled a book of matches from her pocket. 'See here and here,' she said and pointed at the scratches in the wall. 'I drew sketches and Paul wrote verses. It was our secret place.' The match went out and we were in darkness again. 'Touch the stone, Jessie,' Camille whispered. 'Touch it like Rodin showed us how to touch sculptures.'

I closed my eyes and felt the bumps and crevices of the cool rock. 'Do you feel it?' she said in the blackness.

Through my fingertips I felt an energy that seemed to hum from within. 'Yes, I do.'

Her voice, dreamy and low, seemed disembodied in the darkness. 'It's here that I decided to work in stone. I'd already experimented with the red clay that's everywhere in Villeneuve. The artisans make it into roof tiles and *Grandpère* had built a kiln for the pantiles. I used to make tiny people and animals and he showed me how to fire them. But when I touched this rock, the devil's rock, I felt a force go into me. I knew it was my destiny to release the power trapped in stone.'

Camille took my hands and pressed my fingers to her mouth, and I wanted to take off my gloves, feel the tip of her tongue. I imagined it rough, like a cat's. She shifted closer and spoke into my ear, as if frightened of being overheard, even in the heart of a rock.

'It's only to you that I've told this. Even Rodin would think me *fou*.'

'You're not mad.' I put my arms around her and she leaned her head on my shoulder. I realised how thin she had become. 'You're freezing,' I said. 'We should go home.'

'No, let's stay like this for a while. You make me warm.'

I opened my coat and fastened it around us both. We sat in silence in the dark for a while, the heat from each other's bodies spreading through us.

'What about you?' Camille said. 'How did you know you wanted to be a sculptor?'

'I remember the first time I played with clay,' I said. 'I was on my haunches out on the mud flats in East Anglia. I squeezed the mud and watched the ribbons curl between my fingers, and realised I could make shapes, that my two hands could change something as simple as mud into anything I wanted.'

Camille nodded against my shoulder. 'I have a similar memory from playing in the garden at Villeneuve as a child. But it was nothing to how I felt when I first took a chisel to a piece of marble, how brittle it was, how you can snap a thin piece in two like a *langue du chat*, how you can smooth it and rub it and smooth it until it becomes polished and full of light.' She was absentmindedly stroking my waist under my coat as she spoke and I held my breath until she seemed to realise what she was doing and stopped. She sat up. 'I can feel the cold in my bones now, can't you?'

'Yes, we should get back.'

Camille showed me the way to climb back to the top, up a kind of natural staircase.

'You go first. My hip is a little painful. I'll take it more slowly.'

When I poked my head out of the rock, I could see the fog had descended and all I could make out beyond my own hand was a frightening blank. I turned to look down the hole and saw Camille halfway up. Her fingers were reaching for the final handhold when a rock came away in her hand and she fell back, landing with a sickening thud. She cried out in pain.

'Camille! Are you hurt?'

I heard a sob.

'I can't move. I think I've twisted my ankle.'

'Don't move. I'll go for help,' I called.

I scrambled down the curved back of the rock and started to walk in the direction we'd come, but the mist was too thick and I realised I'd be lost on the moor if I went any further. I retraced my steps, climbed back up and called down. 'The fog is too thick. We'll have to wait it out.' I began to panic. Nobody knew where we were. We would be stuck here for hours and Camille would catch pneumonia. I wanted to cry but instead took a breath. What did William always say? For every problem there's a solution. I forced myself to calm down and think. I went back to the rock and called down to her.

'Camille, do you still have those matches?'

'Yes.'

'Hold on, I'll come back down in a bit.'

I began to gather dried bracken and stuff it into my jacket. There were only a few stunted trees in that benighted place, bent over like hags by the relentless winds, but I managed to find some sticks. I broke them over my knee and stuffed them into my pockets and down the front of my coat. I had to make several trips, clambering up the rock to leave the sticks and bracken on the edge of the cave mouth before shimmying back to the ground to look for more fuel. My nails were broken and my fingers torn and bloody by the time I made the last exhausted climb to the top. I called down to Camille to shield her eyes and pushed everything into the cave before sliding back down, the heels of my boots acting as brakes so I wouldn't crash into her.

It was freezing in the cave. She was trembling violently and I rubbed her icy hands and blew on them. I built a fire, stacking kindling onto the larger sticks and covering it all in bracken.

Camille looked on, teeth chattering. 'Where did you learn to do that?'

'From the housemaid back home in Peterborough. She was a lot quicker, though.'

I put my arms around her and we watched the flames poke out little blue tongues. The bracken began to glow orange and the sticks crackled. The air grew smoky but at least we were warm.

Camille leaned her head against my shoulder again. Her hair smelled of bonfires. 'I wish we had some cognac,' she said. 'Where's Henri when you need him?'

I laughed, relieved. If she could joke she had a chance of surviving until we were found – if we were found. Nobody knew we had gone out and it might be hours before anyone noticed we were missing. Meanwhile it was the middle of winter and the fog showed no sign of lifting; the fire wouldn't last long and I'd have to start the search for fuel all over again. I closed my eyes with fatigue and felt sleep taking hold of me. I jerked awake, terrified. If I was going to move I'd have to do it now, before I fell asleep. But Camille was warm against me and I didn't want to go out into the cold.

Her voice was sleepier now. 'What are you going to do?'

'About what?'

She yawned. 'About Georges, what else?'

'I don't know.' I rubbed my eyes, the smoke was making them water. I cleared my dry throat. 'But I'll have to make a decision soon. William sent me a Christmas present, an emerald pendant that belonged to his grandmamma. It's part of a set. There's a ring that goes with it – an engagement ring.'

She went still. 'He'll ask you then, when you go back to England for the summer.'

I nodded.

A small sigh, then her voice again, dreamier this time. 'If you had any sense you would marry him, Jessie. That's what Maman would say.'

'And Georges, what about him? Should I just forget him?'

'I told you before, love always gets in the way. It's a damned nuisance. If you marry William, he'll give you children, your own home. That's what Rodin will give me, if I'm patient, once he gets rid of that hag.'

I put another branch on the fire and watched the sparks twirl up to the natural chimney. Either Rodin had changed his mind about children, or he had told Camille what she wanted to hear. I was careful to keep my voice even. 'Is that what you want – Rodin's children? Is that what he wants?'

She shrugged. 'Of course. Can you imagine what a child we would have?' She laughed and nudged me. 'But don't change the subject. We were talking about how you should stay with William. Georges, now, he's like a stick of dynamite. Maybe he has changed, but you should still be careful.'

I shifted and felt the bracken scratch the back of my legs. 'I don't know what to think any more. What would you do if you were in my place, Camille?' Her breathing was growing even and I shook her shoulder. 'Camille?'

She roused herself enough to answer. 'Me? What I always do: exactly what I want.' She yawned again. 'But in the meantime, make sure William doesn't find out about Georges.'

When she was asleep, I put some bracken behind her head. We'd used up the last of the fuel and I knew what had to be done. I sighed and climbed up and out of the cave and began to gather fallen branches for the fire. By the fifth trip, the fog was so thick I'd had to leave a trail of stones back to the devil's rock so I wouldn't get lost as I wandered further and further away to find wood and bracken. I had lost track of time. It was beginning to get dark and hours must have passed since we left the house. My fingers lost all sensation and I kept dropping the sticks. I was talking to myself, muttering *just one more, just one more* when I saw the light from a lantern swinging through the mist.

'They're over here!' A shape emerged from the fog, the outline blurred like a ghost. It materialised into a familiar figure. William. It must be a fever dream. But he was so real. I shook my head and a ragged wall of fog engulfed him. Someone called my name. I tried to answer but my voice was hoarse from the wood smoke and no sound came out. I jumped up and down and waved. After a few agonising moments, the figure came out of the fog again and he shouted. I would know that voice anywhere. William broke into a run and I stumbled towards him with the last of my strength. He put his arms around me and my knees gave way.

'Jessie, thank God!'

'I don't understand. Is it really you, William? I thought I was dreaming. What are you doing here?'

'I wanted to see you after I got your letter. Such a strange letter, my darling. When I arrived, the house was in uproar – search parties, dogs, the whole village is out looking for you. They've been wading through the river. They said there have been drownings. I don't know what I would have done if –' He tightened his hold on me and I heard the break in his voice. 'Jess, my Jess. I thought I'd lost you.'

CHAPTER 31

Boxing Day, 1884

I slept dreamlessly through until the next evening. When I carefully made my way downstairs, my legs still weak from the ordeal on the moors, William was waiting at the Christmas tree. He was holding two glasses of champagne and handed one to me.

'How is Camille?'

'The doctor has bound her ankle and ordered bed rest.'

'I have you to myself, then.'

He kissed me, his lips warm, and the shape of his mouth familiar. I thought briefly of Georges and the way he'd pressed his mouth against mine, the wild hunger we'd shared. I had been wrong to let him go so far. I'd pulled away from him just in time.

William looked down at my dress. 'I've always liked you in that green velvet.'

'I know it's your favourite.'

'I'm glad you wore it tonight. I want to give you the rest of your Christmas present while it's still just the two of us.'

William reached into the tree, festooned with apples, ribbons and coloured gelatine lights in glass cups. He unhooked an ornamental paper box of the kind my mother filled with sweet treats every Christmas at home.

'William, how did you know I'd be homesick for Ma's sugarplums? Don't tell me you made the box yourself? How sweet!'

Inside was a velvet box. And inside that an emerald ring. My hand flew to my throat. 'Oh, William. I don't know what to say.'

'Say you'll be mine, Jessie. I know it's always been understood we'd be together, ever since you were in pigtails,' he pulled a tendril of my hair loose and wound it around his finger. 'But I want everyone to know. No more waiting. I was so worried when I got your letter. I didn't understand it, and why you kept saying you were sorry. Jessie, I know you've changed since you came to Paris. You dress more unconventionally, but it's not only that. You're more self-assured, more you, somehow. Paris has distilled you, and it's made me love you even more than ever. But I don't want to lose you.' He slipped the ring on my finger. 'Will you marry me, darling Jess?' He smiled. 'Forsaking all others and all that sort of thing? I've been offered a job, a good one, in Manchester, teaching chemistry at a new university. You should see the laboratories – all the latest equipment, and some excellent minds working there. You could still sculpt, maybe give some art classes, until the children come along. We can make a good life for ourselves there.'

I thought of Georges working on a sculpture with his sleeves rolled up and a frown of concentration on his handsome face. I thought of Camille and Rosa and Henri and Suzanne sitting in a Montmartre café, surrounded by a swirl of colour and music. I pictured Manchester: smokestacks belching into a grey sky and rows of houses, each one the same. William mistook my hesitation and laughed.

'It's a surprise, I know, on top of everything you went through yesterday. But you must have guessed when I sent you the pendant. They're a set.' He frowned. 'You aren't wearing it. I've always wanted to see you wearing Grandmamma's emeralds. Where's the necklace?' I glanced upstairs and his expression cleared. 'Of course, in your jewellery box, I'll get it for you.'

I took out the ring and held it against the coloured lights on the Christmas tree. The stone was nearly as large as the one on the necklace. The necklace that was in my jewellery box, sitting on top of Georges' portrait. I turned and gathered my skirts and ran up the stairs two at a time. In my room, William was standing holding the drawing in one hand, the card in the other.

'William, I…'

His eyes were in shadow. 'I understand now.' I'd never heard him sound so cold. 'Here, this is what you want.' The card bit into my palm and a nail from the wooden frame scraped the inside of my wrist. I watched it bead with blood as the door slammed behind me.

CHAPTER 32

THE PARIS SALON

August 1885

William didn't come back. He left France without another word to me and I didn't try to stop him. There was nothing I could say in my defence, nothing that would alter what I had done. I had lost William and it was only in losing him that I realised how much I loved him. I spent that summer in Norway with my parents, numb with misery as we walked through ice canyons, three tiny figures picking our way over turquoise glaciers. My parents worried about my silences but I was too ashamed to tell them what had happened. At night I left the window open and stared out at the pale Arctic sky, unable to cry. In the mornings my quilt was covered in snow.

Paris in August was hot and empty. I returned to a stifling studio buzzing with flies. There was a letter waiting for me: my piece had not been accepted for the Salon. I sank down on my valise and finally wept. When Camille came in some time later I wiped my eyes but she didn't notice I had been crying. She was breathless and laughing as she pulled off her hat and threw it in the corner.

'Jessie! You'll never guess! I've been accepted, for the Salon, my piece. Can you believe it?'

I was crushed. A nasty thought crept into my mind: *no wonder Camille was accepted, she's sleeping with Rodin and he has power and influence.* It was unworthy of me but I couldn't help it. My best friend's victory was a dagger in my heart. First William, and now I had failed in this. I had been wrong about my talent; Paris had taught me nothing and I had lost William chasing an empty dream. Camille was looking at me expectantly and I mustered a smile.

'But that's wonderful, simply wonderful!' I made myself embrace her but she broke away, too excited to be still for even a moment. She paced around the studio, restlessly picking up tools and shifting pieces. Suddenly Camille whirled around.

'*Sang bleu!* The *vernissage*! It's today. Quick, quick, we must get to the Salon at once. Hurry, Jessie, we don't want to be late.' She crammed on her hat and we ran out of the door.

I paused on the stairs. 'My gloves.'

'*Dieu tout-puissant!* Forget your gloves. We don't want to be late for the first night of the Salon.'

The sky was a wash of violet and the evening air was full of conversations. The dead weight that had lain over my heart all summer shifted as we walked through the crowded streets. By the time we reached the Champs-Élysées, everyone seemed to be heading in the same direction, to the *Salon de Paris*, the largest and most important art exhibition in the world. To have a piece accepted by the Salon's jury of established artists was like being given the key to a select club. We reached the steps and I stopped in front of the doors, wide open to let in the last of the light. I straightened my back. Just because I had failed to get in this year didn't mean I couldn't try again. Why, Rodin himself had been rejected over and again. Camille looked at me questioningly and this time my smile was broad and warm and from the heart.

I smoothed a curl behind her ear. 'My dear friend, you deserve this.'

Camille wrinkled her nose and laughed. 'Of course I do! Am I not the hardest-working artist in all Paris?' She linked her arm through mine. 'And next year, Jessie, we will be showing side by side, you'll see.'

We were about to go in when an artist balancing a canvas on his head bumped into us.

'A thousand apologies, *Mesdemoiselles*.' He lowered the painting and clicked his heels.

'Sasha!' Camille said.

The Russian beamed at us and pulled us both into a clumsy hug. Once I was free, I nodded at his painting. 'For the *vernissage*?'

'*Da*. I work on canvas all night, all day, but is not finish and now is too late.' He was unshaved and looked haggard, with dark shadows under his eyes.

I steadied Sasha's picture to get a better look at it, careful to keep my fingers away from the wet oils. A field of golden wheat stretched into the distance under a cerulean sky. Peasant girls with their skirts tucked into their waists were bent over sheaves, their faces and arms browned by the sun. It was well executed but hardly an original subject: everyone from Millet to Courbet and Bastien-Lepage had done it to death. The critics would love it. Sasha headed into the Salon, already busy with viewers and artists frantically varnishing their paintings and making sure they were correctly hung.

Camille grabbed my arm. 'Are the judges blind, to allow such a boring painting and keep out your works?' I was comforted by her words. Camille was a harsh critic, but her judgement was unerring; it was one of the reasons Rodin consulted her before he made any decisions in Studio M. He trusted her. We all did.

Camille and I followed Sasha through the crush of elegant Parisians, the women preening in jewel colours, the men conferring in top hats and tails like crows on a fence.

'Look at her,' I whispered to Camille. 'Over there in the pink ruched silk skirt and burgundy jacket. Isn't she elegant?'

'Ridiculous, I would say. They all look like they should be at the opera, not looking at art.' Camille was wearing a simple dark dress but somehow stood out from the crowd despite her plain clothes. Next to her I looked as overdressed as a tropical parrot in green velvet trimmed with yellow silk. My new dress – bought in London by Ma to cheer me up – was far too warm for the stifling heat of Paris in August. My back was soaking by the time we'd fought our way into the centre of the grand hall where paintings hung two, three and sometimes four deep, from floor to ceiling.

Sasha stopped at an enormous ladder that stretched the height of the hall, and looked despairingly upwards. 'Bastards in Salon hanging committee put me nearly on roof. Am I Michelangelo?

Nyet. Is this Sistine Chapel? *Nyet.*' He ran his hands through his blond hair and looked as if he were about to cry.

Camille patted him on the back. '*Courage, mon brave.*' She gripped one end of the painting and pushed him up the ladder in front of her, shouting abuse at him, using the coarse words of a workman. I held the ladder and called encouragement, shaking with laughter. A small crowd gathered to watch Camille's progress. There were gasps when she neared the top and wobbled under the weight of the painting, applause when she steadied herself and handed Sasha her half. Ignoring her audience, she carried on shouting directions, hands on hips, a small figure backlit by the blazing electric candelabra. Once the painting was in place and Sasha was engrossed in putting the finishing touches to the canvas, Camille began to climb down. I was worried about her weak leg and was so absorbed in willing her not to fall that I didn't notice Georges until he was standing right behind me.

His mouth was sulky. 'I wrote dozens of letters, all summer, but not one reply.'

I noticed with a stab of desire that his hair was longer, curling around the collar of his black velvet jacket. William had taken himself away and left me to face the world without him. But here was someone who desired me, who didn't judge me and find me wanting.

He was looking at me intently, waiting for my answer.

'Georges. You startled me.'

A surge in the crowd pushed us together and his lips brushed mine.

'Jessie, why didn't you answer my letters?'

A space opened up behind me and I stepped back. 'I, I only received them last week when I returned from my walking holiday. I spent most of the summer travelling in Scandinavia with my parents and then I was so busy getting ready to return to Paris, I didn't have time to write back. I'm sorry.' I bit my lip and couldn't meet his eyes.

He frowned. 'What's wrong? Your face is thinner and you look as if you've been crying. What's happened?' Georges was always most irresistible to me when he was being kind. I found myself telling him tearfully about William finding the portrait and reading the note. How I hadn't heard from him since. When I finished I looked up and saw the triumph in his eyes.

'Can't you see how awful all this is for me?' I said, irritated.

'On the contrary, it is exactly what you need, to be freed from that Englishman. Now we can be together. Everything has worked out perfectly, completely to plan!'

I was puzzled. 'What do you mean everything has worked out perfectly. The whole thing is a mess, and it's not as if you planned it.'

He grinned. 'Didn't I? I suppose I can tell you now, you'll find it amusing no doubt. That painting – the one of William and the two prostitutes?'

I winced and nodded. Why had I been so quick to jump to the wrong conclusion?

Georges put his hand on his chest. 'It was I who persuaded Henri to paint that scene, and then to hang it on his studio wall and take you there so you were bound to see it – and think the worse. *Géniale, non?* And as for the portrait and the love note, well, that was a stroke of luck.'

I stared at him while he laughed. I had been a fool, tricked like a child into believing fairy stories that hid the ugly truths of the cruel adult world. Georges stopped laughing.

'Come on now, Jessie, surely you're not angry with me. You can't blame me for doing everything I could to win you. *Après tout*, all's fair in love and so forth.'

I hissed at him. 'Of all the low…'

'*Salut*, Georges!' Camille jumped down the last two rungs. Her face was flushed with the exhilaration of her climb. '*Dis donc*, Duchamp, where have you been all summer?'

Georges kissed Camille three times on the cheek. 'Dying of boredom in my parents' country house, of course. And you, Claudel?'

'Villeneuve with my family, *comme d'habitude*. The country was dull, dull, dull after Paris. I would have gone crazy except for a visit from Monsieur and Madame Rodin. They came for lunch one Sunday.'

There was a short silence. Camille was as shameless as Georges. Rosa was right: the two of them were like wild beasts, ruthless predators who would stop at nothing. And they got away with their behaviour. Here was Camille, rewarded for sleeping with Rodin by exhibiting at the Salon, while I had lost William and the chance of a good marriage and endangered my reputation – for what? A momentary lapse from which I'd pulled back. And here was Camille practically boasting about having carried on her affair not only under the noses of her parents, but that of Rose Beuret. Virtue is its own reward, my mother had always told me. Well, bugger that. I glanced at Georges. He looked amused. I wondered how much he knew, but he folded his expression neatly away.

'Really?' he said. 'I wish I'd been there. Such an interesting mix of people.'

Camille answered carelessly. 'Oh, the visit was a great success. Rodin, Papa and I discussed art while Madame Rodin and Maman talked about the best way to turn a seam and how to boil up bones to make soup.' She laughed. 'They got on famously, those two old women. It's no surprise – they are both classic *bonne femmes*.' Her beautiful face turned ugly for a second and I realised how much she hated Rose Beuret. I understood that this petty cruelty was the only way Camille could strike back at the woman she could not best, despite being younger and prettier than her. Camille was the one to be pitied, not Rose. But what had Rodin been thinking? Camille and Rodin had grown reckless. I realised the affair had taken a dangerous turn and I feared for my friend.

She turned to me and took my hand. 'The rest of the summer passed too slowly. You see, I missed my Jessie so very much.'

Camille had missed me! She had hardly written, not more than a few dashed-off lines, blotted with ink and misspellings and I'd begun to think she had forgotten me as she fell in deeper with Rodin.

Georges' tone was dry. 'Oh, Jessie has been far too busy to think about us. She's been swimming in fjords and scaling glaciers. I've always suspected she was one of those terrifying English ladies who scale the Himalayas with only a donkey for company.'

'Just as well she likes donkeys then, eh, Georges?' Camille said, punching him on the arm.

Georges rubbed his sleeve. 'How ladylike! I wish I could say I've missed you, *chère* Camille, but although deadly tedious, *les grandes vacances* at least gave my bruises time to heal.'

'Oh stop moaning, you're worse than a girl.' She linked arms with us. 'It is good to be back together. *Alors, mes copains*, let's go and see where they've put my sculpture. What did you submit, Georges?'

'I didn't have time over the summer.' He waved his free hand. 'Besides, all this, the Salon, it's old hat. They say there's a new place, *Le Salon des Independants*, it's where all the avant garde are showing. I might try there, when I'm not so busy.'

In the sculpture hall, Georges spotted his old tutor and left us to go and talk to him. Camille nudged me.

'All that talk of the Salon being out of fashion, I don't believe it and neither does Georges. He's just jealous because I'm better than him, the phoney.'

I was furious at Georges but I couldn't let this pass. 'That's unfair. He's well regarded in the studio, and you've seen his work – it's exceptional.'

She shrugged. 'When he sticks at it, or I should say when Jules Debois makes him stick at it. Don't you remember his studio?' I looked at her sharply but her face was innocent. 'It was full of half-finished projects. He's been the same all the time I've known him – lazy. Never mind him, this is my day. Let's find my sculpture.'

We found her *Giganti* peering out from behind a potted palm tree. A few idle stragglers looked up briefly from their catalogues and glanced in passing at it before moving on to the next exhibits. Poor Camille – all that hard work and expectation only to be ignored.

Camille bent down and took hold of one end of the planter. 'Help me move this.' By the time we had heaved it over to a back wall, spilling dirt all over the marble floor, we were bent double laughing.

I grabbed Camille and made her turn round. 'Look, there are two men looking at your *Giganti*. Let's go and listen to what they're saying.' We crept up and stood behind a fat man with a red face and extravagant whiskers who was waving his programme and holding forth. 'This one is by a pupil of Rodin, I can tell.' He leafed through the programme. 'Ah, yes, I thought so. It says here, Camille Claudel. Shows promise, wouldn't you say, Jean-Louis? Well, come on, you're the critic,' he boomed at his companion, a bird-like man with a beady look.

Camille looked elated and I squeezed her hand.

The bird-like man said: 'You have a good eye, Gaston. There is a certain fluidity and lightness of touch, but you can clearly see Rodin's influence, it's unmistakable.' He bent in for a closer look, his hooked nose nearly brushing *Giganti*'s leonine features. Straightening up, he gave a limp wave. 'This is merely an insipid copy of his robust style, too tentative, lacks Rodin's masculine vigour. But what do you expect from a woman? I have always maintained that the female sex is not capable of sculpting. Better they should stick to the decorative arts such as découpage and embroidery. And, if they must paint, let them dabble in watercolours – landscapes and flowers, or sentimental domestic subjects suited to their delicate sensibilities. Not only do these feeble creatures lack the physical strength required by sculpture, it is scientifically proven that their brains are smaller and if they persist in this unnatural pursuit they could lose their minds – a hideous fate. Only men, *mon vieux*, are capable of withstanding the physical and spiritual demands made by Art.'

I'd been hearing this kind of tosh all my life, but to hear it at the Salon where the admission itself qualified Camille to be judged on equal merit was an outrage. The fury that gripped me was for both of us: for Camille and me, and for all women. Can't a woman stand on her own two feet? Must she always be at the whim of men? I had been tossed between William and Georges for too long. No more. Now I wanted to avenge my friend, to knock this snivelling wretch to the ground, and shake his bony little frame until he begged for mercy. I took a step towards him, but Camille held me back, her face pale.

The bird was speaking again. 'Come, Gaston, I'll show you the real thing.' The little man led him to a tight group gathered round another sculpture and we followed. There were gasps and a few sniggers from the viewers. Camille pushed her way to the front of the crowd, pulling me behind her. We came upon one of the most remarkable sculptures I've ever seen. In all my years, I've yet to see a work of art that affected me more. A young woman, carved in snowy marble, knelt before us. Her hair hung loose to hide her face and the nape of her neck was laid bare. Her pale stone back curved like an exquisite guitar down to her perfect buttocks. She was at once sensuously abandoned and vulnerable. I recognised the delicately muscled back and waist: it was Camille.

My eyes widened and Camille nodded. 'It's beautiful. You're beautiful,' I whispered.

She whispered back. 'Do you like the pose? It was my idea.' We shared a smile before she turned her head sharply. The irritating little critic's hand was hovering over the nude as if he were about to touch her.

'Regard, if you will, the continuous line, the expression of emotion through the contorted pose,' he said in a pompous voice to his wider audience. 'I pronounce this one of Rodin's finest works.'

'It's certainly, er, arousing,' said the fat man, his eyes bulging. He licked his lips. 'Rodin must be bedding her, knowing his reputation.'

'I hear she's his latest mistress, a pupil no less, barely out of the schoolroom, the rogue,' said a man with a moustache. More sniggers.

The critic smiled unpleasantly. 'The little slut clearly has hidden talents. Or not so hidden now, eh Gaston?' He nudged his fat friend, who wheezed with laughter and stroked the marble girl's bottom and made a panting face. Camille reached out and smacked his hand away. He looked at her in astonishment. The bird's eyes narrowed. 'Aren't you … ?'

'Mademoiselle Claudel is quite right. I regret it is not permitted to touch the sculptures. Salon rules.' Rodin's cane struck the stone flagstones and the crowd parted for him. He stood in front of the critic and glared at him through his spectacles. I held my breath: was he going to strike him as I had longed to? The little man clearly thought so because he seemed to shrink away. Rodin raised his hand, and instead held it out to the critic. 'Aren't you Jean-Louis Breton? I often read your articles in the art gazette.'

Breton hesitated but Rodin's expression was mild and he hesitantly shook his hand. 'It's a great honour, Monsieur Rodin. Allow me to express my boundless admiration for your work. And this piece, it's simply breathtaking. The line! The luminescence!'

'Thank you.' Rodin clapped him on the back and the bird coughed. 'Now, I hope you have not overlooked the work of my most gifted pupil, Mademoiselle Claudel.' He walked over to Camille's bust of *Giganti* and the crowd followed, as if mesmerised. 'She has a unique style. I showed her where to look for gold, but the gold she finds is her own. Mademoiselle Claudel is certainly worthy of a review all of her own in that newspaper you write for, don't you think, Monsieur Breton? Allow me to introduce her.' He beckoned to Camille, who scowled and didn't move. Rodin waited. After a moment, she walked towards him.

Breton bowed, nearly scraping the floor with his long nose. 'Mademoiselle, may I congratulate you on a fine piece. Such talent in one so young is astonishing indeed. This piece is exquisite, exquisite.'

Camille's voice was cold. 'You don't find it insipid?'

Breton looked nervously at Rodin and back to Camille. 'Insipid?' he stammered. 'Not at all! It has sheer animal power, if you excuse the expression. And the workmanship is extremely accomplished. You must have a skilled *practicien* at your *atelier*.'

Camille put her hands on her hips and glared at Breton. 'Are you mad? I wouldn't allow anyone near my sculptures. This is all my own work.' She jabbed at her chest. '*Je me répéte*. All. My. Own. Work.'

Rodin put a hand on both our shoulder and regarded us with pride. 'I am fortunate to have two gifted pupils working in my *atelier* now, mark their names well, Monsieur, for your articles: Camille Claudel and Jessie Lipscomb. I urge you to review the work of these rising stars. You have a duty to tell your readers about two of the best young artists in Paris.'

He had remembered me after all! Rodin began answering a chorus of questions from an adoring group of women viewers who had clustered around him and I turned excitedly to Camille. We had triumphed and it was one in the eye for that odious little man! But it was never going to be that easy. Behind Rodin's back, the critic smiled slyly at Camille and winked at her.

'You are indeed fortunate to have such a mentor, Mademoiselle. I can assure you, your name will be appearing in my newspaper tomorrow. Not in the arts reviews – no space, I'm afraid – but I'm sure my dear colleague Gaston has room in his gossip column.'

The two journalists leered at her, tipped their hats and walked away, laughing and slapping each other on the back.

Camille clenched her fists and glowered at their retreating backs. '*Salauds.*' She spat and a woman walking past shrank back.

The nightmare I had dreaded was beginning to unfurl and Camille's reputation was heading for disaster. A spiteful item in the gossip column in one of the best-read papers in Paris would be the end of her. Camille was about to fall and there was nothing I could do to help her. She shouldn't have provoked that ghastly man, but she had been pushed beyond endurance. No male artist would have to put up with such insults.

Camille was trembling and I had to half-drag her to the exit, pushing past knots of viewers. Georges spotted us and called out. When we ignored him he hurried after us. Outside, we sat on the steps, careless of the dirt on our skirts and the legs hurrying past. Camille was weeping openly now, and people were looking at us.

I put my arms around her to shield her from their curious stares. 'Hush now, hush,' I murmured. My neck grew wet with her tears.

Georges crouched down beside us. I was grateful for his presence. He took out a handkerchief and wiped Camille's face. 'What happened, is she unwell?' he asked me.

'It was Rodin's sculpture. There was this horrible man, a critic. He was vile, just vile.'

His face was grim. 'I saw the sculpture. All Paris will see it and know who the model was. Tongues will wag.' Georges spoke to the onlookers. 'Please, give us some air.' He lifted Camille into his arms and walked with her towards a line of cabs, where the drivers were smoking and waiting by their horses. He helped me in after Camille and shut the door.

I spoke to him through the window and held onto his arm. 'Aren't you coming too?'

He ignored my question. 'This critic, what was his name?'

'Breton. Jean-Louis Breton.'

He banged the side of the *fiacre* with the flat of his hand and the driver shook the horse's reigns.

As we moved off, I called: 'Georges, what are you going to do?'

'I'm going to sort out this Breton.'

CHAPTER 33

RODIN'S STUDIO

August 1885

The *practiciens* were in a tight circle, sharing a tattered copy of the art gazette. One of the brutes, the worst one, Rodolphe, who had had it in for Camille and me from the start, saw us arriving and nudged the man next to him.

'Here she is, the *exciting new talent*. She must have been kissing someone else's arse to give Rodin's a rest.' He waved the newspaper at Camille.

Camille clapped her hands. 'How clever of you, Rodolphe! I see you are looking at a newspaper that doesn't have any pictures. I had no idea you could read!'

'Oh, I can read all right.' He read aloud in an affected voice. '*Mademoiselle Claudel shows a unique gift for sculpture seldom seen in a woman – especially one of such tender years. This critic wishes to inform our esteemed readers of the most exciting new talent to emerge from under the wing of Monsieur Auguste Rodin.*' He threw down the paper. 'Unique gift, my arse. Who do you think you are? Just in the door and think you're the big noise all of a sudden.'

While he was ranting, I picked up the newspaper and hid it behind my back.

Rodolphe was roaring now, his face puce. 'I'm twice the stone cutter you are, you stuck-up little bitch!'

Camille squared up to him. 'Oh really? I must have missed your piece at the Salon. Or, perhaps you didn't have time to submit as you were so busy scratching your hairy...'

'Mademoiselle Claudel!' Jules Desbois slammed the courtyard doors behind him.

Camille was the picture of innocence. '*Oui, Monsieur?*'

'You may be a rising star but there's still a pile of marble waiting to be cut by your oh-so-gifted hands.'

'*Oui m'sieu.* I'll get straight to it.'

As we walked past Desbois he muttered: 'You deserve every word in that review, and more. Well done. And that goes for you too, Mademoiselle Lipscomb. For once that fool Breton knows what he's talking about.'

Breton had come sniffing around the studio the day after the *vernissage*, all oily smiles and wringing hands, begging my pardon and if I'd only allow him to view my work. I'd gritted my teeth and shown him around the studio, glad that Camille wasn't there. Now he'd apparently written glowing reviews for both of us. I wondered what had happened to change his mind – and what Georges had had to do with it.

Camille and I hurried inside and once we were safely behind the changing screen, tore open the newspaper to find the reviews. Breton had heaped praise on Camille. And on me, too.

Meanwhile, Mademoiselle Lipscomb, another promising pupil leaping from Rodin's stable, shows precision and technical aptitude in Day Dreams, *her sensitive and exquisitely detailed portrait of a young girl. Surely it is only a matter of time before she joins her talented colleague at next year's Salon?*

Exhilarated, I beamed at Camille. We hugged, the humiliation of the first night forgotten.

'He is right, Jessie, your work is sensitive – it's only a shame he didn't mention your *Giganti* as well.'

I was soaring, high above the clouds, on wings. Nothing could stop us now: Jessie Lipscomb and Camille Claudel, up-and-coming artists. This was only the beginning. 'I'm going to submit *Giganti* for the Royal Academy next summer.' I clasped Camille's hands. 'I know what – why don't we show together, both *Gigantis*. It would give the London critics something to talk about.'

She frowned. 'Me? In England?'

'Why not? You can stay with my family and we'll take the train down to London. It would be an adventure.'

I waited while she fumbled in the pocket of her dustcoat for her cigarettes. She lit two and handed me one. She squinted at me through the smoke and grinned.

I opened my mouth in a silent scream of excitement. 'You'll come?'

She laughed and embraced me. '*Mais oui*. How could I resist the sight of all those prim English ladies ogling my gorgeous *Giganti*?'

It was settled: Camille and I would spend the following summer together – the whole summer! I couldn't wait to introduce her to Ma and Papa and show her around Wootton House, with its gardens, where we could talk and work under the shade of the elm trees. I imagined a cool English breeze ruffling my hair, sunlight dappling Camille's face as we sketched side by side.

'Come on, dreamer,' she pulled me to my feet. 'We've got work to do in Paris first.' She tied back her curls, her hands busy behind her head, and said: 'Hurry, Jessie, we don't want to give that *fils de pute* Rodolphe an excuse to say we're passengers on board Rodin's mighty ship.'

'I don't think he'd put it quite that eloquently,' I said.

'*C'est vrai*. He can't open that big mouth of his without speaking about arses. It's an unfortunate affliction.'

Laughing, we climbed the scaffolding around *The Gates*. At first we couldn't resist looking across at each other with wide grins, but soon we became absorbed in our work. When Georges sauntered in at lunchtime I was finishing off a veil that flowed from a tormented soul as she plunged towards the waiting arms of her adulterous lover. Camille was holding an arched foot, teasing out the detail on splayed toes that seemed to grip the air.

Georges called up to us: '*Allô!* I don't suppose you two will consider having lunch with me, now that you're famous?'

Camille threw a rag at him from her perch. 'I think we should buy you lunch, d'Artagnan.' She climbed down and faced him, fists on her hips. 'I don't know what you said to that critic to stop his dirty mouth, but I'm grateful.' She pulled him down by the ears and kissed him noisily on the lips.

He laughed and smoothed his hair. 'What? No punches? And I wore my extra-thick jacket as a precaution.' He looked up into the gloom, shading his eyes. 'And where's the sensitive and exquisitely detailed Jessie?'

I waved and blew him a kiss as I made my way down. I had decided to forgive him his machinations, or at least pretend indifference. And I was beginning to think that William should not have assumed the worst from reading what was, after all, my private correspondence.

Georges fanned his face. 'I'm overcome. That's two kisses. I wonder what would happen if I'd saved your lives?' He closed his eyes and pretended to shudder. Camille aimed a fist at his arm. 'Ow! Camille! Allow me to compliment you on your pugilistic prowess, as Monsieur Breton might say. In other words, you can fairly pack a punch. For a girl, that is.'

When Camille had gone behind the changing screen, I said: 'Georges, what did you do when you found Breton? You didn't hurt him, did you?'

He raised his eyebrows. 'You overestimate me. Let's just say I know his mistress. She's an old flame, which I threatened to rekindle if he spread any vicious rumours about Camille.'

I was crestfallen. 'So he didn't mean what he wrote?'

'Oh he admitted Camille's work was superlative and I don't doubt he was genuinely impressed by your work when he saw it. But before I sorted him out, he was more interested in spreading gossip. That *connard* is not above ruining a woman's reputation out of spite.'

'Thank you, Georges.' I put my hand on his and smiled.

'I would do anything for you, Jessie.'

He pushed me behind Rodin's *The Kiss* and put his arms around me. I let the last of my resistance evaporate. I had lost William; there was nothing left to lose.

I put a hand on his chest. 'Not so fast, d'Artagnan. What would have happened if this *connard* had refused? Would you have carried out your threat?'

He edged closer. 'What do you mean?'

'The old flame.'

'What do you think?' He bent his head to kiss me and I stepped aside, laughing.

'That's enough kisses for one day. Even for a hero.' If he could play games with me, perhaps it was time I had a little fun of my own.

He picked up my hand, turned it around and kissed my palm. 'I've been patient, but it's time to cut to the chase.'

I tried to say something but he moved in swiftly and kissed me, until I stopped caring about what was right and what was wrong. What did it matter? I told myself. I was in Paris.

Finally, I pulled away and smiled to see his breath rising so quickly in his chest. We went out into the street and Camille joined us. The sun was high in the sky, the cobbles so hot I could feel them through the soles of my shoes. I tilted my boater to keep off the glare and closed my eyes to listen to the music of Paris: the clatter of hooves from a passing omnibus, snatches of conversations from the café, the hammering of metal against marble, Camille and Georges teasing each other, a young woman singing with happiness.

CHAPTER 34

PARIS

October 1885

But Georges had not stemmed the gossip. While we revelled in our triumph, word was spreading through Paris. Others had seen Rodin's sculpture and speculated about the identity of the model and soon Camille Claudel's name was on everyone's lips. As summer cooled into autumn, while we worked on, wrapped in the cocoon of Rodin's studio, tiny streams of rumours fed into each other until they became a great river that lapped the walls of the *atelier*. By the following spring, even Rose Beuret couldn't ignore the currents of speculation and spite.

We usually had the *atelier* to ourselves in the evenings and I was surprised when Rose marched into the courtyard. I was waiting for Camille and had become immersed in the new Thomas Hardy, *The Mayor of Casterbridge*. I was at the part where the drunken Henchard was selling his wife and baby daughter at auction so I didn't notice Rose until she was at the inner door to the studio. I sprang up from the bench and the book tumbled down my skirts and onto the flagstones.

'Madame Rodin, please wait.'

Rose ignored me and went inside. I hurried after her, but she was too quick for me. She seemed to know Rodin and Camille's secret meeting place and headed straight to a door hidden by discarded plaster casts. They had forgotten to lock it. The fools – they had grown careless, assuming that everyone would turn a blind eye to the affair between the great man and his gifted pupil. I stood there, powerless, and watched it all happen.

Camille, her clothes dishevelled and her hair loose, ran out of the small backroom into my arms where she hid her face and sobbed. Three scratches beaded with blood marked her cheek. The door banged shut and Rose Beuret's shrieks rang around the empty studio. Camille and I crouched behind *The Gates of Hell*, listening to the rumble of Rodin's voice as he tried to calm Rose's fury. Suddenly it went silent. The air felt heavy, as if we were in a thunderstorm, and I half expected my ears to pop. Then a terrible wailing started up, like the lowing of a wounded farm beast. It was the kind of grief I've only heard since from mothers who lost their sons in the Great War. But at the time I'd never heard anything so desolate. It was the sound of someone's heart breaking.

I plucked at Camille's sleeve. 'Let's go.'

She shook me off. 'No, no, Rodin may need me.'

I spun her round and made her look at me. 'We have to go, Camille. Now.'

There was the cracking sound of a slap. Our heads snapped round and we looked at the door, eyes wide. Camille's fingers found her mouth and she nodded. We ran from the *atelier* like thieves fleeing a crime.

In the sanctuary of our own studio in Notre-Dame-des-Champs we smoked and waited for Rodin. Camille couldn't sit still and paced up and down, her limp more pronounced now since her fall on the moor.

'Where is he? He should come. He must come.' She pushed her fringe out of her face. Her eyes were wild. 'This is good that she knows. It means there's no more need for secrecy. He'll leave her and we can be together. I'm glad it happened.'

'Camille, please sit down. You'll tire yourself out.'

'Is there any brandy?'

I poured out the last of the bottle and went to add water.

'No water.'

She tipped the cup back and drank greedily. I'd never seen her so agitated. I wanted to make it all go away, but there was nothing I could do.

We heard footsteps on the stairs and Camille ran lightly to the curtain to pull it back, expecting Rodin. She stopped when she saw Rose. She was holding a pistol.

'*Putain!*' Rose shrieked.

Camille seemed transfixed by the gun's black mouth. Time seemed to stop, like in a bad dream, and I could not move or utter a word. I watched in horror as Rose squeezed the trigger. Her hand jerked and there was a deafening explosion. The room filled with the acrid smell of gunpowder. In the split second of silence that followed I watched bands of blue smoke hanging in the air. Camille sank to her knees and the trance was broken. I ran to her and caught her bowed head in my hands. No blood. Her skin was warm. I tried to remember what I'd learned in anatomy and searched for the carotid artery. It pulsed in her neck. Thank God, thank God. She moaned and opened her eyes.

I patted her clothes, searching for blood: nothing. Rose Beuret must have missed.

'Camille, can you hear me? Does it hurt anywhere? Do you need a doctor?'

She shook her head and began to sob. I pulled her head to my chest and rocked her. There was a clunk as the gun dropped to the floor. I whipped my head around and glared at Rose.

'Are you mad? You could have killed her.'

'I wish she were dead. I wish I were dead.' Rose put her face in her hands and began to weep.

There were shouts outside, the scuffle of heavy boots on the stairs and Rodin stood at the doorway, taking in the scene: Camille and I kneeling together on the floor, Rose standing over us, the gun at her feet.

Rodin stepped towards Rose, his hands raised. She shrank from him but he pulled her into an embrace. He stroked her hair, which swung wild and loose, heavy skeins of silver and bronze.

'*Allons, allons,* my little bird. You mustn't excite yourself; your heart is not strong. Auguste is here. Don't worry, I'll take you home.' Rose nodded and laid her head on his chest, her breath shuddering like a child after a tantrum. Rodin spoke to me over his shoulder.

'Will you look after Camille?' I nodded, unable to believe what had happened.

When they had left, Camille stared at the curtain as it swung back into place. As we sat there on the dusty floorboards, I began to tremble violently. Nausea rose in my throat and I vomited, splattering our skirts. Camille hugged herself and began rocking violently, her mouth a twisted maw of grief, her face flushed and streaked with tears. I staggered to my feet, kicking the gun into a corner, unwilling to touch it. I shook her by the shoulders until her eyes focused on me.

'What will you do now?' I said.

She took a gasping breath, like a drowning man coming up for air. 'Nothing. It's over. I never want that bastard to touch me again. I'll never forgive him for this. Never.'

She began to weep again and there was nothing I could do to console her.

Camille would not get out of bed the next morning, or the next. She refused to eat, turning her face to the wall when her mother came in with consommés and jellies. I sat by her side, pressing cold cloths to her forehead.

Madame Claudel picked up a plate of untouched food and shook her head. 'She's exhausted. I told her father that sculpture was too hard for a woman.'

Camille, who would normally have sharpened her tongue on her mother's flinty words, merely closed her eyes. Tears leaked into her hairline unchecked.

After a week of this, I went to Rodin's studio.

In the stone-cutting yard, Rodolphe looked up from his hammering and smirked. 'Here comes one of them, anyway. Eh, Mademoiselle Tight-Arse, where's your uppity friend? Too frightened to show her face, I'll bet. I hear Madame Rodin's banned her from the studio. Someone must have been telling tales. Now, I wonder who would do such a thing.' He grinned at his cronies, who fell about laughing.

So that's how Rose Beuret had found out – Rodolphe had tipped her off, the filthy ape. I ignored him and started to throw tools into a

205

carpetbag, all the while keeping an eye out for Rodin. Sure enough, after a few minutes he touched my shoulder.

'Oh, it's you.' I glanced at him and went back to sorting out the tools.

'*Oui, c'est moi. Votre maître.*' He took the heavy bag from my hands and put it gently on the floor. 'How is Camille?'

I wiped off my hands and faced him. 'How do you think she is? She's upset, of course.' I had a hundred things I had planned to say to him, but it was difficult to be angry with him. I was still in awe of Rodin, but I had to try for Camille's sake.

'*Maître*, I don't know what to say to you.'

He smiled and handed me a piece of paper. 'Say you will take this to *notre féroce amie*.' He closed his large hand over mine and held it tight. 'Please, Jessie, *je t'en supplie*. I must see her.'

'She doesn't want to see you, not after what happened.'

He shook his head sadly. 'Ah, *le pauvre Rose*.'

I wrenched my hand free, leaving the letter in his. 'Poor Rose? She tried to kill Camille.'

'Never would she have harmed her. That old pistol doesn't even work properly – it was her father's. Do you still have it?'

I reached into the carpetbag and took out the gun wrapped in an oily rag. He sighed and pocketed it.

'You were never in any danger, I assure you. Rose's eyesight is bad after years of needlework. It was merely a nervous crisis. She… she's had a hard life. Our son, he's not quite … never mind.' He drew a deep breath. '*Enfin*, I spoke to her and she has promised she will not come near Camille again.' He rubbed his chin. 'I don't know what got into *ma petite mignone*. She's always been jealous and fiery with it, but this? I didn't think she suspected anything.'

I pointed at Rodolphe, who was whistling over a piece of marble and pretending not to look in our direction. 'Perhaps there is a simple explanation.'

Rodin shook his head. 'No, it's not that. Rose never listens to gossip about me.'

I'll bet she doesn't, I thought. Better to stay in the dark when you were with a man like Rodin, who loved women of all shapes, ages and sizes. I considered for a moment.

'You must have let something slip, then, an inadvertent confession of sorts. Did you talk about Camille to Rose?'

He looked sheepish. 'Just before this, ah, incident, we were at Georges Petit's gallery for my new exhibition. Rose saw *La Danaïde*. You saw the earlier version of it in the Salon.' He shifted his walking stick from one hand to the other. 'She wanted to know who the model was.'

'And you told her?'

He nodded.

La Danaïde is one of Rodin's most tender sculptures. It's still one of my favourites. While some of his uninhibited female nudes could be crude and shocking, this arousing figure seemed carved out of pure love. No wonder Rose had gone mad. The fool – Rodin was so besotted with Camille he couldn't resist bragging about her, even to his wife.

He touched me on the arm. 'Will you ask Camille to come back?'

'Why would she, after you left her alone in our studio and went away with Rose?'

His mouth tightened. Rodin was still Rodin and didn't like his authority to be questioned. 'I did what was necessary under the circumstances. Rose is my duty, my burden.' His expression softened. 'But I have carried this burden long enough. It is Camille who is in my thoughts every day. Since she's been gone I can't work, I can't think.'

He passed his hands over his reddened eyes and I realised that he was weeping. Rodin and Camille were both in pain without each other, and I was the only one who could help them.

'Give me the letter,' I said.

His face was eager, like a young man in the grip of first love. 'You'll do it?'

'I'll do it.'

It was a decision I would come to regret.

CHAPTER 35

PETERBOROUGH

May 1886

The sun streamed through the morning room bay windows and lay in bright pools on the newspaper spread over the breakfast table. It shone through the marmalade jar, making the orange peel look as if it were suspended in amber.

'What do the reviews say?' Camille said.

'Your *Giganti* was well received.' Camille's English was rudimentary so I translated for her. '*From a fresh new talent, this striking bust shows a confident hand, although the piece appears rather unfinished.*'

She crumbled a piece of toast. 'What else does it say?'

'Nothing much, just some rubbish from a journalist who clearly knows nothing about art.'

'Read it to me.'

I would want to know too, but I wanted to protect Camille. She was still fragile after the shooting. And over the past few months, Rodin had been merciless, both in his attentions to Camille and his professional demands on both of us. We spent every waking hour in his studio working on *The Burghers* and during our breaks he would take Camille aside to talk over ideas for new sculptures. They were working feverishly on a project she wouldn't tell me about. *It will be Rodin's greatest work and we will make it together. It is to be a representation of our love for each other, for all to see.* Her own work lay neglected and unfinished in our studio and by the time we left for England she seemed drained, sleeping for long periods and picking at her food.

In Paris I had watched Camille's cool marble carapace fracture into tiny lines under the pressure of Rodin's love, seen her strong spirit eroded by his demands as she spent her talent on ideas for Rodin's insatiable creative appetite. England would be an escape for her, a cool sanctuary where her turbulent mind would be calmed under the pewter skies. And, selfishly, I wanted Camille to myself again. But Rodin followed us. Under the pretext of visiting an artist in London, he contrived to meet us at the Royal Academy exhibition, where he had charmed my parents into being invited to Wootton House.

Now Camille tapped the newspaper. 'Read the rest.'

Reluctantly, I picked up the paper again. '… *Unfortunately for Miss Claudel, her rather roughly executed and clumsy oeuvre was displayed next to Miss Lipscomb's accomplished and technically perfect bust of the very same model. It was Miss Claudel who came off worse in this particular competition between the fair ladies.*'

There was a moment of quiet while I held my breath. A blackbird sang its piercing melody in the elm outside.

Camille's voice was dangerously quiet. 'And your *Day Dreams*?'

'A mention only.'

'Translate it for me.'

'I'm not sure my French is up to it.'

'What are you talking about? You speak like a native.' When I stayed silent, she snatched the paper from my hand and squinted furiously at the small blurred type. 'It's no good; I can't make out more than two words. *Jessie, tu m'en merdes. Raconte-moi, tout de suite.*'

I quoted from memory. '*The subject's exquisite, tender beauty shines through this sensitive work. Miss Lipscomb shows a remarkable emotional expressivity for such a young artist. The tender subject lends itself perfectly to the light touch and feminine sensibilities of a lady artist. This critic has the pleasure of introducing one of the most promising new artists who will no doubt add to the glory of Brittania and her Empire.*' I paused. 'I told you, awful tosh.'

I watched Camille's face warily, waiting for the inevitable outburst. They had become increasingly frequent. Always tempestuous, since that dreadful shooting she had become more volatile, quicker to anger and prone to bouts of suspicion. Camille knitted her dark eyebrows and I held my breath again. She smoothed out her expression like one would a piece of crumpled paper. When she spoke, her voice was oddly high and bright, like a porcelain bell.

'In England they are not *au fait* with the modern movements in art, as they are in Paris. After all, the Royal Academy rejected Rodin's *Idylle* for that ridiculous collection of sentimental rubbish we saw, full of imbecile knights and princesses with constipated expressions. And did you see that painting of the little girl and her kitten? I thought I was going to vomit.'

She stood up and opened a window. A breeze lifted her muslin sleeves and I could see the outline of her uncorseted body under the white tea dress. For a moment I hated her for the scorn she'd poured on my work by rubbishing the Academy. She couldn't bear for me to be praised instead of her. Well, it was my turn now. I was about to say something sharp to her, when she turned round. Her head was haloed by the sun and she smiled at me.

'I'm sorry, Jessie, I should have congratulated you. Your work put the rest of that exhibition to shame.' She came over and embraced me and once again I could breathe more easily. The storm had passed us by, or so I thought.

Rodin arrived that evening in the middle of a summer thunderstorm. I opened the front door to see our *maître* standing in the downpour, a damp beret mashed on his head and his beard dripping with rain.

'What a climate you endure,' he said, shaking himself out of his coat like a dog and handing it to the new maid, who had just arrived, late and flustered.

'Sorry, Miss,' she said to me, bobbing a curtsy. 'I was in the kitchen helping cook. She's been in a bit of a tizzy trying to follow the recipe for French soup Madame found in Mrs Beeton. Onions and beef broth, it's made from. At least it's not frogs or horses. I don't know how foreigners can eat them things.' She shuddered and made a face.

'Thank you, Liza. I'll show Monsieur Rodin into the parlour. You can go back and help cook. I'm sure dinner will be delicious, as always.'

Rodin came into the hall, rubbing his hands briskly and stood in front of the fireplace. He looked appreciatively around the hall, panelled in kauri pine that shone like honey. 'How is she?'

I didn't need to ask whom he meant. He might have asked how I was, or made some polite conversation first. But Rodin wasn't one for social chit-chat. I swallowed my irritation.

'Her nerves are bad,' I said. 'She's been working too hard and needs a rest. You won't upset her this evening?'

He held out his hands palm upwards, like a magician showing the audience he has nothing to hide. 'Dear Jessie, how well you protect our friend.' He waited until I took his hands. 'Don't worry; I will be on my best behaviour. You know, I can be let loose in civilised company.' He smiled and the corners of his pale blue eyes crinkled.

There was a snort and we both looked up. Camille stood at the top of the stairs, her face a mask of contempt. She greeted Rodin with icy correctness. I sighed. No doubt they'd quarrelled again and I'd be petitioned by both sides until a peace was brokered, and be expected to arrange a safe place for their passionate reconciliation. I was beginning to detest my role as go-between.

Rodin laughed and held out his hands to Camille. 'My dream in stone.'

Baudelaire's line had become his pet name for her, an intimate joke that I should not have been privy to, but I knew everything about their affair. Camille liked to pull me into her bed at night and confide in me in the darkness. She whispered the details until I was both sickened and craving more.

Now she swept past Rodin into the dining room, ignoring his outstretched arms, and I knew the game was on and the part I would have to play in it. Over dinner, while Rodin complimented my mother on the meal and her home and fed my father choice snippets of gossip from the art world that he found so fascinating, Camille did not bother to hide her boredom. She sighed extravagantly and left her food untouched.

Rodin ignored her and kept up his elaborate show of entertaining my parents. Ma nodded politely, bewildered by the torrent of French, while Papa translated the odd anecdote for her between guffaws. Rodin could be charming when he tried, and he was trying hard, in order, I suspected, to spite Camille. Hers was not the only stony face at the table – I was furious at them both for using my parents as pawns in their game.

Papa didn't seem to notice anything amiss but Ma has always been a shrewd judge of people, a skill she'd picked up during her years as a barmaid in a railway hotel. She watched as Rodin stared hungrily at Camille while my father talked about the Irish Question.

Ma dropped her napkin onto the table. 'Jessie, perhaps it's time we retired and let the men enjoy their cigars and port.'

I rose, but Camille stayed in her chair scowling defiantly. For a dreadful moment I thought she was going to refuse to leave the table, but when my mother stared her down, she scraped back her chair and stood. In the drawing room, Camille paced the rug and when it rucked up, she kicked it in a temper.

Ma didn't look up from the cards she was dealing. 'Jessie, dear, tell your friend that carpet is a very expensive Voysey.'

A strained hour passed before Papa and Rodin came in, their faces rosy from too much port.

'A little music would be soothing for the digestion, don't you think, my dear fellow?' Papa said. 'Jessie, give us one of your Scottish songs. My daughter sings like an angel, Auguste.'

'If she sings as well as she sculpts then I will be in heaven,' Rodin said with a broad smile. 'Perhaps Mademoiselle Claudel will accompany her?' He indicated the baby grand piano, its dark wood gleaming in the candlelight.

Camille's expression darkened. 'You know I detest music. An artist paints with her eyes not with her ears.'

Papa didn't seem to notice the tension between Rodin and Camille but I recognised the signs only too well.

'Never mind,' he said. 'Jess can accompany herself. She really is quite talented.'

I saw Rodin smirk at Camille and the look of venom she shot

212

back at him.

'Papa,' I said. 'Perhaps our French friends would not appreciate these simple folk songs. I'm tired, and I think I'll go to bed.'

But Rodin rushed forward, grabbed me by the arm and led me to the piano. '*Mais, Jessie! Chantez, chantez!* Your Scottish songs, they sound so charming.'

Ma frowned at me. 'It's not like you to be shy, or to forget your manners, dear. Do as Mr Rodin asks.'

'If you insist,' I lifted the piano lid and cracked my knuckles to punish Ma. She seemed not to hear and went back to her game of patience. It had been a while since I'd played, but my fingers ran over the keys in familiar patterns and soon I was lost in the ballads about love lost, broken hearts and forced partings. I thought of William, who had not been near Wootton House, even though I'd heard he was in town. He'd taken up his new post in Manchester. I'd finally got up the courage to write to him there, to say I wanted to explain, but he hadn't replied. I'd managed to convince myself I was in the right and that he was being pigheaded. I started another song about forbidden love and my thoughts switched to Georges. He had written letter after letter to me since I'd left France, each more passionate and intemperate than the last. 'I wish you weren't leaving,' he had said before I left, holding onto my hands and speaking urgently. 'Paris without you is torture to me. Everywhere holds the ghost of you. You will come back, won't you? And when you do, I need to know your decision about us. I can't wait any longer.'

I came to the end of the last song in a dream. The last note hung in the air and silence filled the room. It was broken by Rodin, clapping wildly.

'Bravo! Bravo! Encore! *Une exécutation géniale!* To have two such talents – art and music – this is astounding.' Rodin rushed forward with his hands outstretched and kissed me three times on the cheeks. He turned to Ma and said: 'Madame Lipscomb, I congratulate you on your gifted daughter. You must be proud of her – and after such a triumph at the Academy, too.' He glanced slyly at Camille. 'She is, without a doubt, the most talented person in this room.'

I knew what he was doing. But it was rare for Rodin to be this effusive in his praise, and I found myself revelling in his approval despite myself. It was difficult to resist Rodin when he used his full power.

He held out his hands to me. 'Jessie, I have something for you, to thank you for all the help you have given me.' He lowered his voice so only I could hear. 'The help you have given us.' We both looked at Camille. She was staring at a book in her lap and was quite still. Rodin spoke loudly again. 'I have a gift, for you, from one true artist to another. Wait here.'

He excused himself and when he returned he handed me a box. Inside was a small sculpture, a family group. A Rodin, for me!

For a while I couldn't speak. When I did it was with tears in my eyes. 'Thank you, *Maître.*'

Camille's face was thunderous, but I was too swept away by Rodin's attention to notice that a storm was about to burst over me. I was enjoying my moment in the sun. In Paris I was used to playing second fiddle to Camille, both to Rodin and professionally. But this was my home, my family, and it had been I who had the resounding success at the Royal Academy. I see now that I too was being used as pawn in the lovers' game; without me there would have been no sport that evening. In my blind pride, I ignored Camille's fury and graciously agreed when Rodin begged for an encore. I placed the sculpture on the piano lid and placed my hands on the keys once more. But I had sung only a few bars when Camille clapped her hands to her ears and screamed.

My hands stopped. We all stared at her. The only sound was the rain being thrown at the windows. Camille had our full attention.

She threw the book she'd been holding on the floor so hard its spine cracked and the pages spilled over the carpet. 'No more of this! I won't listen to another note of this hideous cacophony. These sugary lyrics and trite melodies – cheap and sentimental, just like your work, Jessie.'

Camille stormed out of the room, leaving my parents openmouthed at her outburst. Ma was the first to recover. 'I have no idea what that was all about, but you'd better go after her, Jessie. She must be feeling unwell, the poor dear.'

I didn't want to go, but my mother had that look on her face, the one that brooks no argument. Ma wanted me to make peace, but I knew she would have had no sympathy for Camille if only she'd understood what she'd said to me. But Ma had no French at all. Papa, on the other hand, was as fluent as me. He stood with his back to us, clearly embarrassed, looking out through the window as if he could see through the black squares to the garden.

Ma glared at me as if it were I that was at fault, not Camille. 'Jessie, what are you waiting for?'

I had no choice – I would have to go after Camille and make peace, even though I was shaking with anger and humiliation. After everything I'd done for her, covering up her affair with our tutor, caring for her and encouraging her during those terrible storms of weeping when she and Rodin quarrelled. And now, in my own home, in front of my parents, she had insulted me in the worst possible way. She had gone too far. I had had enough and I would tell her. At the door, I composed myself and turned to say goodnight to Rodin. He was standing at the mantelpiece, smiling to himself like a cat that has just caught a mouse between its paws.

CHAPTER 36

Camille was not in her room. She had taken to disappearing at night. I'd been concerned the first time she'd done it in London, when she'd walked the streets near the lodgings we'd taken and wandered alone through Hyde Park. At least here she would be safe, and I wasn't going to worry Ma and Papa by telling them. I sighed and settled down on her bed to wait for her. When I woke, the room was light and the birds were calling to each other. Camille had not come back. I pulled on a shawl and ran out of the house. The grass was damp from last night's rain and soon the hem of my dress was soaked. She was nowhere to be seen. I searched the rose garden and went down to the stream that ran through the bottom of the garden, growing more and more frantic. Surely she hadn't gone out the gate. My chest heaving with panic, I ran back up towards the house and stood under the elm tree where I could get a better view of the lawns, which sloped down towards the limestone walls. A twig snapped above me and I looked up into the tree. There was Camille, huddled on a branch, her back to the trunk. She stared down at me sightlessly. When I called to her she shook herself, as if waking from a dream and slowly began to climb down. She stood before me, her teeth chattering, hair hanging in damp tendrils and her clothes wet through. I put my shawl around her and led her back into the house.

I towelled her dry, the way Ma used to do to me after a bath, and put her into bed. I took off my own wet dress and climbed in after her, held her until the warmth of my body crept into hers and she stopped shivering.

Her breathing grew regular and I thought she'd fallen asleep when she spoke. 'Jessie, I'm sorry.' And she began to cry, great heaving gulps, like a child. I held her more tightly and kissed the top of her head.

'Don't fret, my lamb, don't fret,' I said, using the words that had comforted me as a child.

She rubbed at her eyes and sat a little apart from me. 'I didn't mean those things I said about you. How could I? You know that, don't you?' Camille's navy blue eyes were ringed with dark shadows, her brow creased with anxiety. I nodded and she relaxed a little. 'Rodin and I, we had a fight.'

For the first time in a long while I wanted to laugh. 'You don't say?'

A smile tugged at the corners of her mouth. 'Of course, it was obvious. I behaved like an idiot.'

Now that I'd found her and she was safe, I allowed myself to be angry with her again. 'You behaved horribly, not only to me, but to my parents.'

Camille rubbed her forehead. 'I know, I know. But listen to me, and maybe you will understand.'

I crossed my arms and faced her. 'What could possibly excuse such rudeness? In my home, Camille, in my own home.'

'Rodin told me he won't leave Rose. He said we can never be married.'

'What? But he promised! Does that mean you and him…'

She covered her eyes and began to weep again.

Rodin had left before we came down to breakfast. A note on the hall table thanked us for our kind hospitality. *Désolé* but he had to leave immediately for Paris to sort out a problem with his exhibition with Monet. Camille tore the note into pieces so I had to write it out again in an approximation of Rodin's scrawl and give it to my parents at breakfast.

Ma squinted at the note. 'What terrible writing. That's a shame he had to dash off, such a nice man.' She smiled at Camille. 'Are you feeling better dear? You look a little peaky.'

It was an odd summer – not at all like I'd imagined it would be. Camille's moods were changeable: affectionate towards me one day and the next she'd be distant and cool. She went away to stay with Amy Singer's family, making it clear she wanted to be on her own. And when she returned she talked incessantly about the Singers, a large, artistic family. Their bohemian home seemed more to her liking than Wootton House and its quiet pace. We went to stay on the Isle of Wight with an old schoolfriend of mine, Florence, and I thought we'd finally have time together, walking along the cliffs and sketching. But Camille struck up a close friendship with Florence and I'd often find myself excluded in those subtle but devastating ways women employ to make it clear you are not wanted.

But still I kept making excuses for Camille. She was confused; she was heartbroken over Rodin; she was fragile. The stream of letters continued to arrive unabated from Paris in Rodin's unmistakable hand. Some she'd tear up and stamp on the pieces, others she'd press to her lips and tuck into her pocket to read again later.

Finally, September arrived and it was time for her to go back to Paris. Ma had asked me to stay on for Christmas and I'd agreed. As their only child, I knew they missed me dreadfully. Besides, Camille's long visit had put a strain on our friendship. Perhaps we needed a break from each other.

I knelt on the floor, helping Camille to pack. We layered her dresses with tissue paper and folded them into her trunk. We worked in silence and I thought how different it used to be with her in the early days of our friendship, when I could say anything to her, no matter how irreverent, my candour rewarded with shouts of laughter and an answering jibe. Instead I'd taken to choosing my words carefully, watching her face anxiously for the first signs of an outburst. I'd always prided myself on my courage and hated this new tentativeness. And, it only seemed to make Camille more impatient with me. I'd watch powerless as her lips curled with disdain as I stuttered some inane pleasantry. She was slipping away from me and I knew unless I fixed what had broken between us, I'd lose her. I sat back on my heels and summoned the Jessie who was afraid of nothing.

'Camille, look at me.'

She glanced up and went back to folding a shawl. I grabbed her wrist. She tried to shake me off but I held on.

'What is it?' she said.

'This summer, I've found it difficult, found you difficult. At times you've behaved as if you were my enemy, not my friend.'

Camille sighed and I released her wrist. 'You're right,' she said. 'I've not been myself, I'm sorry. Can't we be friends again?'

'No we can't, not until we sort this out. Sorry just isn't good enough.'

Camille stood up and walked towards the window. She looked out at the elm leaves, which were turning to copper. 'It's all Rodin's fault,' she said with her back to me. 'He ruins everything. He wants to control everything – me, you. I haven't been able to think straight.' She turned around. 'But it's true that things can't go on like this. It's intolerable for all of us. When I go back to Paris, I promise I'm going to sort everything out. I know you've hated acting as our go-between and putting up with my moods, but you won't have to do that any more.'

She came and knelt beside me and put her arms around me. I closed my eyes. These were the words I'd wanted to hear. I'd talk to her about spending more time in our own studio, working on our own pieces. Perhaps everything would go back to how it used to be when we'd sit and drink tea, and smoke and talk about our plans. It would be Camille and I against the world once more.

'Jessie,' she whispered. 'You are my one true friend. I don't know what I'd do without you. Can you forgive me?'

I nodded through tears. She was my Camille once more. Everything was going to be all right.

I disentangled myself. 'There's nothing to forgive. Come on, we'd better get your packing finished.'

She dug into her skirt pocket and grinned at me. 'Not before we have a last cigarette.'

CHAPTER 37

Peterborough

February 1887

Once again I was knee-deep in tissue paper but this time it was Ma and I smoothing silk skirts and brushing out furs. I was lost in a daydream, the boulevards of Paris already stretching before me as I walked arm in arm with – with whom? Certainly not with William. My letters to Manchester had met with flinty silence and I'd stopped writing after a while. Instead I pictured Georges, a scarf tied loosely around his neck to ward off the crisp early-spring air. Another of his letters had arrived the day before.

Jessie! Where are you, for God's sake? I am dying from boredom. Paris is a desert without you. Come quickly! It's time you came back to where you belong – to Paris and to me. Je t'embrasse mille fois. Georges.

'Penny for 'em.' Ma raised her eyebrows.

'Mmm?'

'Jessie dear, you're a million miles away.'

'Sorry, I've a lot on my mind.'

'Come here, my lamb, I'll miss you.' She put her arms around me and I sank into her warm embrace, her cheek soft against mine.

Suddenly I was tired of fighting my feelings, of the push and pull between William and Georges. William had made it clear he didn't want me, and Georges was waiting.

'Ma, you know how you always said I could tell you anything?'

She stiffened and held me at arm's length. 'You're not … We can bring the wedding forward and nobody will be the wiser. William won't mind. Plenty of girls have early babies.'

I stared at her open-mouthed before bursting into laughter. 'Ma, I'm not pregnant! Besides, we're not engaged. And you know William and I haven't been speaking since he came back from France. Ma, I told you we'd quarrelled.'

She waved her hand dismissively. 'Don't try to pull the wool over my eyes, Jessie Lipscomb, I'm your mother, I know everything. William's mother told me he'd taken the family emeralds out of the safe and had them cleaned and remounted – and that means only one thing, a wedding. I just assumed you'd come to your senses and make it up with him. But still, it's a blessing you're not in the family way, not just yet anyway.'

I couldn't help laughing. There I was, my precious virginity intact, no thanks to Georges' attempts, and there was certainly no danger now of William ever breaking down my defences.

She frowned at me. 'I don't know what's so funny. You wouldn't be the first girl to walk down the aisle with a big bouquet.'

Thinking about William had been a mistake. My laughter turned into a sob before I could disguise it.

Ma took my hand and patted it. 'What's troubling you? Out with it – don't worry, I've heard it all after years standing behind a bar. Lord, the tales I could tell! Come, tell Ma what's troubling you.'

Surely, anything I said about Georges would seem trivial after my mother's vision of me waddling up the aisle.

'Ma, William did ask me, but we're not engaged.'

'What? Jessie, don't tell me you've gone and turned down the best chance you'll have of a good marriage.' She crossed her plump arms and waited.

My words tumbled out, my cheeks pinking. 'The reason we quarrelled, well it was my fault. You see, in Paris, there's this other man. A Frenchman. He's an artist, but oh, he's so talented, he'll go far just as soon as he gets a break. And he's handsome and funny and, and *romantic*. Oh Ma, I'm mixed up, I don't know what to do. One minute I know William is the one I should be with for the rest of my life, and the next Georges just has to write to me or to, to kiss me and…'

Ma gripped my arms so hard I gasped. Her voice was hard. 'Now, you listen to me, Jessie Lipscomb. You've been cosseted all your life. It's probably your father's and my fault for spoiling you, but the upshot is you've always got what you wanted. You don't know a thing about real life.'

'Ma! You're hurting me.' She let go my arms and I rubbed them. I could hear the petulance in my own voice. 'I do so know about real life; I'm not a child. Haven't I lived on my own as an independent woman in London and Paris?'

'Independent!' She snorted. 'On your father's money, more like.'

'Ma! Let's not talk about money, it's vulgar.'

'Vulgar! I'll tell you what's vulgar my girl – a woman having to break her back to earn her own living. Have you thought for one minute how this whatsisname is going to provide for you?'

This wasn't going the way I'd expected it to. Why was Ma being so cruel? If only I could make her understand.

'His name is Georges. And I don't need anyone to provide for me. I could work. Once I get a few commissions…'

She cut me off with an exasperated sigh. 'Work! You don't know the meaning of the word. Do you think art will pay your rent? Put food on the table? You want to try fourteen hours on your feet behind a bar, listening to the muck men talk, or sweating away in the din of a factory, going to bed in a freezing room, so tired you don't know whether to cry or sleep.'

I opened my mouth but she held up her hand. 'Hold your tongue, I haven't finished yet.' I closed my mouth. Ma had never spoken to me like that before.

'What happens when you do fall pregnant?' she said. 'How are you going to work then? You'd have to leave the babby with some old drudge for a few pennies and hope she doesn't feed it gin to keep it quiet. Soon you'd be too tired and worn out to go on and there's a worse fate waiting. A few moments on your back and you could make more in a night than you could in a month, and not have to leave the little one. I had a *Georges* buttering me up and chasing after my skirts, but men like that don't stay the course. Thank God for your father. He saved me from a bad end.'

I couldn't speak. I pictured my mother at my age, alone and heartbroken, abandoned by some awful man after he'd taken advantage of her.

But that wouldn't happen to me. These were modern times, the world had changed and women could be independent if they wanted to be. I tried again to reason with her.

'I know women – poor women – have to work hard, but I love my work, and besides, Papa is wealthy.'

Her voice was hard. 'You think Papa is going to make it all better? Do you think he'd forgive you for throwing William away and taking up with some penniless artist?'

'He forgave you, for your past.'

Her face grew red with fury and she clasped her hands together, as if to prevent herself striking out. I drew back but she only took a deep breath and closed her eyes. When she spoke again her voice was low and controlled.

'Listen to me, Jessie, and then we'll never talk of this again. Your father married me because he was in love with me and he's a good man who forgave my past mistakes. But it's different for you – you're his precious little girl. He's always put you on a pedestal, but if you break off your engagement to William and disgrace yourself – and us – by running away with a foreigner of no character and become his mistress, he'll cut you off. Make no mistake about it. Decent society will turn its back on you. And so will your father. You'll be ruined.'

I bit my lip to stop myself from crying and looked out of the window, where the elm tree's bare branches were moving in the wind.

Ma sounded tired. 'Even if Papa were to forgive you, the money's not there like before. I didn't want to have to tell you this, but he's had a bad year and lost a fortune on the stock exchange. We weren't sure if we could afford to send you back to Paris. The rent for your digs at the Claudels and the studio are really more than we can afford now. But, as usual, your father insisted his Jessie is not to want for anything.'

She stood up stiffly, her knees creaking. 'I can't make up your mind for you. But if you go off with this man, you'll have to stand on your own two feet.' Ma narrowed her eyes at me. 'And perhaps your fancy Frenchman won't be quite so keen when he finds out you're not an heiress any more.'

I was stung. How dare she? My fists closed, crushing the silk dress I was holding. 'Georges loves me. It wouldn't make a blind bit of difference if I were a pauper.'

She laughed and shook her head. At the door she turned to me again. 'You're a fool if you leave William. You don't know how lucky you are to have the chance of a husband like him. Handsome young men with no prospects who promise you the moon are ten a penny. You don't have to go to Paris to find one – the streets of London are full of 'em. I know it's hard, Jessie, but love – that kind of love – isn't worth throwing your life away for.'

I waited until I heard her footsteps on the staircase before I took out Georges' letter from my skirt pocket, smoothed out the creases and read it again, my eyes blurring. He did love me. He did. I didn't care what they all thought.

CHAPTER 38

Paris

February 1887

On my return to Paris I rushed around to Rodin's studio to find Camille. She had not been at the apartment and I had brushed off Madame Claudel's entreaties to rest after my journey and paused only to wash and change my travel-stained clothes. In Studio M, I breathed in the familiar scent of wet plaster and marble dust. It was nearing the end of the working day but the courtyard, which should have been full of *practiciens*, was strangely empty. I pushed through the interior doors and was met with an arresting sight. Camille was standing on a table with a dustsheet wound about her like a Roman matron and there was a paper crown on her head. She waved a bottle of wine in the air, like a beacon, and was surrounded by *practiciens*. Camille took a swig and they cheered and whistled.

'How do I look, Rodolphe?' Her words were slurred.

'Good enough to eat – like a *bonbon* waiting to be unwrapped.' Rodolphe's simian face leered at Camille and she threw back her head and laughed.

'Behold the Statue of Liberty!' she shouted. Camille drank deeply again and staggered, nearly losing her footing. Rodolphe caught her around the waist to steady her. 'Here, *mon ami*, have a drink,' she said to him. She was pouring wine down his throat when she caught sight of me.

'*Salut*, Jessie!' Camille beckoned to me. 'Come and join the fun. We've just heard Eiffel is to build a colossal tower over Paris, even more vulgar than the Statue of Liberty he worked on with

Bartholdi.' She put the bottle to her lips again and wiped her mouth with the back of her hand. 'Those poor New Yorkers have to look at that abomination every day. Now we in Paris are to have our own monument to bad taste.'

I didn't know what to say or do. Before we had left for England, Camille and I had been excluded from the tight-knight group of *practiciens* who had sneered at our work and insisted that women had no place in any *atelier*, let alone that of Rodin. But here she was, acting as their ringleader. It dawned on me that Rodin must have promoted her to stone carver and that she was one of them now. While I had been in Peterborough, counting the days to our reunion, she had been forging new alliances and playing studio politics, befriending the same brutes who had done everything in their power to thwart us. Now they had accepted her as Rodin's protégée – no doubt to curry favour with the great man.

Camille jumped down and flung her arms around me. Her breath smelled of wine and her lips were stained with a ruby tidemark. 'Drink?' She waved the bottle in my face and I pushed it aside.

'No thank you.'

'No thank you,' she mimicked in a prissy voice and grinned at the *practiciens*, who obligingly screamed with laughter. Camille closed one eye to focus on me and placed the bottle on a table. 'If you're too high and mighty to have a bit of fun with the workers, you'd better get on with your work then, English Miss. *Allez!*' She clapped her hands at me, as if she were the studio manager and I a new start. She turned her back on me as if to dismiss me, and her cronies gathered around to slap her on the back.

I gathered what was left of my dignity, like a beggar woman picking up her ragged skirts, and walked out of the studio. I waited until I was in the street before I allowed my shoulders to drop. I slid down the courtyard wall until I was crouched on my haunches and buried my face in my arms. I had been humiliated. Camille had humiliated me. I lifted my head and wiped away the tears with the heels of my hands. I spoke aloud, oblivious to anyone who might be passing.

'How dare she? That bitch! How could she? After everything I've done for her!'

'Are you all right, dearie?' An old woman leaned over me. 'It can't be that bad, can it?' She patted my shoulder with one hand and I began to cry again. I heard a rustling and with a start of fury, realised she was rummaging through my satchel, which had fallen open beside me. The old cow was trying to steal from me.

'*Va t'en!*' I screamed in her face and she started back. I got to my feet and she scurried off. I searched for the vilest words I knew in both English and French and hurled them at her until she'd rounded the corner.

Camille came to breakfast the next day clutching her head. I stiffened when I saw her but she didn't seem to notice and came barrelling over to embrace me, as if nothing had happened. She clearly had no recollection of what she'd put me through. I didn't return her embrace; I was growing tired of dealing with her outbursts. I didn't know where they came from, these unpredictable scenes. I was beginning to wonder if she were a secret drinker – I'd already seen some artists succumb to the grip of drink and become tiresome to be around – but my suspicions only masked a more terrifying prospect: that Camille may have been losing her mind.

She smiled at me and I looked away from her. 'What's the matter, Jessie, I thought you'd be more pleased to see me?'

'I saw you, yesterday afternoon. You were with the *practiciens*.'

Camille rubbed her temples. '*Sang bleu!* That swine Rodolphe got me drunk and I can't remember a thing. Did you come to the studio? Remind me never to drink with those apes again.' She took my arm and leaned her head on my shoulder. 'I missed you so much, *ma petite anglaise*. Don't leave me alone again.'

My anger began to drain away. Camille had given me an excuse to forgive her and I grabbed it. The alternative was too desolate to contemplate.

CHAPTER 39

Paris

April 1887

In the end, it was money that came between us and cast a shadow over the last three months I spent in Paris.

It all came to a head in April, when the city is at its most breathtaking. I'd hardly seen Camille since my return. She taken to sleeping in our studio and would leave early in the morning and come back late. Rodin had indeed promoted her to *practicien* and the hours were punishingly long. As for me, the studio manager, Jules Desbois, thanked me for my work on the draperies for *The Burghers*, which were now complete. I was no longer needed.

I kept to our studio where Emily Fawcett became my daily companion. We worked quietly and diligently, breaking for tea in the morning and bread and cheese at midday. She was a pleasant companion, but it wasn't the same. The only sign of Camille was a trestle bed in the corner and a small trunk. Sometimes there would be a couple of dirty glasses or a discarded chemise lying on the floor in the morning. She was obviously still deeply involved with Rodin. I was always careful to tidy up the evidence of their trysts before Emily arrived. It was hard to give up the habit of covering for the lovers and I missed the role of go-between after having found it irksome.

Of Rodin there was no sign. My father had written a cheque for his tutoring fees after a whispered argument with my mother, who had sighed heavily as she placed it in an envelope for the post. I'd been back in Paris a month and had still received no tuition from our *maître*. I was complaining about the situation to Emily one day after I'd sent a note to Rodin asking when he would resume his tuition. I'd waited a fortnight, but he hadn't bothered to reply.

'It's really too bad,' I said. 'What's the point of being here if we are to learn nothing?'

Emily made a wry face. 'I'm afraid our role is to provide a convenient fee for the *maître*, and a free studio for Camille.'

'What do you mean? Camille pays her share.'

'No she doesn't. Look, I'll show you.' Emily fetched a large black book from inside the tea chest we used as a table. 'I found this the other day. It's a ledger with the payments to the landlord. See, here's the total rent – I pay nearly half of that.'

I took the book from her and ran my finger down the page. 'And I the other half.'

'You see, Camille pays next to nothing.'

It's strange how you can put up with so much – the tantrum in Peterborough when I'd sung for Rodin, the cold shoulder when she'd taken up with Florence, my humiliation in front of the *practiciens* – but a relatively trivial matter can tip you into fury. Camille was cheating me. What else had she done? I recalled a sarcastic letter I'd received from her just before my return to Paris. I'd queried a foundry bill she'd sent me for one of my busts. It had seemed excessive and I was conscious of my parents' financial plight. There was even talk of putting Wootton House up for rent. I hated to see my parents so worried and was trying to make economies where I could. I had begun, for the first time, to scrutinise the bills coming from France. Camille's reply was highly indignant and I'd dropped the subject, embarrassed. Now I was convinced the foundry bill had been padded.

I looked again at the ledger. The figures in black ink told their own story. Camille had made remarks about my family's wealth, and the cost of my clothes. Did she take me for a fool – a rich fool?

I slammed the book shut. 'Right, that's it; I'm going to ask Camille for a large reduction in rent. I'll put it in writing so she knows I mean business.'

Emily's eyes grew wide, but she nodded. 'I think that would be best.'

A few days later I found my letter to Camille torn to shreds and scattered on the studio floor around her makeshift bed.

I also wrote to Rodin and this time he did reply, but it was infuriating. He ignored my complaint, asked if I'd seen Camille and begged me to bring her to his studio with Emily and he would give the three of us tuition. I assumed Camille and Rodin had had one of their tiffs and he was using our lesson as a pretext to see her again. I wrote back to say I would come with Emily. In the meantime, quite by chance, I discovered the reason Rodin had neglected his teaching duties.

It was the end of a long day at the studio in rue Notre-Dame-des-Champs. Another interminable evening at the Claudel apartment stretched before me, listening with one ear to Louise playing the piano and with the other to Madame Claudel's complaints. I missed Camille. I hadn't realised how much of my time was taken up with her and I hadn't been able to fill the gap she'd left, even if I'd wanted to: Rosa was busy with a new commission and Georges was at his parents' house in the country. It was just as well he was out of town – without Camille or Rosa as chaperone, I wouldn't have been able to see him on my own. And if I did see him alone, and if Madame Claudel found out, I would be sent home on the next train. I was lonely.

I dawdled along the pavement that evening and passed a café. I was looking wistfully at the people chatting when I heard my name called.

'*Hein*, Jessie! Over here!' Suzanne Valadon and Toulouse-Lautrec were waving wildly from a far table.

My heart lifted to see them and I hurried to their table. I bent to kiss Suzanne and smiled at Henri, who unscrewed the silver top of his cane and poured me a brandy.

He spoke to me in his heavily accented English: 'Why so glum, my little English plum? Do you see how I make this clever rhyme? My vocabulary has improved wonderfully since we last met, don't you agree?' He bent closer to me and lowered his voice. 'I have been sleeping with a prostitute from Leeds – most educational.'

I could have hugged myself; it was bliss to be in this kind of company again. But Suzanne looked put out.

'French, please, Henri. Are you boasting about your adventures with tarts again? Do you think I'm stupid? The word is not so different in English. I'm sure Jessie doesn't want to hear your dirty little confidences, she is a respectable young woman, *après tout.*' She raised an eyebrow and caught me taking a large swig of brandy; I couldn't help laughing. 'An English lady with cognac coming out of her nose,' she said. 'Henri, give her your handkerchief.'

Suzanne leaned her arms on the table, revealing the snowy tops of her breasts in all their splendour. A man walking past whistled and she treated him to one of her dimpled smiles. She turned her attention back to me, all business again.

'I need a favour.'

'What kind of favour?' I said.

'Will you put in a good word for me with Rodin? I've been begging him for classes all winter. I've promised to model for him – even doing those sexy poses he likes, you know, with other girls – but he says he can't.'

'Did he say why?' It was unlike Rodin to turn down such a blatant offer from someone as desirable as Suzanne.

She banged down her glass. 'That *salope*, Camille, that's why.'

I frowned. 'Camille? What has she to do with it?'

'He's under contract to her, he says.'

'What do you mean?'

'It's so absurd, I can barely tell you. I thought you'd know all about it.'

I shook my head. I didn't want to admit I had hardly seen Camille, and that when I did she was off-hand, making it clear she was in a rush to be somewhere – or with someone – more interesting.

'Camille has forced Rodin to sign some stupid piece of paper that forbids him from teaching anyone apart from her,' Suzanne said. 'I can't even get to him under the pretext of modelling for him. This stupid contract also says he must employ models only if she approves them first. Can you see Camille approving me?' Suzanne had a point – she and Camille had never liked each other. 'In return the little trollop has agreed to "visit" Rodin so many times a month.' Suzanne snorted. 'Open her legs, more like.'

It took me a while to understand what Suzanne had just told me. But when I finally did, it explained why Rodin had not been to our studio lately, and perhaps why I had been effectively dismissed from his studio, why my letters asking for the tuition I had paid for went unanswered. Camille had gone too far this time.

'This is outrageous,' I said.

She shrugged and ground out her cigarette on her plate. 'You should talk to Rodin; he's always liked you and he'll listen to you,' Suzanne said.

Henri reached across the table and picked up my hand. 'Perhaps you would accept me as your new tutor. I could teach you all manner of interesting *techniques*.'

I shook my head and smiled at him. It was impossible to take offence at Henri; he was one of those people who could say the most outrageous things and get away with it.

'Henri,' I said. 'You'd make an excellent *maître*. If only I were a painter!' I gathered up my things and said to Suzanne, 'I find it hard to believe this contract really exists. Are you sure?'

'Rodin himself showed it to me,' Suzanne said. 'It's all written down. He even had to sign it. You should ask Camille about it; maybe even give her a few home truths. It's about time she was taken down a peg or two. She's getting too big for her boots, the way she queens around the salons these days with Rodin. He's started taking her out to dinners and exhibitions with him; they don't care who knows about their affair. It doesn't bother me, that sort of thing, but what gets me is Camille thinks she is better than me. After all, she is just another model sleeping with an artist.'

I hurried away. I had a lot to think about. Thanks to Camille, Rodin clearly had no intention of honouring his commitment to teach me or anyone else. Suzanne was wrong: I had no influence over Rodin. He listened only to Camille. I would have to speak to her and make her release him from this absurd contract. It was the least she could do for me.

CHAPTER 40

'Get out! And never come back, do you hear me? I never want to see you again!'

The studio door slammed behind me and I stumbled down the stairs. All the way down I could hear Camille raving and the sound of crashing. I burst out of the doors into the street just as a plaster sculpture smashed at my feet. I looked up and saw Camille hanging out of the window. I fled from rue Notre-Dame-des-Champs, the street I'd come to love so much and that would now forever remind me of this terrible fight with Camille. I stumbled on a café – the one where I'd met Henri and Suzanne – and sank down onto a chair and asked for an *eau de vie*. My hand shook as I lifted the glass to my lips, not from sorrow but with rage. Camille had turned the tables on me when I'd gone to speak to her about studio fees and this ridiculous contract she'd made Rodin sign. I had gone to the studio early, at dawn, to catch Camille. I waited outside until Rodin had left and went up to confront her. She'd listened in silence while I put forward what I thought was a reasoned argument. I was careful to keep my temper and be the adult to her spoilt child. When I'd finished she looked at me with a pitying smile.

'Jessie, you are not yourself, to come out with these fantastical accusations – what an imagination you have! I forgive you.'

'*You* forgive *me*?' My calm was beginning to evaporate.

'*Ah, oui, toi!*' She gave a little chuckle. 'Of course, I understand, Jessie. You've had a quarrel with Georges, no doubt. I knew he'd been in the country mooching off his parents again, but I heard he's back in town.' She picked up a carving tool and began to work. 'You'll know by now of course that he hasn't a *sou*.'

'What are you talking about?'

Camille turned back to me, her expression innocent. 'Hasn't he told you? Ah, that's too bad. I hope Georges hasn't been taking advantage of your trusting nature. *Tu êtes une petite ingénue, toi.*'

I had been about to lose my temper, but my anger had been snuffed out. A cold gust of wind came through the open window and made me shiver.

I sat down, suddenly weary. 'What do you mean, Camille?'

She took out a cigarette, made me wait while she lit it and took a drag.

'Camille!'

'Very well, I didn't want to say anything before, but it's about time you found out the truth. It's my duty, as your friend, to tell you that Georges is interested only in your money.'

A cold worm turned in my stomach. 'That's ridiculous!'

Camille picked a strand of tobacco off her tongue. 'Is it? You know the Duchamps don't have a pot to piss in? No, perhaps you don't, but all Paris does, you poor thing.'

I was dumbfounded. 'But he lives so extravagantly – his clothes, the gold cigarette case, the endless cabs, the restaurants.'

'He spends his small allowance as soon as he gets it and borrows the rest. Half the moneylenders in Paris know his address.'

I searched my mind for any clues that Georges was a fortune hunter but came up with a blank. And while I had never hidden my background, I couldn't remember telling him that Papa had become a rich man by investing in the coal exchange just at the right time. Georges and I, we talked about art, about our work. We had never talked about money. Certainly, Papa was generous to me and I never wanted for clothes, furs and jewellery, but in Paris I'd learned to dress more simply. Camille must be mistaken, or worse, spinning a malicious lie.

I stood up and faced her. 'Let me get this right, you think Georges, your friend and mine, is only interested in me because my parents are wealthy? That's absurd. How could he possibly know that?'

She shrugged her shoulders in that French way I'd once found so charming and now despised for its casual disregard of the other person's feelings.

'I told him,' she said.

'Why? Why would you talk about that?'

'Because he asked me. I told him your father was as rich as Croesus. You know Georges, he likes fine clothes. He has no money but he's always been good at sniffing it out. Look at you, in your Worth dress and furs. It doesn't take a genius to see you're rich.' She looked at me carefully. 'You're not upset are you?' Her laugher had a metallic ring. 'Now, don't be angry with Georges. Did you think he was blind to the advantages your wealth would bring him – the freedom to do as he wants? Come now, don't be such an innocent, you're worse than the *grisettes*.'

'But the drawing with the note, all the love letters he sent me in England.'

Camille waved her cigarette in the air. 'Of course, he *thinks* he loves you. Georges is a scoundrel but he is a romantic one. *Après tout*, he is a French man. He has convinced himself he is in love. He loves you, in his way. But he is incapable of putting his own interests to one side. Not like William, he's a true English gentleman. But you let him get away. If you'd been clever, you would have hung on to him, and if you'd been a French woman, you would have had both of them.'

Camille walked over to me and pinched my chin, the way I remembered her doing to the maid the first day we met. 'Dry your tears. I tell you this only because I love you. I'm glad we are friends again. Now, forget all this silly nonsense. We all share the same rent.'

That's when I went to the tea chest and pulled out the ledger, silently pointed to the figures that told their own story. And that's when she flew into a rage. She threw accusations at me like missiles: I was a viper in her bosom, I had stolen ideas from her, I wanted to steal Rodin from her, I didn't have a shred of real talent, I should marry William and have his brats because that's all I was good for.

It was like a typhoon ripping through me. When she came at me with her hands clawing I knew I had to get away from her. In the relative safety of the café, I took another gulp of *eau de vie* but it didn't do any good. I lay my head on the table and began to cry. People were staring at me, but I couldn't stop. Camille hated me: she must to make up such lies about Georges. I dried my eyes. Georges. She said he was in Paris. I needed to see him. I would go by myself, without a chaperone.

CHAPTER 41

'Jessie!' Georges was in his shirtsleeves when he opened the door to his studio. 'You're alone.' He looked closely at me. 'You've been crying.' He checked the street was empty before he let me in.

It was dark inside, the shutters closed, and there was no sign of Sasha. Georges saw me looking at the bed with its bearskin counterpane.

'Don't worry, he's out.'

We sat down together and I told him about Camille's outbursts in England, about her coldness towards me, and about the contract she had made Rodin sign. When I finished, I put my head in my hands and wailed.

'I've lost my *maître*, my studio. Why is Camille doing this? She's supposed to be my friend.'

Georges waited for me to calm down. He cleared his throat. 'Camille has changed. In Rodin's studio she struts about with the *practiciens*, holding court while they hang on her every word. They know she is Rodin's favourite and not to be crossed. One word from her and a man could find himself without a job.' He took out his cigarette case and offered it to me. I noticed the gilt had worn off. He struck a match and held it out. I leaned towards his hand, cupped it with mine.

'I looked for you in the studio when I came back from the country,' he said. 'But they said you didn't work there any more. Is it because of me, Jessie? Are you trying to avoid me?'

I shook my head. 'Jules says I'm not needed now *The Burghers of Calais* is finished,' I said.

'But you were also working on *The Gates of Hell*, which is never going to be finished, the way Rodin changes his mind.' He thought for a while. 'Camille must be behind this, she's frozen you out. The power has gone to her head. She grows more reckless every day, in her affair with Rodin.' I started and he smiled. 'You think I didn't know?'

'I thought you might have guessed. But I wasn't sure.'

'I've always known. And now so do many others. They don't bother to hide it any more. It's common knowledge in our circle that Camille is Rodin's mistress and it won't be long before it's all over Paris.' He ground the end of his cigarette beneath his heel, leaving a black smear on the bare floorboards. 'Camille ought to take care. What is amusing in the Latin Quarter becomes a scandal in *le faubourg* Saint-Germain. The critics, the art gallery owners, the ministers who commission artists, they like to think of themselves as respectable, and their wives love nothing better than to judge a women like Camille. She'll never get a commission. And once her family find out – as they inevitably will – they'll turn their backs on her. She'll be finished.'

Georges was right, Camille was flouting every rule that bound women of our class. I remembered my Ma's words of warning and went cold. 'I have to do something.'

He stroked my cheek and I leaned into his warm palm. 'Loyal Jessie! You still love her after everything. But there's nothing you can do. She's like a woman possessed. I know her. When she gets in these moods she doesn't listen to anyone. My advice? Forget about Camille. You don't need her, you have me.' His eyes gleamed in the darkness and he pulled me back onto the bed.

His lips were warm, his tongue teasing. I did not resist his kiss and allowed myself to sink back against the bearskin as he pressed against me. There was a rustling and his hand was under my skirts, moving up my thigh, pushing aside the thin cotton.

I wrenched my mouth from his. My voice was unsteady. 'No, Georges, I can't, not now.'

He groaned. 'I can't stop. I want you.' His hand worked its way higher until I sighed and moved against him. He kissed me again, his tongue deeper, his other hand slipping the buttons down the front of my dress out of their loops. He stopped and laughed softly. 'It's like breaking into the *Banque de France*.' He kissed the top of my breasts, then pulled down my chemise and began to lick and suck at my nipples. I put my hands on his head and pulled him closer. He lifted up my skirts and ducked between my legs. I felt his lips brush the inside of my thighs, his tongue darting, and suddenly his hot mouth was there, licking and licking until I closed my eyes and arched my back, forgetting everything, the pleasure blacking out any thoughts of Camille.

Georges helped me with my buttons. 'You know of course that I'll have to marry you now.' He stopped and took my face in his hands to kiss me again. My mouth felt bruised but I didn't care.

The fog in my mind began to clear. I put my hand against his chest. 'Are you serious?'

He looked at me steadily. 'Never more so.'

'Even if I could do that to –' I couldn't bring myself to say William's name. 'It would be difficult for us.'

He nipped the soft pad under my thumb with his teeth. 'Why?'

I sat up and smoothed down my skirts. 'There are practical matters to consider.'

He sighed and I heard the snap of his cigarette case. 'Practical. I hate practical.' The flare from the match lit up his face and I caught sight of his beautiful mouth for a second before we were once again in the dark.

'Well, there's the matter of a settlement,' I said. 'If we were to marry we would be penniless.'

'Of course, your parents will be angry for a while when you break off the engagement, but they'll soon forgive their only daughter. Surely they won't withhold your inheritance?'

'That's just it, Georges, it's what I've been trying to tell you. There isn't any money left. My father made a bad investment and lost his fortune.'

The tip of the cigarette glowed as he drew in the smoke. I waited for him to say it didn't matter, that money, my money, meant nothing to him. That he would take up a profession and his family, with its vineyards and *château*, would help us. The silence stretched.

'Jessie, I can't…don't you see…I need to marry money. I'm not made for poverty.'

I got up and reached for my hat. 'It's true, then, that you are the worst kind of man, a fortune hunter. Camille was right – I have been naive.'

I walked out of the studio. A cab was passing and it wasn't until I was getting into it that Georges called my name. His footsteps rang out behind me as I slammed the door shut. It was only when I heard the horse's hooves pick up speed that I allowed my face to crumple.

CHAPTER 42

I couldn't go back to the Claudels' or my studio, so I fled to Rosa's apartment. She was a well-known figure in Montmartre – all the cabbies knew the woman who dressed as a man, and one took me to where she lived.

A maid led me into a room where a matronly little woman in a black silk dress and lace cap sat embroidering by the fire, a pot of coffee keeping warm at her feet. Her smile was sweet.

'Rosa has told me so much about you.' She held out a small hand to me. 'I'm Nathalie Micas. I'm so happy to meet you at last.' She had a high, flutey voice and her hands fluttered like butterflies as she poured coffee into a tiny porcelain cup. I stood without speaking, too stricken with misery and shame to do more than stare into the hearth at the crackling logs. Without asking me, Nathalie added crystals of sugar and a splash of cognac. 'There, drink that and you'll feel better, *chérie*. Come and sit by the fire with me. Rosa won't be long. Just move the otter.'

I looked down at the sofa and what I had taken to be a small dog looked back up at me with unblinking eyes. It opened its blunt whiskered snout and gave an odd little bark, showing sharp teeth. I took a step back.

'Don't worry, Zola is quite harmless, aren't you *mon petit chou*?' Nathalie lifted the otter and sat down with it on her lap. She stroked the gleaming fur and it paddled its webbed paws with pleasure.

I sipped the potent coffee. The cognac began to have its effect and I sagged back into the sofa. I looked glassily around the crowded room. There were stuffed animals on every surface – on the table uncomfortably close to me, a fox fixed me with its beady eyes, a vole dangling limply in its mouth – the walls were crammed with paintings of animals of every sort, domestic, working and wild. I was admiring a fine bronze of a hunting dog when I yelped and nearly dropped my coffee canteen. A pair of claws dug into my shins as a heavy, furred creature pulled itself up onto my knees.

'I see you've met Rimbaud.' Rosa stood in the doorway dressed in an artist's smock, bell-bottom sailor's trousers and labourer's boots. 'Don't worry, he's quite tame, aren't you, *mon petit ange?*'

The lion cub turned its head towards its mistress, its eyes glowing amber in the firelight. I ran my fingers through coarse fur and it began to knead my skirts, opening and closing its paws in ecstasy.

Rosa came into the room, wiping her hands on a rag. 'Welcome, Jessie. I'm sorry I wasn't here to greet you, but I was busy with a dissection.'

'*Putain! Putain! C'est combien? Je suis un bon coup, tu sais!*' A rasping voice shouted and a clatter of feathers landed on my shoulder. The lion cub gave a warning growl and a black bird with a large yellow beak flew up onto the mantelpiece. Lifting a wing, it deposited another streak of white guano onto the marble fire surround.

Rosa bent down and kissed me roughly on the cheek. 'Don't be alarmed. It's only Baudelaire, my impertinent Mynah bird. You must excuse his language, but he can't resist chatting up a pretty face. Baudelaire, mind your manners!' She stroked his back and the bird clucked in its throat. 'He used to belong to a sailor who traded down the coast of Africa, so he speaks French, Swahili and Afrikaans. Don't you, you clever little thing!'

The Mynah bird put its head to one side and opened its beak '*Fokof jou bliksem!*'

'Filthy little beast,' Rosa said. 'And I see you've met my darling Nathalie, the gentlest woman to walk the earth and a damn fine artist. God knows what she sees in me.' She sat down next to Nathalie and put an arm around her. 'Now, you must tell us what is wrong, dearest Jessie.'

'Is it obvious that there is something wrong?'

'Yes. *Allez, raconte-nous.* You know you can tell us anything.'

I pulled at the ears of the lion cub, which had fallen asleep, and told them everything from the start: how Georges had tricked me into thinking William had been unfaithful, how William had left me after finding Georges' portrait and note. I couldn't bear to tell them yet about what I'd just done with Georges, so I told them about Camille first. When I had finished, I was trembling with anger once more.

Rosa put her head to one side, as if considering a mathematical problem. 'Camille is drunk on love and professional success. That's a powerful mixture and enough to turn any artist's head. But she's a damned fool to shun her friends. You're not the first she's behaved badly towards – lately she's been casting us off, one by one. The little upstart even tried to snub me at a dinner for Puvis de Chavannes, but I put her in her place. Nobody snubs La Bonheur.'

I leaned forward and the lion cub grunted. 'Won't you talk to her, Rosa? She seems to think I'm some sort of threat to her.'

'I could try, but I doubt she'll listen. As you know, Camille's stubborn and always, always thinks she's right.' Rosa ran a hand through her hair, which was cut short like a choirboy's. 'I'm worried about her – there's a lot of talk about her, and none of it flattering. This business with Rodin won't do her reputation as an artist any good. The best she can hope for is that he marries her and she becomes respectable in the eyes of society, but men like him are not easily yoked. And there is the matter of Rose Beuret – Rodin will never leave her.'

'But, he doesn't love her,' I said. I couldn't believe that after all Camille had said to me and put me through, my first instinct was still to spring to her defence.

'How do you know?' Rosa said. 'Rodin's comfortable with La Beuret. And she was a great beauty in our day – we all longed to sleep with her.' She smiled at me. 'Yes, even me – especially me. No, Rodin won't leave his first love. When you get to our age, young lovers are a delightful pastime, but in the end exhausting. What you want is someone who has known you in your youth – and still sees you as the young person you once were.'

Rosa smiled at Nathalie and kissed her tenderly. I thought about the warmth of Camille's breath on my neck in the cave at *La Hottée du Diable*, the softness of her mouth when we kissed before the Madwomen's Ball, and wondered what it would be like to live like this with Camille, as a couple; to sit side by side in the twilight of our days in a room full of our sculptures, after a long life of work, unfettered by the demands of men and children.

I shook my head as if it still held wisps of fog from the Villeneuve moors. 'Surely, you live as you choose with Nathalie,' I said, my voice rising. 'You don't care about respectability or about what society says; why should Camille and Rodin?'

Nathalie had been listening quietly, but spoke up now in her clear, high voice. 'Rosa and I can live in peace the way we do only because we have our own money, and we earn plenty more by making conventional art that people want to buy – the kind of art that some of your friends might sneer at, I suspect.'

She was right: Georges or Henri and the rest of the Montmartre crowd would hoot with laughter at the realistic scenes of hunting horses and spotted sows that hung on the walls.

Rosa took up Nathalie's argument where she left off, in the manner of an old married couple. 'You see, Jessie, we are not dependent on anyone. We have no disapproving family breathing down our necks and ready to cut the purse strings. Camille is different entirely from us. Her work is unorthodox – some would say shocking – for a woman, she has no money of her own and is dependent on her family's good will. She desperately needs Rodin's influence to get her commissions. But the little fool is making the classic mistake so many women make – she is pouring all her energy into Rodin's work and giving him her ideas, the little fool. But I don't know why I should feel sorry for her – she's been a bitch to you, Jessie.'

I could feel the heat rising in my face. 'Don't call her that. I love her.' I had been frozen until now; stunned by the blows I'd received in quick succession from Camille and then Georges. But speaking those words out loud broke the dam holding back my pain. I began to cry in earnest for all that I had lost: first William, then Camille and now Georges. Alarmed, the lion cub jumped off my lap. Nathalie and Rosa came to my side, put their arms around me and rocked me. In the shelter of their embrace, I closed my eyes and told them my secret – about Georges and what I had done with him and how he had dropped me when he found out I would have no fortune and was of no use to him.

'My poor darling,' Rosa said. 'Didn't I warn you about them? Those wild animals! And now they have hurt you.'

'I'm so alone,' I said between sobs that tore at my throat.

'You are not alone,' Rosa said. 'You must stay with us. I'll send word to the Claudels – Louis-Prosper knows me. We will look after you.'

I don't know why they call it heartbreak, it feels more like your heart has become too big for your chest, so swollen with pain it nearly chokes you. The curse of a childhood like mine is that it doesn't prepare you for being hurt. I had always expected to be loved and didn't know – not really – that love could be taken away. And when you're young, you think you'll never get over it, never laugh or love or be happy again, but of course you do, and that makes me sadder than it should. Time heals, so they say, but losing Camille and Georges, it changed me, made me less brave.

In the days after it happened, I couldn't work or eat; even sleep was a false friend. In my dreams, Camille was the Camille I'd first met, laughing as we shared a cigarette, scowling in concentration as we sculpted, her beautiful face clearing when she looked up at me. I would wake happy, only to remember all over again that Camille had destroyed our friendship, and that Georges had made the worst kind of fool out of me. The wounds would open again and my helpless sobs would bring Nathalie to my side with cold cloths and laudanum-laced tinctures. The animals seemed to sense my pain. The lion cub took to sleeping next to me on the bed Nathalie had made up in the corner of the parlour: my nest they called it. At night, the cub stretched out next to me, its breathing a hot rasp against my neck. When the tears came it would sit up on its haunches and lick the brine from my face, its rough cat tongue tangling in my hair. During the day, the otter tumbled and played at the foot of the bed, nipping my toes through the counterpane and kicking at them with his hind legs. The Mynah bird kept a respect-ful distance, rumbling and whistling.

Rosa was stroking my forehead one evening as the tears ran down my face unchecked and wet my ears. 'I know it is hard to believe now, Jessie, but the pain will ease with time. You will think of them less and less and then one day you will realise you can't remember what they look like.'

'I can't forget Camille. I keep going over it again and again. I don't know what I did to her, to make her turn against me. Did our friendship mean nothing to her? I would never have thrown it away so lightly. I don't understand why she has done this to me. If only I knew why, I would have some peace.'

Rosa handed me a small bottle. 'Drink this and sleep now.'

I fell back against the pillows. As the laudanum fog rolled through my mind, I felt the bed shift. Rosa stood and through half-closed eyes I saw Nathalie beckon her from the door.

'Is she asleep, Marie-Rose?' Nathalie said.

'Yes, *la pauvre*. Dreaming of that she-wolf, no doubt. What is it?'

'Georges Duchamp is here. He wants to see Jessie.'

Suddenly I was wide awake.

Rosa sighed. 'He'd better not see her like this. Help me put the screen around her then we'll hear what Monsieur Duchamp has to say for himself.'

When the screen was in place I sat up carefully in bed so as not to make a noise and looked through the space between the hinges. Georges came in and sat by the fire. He put his face in his hands and a lock of his hair fell forward. He was unshaved and his jacket was rumpled. Nathalie disappeared, leaving Rosa standing before him, her arms folded.

'So, Duchamp,' she said. 'What brings you here?'

'It's Jessie. I'm afraid I haven't behaved well.'

Rosa snorted. 'Really? You surprise me! There's not a work-ing girl in Montmartre or a countess in *le faubourg* Saint-Germain whose heart you haven't broken with your empty promises. It's just as well Jessie is made of sterner stuff.'

246

He stood up and grasped Rosa by the arms. 'Have you seen her? I've been looking for her everywhere. Is she here?' He looked around the room and I instinctively drew back from the screen.

Rosa shook him off. 'She's come to visit for a few days, yes, but she's out for a walk just now with some friends. What is it you want from her, Georges?'

'What friends? Who is she with?' He sat down again and covered his eyes. 'This is absurd. What's wrong with me?' He leaned forward and took Rosa's hands and pulled her down to the sofa. 'Rosa, *je t'en prie*, you must persuade Jessie to see me. She'll listen to you.'

'Don't be ridiculous. Jessie is her own woman. She doesn't want to see you, and I don't blame her, quite frankly.'

'She told you what happened?'

'Yes, she told me everything. Nice work, Duchamp.'

He groaned. 'You must understand I was taken by surprise when she told me about her family's situation. I assumed she was rich – the clothes, the hats, the grand house in England, the way she talks and dresses. I can tell these things.'

'Yes, you are quite the connoisseur of wealthy young women.'

'It's not my fault. My father, the bastard, squandered most of my inheritance on cards and his mistresses; he brought me up to have the tastes of a gentleman, but left me with the income of a clerk. The money – what's left of it – is running out and in a few years, I'll be penniless. It's true that Jessie's fortune drew me to her at first, but then I fell in love with her.'

I clutched at the quilt.

Georges rubbed his eyes. 'If Jessie will have me, we can live together in my studio, working as equals. Damn the money.'

'Really?' Rosa said. 'In that squalid little studio with your crazy Russian friend? And what will you live on?'

'Art and love.'

Rosa laughed. 'Oh that's a good one. I haven't laughed so much in years. Art and love! I can see it now – Jessie freezing in the winter in that hovel of a studio. How long before her looks fade with poverty and pregnancies and you go looking for excitement? And no talk of marrying her, I see. Art and love! Pah!' She spat into the fire and the coals sizzled.

Georges stood up and put his hands in his pockets. He looked like a sulky schoolboy being told off by the head beak. 'Suzanne Valadon is not married,' he said. 'She's a free spirit, a modern woman with a child out of wedlock, and she has survived.'

'Her mother looks after the boy,' Rosa said. 'And La Valadon comes from the streets, she knows how to survive. Jessie isn't like that, she'd be ruined and eventually you'd leave her. Is that what you want for her?'

The Mynah bird called out: '*Crétin! Crétin! Va t'en!*'

Georges jumped and when he saw the bird behind his shoulder, laughed for the first time. The familiar curl of his mouth sent a shaft of pain through me.

'Even your animals conspire against me,' he said. 'You're right, of course. I'm being selfish about Jessie.'

Rosa stood up to poke more life into the fire. 'Yes you are. You are a handsome, amusing, selfish bastard, and Jessie will get over you, but only if you leave her alone.' She sighed. 'You and Camille have behaved very badly towards her.'

'You have spoken to Camille – since the girls quarrelled?'

She nodded and I wriggled nearer the screen and knocked my knee against it. Georges turned his head sharply towards me and I held my breath.

'What was that?' he said.

'Rimbaud or Zola. They are always playing hide and seek together in that corner.'

'Why you cannot keep poodles like any other Parisian *grande dame*, I will never know.'

'Where would be the fun in that?'

Georges put his hands in his pockets. 'Won't you give me a drink, Rosa?'

When she'd poured them both a brandy, Rosa said, 'Camille wouldn't listen to me, of course, when I told her she was a fool to turn her back on Jessie, that she needed a friend like her. I pointed out the whole of Paris was gossiping about her and Rodin, but she started screaming like a fishwife and ranting about a conspiracy. It would appear we are all in this conspiracy together, most of all Jessie, whom she calls *a viper she nurtured in her bosom*, and some other, choicer names I don't care to repeat. *Enfin*, she believes that Jessie wants to take over the running of her studio and is turning the models against her, complains that she's been teaching her own students.'

It's true I had been tutoring young English girls to stretch out my allowance after Papa had been forced to reduce it, but where was the harm in that? If I had hoped to find out why Camille had turned against me, I was none the wiser. Her accusations still didn't make sense.

Georges echoed my thoughts. 'Why shouldn't Jessie take in students? I do it myself when I'm hard up – if they're pretty enough. And what does Camille mean by a conspiracy?'

'I have no idea, *c'est complètement fou*. It's all in her mind, of course. The important thing is that Camille believes Jessie is her enemy and won't be persuaded otherwise. There's nothing more I can do.'

Georges stood up. 'And, I suppose there is nothing more that I can do. About Jessie I mean.'

'No, there isn't.'

'Will you give her my love?'

'It would be kinder not to.'

And he was gone.

I sank back on the pillows and tried to make sense of what I'd learned. I had lost William because of Georges, but now that Georges wanted to be with me, money or no money, I didn't want him. He had shown his true colours when I needed him most and taken what he should not have. William would never have behaved like that, and I had thrown the chance of a life with him away because my head had been turned. There was nothing left for me in Paris, not without Camille, or Georges. And professionally I was wasting my time. Without Rodin as a mentor, without even a studio, what was I doing here? My chest hurt as if I were lying under a boulder. If only William were here – he alone had the power to lift this burden from me. But it was too late, I had lost him. I buried my face in the pillow and began to cry again.

Rosa folded back the screen. She whispered, 'Jessie, are you awake?'

'Yes.'

'Then, you heard everything?'

I sat up and wiped my eyes. 'Yes, I heard.'

She sat beside me and I leaned against her. She patted my shoulder and kissed my forehead. 'I am going away for a few days. But Nathalie will look after you while I'm gone.'

The blossom dusting the trees in the Tuileries looked so like candy floss that I wanted to put out my tongue and taste it. Nathalie had bullied me in her gentle way to get out of bed that morning. She had bathed me like a child with a sea sponge in a copper bath in front of the fire. I had not wanted to eat but she tempted me with hot chocolate and a brioche in a little café in the park. We sat in the spring sun and watched some children ride past on hired ponies. One tubby little boy kept pulling at the reins until his mount bucked. He slipped from the saddle, grabbed its mane and dangled there while the pony bent to chew some grass. There was a great scolding and fussing from his nanny and I found myself laughing. The heaviness in my chest shifted and I thought: I could be happy again in Paris, on a day like today. That's when I saw Camille.

She was with Rodin and they were coming from the Louvre. They were talking, her face animated as he laughed at something she said. I watched them approach and resolved I would speak to her. As they drew near, Camille must have sensed she was being watched because she turned her head towards me. I lifted my hand in greeting, but her expression froze and she looked away too quickly, as if she had not seen me. But of course, she had. How could she not? She pulled at Rodin's sleeve and I saw her lips move: *Let's go.* Rodin looked over at me from under the brim of his hat. He shrugged his shoulders as if to say *What can I do?* Camille dragged on his arm and they turned round and walked back towards the Louvre. Camille was moving fast, as if she could not get away from me soon enough.

Did she imagine I might make a scene? Shout at her or claw at her face like a drunken streetwalker? It was as if I had been slapped. I sat there enraged, helpless. Perhaps she was right to hurry away: I had an urge to run after her, pull her around to face me and shake her by the shoulders. Had it come to this – that she could not bring herself to exchange a few civil words in a public park? I clenched my fists. She *would* speak to me. I stood up as if to follow them, but Nathalie put her hand on my arm. I sat down and craned my neck to see if Camille would look back at me. She didn't. I watched her walk out of my life. I didn't know then, but it was the last time I would see her for more than forty years.

On the walk back, I was gripped first by fury then by a sort of empty despair. There was nothing for me left in Paris but I could not go home to Peterborough where I would be reminded daily of William. He would meet someone else, no doubt, and I would have to smile when his sisters broke the news of an engagement. I had been a fool, such a fool. I was too busy imagining my bleak future to look where I was going and a cab nearly ran me over as I crossed the road to Rosa's apartment. The horse shied clear of me just in time but I slipped, catching my heel, and fell with a sickening jar. Shaken, I felt a man's hand pull me to my feet. I brushed the dust and horse dung from my dress and turned to thank the Good Samaritan.

'Hello, Jess.'

It was William. He looked thinner and there were dark shadows under his eyes. But it was William, my William.

'I've come to bring you home, darling. Oh, Jessie, I've been such a fool. Can you forgive me?'

I sagged at the knees and he caught me in his arms and kissed me.

I had been saved and it was Rosa I had to thank. She had gone to England and found William.

'It wasn't difficult,' she told me later. 'I have contacts. I told him I had a confession to make, that it was I who had drawn that portrait of you and written that note. That I had plied you with drink one night at my studio and tried to seduce you, as I do with all my pretty young artist friends. But you turned me down in the most gracious way, that we remained friends and that you kept the portrait as a mark of our friendship.'

I turned the emerald ring around on my finger. 'And he believed you?'

'Of course. He loves you, Jessie.'

'I don't know how to thank you Rosa.'

'There is a way. You must promise me something.'

'Anything.'

'You will never tell him the truth about Georges. You owe him that. Do you promise?'

I hung my head. 'Yes, Rosa.' I locked away my shame and kept my promise.

CHAPTER 43

PARIS

1929

Paul had agreed to meet me in Maxim's for dinner so I spent the day walking around Paris, and ended up in rue Notre-Dame-des-Champs. There were now cars in the street and women's skirts and hairstyles were shorter, but otherwise nothing had changed. The noise of hammering still filtered from artists' studios and the smell of fresh bread wafted from the same *boulangerie*. A young concierge opened the double green doors of our old studio and banged a rug against the wall.

'Bonjour, Mademoiselle,' I said.

She smiled and carried on with her work.

'This used to be my studio, a long time ago, when I was your age.'

'*Ah, oui*? I would let you come up and see it, Madame, but it's occupied by a notaire, a respectable man. The landlord refuses to rent to any more artists since the last tenants – a young couple who left the place in a terrible mess. They were Americans, with a little boy. She was of good class and the baby *un vrai bonbon*, but the husband –! A writer, what do you expect? Out all hours drinking – they left the little one with me, *Dieu merci* – and the fights! Bottles smashing, shouting and screaming until the police had to be called. Artists, they are nothing but trouble.'

'*Oui, c'est vrai, ça.*' I said, with a smile.

Paul was late and full of apologies. He was balding and had grown heavy around the waist with a correspondingly ponderous air. His mouth was pinched under a pencil moustache. I'd never have recognised him if it were not for the strong resemblance to his father.

He rose to his feet and kissed my hand. 'Jessie, how marvellous to see you again, you haven't changed at all. I recognised you at once.'

'How kind you are, but I hope I didn't look this old in my twenties.'

'Ah, we are all getting older. You left Paris – when was, it? I had finished *lycée* the year before. *Mon Dieu*, can it be so long? More than forty years ago. Where do the years go? I am sixty-one but in my heart I am still a youth.'

'It's the same for me,' I said. 'Yet we are not the same, everything has changed.'

'*Oui, la Grande Guerre.*'

We were silent a moment, lost in our own memories. The War had shattered all our lives. I was one of the lucky ones. My prayers were answered and my three sons spared. During those terrible years I held my breath every time the postman came to the door. I hadn't wanted to imagine what my sons were going through in a France that had been turned into a muddy battlefield where young men barely out of school were slaughtered.

'It's a different world now, although you wouldn't think so sometimes,' I nodded at the Art Nouveau fantasy with which we were surrounded. Paris of the Belle Époque, with its gilt mirrors and floral curlicues, was alive and well in this restaurant, as if the War had never been.

Over the rich meal, Paul told me what had happened to Camille after I'd left Paris.

He picked up his knife and began working the spine free from his fish. 'I had no idea why you left so suddenly. Camille wouldn't say when I asked her, only that you had to return to England. Next I heard you were married.'

'Yes. I'm not sure whether you met William.'

'No, I'm afraid I didn't have the pleasure, but he is a fortunate man to be married to you, *chère* Jessie. Now that we are older, I can confess that I had rather a crush on you, as the Americans say. You were so kind to me.'

I smiled, remembering Paul at seventeen, so serious, a sensitive boy with delicate features.

He folded and refolded his napkin. Then he told me what I wanted to know.

'After you left, we hardly saw Camille at home. She slept in the studio – the one you shared – or so she said. Then one day, one of Maman's friends told her the gossip. Was she aware that her daughter was Rodin's mistress? That he'd set her up in a semi-ruined château? There were rumours of obscene sketches he'd made of her displayed openly at their wild parties.'

He brushed at some crumbs on the tablecloth and I had the urge to stab his hand with my fork.

'Wild parties? Sounds wonderful,' I said.

Paul looked startled, and then he chuckled, as if he'd decided I must be joking. 'So, you can imagine our mother's reaction.'

'What did she do?'

'Oh, there was a terrible scene,' he said. 'Camille was summoned to the apartment where she admitted it all, without the smallest particle of remorse. If it had been up to Maman, Camille would have been exiled from the family, cut off without a *sou*. She was particularly offended because Camille had tricked her into inviting Rodin and Rose Beuret for lunch in Villeneuve.'

I shook my head. How typical of Madame Claudel to be more concerned about being made to look a fool than by her daughter's affair with an older man. I would go to my grave unable to understand that woman.

Paul said, 'Camille was saved only by Papa. He was pragmatic, said we should set her up in her own studio apartment and give her an allowance. At least that way she would not be seen to be living with Rodin.'

I had wondered how Camille had weathered the storm and marvelled at her ability to survive a social catastrophe that would have ruined a woman with a less indulgent father. I warmed again to Louis-Prosper. For all his sarcasm and affectations, he had protected his gifted daughter from destitution, if not social disgrace.

'Good for him,' I said.

Paul's mouth fell open. 'Do you think so, really? Come now, you yourself are a parent. If he had been a proper father, taken a stronger line, forbidden her to see Rodin again, and kept her at home, it may have saved her from further sin.'

I pushed my plate from me and a waiter took it away with a sorrowful look.

'Why so harsh, Paul? Camille has always loved you. When I visited her in that, that place, she spoke so warmly about you. And you haven't even asked me how she was.'

Paul lowered his voice, as if to guard his family shame from the next table. 'I know exactly how she is: mad, insane, out of her mind.' He threw down his napkin and glared at me. 'You think me unforgiving, intolerant? Who are you to judge me – you don't know the full story, of the depths, the moral abyss, into which Camille sank.' He banged his fist on the table when he said 'abyss' and the cutlery bounced on the tablecloth. The waiter came over but Paul waved him away. 'Bring us coffee and then leave us alone.' He leaned towards me, his eyes blazing. 'Despite being caught out in her sin, she continued to see that adulterer.'

'Hardly an adulterer – Rodin wasn't married.'

'He was in God's eyes. He and Rose Beuret, they had a son.'

I couldn't bear his preaching at me any more; he was like an overheated evangelist. 'Camille was in love. There are worse crimes. For God's sake, Paul, can't you show her some pity?'

He sighed and his shoulders dropped. 'You're right, I'm a hypocrite. In truth, I have come to look at their affair with less condemnation over the years. I myself am not without sin. In China I fell in love with a married woman. I couldn't stay away from her, even when she refused to leave her husband. So, you see, I know only too well the pull of love, and how it can make you behave.'

He looked so miserable and for a moment like the Paul I remembered. I touched him lightly on the back of his hand. 'It's hard to draw away from temptation when you're in love. We've all made mistakes. But you did the right thing in the end – I know you did because you sent me photographs of a wife and children.'

He held my hand. 'Yes, Reine is my salvation – and our five

angels.' His face darkened. 'But there's more, about Camille, that I find hard to accept, that I can't accept, as a Christian. You were right when you say there are worse things.' He passed his hand over his face and looked at me bleakly. 'Like the murder of an innocent child. Ask yourself this: how could anyone live with such a crime upon their conscience?'

I pulled my hand away. 'What are you talking about?'

'One day I went to see Camille and she was sobbing. The studio was a mess, her *maquettes* all smashed. She was tearing her hair and screaming, beside herself. I wanted to fetch the doctor but she begged me not to. She was going to have a baby, Rodin's baby. But he would not leave Rose Beuret, even though he'd fathered a bastard child on my sister.'

I imagined Rodin's horror at the thought of his dream in stone growing heavy with child. He wouldn't be the first artist to shudder at the prospect of his muse turning into a tired, blowsy mother. When the waiter came back to the table, I asked for cigarettes. I hadn't smoked since I'd left Rosa's apartment all those years ago. The dining room was nearly empty and the waiters were putting new linen out and polishing glasses. Paul waited until my cigarette had been lit before he began again.

'Rodin wanted her to get rid of the baby. I asked her if she was going to do it. Do you know what she said to me? *I have no choice.* I tried to reason with her, told her we always have a choice. God gave us free will to choose between good and evil and now he was calling on her to do the right thing. Do you know what she did? She laughed in my face. *Oh, mon petit Paul, you have cheered me up. What a ridiculous creature you are with your Church and your God.*'

'What happened?' I knew what he was going to say next, and I wasn't sure I wanted to hear it.

He shaded his eyes as if from a bright light, and sighed. 'She'd do anything for Rodin, for art and love. Wasn't that your mantra, then? The two of you used to say it all the time: *Art and Love.*'

I ignored him and tried to imagine what Camille must have gone through: the searing pain, the fever and loss of blood afterwards. The models in Rodin's studio talked of sharp wires and bitter potions swallowed down or pushed up inside the poor girl who had fallen pregnant, the doctor who would 'take care of it' for the right fee. Poor Camille.

'It's hard to contemplate having a baby alone,' I said. 'It must have been awful for her – a terribly difficult decision.'

'What about the child she killed?' His voice had risen and the waiter hurried over. Paul waved him away, lifted his wine glass with a trembling hand. When he had finished his drink, he seemed more collected. 'Camille was never the same after that. It unbalanced her mind. And in the end, it did her no good with Rodin. When she finally realised he was never going to leave Rose Beuret, Camille left him. It destroyed her career. He destroyed her career. She'd been having a degree of success, but suddenly commissions were cancelled and she blamed Rodin.'

'Was it true? Surely he wouldn't be so vindictive.'

'I wouldn't put it past a man like that to not only ruin my sister but steal her gifts, even though he always claimed he tried to help her and put in a good word for her whenever he could.'

'But you didn't believe him?'

Paul shook his head. 'He crushed her.'

I couldn't accept that Rodin would act in such a way towards Camille, even when their affair was at an end. He was not a cruel man and it was he who called her a genius, *une femme de génie*.

Paul smoothed the tablecloth with his hands. 'Camille started drinking heavily, spent her allowance on wine, and ate out of rubbish bins in the street. She'd go down to the Seine and invite the tramps back to her studio to drink with her. The neighbours complained to the police and Maman sent me to speak to her. She'd boarded up the windows, wedged the door shut. I had to prise it open with a chisel. Inside it stank of cats; there were strays everywhere. The only light was from the fire she was feeding with wax moulds of her work. When I asked her why she was burning them and why the windows were barred, she said *so that son of a whore Rodin won't steal my work*. Her voice was metallic, her body bloated with alcohol. My beautiful sister.' He put his hand on my wrist. 'You have to understand, Jessie, I had to do it. When father died, it fell to me as head of the family to do the right thing.'

I loathed him now, for his hypocrisy, for betraying Camille, burying her alive.

'Don't tell me,' I spat. 'You had no choice.'

He didn't answer, wouldn't look at me. I waited for him to speak, to explain why he had done what he had done. When he spoke, his tone was flat.

'They came for her in the middle of the night. Broke open the boarded-up shutters with crowbars and pulled her out of the window. She was screaming that Rodin and his *bande* were abducting her, that he'd been poisoning her food and stealing her work. They took her away, to a house for the insane.'

'You had no right.'

Paul still would not meet my eyes. 'It was the right thing to do. Camille would have ended up murdered, or worse. What else could I do? I was abroad most of the time, Louise was busy with her own family, and Maman was getting older and couldn't cope.'

'Paul, look at me.'

When he looked up, his face was tormented.

'You did a terrible thing to Camille, you abandoned her.' He flinched but I carried on. 'There's still time to make it right. You have the power to make amends, to release her. I've seen her, she's harmless, a poor creature. If you won't care for Camille, then let me, I'll take her to England, make sure she wants for nothing.'

He looked at me for a long time, and I hoped. Then he dropped his eyes.

'Go home to your family, Jessie, and forget about my sister. I will not sanction this foolish plan. There's nothing you can do for her.'

'Paul, please.'

After he left, I put my head on my arms and started to cry. I had lost Camille all over again. Through bitter tears, I remembered the day I started the search for my old friend.

CHAPTER 44

PETERBOROUGH

1897

'Who is this pretty lady, Mama?'

I did not look up from the bust I was working on of my seven-year-old son. I was concentrating on the tricky business of carving the whorls of his ears.

'Mama!'

I put down my knife and sighed. 'What is it, Sydney?'

When I looked up, Camille stared back at me. Sydney held the bust in both arms. He'd been looking through an old tea chest in the potting shed I still used as my studio and found the portrait I had made of Camille ten years earlier. I took the terracotta head from him and brushed the cobwebs from her face. Her expression was austere, despite the youthfulness of her rounded cheeks. How old would she be now? Thirty-two? I'd kept in touch with Rodin over the years, sent him news of my wedding and the births of my children. Brief, polite letters came back in his illegible hand. Camille never answered my letters and after a while they were returned 'address unknown'.

I had tried to put our broken friendship behind me, but I couldn't forget Camille. When I had my first baby – a little girl with navy blue eyes – I was so full of love and tenderness all traces of anger fell away from me and I was able to forgive Camille. It was as if a shard of pain inside me had melted. As a young mother, in the quiet moments after the children were asleep, I liked to think back to the beginning of our friendship, and to the happiest days of my life. But I hadn't thought of Camille in years. Now I ran my fingers over the clay bust over the contours of her face, and I was filled with regret. I should have fought harder to keep her. I would never meet another friend who would mean as much to me.

'Mama, why are you crying?' Sydney put his small hands on my knees. I pulled him into my arms and covered him with kisses until he squirmed away.

'Mama's a little sad, that's all. I was remembering a girl I used to know – my best friend.'

After William came to fetch me back to England, I has been ill for a long time. I'd caught a chill on the ferry home that turned into pneumonia. For the rest of that summer I lay in my old bed in Wootton House, watching the leaves of the elm tree turn from green to russet. Ma fussed over me but she was too relieved to learn about William's and my engagement; she knew better than to ask too many questions.

At first I wrote to Camille in a fury, dashing accusations across the page, smearing the ink. *How could you treat me so after everything I did for you and Rodin? I thought I knew you. Now I wonder if I ever did.* But I burned those letters. I couldn't face the accusations she would no doubt throw back at me and they would somehow seem more horrible in writing. And I couldn't bear to think of her reading the harsh words in the letters I never sent.

While I burned with fever, I asked myself over and over why she had broken our friendship. How could she just forget about me? Why did she no longer love me as I loved her still? I couldn't bear to think she was carrying on her life in Paris without a thought for me. I wondered what she was doing, where she was going, who she was seeing. I pictured her in Rodin's studio, high up on the scaffold, intent on *The Gates of Hell*, or at *Le Chat Noir*, laughing as Georges sat with a girl on his lap, trading insults with Rosa.

William came often, pressing my hand in his and speaking about mutual friends and exhibitions coming up in London: anything to take my mind off Paris. But like an animal gnawing at a wound, I returned again and again to Camille. As for Georges, I wouldn't let myself think about him.

'I don't know what to do, William. Should I write to her?'

He sighed and looked out at the spreading elm, its branches now almost bare beneath a pewter sky. 'If it would give you peace of mind.'

'And what shall I say? Shall I ask her why she turned on me? Oh, why did she do that, William?' I could hear the whine in my voice and hated myself for it. I held onto my grief as I could not hold onto Camille.

William's sigh betrayed his irritation. I could tell that he was wondering what had happened to his courageous girl.

'There, Jessie, don't fret. You'll only make yourself ill again and you are looking so much stronger.' He got off my bed and stood in front of the fire. 'You've done nothing wrong, Jess. You should write her a civilised letter; show her she hasn't hurt you.'

William helped me write a short note to Camille. Instead of a plea for love and friendship to be restored, the letter was polite and friendly, enquiring after her family and her work. I wrote about our wedding that would take place that December in London. It was to be a big affair as Papa had saved our fortunes after all with a timely investment in paraffin oil, which could now be mined from shale in Scotland. But I didn't tell her about that. Instead, I hoped she was well and added, almost as an afterthought, that I regretted any misunderstanding between us and hoped we could still be friends.

William put the letter in his pocket. 'I'll put it in the afternoon post.' He kissed me on the forehead. 'Forget about Paris. You're home now.'

A week later I received a letter postmarked Paris. My heart lifted when I recognised Rodin's lavish scrawl. It was a strange, rather dear little note wishing William and me well. I wondered if Camille would write too, but day after day arrived with no letter from her and after a time, I became caught up in the preparations for my wedding and tried to put her from my mind.

On our wedding day in London, yellow roses were twined around the pillars and sat in fat bunches at the end of the pews at Great St Helen's. I wore my emerald pendant and ring. William looked so handsome, a yellow rosebud in his buttonhole. He held out his hand to me and I felt as if I had sailed into a safe harbour.

'Jessie. My beautiful Jessie.'

As we walked back down the aisle, there, among my English aunts, uncles and cousins, sat an incongruous figure – Rosa in full morning suit with Natalie on her arm. They seemed unaware of people staring.

'*Salut*, Jessie! We came to make sure William was looking after you.'

A seed of hope burst open inside me and I looked along the pew for Camille. But she had not come. I held onto William's arm a little tighter and he bent his head to mine.

'Everyone who loves you is here, Jessie,' he whispered.

He kissed me and the congregation cheered and clapped.

I smiled at him as Widor's Toccata burst through the church. 'Let's go and drink champagne.' We walked out into the bright, clear morning of our marriage.

William settled into his position at Owen's College in Manchester and I began a new life as the wife of an academic. I tried not to miss Paris and busied myself with hosting tea parties for the other masters and William's students, clever and serious young men who talked in chemical formulae. But while I handed out sherry and fruit cake, my mind would slip back to *Le Chat Noir*, to the studio in Notre-Dame-des-Champs, to Georges and Camille. I had tried to bring Paris into our new home, dressing tables in embroidered shawls, hanging sketches by Henri and Rosa. The little sculpture Rodin had given me sat on the mantelpiece, and it gave me strength during those dry gatherings.

But when I came to bed, after yet another dreary evening stuck in a corner with the rest of the wives, William would take me in his arms and whisper into my hair. The passion of our nights together took me by surprise, bound us tightly together. William had been right: we were of different metals but together we were the perfect compound.

And then there was the wonder of becoming a mother. Helen was born and with her dark blue eyes she reminded me of Camille. She loved to play with my clay and it was no surprise when she became an artist. Had some of Camille's spirit entered my heart and made its way into my child? It was a fanciful notion and one I have never shared with William.

We had three more children, lively sons, and I began to disappear, bit by bit. I tried to keep sculpting, but it was impossible during those early years of motherhood, when my children filled every corner of my life.

When Papa died, Ma was distraught and we moved back into Wootton House with her. Father's estate had been decimated by the recession of the 1890s and I found myself running a large household on a small budget. I taught the children at home to save on school fees and balanced the books.

When the children grew bigger, I went back to sculpting. I made portraits of the children and took on commissions, but it was never the same: my ambition had gone along with my youth. Sculpting the perfect heads of my children in my old potting shed of a studio was what I loved best. And my favourite model was Sydney, my beautiful boy.

The day he found Camille's bust, Sydney was leaning into the tea chest, looking for more treasure.

'Mama, you know how you're good at finding things? Like my wooden horse that was buried in the garden all winter?'

'Yes, darling.'

'Well, why don't you go and find your friend?'

I stopped what I was doing. 'You're right. That's what I'll do.'

But it was years before I found her. I made a few attempts to write to her family but never received a reply. Then war broke out and we were all in turmoil. But I didn't give up and after the war I tracked her down through Paul. A friend of ours in the Foreign Office mentioned he was working in the French Embassy in Copenhagen. *Chap's a poet, quite famous it would seem.* Paul's reply came back months later: Camille had been ill for years and was in hospital in the south. He thanked me for my kindness. I wrote again asking for details but he had moved. For years my letters went unanswered, until a postcard came one morning. My letters had been lost and had only just turned up. Paul was the French Ambassador by now in Washington, but writing was still his passion. Had I perhaps seen any of his plays on the stage? He enclosed photographs of himself outside the White House and said he remembered me fondly. His poor sister Camille was still in the same situation. I wrote by return of post. Where was Camille? Could I write to her? William and I were travelling to Italy by train and we would pass through the south of France. Could I perhaps visit her?

CHAPTER 45

ASYLUM OF MONTDEVERGUES

April 1930

I gave up on Paris, disheartened, and returned home to Peterborough. A few months later, I went back to the asylum, a desperate plan hatching in my mind. Camille was waiting for me in the hospital's parlour, a dingy little room where the patients could receive visitors. She wore a crumpled hat and the same shabby coat.

She reached for my hands. 'Jessie, *ma petite anglaise.*'

We embraced and I whispered to her: 'Go and pack, Camille, I'm taking you away from here. We'll run away together. You can live with me in England.'

Camille began to tremble violently and grew agitated.

'Are you all right?' I said, panicked. I helped her sit down and held her hand as the colour slowly returned to her face.

'I can't, Jessie, I can't.'

She began to cry and I realised how selfish I had been. Camille had been in an institution since 1913. Outside these walls, the world had changed. Her world, the world I returned to again and again in my dreams, had gone forever. She was too weak and frail. If I took her away it would kill her.

I watched the relief in her eyes as I told her I could not take her with me after all.

'I'm sorry, Camille.'

She nodded her head and closed her eyes as if weary. We sat in silence for a while. When she spoke, Camille's voice was distant, as if she were half-asleep.

'Do you remember the last time we saw each other? In Paris, I mean, not here.'

How could I forget that morning? I didn't trust my voice.

Her hand crept into mine. 'Are you still angry with me? I'm sorry, Jessie. I was upset, but not with you. You see, I had just found out I was pregnant.'

I turned in my seat and brought her hand to my lips. 'Oh, Camille.'

She dropped her eyes. 'I didn't tell anyone, not even Rodin. Not that time anyway. In the end, it didn't matter. I lost the child. And the next one, and the one after. I thought at first it was some kind of judgement.'

'It's only natural to feel like that, but it wasn't your fault.' I pressed her hand, but she withdrew it.

She clenched her fist, shook it in the air, for a moment no longer a weak asylum patient, but spirited Camille once more. 'You are right, Jessie, it wasn't my fault. It was that bastard Rodin's. After I lost the first one, I told him and I thought he would be sad, but he was relieved, I could see it in his face, *le connard*. When I lost the others he didn't bother to hide his satisfaction, said it was better that way.'

'Men don't feel it the same as we do,' I said. William had explained to me that miscarriage was natural selection, a way of weeding out the deformed. When I'd had one, he'd drawn diagrams and spoken to me as if I were one of his students. I had wanted to strike him.

Camille's voice dropped to a whisper and she put her face close to mine so I could see the stumps where her teeth had once been. 'Rodin poisoned me, and he poisoned my babies. What a monster! A monster!' She began to weep and I put my arms around her thin shoulders.

These must be delusions, a symptom of the paranoia Dr Charpenel had warned me about. I murmured to her, as I used to soothe my children, and she grew quiet. I thought the storm had abated, but I was wrong.

Camille stood up and began to pace up and down. 'I've worked it all out – why he was doing it. You see, he couldn't steal my ideas any more if I was nursing a baby. He needed me working, thinking, creating. As soon as the doctor left me in my bed, a covered metal dish in his hand, the sheets still running with blood, Rodin would be back at my side, telling me that work was the answer, the only cure for my sorrow.'

Camille beat the air with her fists. 'Like a fool, I believed him and went back to my sculptures, which he copied, every single one of them. Oh, he was clever about it, so clever that at first I didn't notice. We shared the same models, you see, and I'd suggest the poses, talk through my ideas while he nodded his head and I'd be thrilled he approved. Idiot! And all the time he was stealing from me.'

Camille sat down again and scrabbled at my hands; I shrank from her, I couldn't help it. Her eyes were unfocused, as if she couldn't see me, and she was ranting, spittle flying from her mouth. I couldn't untangle the truth from her delusions.

She seemed to sense my disbelief and threw my hands away in disgust. 'I'm wasting my breath on you, you were always on Rodin's side, you worshipped him like a schoolgirl with a crush.'

Even weak and broken, Camille had the power to wound me. I could feel my temper rising, old resentments breaking the surface.

'I was always on your side,' I said. 'Though, much good it did me.' I had had enough of her temper. She'd raved at me once before and I'd put up with it, but this time I would argue back, rationally. 'As for these accusations of stealing your ideas – they don't hold water. Artists steal from each other all the time, work on the same subjects, it's not fair to blame one's failure on another's success.' I thought of my *Giganti*. I had worked so hard, but it never made the cut at the Paris Salon, while Camille's version was declared a work of genius. That was no one's fault, other than God's for giving her more talent than me.

Camille narrowed her eyes. 'You don't think I know that artists borrow from each other? Do you think I'm an imbecile? But this was different, I tell you.' She banged her fist into her palm. 'Rodin stole my ideas. Why don't you believe me, if you're such a good friend? All you have to do is look at my *Sakuntala* and his *Éternelle Idole* – the exact same pose, the man begging forgiveness. It was my idea. Mine! Mine! Mine!' She jabbed her finger at her chest and I winced at the force she used. 'I was blind, I couldn't see it. Not until the critics saw my *Sakuntala* and mocked me for copying Rodin. But who do you think gave him the idea for that piece and for so many others?'

She grasped my arm and I was amazed by the strength in her bony fingers. 'Rodin took everything from me,' she said, her breath rank in my face. 'He was getting older and losing his inspiration. I was young, my creativity strong. He sucked it out of me and injected it into his own dry husk. Rodin stole everything: my ideas, my youth, even my children.'

All of a sudden she lost her wild anger and stared bleakly at her hands in her lap.

I was sorry then. I had been too hard and expected too much from her poor injured mind. She looked weighed down by misery. If only I could draw the bitterness from her wounds, help her remember the sweetness of the past.

'Camille, you loved Rodin once. Won't you tell me about the times you were happiest with him?'

She sat back in the chair and closed her eyes. I thought she'd fallen asleep but she spoke softly, as if a young woman again.

'Rodin rented this house for us, La Folie Le Prestre, where George Sand used to meet de Musset. When he led me through the garden and through the doors, he covered my eyes. When I opened them it was like being in a fairy tale, you know the one, where the princess wakes up after a hundred years. It was a ruin, dust everywhere, crumbling plaster, statues of goddesses in alcoves. I loved it, our *atelier*, Rodin's and mine, our secret place in the middle of Paris.

'We would lie naked in each others' arms in this great ruined chateau … the overgrown vines in the windows turned the light green, as if we were underwater … the only sound was his heart beating … his eyes were pale as opals and burned with the same cold flames …'

She shook her head as if to clear water from her ears. 'No. Not that. His spell is still on me, the poison he fed me still in my veins. He whispered his lies in my ears while he stroked my skin, white as marble … *my dream in stone*, he called me. *We'll be married soon, soon ma belle rêve, spend the rest of our lives together. We're partners you and I, twin geniuses, we'll rise together, our powers entwined like flames.'* She opened her eyes as if waking from a dream and gave a strange metallic laugh. 'And I believed him.'

There was a sadness about her now but a luminosity, too, like light shining through a Bernini. I could see once more the Camille I knew in Paris and I wanted to kiss her ruined face. Rodin was a fool to have let her go.

'What changed?' I said. 'Why did you leave him?'

Her shoulders dropped and she seemed to age again before my eyes. 'I got pregnant again. I had lost so many babies and I was thirty-six, but this one was a survivor. I could feel him kicking inside me, strong, full of life, a child of my own.' She placed her hands over her belly and smiled. 'Rodin wanted to fix me up with a doctor, some butcher who took care of the models. I said I would do it, agreed to everything, even told Paul. He was shocked, of course, called me a murderer.'

I put my hand over hers, where it rested on her stomach. 'Paul told me, when I met him in Paris.'

She looked into my eyes. 'Were you shocked?'

'No, I just thought about you, how terrible it must have been.'

Camille touched me lightly on the cheek. She walked towards the window and looked through the bars to the bleak garden. When she turned around she was radiant.

'I left Rodin. Found my own apartment and locked myself away. A long illness, I told everyone. Paul and Rodin thought I was ill after the abortion. But I had the child. I have a son, Jessie.'

In Camille's room, she pulled the box out from under the iron bed. Inside was the head of a young boy of about five with a tilt to his chin and a bold look. His resemblance to Camille was unmistakable. She took a slip of paper from the pocket in her skirt: an address in Villeneuve.

'I gave him to my old nursemaid to look after. She was always kind to Paul and me. I wanted to hide the baby from Rodin, I didn't want him to come to any harm. Will you take this to him?'

She handed me the bust. 'Jessie, *mon amie*, will you find him for me and tell him about his mother?'

'How will I find him?' I said.

'It's a small village.'

I cradled the bust in my arms and looked at Camille's son. It seemed too perfect, like an image of a dream child. Like the poisonings and Rodin's conspirators, was this child also a figment of her broken mind? I put the bust in its box and embraced Camille for the last time. I was being asked to play one more part in her life and I would not let her down.

As the car took me away from Montdevergues, I opened the window and felt the wind on my face and thought of Camille, shut up in that place for sixteen years, all alone. How could anyone bear that and not be broken? I allowed myself to cry for Camille, for the wasted years, for the ruined talent, for my friend. But hadn't I wasted my own talent? When Camille was making works of genius, I was totting up grocery bills, soothing fractious babies. I should be grateful for what I had: a good husband and four children. But I remembered the sharp tang of lemon cologne, the golden sunlight of a Paris afternoon. And I wept for us all, for Camille, for Georges, for myself.

CHAPTER 46

VILLENEUVE

May 1930

I looked at the name on the piece of paper Camille had given me. 'I'm looking for Louis Claudel. He would be in his late twenties now.'

The young woman wiped floury hands on her apron and frowned. 'There's no one here by that name, Madame.'

'Are you sure? This is the address I was given, the cottage next to the priest's house in Villeneuve.'

She shook her head again and began to close the door. A man appeared behind her.

'*Qui est là, Francine?*'

'An English lady, asking for – who was it again?'

'Louis Claudel. He would be about your age.'

He shrugged. 'My name is Jean-Luc, this is my wife, Francine. No one else lives here apart from our daughter.'

I drooped. Camille's tale of a stolen child was one of her delusions, like being poisoned by Rodin's gang. I should have listened to William. I had been a fool to come all this way, a fool on a fool's errand. I turned to leave, the box still in my hands.

The young man put his hand on my shoulder and I turned to face him. 'I'm sorry, you could try the big house outside the village. The family there are the Claudels. My grandmother used to work for them.'

I looked at him again, more carefully this time. He was nothing like Camille, but his chest was broad and his head jutted forward like a bull's. I tried to imagine him with a long, tangled beard, and dressed in a suit stained with clay. Was I clutching at straws to imagine he looked like Rodin?

He gestured me inside. 'You look tired, Madame. Perhaps you would like to come in and rest and have a glass of wine? It's from our own vineyard.'

I followed him and his wife inside. The cottage was small but the copper pots above the sink gleamed and there were bunches of herbs hanging from the beams. A little girl was drawing at the scrubbed wooden table, her face a scowl of concentration. When she looked up her eyes were navy blue.

'What's in the box?' she said.

'Marianne, don't be nosy,' but her mother's voice was gentle as she smoothed the child's dark curls from her forehead.

I put the box on the table. 'Would you like to see?'

Marianne knelt on her chair and I took out the bust and put it in front of her. A small hand, grubby with charcoal, reached out and ran over the contours of the plaster face.

She put her hands on her hips. 'Can I have it?'

I picked up her drawing. I looked at her wide mouth and the tilt of her head and my heart contracted.

I nodded. 'It's yours.'

AUTHOR'S NOTE

Camille Claudel died on 19 October 1943 at Montdevergues Asylum after having lived there for thirty years.

Jessie Elbourne always insisted her friend had had a child by Rodin.

In 1951, Paul Claudel organised an exhibition of Camille's work at the Musée Rodin, which continues to display her sculptures. She was largely forgotten until a major retrospective of her work in 1984.

Paris Kiss is inspired by real events, although I used dramatic licence to give Jessie a romantic involvement in Paris and for the women to befriend Rosa Bonheur, Toulouse-Lautrec and Suzanne Valadon, who were in Paris at the same time.

During my research, I consulted many books, too numerous to list here. They include: *Camille Claudel, A Life* by Odile Ayral-Clause; *Camille, The Life of Camille Claudel* by Reine-Marie Paris, translated by Liliane Emery Tuck; *Rodin, The Shape of Genius* by Ruth Butler; *Rodin, Eros and Creativity*, edited by Rainer Crone and Siegfried Salzmann; *Women and Madness, The Incarceration of Women in Nineteenth-Century France* by Yannick Ripa; *A Wanderer in Paris* by E.V. Lucas; *Jessie: Study of an Artist* by Abi Pirani (MA Thesis, University of York, 1987); *The Journal of Marie Bashkirtseff*, translated by Mathilde Blind; *The Invention of the Model: Artists and Models in Paris, 1830–1870* by Susan Waller; *Women Artists: a Graphic Guide* by Frances Borzello and Natacha Ledwidge; *Nineteenth Century Fashion in Detail* by Lucy Johnson with Marion Kite and Helen Persson.

ACKNOWLEDGEMENTS

I could not have written *Paris Kiss* without my husband Michael who gave me the time, encouragement and confidence I needed.

I'm grateful to my agent Jenny Brown who believed in *Paris Kiss* enough to see me through several rewrites, and to Sara Hunt of Saraband and editor Ali Moore for their expertise and sensitivity.

I'm indebted, too, to the staff on the University of Glasgow's Creative Writing Department for the generosity with which they shared their craft and knowledge. Thank you Laura Marney, Elizabeth Reeder, Zoe Strachan, Kei Miller and Michael Schmidt.

Every author needs readers, so a big thanks to Carmen Reid for her insights, and for the unstinting support, wisdom and laughter I found at G2 Writers, with special thanks to George Craig and Philip Murnin.

ABOUT THE AUTHOR

A journalist, Maggie Ritchie graduated with distinction from the University of Glasgow's MLitt in Creative Writing. She won the Curtis Brown Prize for *Paris Kiss* and was shortlisted for the Sceptre Prize and the Mslexia Novel Competition.

Maggie lives in Scotland with her family. You can follow her on Twitter @MallonRitchie.

MORE HISTORICAL FICTION
FROM SARABAND

An Exquisite Sense of What Is Beautiful
J David Simons' sweeping novel of East and West, love and war.

The Physic Garden
The moving and poetic tale of a 19th-century physic gardener, by Catherine Czerkawska.

The Land Agent
A remarkable and moving story of love, land, community and identity from J David Simons.

Making Shore
Sara Allerton's World War II drama, based on a true story. Winner, People's Book Prize 2011.

A Capital Union
Victoria Hendry. Shortlisted for the 2014 Historical Writers' Association Debut Crown.

Unfashioned Creatures
Lesley McDowell. A Gothic thriller of madness, love, ghosts – and Mary Shelley.

GREAT READS
PUBLISHED INDEPENDENTLY